Enjoy!

Susan

Mallery

W9-AWO-644

GARFINKEL

Select praise for Susan Mallery's Mischief Bay novels

The Girls of Mischief Bay

"Mallery skillfully depicts three very different women in different stages of their romantic relationships who enter into unbreakable friendships... Will appeal to fans of women's fiction, especially such friendship books as Karen Joy Fowler's *The Jane Austen Book Club*."

—*Booklist*

"Romance superstar Mallery begins a new women's fiction series with a novel that is both heart-wrenching and warmhearted... A discerning, affecting look at three women facing surprising change and the powerful and uplifting impact of friends."

—*Kirkus Reviews*

"Once again, Susan Mallery has created an inviting world that envelops her readers' senses and sensibilities. It's not just a tale of how true friendship can lift you up, but also how change is an integral part of life... Fans of Jodi Picoult, Debbie Macomber, and Elin Hilderbrand will assuredly fall for *The Girls of Mischief Bay*."

—*Bookreporter*

"Fresh and engaging... There's a generational subtext that mirrors reality and the complexities of adult relationships...filled with promise of a new serial that's worth following."

—*Fort Worth Star-Telegram*

The Friends We Keep

"Gabby, Haley, and Nicole are down-to-earth real women with whom readers will be able to identify, and Mallery successfully balances each story line. The women's stories and the depth of support they provide one another make this an engaging read to be savored all the way through."

—*Publishers Weekly*

"Another terrific read from Susan Mallery! Very highly recommended."

—*Midwest Book Review*

SUSAN MALLERY

Sisters Like Us

mira

mira

ISBN-13: 978-0-7783-6880-9

Sisters Like Us

Recycling programs
for this product may
not exist in your area.

For questions and comments about the quality of this book, please contact us at CustomerService@Harlequin.com.

MIRABooks.com

BookClubbish.com

Printed in U.S.A.

I acknowledge it is very, very wrong for an author to have a favorite book. Books are like children and we should love them all equally. Yet I will confess (but only to you) that I had great fun writing this one. So much fun. And I love all the characters, even Bunny, and I admit that Lucas turned out to be much more amazing than I'd ever anticipated.

This book is for those of you who will unexpectedly fall wildly in love with Lucas...even though you think you shouldn't!

Also by Susan Mallery

Secrets of the Tulip Sisters
Daughters of the Bride

Happily Inc

Second Chance Girl
You Say It First

Mischief Bay

A Million Little Things
The Friends We Keep
The Girls of Mischief Bay

Fool's Gold

Best of My Love
Marry Me at Christmas
Thrill Me
Kiss Me
Hold Me
Until We Touch
Before We Kiss
When We Met
Christmas on 4th Street
Three Little Words
Two of a Kind
Just One Kiss
A Fool's Gold Christmas
All Summer Long
Summer Nights
Summer Days
Only His
Only Yours
Only Mine
Finding Perfect
Almost Perfect
Chasing Perfect

For a complete list of titles available from Susan Mallery,
please visit www.SusanMallery.com.

Sisters Like Us

Chapter One

THERE WASN'T A HOLIDAY ON THE CALENDAR THAT Harper Szymanski couldn't celebrate, cook for, decorate, decoupage, create a greeting card about or wrap in raffia. There were the biggies: birthdays, New Years, Fourth of July. But also the lesser celebrated: American Diabetes Association Alert Day, Auntie's Day, National Massage Therapy Awareness Week. Why weren't there greeting cards to honor that? Didn't everyone need a good massage?

Despite a skill set that made Martha Stewart look like a slacker, Harper had never figured out a way to monetize her gift for setting a table to commemorate anything. She'd tried catering about ten years ago, but had quickly discovered that her need to overbuy and overdeliver had meant losing money on every single job. Which left her in the awkward position of trying to make a living the hard way—with two semesters of community college and sixteen years of being a stay-at-home mom.

Retail jobs and the pay that went with them hadn't been close to enough to support herself and her daughter post-divorce. Three online aptitude tests had left her even more confused—while getting her degree in biochemistry and going on to medical school sounded great, it wasn't actually a practical solution for an over-forty single mom with no money in the bank. Then an article in the local paper had provided an interesting and almost-viable idea. Harper had become a virtual assistant.

If there was one thing she knew it was how to take care of the details. You didn't get good at a basket weave Fourth of July cake without paying attention. One year after filing her business permit, Harper had five main clients, nearly a dozen more who used her services intermittently and almost enough income to pay her bills. She also had her mother living in the apartment over the garage, an ex-husband dating a gorgeous blonde who was—wait for it—exactly fourteen years younger than Harper because they shared a birthday—a sixteen-year-old daughter who had stopped speaking to her and a client who was desperately unclear on the concept of *virtual* in the world of virtual assistants.

"You don't have to drop off your bills every month," Harper said as she set out coffee, a plate of chocolate chip scones that she'd gotten up at five-thirty that morning to bake fresh, a bowl of sugar-glazed almonds and sliced pears.

"And miss this?" Lucas Wheeler asked, pouring himself a mug of coffee. "If you're trying to convince me coming by isn't a good idea, then stop feeding me."

He was right, of course. There was an easy, logical solution. Stop taking care of people and they would go away. Or at least be around less often. There was just one problem—when someone stopped by your home, you were *supposed* to take care of them.

"I can't help it," she admitted, wishing it weren't the truth. "It's a disease. I'm a people pleaser. I blame my mother."

"I'd blame her, too, if I were you."

She supposed she could take offense at Lucas's words, but he was only stating the obvious.

In some ways Harper felt as if she was part of the wrong generation. According to celebrity magazines, fifty was the new twenty-five, which meant almost forty-two should be the new what? Eleven? Everyone else her age seemed so young and carefree, with modern attitudes and a far better grasp of what was in style and popular.

Harper was just now getting around to listening to the soundtrack from *Hamilton* and her idea of fashionable had a lot more to do with how she dressed her dining room table than herself. She was like a 1950s throwback, which might sound charming but in real life kind of sucked. On the bright side, it really was her mother's fault.

"Speaking of your mother, where is she?" Lucas asked.

"At the senior center, preparing Easter baskets for the homeless." Because that was what women were supposed to do. Take care of people—not have actual careers that could support them and their families.

"I, on the other hand, will be paying your bills, designing T-shirts for Misty, working on the layout of a sales brochure and making bunny butt cookies for my daughter."

Lucas raised an eyebrow. "You do realize that *bunny butt* is just a polite way of saying *rabbit ass*."

Harper laughed. "Yes, but they're an Easter tradition. Becca loves them. Her father is dropping her off tomorrow afternoon and I want the cookies waiting."

Because maybe if there were bunny butt cookies, her daughter would smile and talk to her the way she used to. In actual sentences that shared bits of her life.

"You sorry you didn't go?" Lucas asked.

"To the memorial? Yes." She thought for a second, then added, "No. I mean I would have liked to pay my respects and all, but Great-Aunt Cheryl is gone, so it's not like she would miss me showing up."

The drive from Mischief Bay to Grass Valley would take practically the whole day. Harper couldn't imagine anything more horrible than being trapped in a car with her ex, his girlfriend and her daughter. Okay, the Becca part would be great, but the other two?

The worst of it was that while Great-Aunt Cheryl was actually Terence's relative, Harper had been the one who had stayed in touch, right up until her death two months ago.

"Terence is forty-four. What is he thinking, dating a twenty-eight-year-old?" She glared at Lucas. "Never mind. You're the wrong person to be having this particular conversation with."

Because while her client was a handsome, single, fifty-year-old man, he also dated women in their twenties. In his case, their early twenties.

"What is wrong with you?" she demanded. "Is it all men or just you and my ex? Oh, dear God, the one thing you have in common with Terence is me. Did I do something to make you all date twentysomethings?"

"Calm down," Lucas said mildly. "I was dating younger women long before we met. It's not you, it's me."

"Where have I heard that before?" She glanced pointedly at the clock on her microwave. "Don't you have crimes to solve?"

"Yeah, yeah, I'm going."

He rose and carried his dishes to the sink. Lucas was about

five-ten, nicely muscled with a belly way flatter than hers. He wore jeans, cowboy boots and a long-sleeved shirt. He was a detective with the LAPD, and from what she'd learned about him in the nine months she'd been working for him, he'd always been a cop.

He returned to the table and slipped on his shoulder holster, then grabbed his blazer. "How do you make bunny butt cookies?"

She laughed. "It's easy. You take a round sugar cookie frosted in pink icing, add two small oval sugar cookies decorated with pink candy for feet, use a miniature marshmallow for the tail and viola—bunny butt cookies."

"Save me a couple."

"I promise." She would put them in a little box that she would decorate for the holiday. Because she simply couldn't hand someone cookies on a plain paper plate. If she tried, the heavens would open and release a plague of locusts at the very least.

Oh, to be able to buy packaged cookies from the grocery store. Or prepared spaghetti sauce. Or a frozen entrée. But that would never happen because it wasn't what Harper was supposed to do.

She carried the rest of the dishes over to the sink, packed up the uneaten food, then retreated to her large craft room with its built-in shelves and giant tables and cupboards. After finding a nice bunny-butt-cookie-sized box, she studied her ribbon collection before selecting one that would coordinate. While her glue gun heated, she sorted through her fabric remnants to find one that was Easter appropriate and wondered what other women did with the time they saved by not making every stupid thing by hand.

But Harper was her mother's daughter and had never been

very good at bucking tradition. Her sister, Stacey, was the rebel while Harper did what she was told. It wasn't that she didn't like making bunny butt cookies or decoupaging gift boxes, it was that she wanted just a little more in her life. More challenges, more money, more communication with her daughter. And while it was fun to blame all her problems on her mother, Harper couldn't help thinking that in reality, everything she wanted but didn't have was very likely her own damn fault.

The smell of waffles and turkey sausage filled the kitchen and drifted down the hall toward the master bedroom. Stacey Bloom slipped on her sleeveless dress, then glanced at herself in the mirror. With the loose style and knit fabric, not to mention her body shape, she looked as she always had. No one would guess, which was the point. She didn't want the questions that would inevitably be asked—mostly because she didn't want to be judged for her answers.

She knew that was her problem, no one else's. The judging thing. If it were any other topic, she would be able to provide a brief but accurate response, one that would explain her position while making it clear that while the questioner might think his opinion was important, she did not. Except for this time.

She stepped into her lace-up hiking boots and tied them, then pulled a blazer from the row of them in her closet. She had learned years ago that having a kind of work uniform kept her mornings simple. She bought her black sleeveless dresses online, three or four of them at a time. Her blazers were of excellent quality and lasted for years. She changed them out seasonally—lighter fabric in summer, heavier in winter—although the temperate climate in Mischief Bay, California, meant her decision to switch one for another was based purely on convention and not necessity.

As for the hiking boots, they were comfortable and offered a lot of support. She spent much of her day standing in a lab or walking between labs, so they made practical sense. Her mother kept trying to get her to wear pumps and stockings, neither of which was ever going to happen. The shoes would cause foot pain and pressure on her lower back—these days more so than ever. Besides, something about her hiking boots seemed to intimidate the men she had to work with, and although that had never been her purpose, she wasn't going to deny she liked the unexpected benefit.

She walked into her kitchen and hung her blazer on the back of her chair. Her husband, Kit, stood at the stove, humming to himself as he turned the sausage. The table was set and there was a bowl of sliced fruit by her place mat. A thermal to-go cup stood next to her backpack. She wanted it to be filled with delicious hot coffee, but knew instead it contained a vegetable-infused protein shake. Without looking she knew that her lunch was already packed in her backpack.

Kit turned and smiled when he saw her.

"Morning, sweetie. How are you feeling?"

"Good. And you?"

"Excellent." He winked, then went back to his cooking.

As it was the last Friday of Spring Break, he wasn't teaching today, so instead of his usual khakis and a button-down shirt, he had on sweats and a T-shirt with a drawing of a cat on a poster. Underneath the poster, it said Wanted Dead or Alive: Schrodinger's Cat.

She wasn't sure which she loved more—that he fussed over her by fixing her meals and making sure she was taking her vitamins, that he called her sweetie, or that he had a collection of funny science T-shirts. She supposed there was no rea-son she had to pick any one thing. Until meeting Kit, she'd never been sure that she believed romantic love existed. She could have explained the chemical processes that took place in the brain but that wasn't the same as believing in the feel-ings themselves. Now she knew differently.

He set two plates on the table, then sat across from her. A pot of herbal tea sat in the center of the table. She poured them each a cup. Kit wouldn't drink coffee in front of her although she guessed he had it when she wasn't around.

"Harper called," he said. "She invited us over for dinner tomorrow night. Becca will be home from the memorial." He frowned. "Who is Great-Aunt Cheryl? She didn't come to the wedding."

"She's not related to Harper and me. She was Terence's great-aunt, but she and Harper were always close, which our mother found threatening. Great-Aunt Cheryl was an army nurse during World War II and some kind of spy in the 1950s. She raised dogs."

"Like poodles?"

Stacey smiled at her husband. "No, these were specially trained dogs used in spy missions. Apparently their training was far more advanced than regular military canines. I tried to get her to talk about her work, but she said it was all top secret and I didn't have clearance. Still, what she did tell me was fascinating to hear about. I was most intrigued by the lack of morality involved. When someone is trained to kill, there are psychological ramifications, but with animals, there is simply the task. Pushing a button that will ultimately arm a bomb requires little more than the command and subsequent reward for good behavior."

Kit chuckled. "That's my girl, always with the cheerful breakfast conversation."

"So much of life is interesting to me."

"I know, and you are interesting to me. Now, about the elephant in the room..."

She automatically glanced at the calendar on the wall. It was about one square foot and rather than show the date, it counted up to 280. Kit tore off a sheet each morning. Today was day 184.

Stacey involuntarily put her right hand on her round belly. Right hand rather than left because she was right hand dominant and therefore would be in a better position to protect with said right hand. Not that there were any threats in the room—they came from outside the haven that was their home.

Her gaze returned to her husband. Kit's kind expression never changed. His brown eyes danced with amusement from behind his wire-rimmed glasses, his mouth smiled at her. He needed a haircut because he always needed a haircut.

They'd met nearly three years ago, when Stacey had spoken at the Mischief Bay High School career day. As a science teacher, Kit had reached out to Stacey's biotech company and asked for someone to address his students. He'd specifically requested a woman to inspire the young women in his classes.

Stacey had volunteered. She spoke regularly at conferences and symposiums, so had no fear of talking in front of a crowd. Lexi, her assistant, had helped her put together a presentation that assumed little or no knowledge of disease pathology, or science, for that matter. The students had appeared interested but the bigger surprise of the day had been meeting Kit.

She'd found herself flustered in his presence and when he'd invited her out for coffee, she'd accepted. Coffee had turned

into a long weekend and by the end of their third week together, he'd moved in with her.

She had never been swept away before, had never fallen so
completely for anyone. More importantly, she'd never felt so
accepted by a man who wasn't family.

In the vernacular of the day, he got her. He understood
how her brain worked and wasn't the least bit intimidated by
her intelligence or success. When regular life confused her,
he was her buffer. He was *normal*. Just as important, he took
care of her in a thousand little ways that made her feel loved.
While she tried to do the same with him, she was confident
she failed spectacularly, but Kit never seemed to mind.

"I'll tell her," she murmured, getting back to the topic at
hand.

"Technically you don't have to. In about ninety-six days
you'll pop out the baby. I'm pretty sure Bunny will be able
to figure it out from the broad strokes. You know, when she
holds her granddaughter for the first time." He paused to sip
his tea. "Unless you weren't going to say anything then. I
mean, we can wait until Joule learns to talk and we can let her
tell Bunny herself. Most kids start forming sentences around
eighteen months or so but with your genes floating around
in our daughter, she will probably be on her second language
by then. I say we let her tell her grandmother who she is."

She knew Kit was teasing. She also knew the problem was
of her own making. She'd been the one to put off telling her
mother she was pregnant. She'd told Harper right away because Harper was her sister and they'd always been there for
each other. Harper was easy and accepting and would understand. Bunny wouldn't. Bunny had very clear ideas on what
women should or shouldn't do in their lives and Stacey was

confident she'd violated every one she could so far. Having a child would only make things worse.

One week had slipped into two. Time had passed. Stacey had told Kit she was going to wait until after the amniocentesis, but they'd had the results weeks ago and still Stacey hadn't said anything to her mother.

She got up and circled the table. Kit pushed back enough for her to collapse on his lap. He wrapped his arms around her as she hung on, burying her face in his shoulder.

"I'm a horrible daughter," she whispered.

"You're not. You're wonderful and I love you. As for Bunny, if she can't take a joke, then screw it." He touched her cheek until she looked at him. "Stacey, I'm serious. You do what you want. I'm with you. If you don't want to tell Bunny ever, then that's okay. I'm just trying to point out, she will find out at some point, and the longer you wait, the harder it's going to be."

"It's already hard."

"I told you so," he said gently, before kissing her. "Go finish your breakfast."

"I will. I love you, too."

He smiled at her. She returned to her seat and began to eat. Because she had to stay healthy for the baby. She was comfortable being a vessel—she could do the vessel thing. It was the idea of parenting that tormented her. Who was she to think she could be a mother? She wasn't like other women—she didn't want what they wanted. She had different priorities, which she probably could have lived with, if not for her mother.

Because Bunny knew Stacey wasn't like everyone else and she had no trouble pointing out that fact. Once she found out about the baby… Well, Stacey could only imagine.

"I'll tell her tomorrow at dinner," she said.

"Good for you."

Which was his way of saying *There is not a snowball's chance in hell I believe you, but sure, say it because it makes you feel better.*

"She's going to be mad I waited so long."

"That she is." He smiled at her. "But don't worry. I won't let her hurt you. I promise."

She knew he meant what he said—that he would do his best to protect her. The problem wasn't that her mother would physically abuse her—the problem was what Bunny would say. In the Bloom family, words were the true weapon, and expectation was the ammunition. The rest of the world considered Stacey a brilliant scientist with a string of credentials and awards. Bunny saw little more than a daughter who refused to be conventional in any way that mattered—in other words, a failure. What on earth was her mother going to say when she found out her daughter was six months pregnant and had never said a word?

Chapter Two

HARPER CHECKED HER DAILY CALENDAR TO CONFIRM all she had to get through that day. As it was the end of the month, she would be billing her clients for her work. In addition, she needed to email Blake and remind him that his mother's birthday was in two weeks. She already had several gift ideas noted in case he wanted her help with that.

She wrote the email to Blake, a Boeing sales executive who spent his work life traveling the world. Blake sold private jets to the über-rich, and then made sure the customization of said planes was to their liking. She never knew where he was at any given time, or who he was meeting with, but it all sounded very exciting. She thought of him as the sales world's James Bond.

Her regular clients were Blake, Lucas, a nurse turned stand-up comedian named Misty, Cathy, a party planner, and the City of Mischief Bay. When she'd first started her business, she'd had no idea what she was doing. A half-dozen college extension courses later, she'd mastered several computer programs, learned the basics of a handful of others, knew how to file a DBA, keep basic records for her business and pay her taxes. Harper Helps had been born.

Lucas had been her first client—she'd met him through a friend of a friend. After being shot on the job, Lucas had spent several weeks recovering. During that time, his bills had gone unpaid and his lights and water had been turned off. When he'd recovered, he'd decided to let someone else handle the details of his life and had hired her. Blake had found her through a Facebook ad, of all things, and Misty was one of Lucas's former nurses.

The work with the city had come through an online posting requesting a bid to design a mailer. She'd applied, offered samples of her work and had been hired.

The irony was Harper had started her home business because she didn't have any skills—now she would certainly be qualified to work in an office, only to find she didn't want to. She liked making her own hours and being around for her daughter—not that Becca was especially interested in her mother these days, but still. Harper was here should her daughter ever want or need her.

Harper went into the kitchen and poured herself another cup of coffee. The back door opened and Harper's mother walked in. Bunny Bloom was petite, slim and in her early sixties. She dressed in high-end knits, wore her dark hair short and spikey and always, *always* put on makeup before stepping outside her apartment.

Bunny had lost her husband a couple of years ago and while Harper had been a mess in the months following her father's death, Bunny had soldiered on, taking care of what needed doing. Once the dust had settled, she'd moved into the apartment above Harper's garage both to be close to her only grandchild and to help Harper financially. There were months when

Bunny's thousand-dollar rent check meant the difference between hamburger for dinner and a box of mac and cheese. Figuratively, Harper thought as she smiled at her mother. She would never use boxed mac and cheese. She would make it herself, from scratch, including the noodles.

"Hey, Mom. How are you?" Harper asked, automatically pouring a second cup of coffee before pulling a freshly made coffee cake from the bread box and cutting off a slice.

"Old. Have you heard from Becca?"

"Just that they're planning on heading home tomorrow." She didn't mention that since the text two days ago saying her daughter had arrived, she hadn't heard a word. These days Becca just wasn't talking to her and for the life of her, Harper couldn't figure out why.

They settled at the round kitchen table and she gave the plate of coffee cake to her mother. Each of the four matching place mats had a rabbit motif, as did the salt-and-pepper shakers in the center of the table. The sugar bowl and creamer had rabbits *and* tulips, celebrating the holiday and the fact that it was spring.

"Good." Bunny poured cream into her coffee. "I need to see my only grandchild for Easter. Have you started preparing dinner?"

"I have."

Although no matter how much she prepped, she would spend most of Easter Sunday in a frenzy of cooking. The menu this year included strawberry avocado salad, a glazed ham, Potatoes Grand-Mère, both roasted asparagus and creamy spring peas, along with lemon meringue pie and an Easter Bunny cake. Oh, and appetizers.

All that for five people, or possibly seven if Lucas came and brought a date. She was never sure with him. Regardless, there would be food for twenty and lots of leftovers. And none of that counted the special "welcome home" dinner she would make tomorrow.

"Do you need help?" her mother asked.

Harper did her best not to scream. Of course she needed help! She was working sixty hours a week in a desperate attempt to stay afloat financially, taking care of her house, dealing with a sixteen-year-old, decorating for the holiday and getting ready to cook a fancy meal. Help would be nice. Help would be grand. But, in Bunny's world, the woman of the house did not ask for help. No, she did it all herself, seemingly effortlessly. Family came first. The measure of a woman was how well she looked after her family and so on. Harper knew it all by heart. The problem was, from her perspective, the only person who cared about all that was Bunny herself. Bunny who no longer had to do anything for anyone because somehow all that responsibility was Harper's now. Bunny was free to spend the day with her friends, dress perfectly for every occasion and judge her oldest daughter.

Harper smiled at her mother. "I'm good, Mom. I have it all under control. You just show up and look pretty."

"All right. Stacey and Kit are coming to dinner?"

"Last I heard."

Which could be interesting, Harper thought. At some point her sister was going to have to reveal her pregnancy and wouldn't that be a conversation starter? She wasn't sure if she wanted it to happen at Easter dinner, though. Not with all the work that went into the meal. Maybe after would be better, when everyone was still digesting, although that could be problematic, as well.

She supposed the actual issue was that there was simply no good time to confess to your mother that you were six months pregnant. At sixteen it made sense to hide the truth, but Stacey was forty.

Harper held in a sigh. She knew exactly why Stacey wasn't eager to share the information. Their mother would have a million rules and shoulds, all of which Stacey would ignore. Then there would be fighting. Given that scenario, keeping quiet sort of made sense.

"Do you think she left you anything?"

Harper stared at her mother. "I'm sorry, I have no idea what you're asking."

"Do you think she left you anything?"

"Saying the same thing again doesn't make it any clearer, Mom."

Her mother sighed. "In *the will*."

Oh, right. Because Bunny would rather buy store-bought bread than actually say Great-Aunt Cheryl's name. Which would be really funny except Harper had a similar problem with her ex's girlfriend. She went out of her way to never say *Alicia* if at all possible. Although there was a huge difference, what with Alicia being twenty-eight and gorgeous and Great-Aunt Cheryl not being a relative at all and, well, dead.

"I have no idea," Harper admitted. "A couple of years ago she asked me if I would take her dogs. I made it clear there was no way."

Great-Aunt Cheryl had been many things, including a former army nurse who had somehow become a spy during World War II. After that, she'd traveled the world, taken lovers and generally lived a life that would have left anyone else exhausted. In the past decade or so, Great-Aunt Cheryl had taken to training dogs for the government. Harper was pretty sure they could arm a nuclear missile if instructed. They were also huge, slightly scary-looking Dobermans that she in no way wanted in her house.

"So no jewelry? No antique silver tea service?"

"Great-Aunt Cheryl wasn't the antique silver tea service type."

"Pity."

They both knew that wasn't true.

"I'm not expecting her to leave me anything, Mom. She was Terence's aunt, not mine."

"Yet you were always so close."

There was a slight sniff at the end of the statement, but Harper ignored it.

"We were. She was lovely and I miss her a lot." Great-Aunt Cheryl had always encouraged her to do more with her life than just take care of her family. When Becca had started kindergarten, Cheryl had offered to pay for Harper to go to college.

Harper, being an idiot, had refused. Why should she take time away from caring for her family to do something as ridiculous as going to college? It wasn't as if she was ever going to be on her own and having to support herself and her daughter.

After the divorce Harper had wanted to tell Great-Aunt Cheryl how much she appreciated the offer, even if she hadn't taken it. But at that point she'd been afraid it would sound too much like begging for money, so she'd never said the words. Now she couldn't.

Regret was a mean and vindictive bitch.

Harper heard a knock at the front door, but before she could run to open it, she heard a familiar "It's me."

"In the kitchen," she yelled as she deftly maneuvered hot lasagna noodles into the casserole dish. She wiped her hands on a towel, then reached for the bowl of marinara sauce—homemade, of course—and a spoon.

She glanced up as Lucas strolled into the room, then returned her attention to what she was doing. There was no point in looking at what she couldn't have, she reminded herself. Not that she wanted Lucas—not exactly.

Yes, the man was ridiculously good-looking. Tall and fit, with an air of confidence that was just shy of being a swagger. He was fifty, so older than her, and unexpectedly kind. While he was always underfoot, he was rarely in the way and whenever he came to dinner—which was surprisingly often—he always brought thoughtful little gifts.

He stood on the other side of the kitchen island and studied the ingredients she'd set out earlier.

"Let's see," he began. "Lasagna goes without saying, so there will be garlic bread. Some kind of salad." He paused. "The chopped one with the homemade basil dressing. Which means we're having Becca's favorite dinner."

"In celebration of her return."

"She was gone three nights. How are you going to show she's special when she heads off to college for months at a time?"

"I don't want to think about that," Harper admitted. Not her only child being gone nor how she was supposed to pay for out-of-state tuition. "I made a chocolate cake."

"Of course you did. What time is dinner?"

"Terence said they'd be back between four and five, so maybe five-thirty or six."

"I'll be here." He looked around at all the mess. "This big dinner is in addition to the Easter feast tomorrow?"

"Of course. They're totally unrelated."

"And we couldn't just let one of them go?"

"Seriously? You're asking that?"

"Yeah. You're right. What was I thinking?"

She finished sprinkling on a layer of grated cheese, then glanced at the clock. It was nearly three. She figured she could risk leaving the lasagna out on the counter until she popped it in the oven at four-fifteen. She'd made the bread days ago and had defrosted a loaf already. The garlic spread was done and the salad was in the refrigerator. She only had to pour on dressing and that was good to go. There was still the table to set. She returned her attention to Lucas.

"Are you bringing someone?"

One corner of his mouth turned up. "Persimmon."

Harper wiped her hands on a towel. "You have got to be kidding. That's her real name?"

"It's on her driver's license."

"Which you saw because you check their ID before you date them?"

"I like to be sure."

"That they're not underage or that they're not too old?"

"Sometimes both."

"I get the biology," she said, studying him across the kitchen island. "The young, healthy female should produce the best offspring. But we're not living in caves anymore. You drive a Mercedes. If you've evolved enough to handle freeway driving, why can't you date someone remotely close to your own age? I'm not suggesting an old lady, but maybe a woman in her thirties." She walked to the pantry and got the small box of cookies she'd set aside for him.

"Never mind," she told him as she handed him the decorated box. "You don't have an answer and I have no right to question your personal life. I just work for you."

"And give me cookies." He studied the ribbon and appliques. "It's beautiful, but I would have been happy with plastic wrap."

"That's not how we do things around here."

"Which is part of your problem."

"I know that. Unfortunately, knowing and doing something about it are two different things. Go wash your hands, then you can help me set the table."

"Yes, ma'am."

He did as she requested, then met her in the formal dining room. Harper remembered when she and Terence had been looking for a house in the area. They'd passed on several because the dining room wasn't big enough. When he'd pointed out their family wasn't that large, she'd reminded him that she had a huge table, a giant hutch and massive buffet to find room for. He'd grumbled about her having too many dishes—every now and then she thought maybe he was right. After the divorce she'd sold two full sets and still had more stock than the average department store.

Her basic set of dishes were white, allowing her to use them as a base for any holiday or event. Now she studied her tablecloths and napkins, then thought about the bunny fest that would be tomorrow's table.

"Becca likes pink," Lucas offered. "Isn't pink a spring color?"

"It is, and that would work. Thanks."

She pulled out a pale rose tablecloth with matching napkins. She would use gold as the accent color, along with a little dark green. The dinner would be attended by Bunny, Becca, Lucas, fruit date, Kit and Stacey, and Harper, so seven.

She handed Lucas the tablecloth before digging out seven dark green place mats. The rest was easy: seven gold chargers, seven sets of gold flatware, her favorite crystal glasses, white plates. She had a collection of salad plates in different patterns, including eight that were edged in gold. She would make custom napkin rings by dressing up plain ones with clusters of silk flowers. She had three hurricane lamps with gold bases.

She left him to put the linens on the table, then hurried into her craft room to double-check supplies. Honestly, she should have planned her table a couple of days ago, in case she needed to go to the craft store. Now she was going to have to wing it.

She plugged in her glue gun, then dug through a large bag of silk flower pieces and found several tiny pink blossoms, along with some greens. She had glass beads, of course, and plenty of ribbon. Ten minutes later, she had secured the last of the flowers to the clear plastic napkin rings she bought in bulk. She picked up bags of colored glass beads and the ribbon, then turned and nearly ran into Lucas.

"What are you doing?" he asked, sounding more amused than concerned.

"Decorating the table. Can you get those hurricane lamps, please?"

"There's something wrong with you," he told her as he picked up the lamps and followed her back into the dining room. "Your crafts don't make you a penny, yet you have that huge room for them. At the same time, you cram your office into that tiny bedroom in back."

"Sometimes I have to use my craft room for work," she said, trying not to sound defensive. "When I work for my party planner, I do."

"Yeah, sell it somewhere else. Harper, no one's going to take you seriously until you take yourself seriously."

She thought of the stack of bills on her desk and how every month was a struggle. It was the house, she admitted to herself. She'd wanted to keep it after the divorce so that Becca wouldn't have to move and she didn't want to be forced to sell it when her daughter turned eighteen. Buying out Terence had decimated her half of their joint assets, meaning he got to keep all the cash, savings and most of their retirement accounts. In return she had the house and little else.

"I take my income very seriously. At some point I'll switch out the craft room with my office, but not yet. The craft room makes me happy."

"I doubt that. It's a constant reminder of how you have to be perfect."

The unexpected insight caught her off guard and made her feel embarrassed and exposed. Like he'd walked in on her going to the bathroom.

Lucas was like that. Not that he walked in on her doing anything, but every now and then he was uncomfortably intuitive.

They returned to the living room, where he put the hurricane lanterns on the sideboard. She wrapped rose and gold ribbon around the bases before setting them in place. After scattering the glass beads down the center of the table, she studied the effect.

"It's beautiful," Lucas told her. "Becca's going to love it."

"Bunny will complain I haven't done enough."

"Want me to take her on for you?"

"You'd never take the chance," she told him. "What if you got old lady cooties?"

"There is that." He followed her back into the kitchen where she pulled the garlic spread out of the refrigerator.

"So who is Great-Aunt Cheryl anyway?" he asked.

"Terence's great-aunt. I first met her when he and I were still dating. She was wonderful. Funny and irreverent. She never married, but there were always very interesting men hanging around. She had a million stories and they were all so interesting. Just when I started to think she was making it all up, she'd pull out something like a letter from President Truman thanking her for her invaluable aid to our country."

She sliced the French loaf lengthwise. Lucas leaned against the counter.

"You admired her."

"I did. Very much. She was always very sweet to me."

"Bunny hated her and was jealous of your relationship."

Harper stared at him. "How did you know?"

"Come on. Really? Your mother is the most traditional person I know, and she's convinced you that if you buy bread instead of making it, the sun won't rise in the morning. Bunny is all home and hearth. Great-Aunt Cheryl would make Bunny's teeth hurt. Worse, she would have violated every one of Bunny's core beliefs."

"They weren't close," Harper admitted. "Over the past couple of years, Great-Aunt Cheryl and I weren't in touch as often. I thought she was busy. It was only after I found out she'd died that I learned she'd been sick."

Harper still felt guilty for not pushing harder to find out what was going on. "She didn't want to be any trouble, or something like that. I wish I'd been with her at the end."

"Was she alone?"

"No, she had Ramon."

He raised his eyebrows. "Ramon?"

"Great-Aunt Cheryl was a little like you when it came to her lovers."

"Good for her. Why didn't you go to the memorial?"

Harper had all her socially correct excuses at the ready, but with Lucas, she found herself blurting out the truth.

"It's nearly a day to drive to Grass Valley and I didn't want to be in the car that long with Terence and *her*."

"Alicia?" Lucas asked sweetly. "Is there a reason you can't say her name?"

"Yes. It's like Beetlejuice. If you say her name too many times, she'll rise up with horrific powers and do unspeakable things. I'm being cautious."

"The world thanks you."

"As it should."

She finished coating the bread. After slicing it, she wrapped it in foil so it was ready to pop in the oven.

"Expecting anything from Great Aunt Cheryl?" he asked.

"No. We were friends and that's plenty."

She went into the pantry and scooped flour into a sifter, then sorted through her folder of stencils before finding the one she needed. Technically it wasn't Easter until Sunday, but she wanted something fun for her daughter's return.

Lucas didn't speak as he followed her outside. She stopped at the end of the walkway, then put the stencil on the concrete path before straightening and gently turning the handle on the sifter.

Flour drifted down, landing on the stencil. When she lifted it up, there was a perfect set of rabbit footprints.

Lucas stepped around her and headed for his car. "You're a scary woman, Harper Szymanski. I'll see you in a couple of hours."

"With Pomegranate."

"Persimmon."

"Does it actually matter?"

He got into his white Mercedes convertible, turned to her and winked. "Honestly, it doesn't."

Chapter Three

STACEY TOLD HERSELF THAT EVERYTHING WAS GOING TO be fine. The scientific research on the power of positive thinking was extensive. When an outcome was uncertain, focusing on optimistic possibilities relaxed the body and cleared the mind. Otherwise, thinking could be crippled by fear, like hers, right now.

"She's going to kill me when I tell her about the baby," she murmured, glancing at Kit as he drove the handful of blocks to her sister's house.

"Bunny would never do that. You're her daughter and she loves you."

"She's going to be disappointed in me. She's going to give me that look that makes me feel inadequate and small, as if I'm the most disappointing daughter ever. Then she's going to tell me there's something wrong with me."

Kit reached across the console and took her hand. "There's nothing wrong with you, Stacey. You're brilliant, loyal, kind and funny."

"But she *is* going to yell at me and be upset."

It was the latter that would be the most difficult for her to handle. Stacey might not get along with her mother, but she didn't want to hurt her feelings, either.

"She's not going to understand why you didn't tell her before," Kit said quietly.

She squeezed his fingers as tightly as she could. "I couldn't. She's going to say things that I don't want to hear." Stacey was terrified enough about the baby as it was—she didn't need her mother making the situation worse.

Most mothers worried about their child having a problem or about the pain of delivery or if they could handle the reality of juggling their already-busy life with an infant thrown in. She got that and shared some of those concerns, but her real worry—her real *fear*—was that she wasn't going to be an adequate mother.

The baby wasn't real to her. Hearing the heartbeat had brought Kit to tears while she'd simply monitored the rhythm and strength and found it to be within the normal range.

She had no sense of life growing within her. Yes, she understood the biology of what was happening, but that was simply science. Emotions were different. She could see herself as the vessel in which the baby grew, but not as the infant's mother. She couldn't imagine holding her daughter or rocking her. Kit talked about how excited he was for her to be born while Stacey had no sense of after.

"I just need to get through this," Stacey whispered, thinking both of telling her mother and having the baby. "Once I know how she's going to react, I'll be fine."

"Even if you're not, I'll be right there, next to you." He drew back his hand and flashed her a grin. "Harper will provide cover while we'll be ready to run if Bunny starts swinging."

Stacey managed a slight smile. "She would never hit you or even say you were wrong. You're the man and, by default, special."

"It's good to be me." His grin faded. "I know I've asked before, but I want to double-check that you're okay with Ashton moving in with us."

The change of subject was welcome but the new topic matter confused her. "Why would there be a problem with Ashton?"

Kit pulled up in front of Harper's house and turned off the engine. He faced Stacey. "You barely know him. He's going to be living with us through the summer. The baby is due in late June. Any one of these could be considered a problem for most women."

Kit was a rock-solid guy, but his sister was not. She'd spent most of her life in and out of drug rehab. Every now and then Stacey wondered if she should have specialized in addiction. The brain had an amazing capacity to fixate on pleasure— whatever its source.

Kit's sister's lifestyle had played havoc on her son's life. Ashton had bounced around, living with friends and distant relatives while his mother dealt with her issues. Over the years Kit had tried to bring Ashton to California to live with him, but his sister wouldn't allow it.

Now that Ashton was eighteen, he was free to do what he wanted. Kit and Stacey had agreed the young man could live with them until he started MIT in the fall. He only had two classes left to complete his high school diploma and he would take both of those online.

"He's been very responsible and pleasant both times I've met him," she said. "I'm sure we'll get along."

Plus, having another person in the house would allow her

to be distracted from the impending birth. Not that she would admit that to Kit.

"You're being very generous," Kit said.

"I'm not. I like Ashton."

"I meant about us supplementing his college."

Ashton had a scholarship that covered his tuition but little else. Kit and Stacey would take care of his room and board, along with whatever else he might need.

"I've always been well compensated and the house is paid for. We have money set aside for Joule's college fund. Helping Ashton is our way of paying it forward." Perhaps if she put out enough good deeds, the Universe wouldn't notice that she had no interest in her daughter.

Kit leaned close and kissed her. "You're the best wife ever."

"I wish that were true."

They got out of the car and started for the front door. Stacey paused to study the bunny footprints on the walkway. Inadequacy gripped her with cold, bony fingers.

She would never be able to do anything like that, she thought, trying not to panic. She wouldn't even think to do it, let alone be clear on how to execute the plan. Yes, Kit would be the one staying home with their daughter, but still—she was completely and totally clueless.

Harper opened the front door and smiled. "Hey, you two." She ran down the steps and hugged her sister before embracing Kit. "I hope you're hungry. I made lasagna."

Because it was Becca's favorite, Stacey thought automatically. Harper always did that sort of thing. She took care of the details of life. Details Stacey rarely noticed.

They went into the house. From the foyer Stacey could see the decorated table, the place settings and the crystal glasses.

She thought of the plain dishes she and Kit had at home and wanted to whimper.

"Come on," Harper said, leading them into the kitchen. "I'm trying a new herbal tea I read about online. It's supposed to be perfect for pregnant women. It supports both the baby and the mother." She grinned at Kit. "For you, I have a beer."

"You're my favorite sister-in-law," he told her.

Harper laughed. "Of course I am."

Stacey watched Harper pour hot tea into a mug. "I'm going to tell Mom today."

Harper rolled her eyes. "Uh-huh. Sure you are. I usually resent you being both the pretty and the smart sister, but right now you do have your issues. I say wait until Joule is born, then hand her over. Mom will get the message."

Kit got a bottle of beer from the refrigerator. "That's what I said."

The back door opened and Bunny walked into the kitchen. "You're here," she said, smiling at Stacey and Kit. "Why didn't anyone tell me?"

She hugged them both, then looked around at the kitchen. "Do you need help with dinner?" she asked Harper.

"Thanks, Mom, I'm good."

Stacey sipped her tea. Harper always made everything domestic look so easy. Her house was perfectly decorated for whatever season and always tidy and clean.

Bunny took a mug of tea and sat at one of the counter stools. She looked at Stacey. "So what's new?"

The room went totally silent. Stacey could feel her husband and her sister both watching her, waiting to see what she would do.

She had to come clean—she understood that. If only her mother would understand. But Bunny wouldn't. She hadn't approved of Stacey keeping her own last name when she married Kit, that she still worked full-time, that her job had always been the most important part of her life, at least until she'd met Kit.

Stacey sucked in a breath and opened her mouth. "Mom, I—"

"Knock, knock!"

The call came from the front of the house. Harper walked by and murmured, "Saved by the bell, so to speak. I can't figure out if you have the best or worst luck."

"Me, either."

Harper's client Lucas walked into the kitchen with a tall, thin redhead at his side. The young woman looked to be maybe twenty or twenty-one. She held a large, fabric-covered box, which she handed to Harper.

"Lucas said this is for you."

"It's beautiful," Harper said as she set it on the counter. "Where did you find it?"

"Etsy," Lucas said, handing Bunny a bouquet of flowers. "Hello, Bunny."

Her mother batted her lashes and smiled at Lucas. "Hello, Lucas." She turned to his date. "And you are?"

"Persimmon," Harper said with a grin.

"Oh, dear." Bunny's mouth grew pinched. "That's an unusual name."

"I know, right? I have a sister named Kumquat."

"I can't imagine what your parents were thinking." Bunny gave her an insincere smile. "Let me get these in water."

With Lucas and Persimmon around, Stacey was able to relax. There was no way she could tell her mother the truth now. Maybe after dinner, when Lucas and his date had left.

Stacey settled on one of the bar stools at the kitchen counter and prepared to watch the dynamics of the interactions between Lucas, Harper and Bunny.

Harper got her guests drinks. Lucas took a beer and Persimmon wanted to try the herbal tea. Stacey wondered if she was old enough to legally drink alcohol. Bunny fussed with the flowers, all the while eyeing Lucas's date.

In a way, Bunny's dilemma was interesting to observe. She didn't approve of his young girlfriends, yet he was a man and therefore right by default. Stacey wondered about his preference for dating women so much younger than himself. He was attractive, intelligent and had a very responsible job. By all accounts he should be more comfortable with women closer to his own demographic. Yet he clearly favored young, beautiful but vapid women.

Kit's theory was that Lucas had had some trauma in his life. Stacey had asked Harper, but she didn't have any insights.

Lucas settled next to Stacey, then leaned close. "Still not coming clean?" he asked quietly.

"How did you know?"

"There's no screaming and Bunny isn't hyperventilating. Want me to tell her? She doesn't scare me."

"She doesn't scare me, either."

Lucas raised his eyebrows.

"Okay, she doesn't scare me much."

He winked at her and she laughed.

Harper pulled her cell phone from her jeans pocket and glanced at the screen. "That's Becca," she said, sounding relieved. "They're pulling up now."

Everyone walked toward the front of the house. Kit grabbed Stacey's hand and squeezed her fingers. She looked at him and sighed.

"I know," she told him.

"You'll get there."

Stacey hoped he was right.

They all went out front, careful to avoid the rabbit footprints. A large black BMW pulled into the driveway. Stacey noted that Terence's girlfriend was driving rather than him, which was unusual, but not as unexpected as the three incredibly large dogs in the back seat with Becca.

The car came to a stop and Terence nearly fell out of the passenger's side. His face was red, his eyes practically swollen shut and he was coughing and choking. Alicia, his girlfriend, got out and shook her head.

"I guess he is really allergic to dogs, huh?"

Becca was the last to leave the vehicle, followed by three huge Dobermans. The dogs were sleek and muscled, black-and-tan, with alert but wary expressions. Stacey watched her sister stare at her daughter, then at the dogs.

"No," Harper breathed. "She didn't."

"Mom, it's not what you think!"

All the Bloom women had dark hair and blue eyes, with heart-shaped faces. Stacey was the tallest at five-seven. Bunny and Harper were both a few inches shorter, and Becca was in the middle. Seeing them together, no one could miss the family resemblance.

Alicia sighed. "Don't get your panties in a twist, Harper. Great-Grandmother Cheryl or whatever she was to you didn't leave you the dogs." The blonde woman's expression turned smug. "She left them to Becca. All three of them. Good luck."

Harper took a step toward her daughter. "She left *you* the dogs and you never thought to give me a heads-up?"

Her daughter's chin rose. "I knew you'd overreact and tell me I couldn't bring them home."

Terence continued to choke and cough. Becca looked at him.

"Dad is allergic to dogs, like you said. He took all kinds of meds but he still had a hard time. I guess it was being in the car and everything."

Harper barely glanced at her ex, instead keeping her attention on Becca. "We cannot have three dogs."

"They're huge and dangerous," Bunny piped in. "And that one's pregnant."

"Her name is Bay," Becca said, still sounding defiant. "And they're mine. Great-Aunt Cheryl wanted me to have them and you can't take them away from me."

Kit put his arm around Stacey. "To think we almost named our daughter Bay," he murmured. "Awkward."

She appreciated his attempt at humor but was more concerned about Becca and Harper fighting. If her sister couldn't get along with her daughter, what chance did Stacey have with her child? Harper was the perfect mother. She knew how to do *everything*.

"Becca, be reasonable," Harper said. "They're huge dogs. We don't have enough room for them. Plus, they're specially trained. Shouldn't the government take them?"

Becca's eyes filled with tears. "I knew you'd be like this. You never want me to have what I want."

Alicia had opened the trunk. She started pulling out bags and boxes. "No one needs to help me," she said sarcastically. "I'm fine."

Both Kit and Lucas walked over and finished emptying the trunk. Terence stumbled into the car while Alicia got behind the wheel. They drove off without saying a word.

Lucas glanced at the dogs. "What's the boy's name?" he asked.

"Thor and the other one is Jazz."

"Thor, come."

Lucas's voice was firm. The male Doberman trotted over and sat in front of him. Lucas held out his hand. Thor sniffed, then looked at him.

"Good boy." Lucas patted him on the head. "I'll take him."

Harper spun to face him. "You'll what?"

"I'll take him. I have a yard and I've always wanted a dog. It'll be great."

Becca sniffed. "That would be okay, if you promise to be a good puppy dad."

"I do promise."

Staccy met the gaze of the pregnant dog. The animal looked calm and kind of sweet, in a very large, I could eat you in a hot minute kind of way.

"We'll take, um, Bay," she said without thinking. Maybe she could learn something when the dog had her puppies. If nothing else, it would be nice to have another pregnant female around.

"Stacey," Bunny said disapprovingly. "You can't just blurt out things like that. You have to talk to your husband first. What if Kit doesn't want a dog?"

Kit met Stacey's gaze. She saw the understanding in his eyes and knew he got what she'd been thinking. Still, she should have asked him—a dog was a big responsibility and she spent her days at the lab.

Kit smiled at her, then he called Bay. The Doberman hurried to sit in front of him.

"Want to come home with us?" he asked.

She tilted her head as if considering the offer.

Persimmon clapped her hands together. "This is so wonderful. Like a Hallmark movie. The whole family pulled together." She smiled at Harper. "Now you have to let your daughter keep the dog because it's just one. I could so cry right now."

"Me, too," Harper muttered. "Becca, the only way we're keeping a dog is if you take responsibility for it. I mean that. You have to do everything. If you don't, it goes. Am I clear?"

"I'll do it, Mom. You'll see. I'll handle it all."

"I want to believe you," Harper began, then stopped herself. "All right. Let's sort through all this stuff and figure out what goes where. Did Great-Aunt Cheryl leave an instruction sheet or something?"

"There's a whole book," Becca said eagerly as she wiped away tears. "They know some really cool stuff, Mom. You'll see."

"I'll do research on pregnant dogs," Kit said. "We're going to have puppies."

And a baby, Stacey thought, knowing there was no way she could tell her mother the truth today. As Harper said, Stacey either had the best or worst luck in the world. She just couldn't decide which.

Chapter Four

BECCA SZYMANSKI CARRIED HER SUITCASE AND BACK-pack into the living room and let both fall to the carpeted floor. She was happy, sad, mad, annoyed and relieved all at once, and her chest wasn't big enough for that much emotion.

She'd known her mom was totally going to overreact to the dogs and she hadn't been wrong. Just once, just one single time, she would really appreciate it if her mother would listen and respond like a thoughtful person instead of always jumping to the conclusion that not only would it go badly but it would all be Becca's fault because she wasn't responsible enough.

Becca *was* responsible. She'd gotten through her parents' divorce without letting either of them know how devastated she was. She'd gotten through her best friend's moving away without anyone seeing how shattered she was inside. She lived a thousand emotions her mother knew nothing about…and never would.

Becca collapsed to the floor and started to cover her face with her hands only to hear a faint whimper. She looked up and saw Jazz standing just inside the front door, her expression worried, her brown eyes questioning.

"Oh, Jazz, I'm sorry. I forgot you were there." Becca bit her bottom lip. Did saying that make her mother right?

No, she told herself quickly. Of course not. She'd been home five seconds—it would take a while for them all to adjust to a pet.

She shifted onto her knees, then held out her arms and said softly, "Jazz, come here."

The black-and-tan Doberman approached, then sat obediently. Becca threw her arms around the dog and hung on. "It's okay," she whispered against the dog's warm body. "You're going to be safe now, I promise. I'm going to be here for you."

She drew back and looked into Jazz's face. "Thor is going to stay with our friend Lucas, and Bay will be with Aunt Stacey. Lucas is a good guy. He's a detective with the Los Angeles Police Department. He's been my mom's client for about a year now." She smiled. "He's a grown-up, so you know what that means, although he's pretty cool with me." She wrinkled her nose. "He always has really young girlfriends. It was creepy at first, but finally I asked him if I had to worry that he would want to date one of my friends in a couple of years."

Jazz's ears perked up, as if she were interested in the answer.

"He said the younger woman thing was because of trauma and that he promised he would never embarrass me that way. He said he wanted me to know that he totally respected me and my mom and that he would be there if we needed something." She stroked the dog's head. "To be honest, he has been really supportive and stuff with us. I'm telling you this so you won't worry about Thor."

She thought about her aunt Stacey. "I'm sure Bay will be good with Kit and Stacey. They have a nice house and a yard.

Uncle Kit's really fun and Aunt Stacey is super smart. She's going to cure MS or maybe help people with MS have less symptoms. I'm never sure when she talks about her work." She hugged Jazz. "I get it. Even though you know everyone is okay, you're going to miss your friends, though, aren't you? I *so* get that. I miss Kaylee, but she's off having fun with her new friends. You should see what she posts on Instagram all the time." Becca waved her hands in the air. "Look at me! Look at me!"

Jazz's steady gaze never wavered. Becca dropped her arms to her side.

"You have no idea who I'm talking about, do you," she said with a sigh. "Sorry." She thought briefly of pulling out her phone and showing Jazz the videos, then told herself the dog still wouldn't care. Because this was all new to Jazz and no matter how well trained she was, she had to be scared.

"I remember the first night my dad left," Becca admitted in a low voice as she sat on the floor and continued to pet the dog. "I was crying, my mom was crying, my grandmother kept asking my mom what she'd done wrong. It was horrible. Uncle Kit and Aunt Stacey had just gotten married and were on their honeymoon, so she wasn't here."

Becca sighed. "I don't know if anyone's told you this, but Great-Aunt Cheryl is gone. She was really old and she died." She shifted so she sat directly in front of Jazz. "I promise I will always take care of you, Jazz. I'll be here. I have to go to school and stuff, but then I'll come home. You belong here now. With me."

She smiled. "I always wanted a dog, but Mom said we couldn't because Dad was allergic. After the drive home, I guess he really is. Anyway, I want you to know I'm going to take care of you. I have the book of instructions Great-Aunt

Cheryl left me. I'll get copies to Stacey and Lucas. You have to believe in me, okay? I'm going to be here. I'm not going to die like Great-Aunt Cheryl, and I'm not going to leave you like my dad."

Tears unexpectedly formed. Becca brushed them away. It was one thing to be upset about the dogs, but she refused to cry over the divorce. It had been two years and she should be over it. At least that was what everyone else seemed to think.

She knew, compared to some of her friends, she had it easy. She wasn't shuffled from house to house and she didn't have to deal with a bunch of new stepbrothers and sisters. In fact, she rarely saw her father. He was too busy with his new life and Alicia.

"How's it going?"

She looked up as Lucas walked into the living room, then leaned her head against Jazz. "We're still getting to know each other. It's only been a couple of days, so Jazz is a little scared."

"Sure." He sat in a club chair across the room. "There's been a lot of change. How are you holding up?"

She glanced at him and rolled her eyes. "Why are you asking? You know I'm mad at my mom."

"Yes, I do. Want to tell me why?"

She didn't know what it was about Lucas, but she could always talk to him. Maybe it was because he didn't speak to her like she was a kid—he treated her as if she were a regular person with thoughts and opinions and feelings.

When she'd first met him, she'd wondered if he was one of those creepy old guys she and her friends were always being warned about. One of her friends had a stepdad who'd tried to touch her, which was horrible and disgusting.

But Lucas wasn't like that. He was nice. He listened and when he was around, her mom was a lot calmer. Becca had even gotten used to the really young girlfriends. Some of them were complete airheads, but a few had given her some fashion advice. Still, what was with naming your kid Persimmon?

"She always says no," Becca grumbled, remembering the question. "I've begged for a dog forever and she said it was because of my dad. Then he moved out and she still said no. Great-Aunt Cheryl left the dogs to me in her will. They're mine. Mom should respect that."

Lucas didn't say anything, but then he didn't have to. She squirmed slightly. Jazz gave her a quick lick on her cheek before flopping to the floor. Becca sprawled out next to her and held her paw in her hand.

"Fine," Becca said with a sigh. "Three dogs would be a lot, and I've never taken care of a dog before." She glared at him. "There are instructions in the book and I've been reading them. I know how much they eat and when they have to be walked. I'm going to take care of Jazz. I'll feed her and play with her and pick up after her."

She shuddered as she thought of the volume of poop the three dogs had generated over the past couple of days. Gross didn't come close, but everything had a price.

"I'll even clean up the yard. I'm going to be a good dog mom. You'll see."

"Sounds like you have a plan."

"I do." She sat up. "Are you really taking Thor?"

"I am. He'll be spending his days here while I'm at work, so Jazz won't be alone."

"Does Mom know?"

"I'll tell her after dinner."

Becca chuckled. "Thanks. She can't tell you no and there's no way she can watch Thor and make me get rid of Jazz, so thank you."

"That wasn't my master plan but it does seem to solve a lot of problems."

He reached into his jacket pocket and pulled out a DVD case, then handed it to her. Becca look at the cover and laughed.

"You didn't! *Sixteen Candles*. Thanks, Lucas. You know it's my favorite."

"I do know."

Becca had a thing for the '80s. The clothes, the overstyled hair. How on earth did anyone ever wear leg warmers? But Madonna's music was great and the John Hughes movies were always fun to watch.

"Come on," Lucas said as he rose. "Bay and Thor are playing outside. Jazz should be with them to get the kinks out from her long drive down."

"Okay." Becca turned to her dog. "Come on, Jazz. Let's go in the backyard."

The slim, muscled dog rose and stretched, then walked at Becca's side. Becca stroked her head and ears. She was all Jazz had now.

"I'll be here," she told the dog. "You can depend on me." Because she knew all about what it was like to be an afterthought, and she never wanted Jazz to feel that way.

Stacey arrived at her office shortly after seven Monday morning. On days Kit had to get to school, their mornings were less leisurely and they both liked to be at the office early.

Except for dinner at Harper's, they'd spent Easter Sunday getting Bay acclimated to her new home. Stacey had lost her nerve again and didn't tell her mom about her pregnancy, rationalizing that she didn't want to monopolize everyone's attention on the holiday.

She and Kit had taken Bay on two long walks so she could get familiar with the neighborhood. Stacey had read up on pregnant dogs and had researched veterinarians in the office, while Kit had installed a doggie door so Bay could come and go as she liked during the day.

Bay was exceptionally well behaved. She'd slept in her dog bed in their room and had eaten. According to all Stacey had read, the dog seemed to be adjusting.

Stacey reviewed the latest test results from their new research direction. Proteins were an obvious area to investigate, but narrowing down exactly which ones and how they reacted was the tedious challenge. Still, progress was being made.

"Morning."

Stacey looked up as her assistant, Lexi, walked into her office. Lexi, a tall redhead in her midthirties, placed a mug on Stacey's desk.

"Herbal tea," she said with a grin. "In case you were hoping I was going to slip you a little caffeine."

"You'd never do that," Stacey said with a smile. "You always take excellent care of me. How was your weekend?"

"Good. Busy. The Easter Bunny did his thing on Sunday morning. Oh, Sam fell out of a tree, which had me sweating a broken arm, but he's fine. Still, what is it with kids and trees? It's not like the trees climb all over them. It's a tree—leave it alone."

Stacey wanted to say that Lexi could simply tell her son not to climb trees, only she knew that advice would not be welcome. She wasn't sure if it was all children or simply Lexi's, but hers didn't listen very well.

Her assistant was bright and capable. As she frequently did, Stacey thought it was a shame that Lexi hadn't gone to college. She could have been successful in many different areas.

Not that she wasn't an excellent assistant—she was. But with three kids to support, Lexi was frequently scrambling to make ends meet. A career with a more lucrative pay scale would have been appreciated.

But Lexi had gotten pregnant in high school and then again a couple of years later. She'd married in her late twenties and had her third child by her now ex-husband.

People made interesting choices, Stacey thought. Some made sense while others simply confused her. She was never sure how much of that was her inability to relate to them versus the decision not making sense in the first place.

"How was your Easter?" Lexi asked as she took a seat across from Stacey's desk.

"Very nice. Harper prepared a wonderful meal. I brought plenty of leftovers for lunch if you'd care for some."

Lexi closed her eyes and moaned. "You know I love your sister's cooking. What that woman does with brownies should be illegal."

Lexi's interest in food greatly contributed to her weight problem. Stacey had tried to explain that she should think of food as fuel—like gas for a car. Perhaps that would allow her to lose weight. Lexi had told Stacey that while she was the best boss ever, she wasn't allowed to comment on her personal appearance and if she did it again, Lexi would write her up.

It had been the only moment of tension in their otherwise-successful working relationship.

Stacey honestly hadn't understood what she'd done wrong. Kit had tried to explain that Lexi probably knew she had a weight problem and wasn't looking for Stacey to try to solve it. Which made absolutely no sense. Not only were there health risks, but Lexi was always complaining about being tired and that she couldn't buy cute clothes. Simply eating less would make it all go away.

But Stacey appreciated Lexi and wanted to keep her happy, so she had vowed not to say anything ever again. She'd brought in brownies Harper had made as a peace offering and all had been well.

Lexi opened her eyes. "Did you tell her?"

No need to ask, *tell who what?* Lexi had known about the pregnancy since Stacey had had her first ultrasound. She wanted to pretend confusion as to why it had been so easy to tell Harper and Lexi about the baby, yet so hard to tell her mother, only she couldn't. She knew exactly why she didn't want to confess all to Bunny.

Maybe it was a bit like Lexi and her addiction to food. Knowing the right thing to do didn't make it any easier to accomplish.

"We have a new dog."

Lexi blinked at her. "There's a non sequitur. You have a dog?"

Stacey explained about Becca and the inherited dogs. "We took Bay. She's beautiful and so well trained. With all the confusion, it didn't seem like a good time to tell my mother about the baby."

"Uh-huh. I'm sure someone believes that, but it wouldn't be me. You are lucky you're tall enough that your pregnancy doesn't show or she would have guessed by now anyway. You're going to be one of those annoying women who doesn't look pregnant until the last three days." She folded her arms across her chest. "Stacey, you know it's only going to get harder to tell her the longer you wait, right?"

Stacey nodded, although she couldn't imagine it being any more difficult than it was right now.

"You also have to let Karl know," Lexi added.

"I've told HR," Stacey said defensively.

She'd already filled out all the required paperwork and requested her leave. The chain of command had been alerted. Which was not, she admitted to herself, the same as telling the head of her department.

Karl wasn't exactly her boss—Stacey had autonomy in her department. As long as her team produced results, she was left to her own devices. Still, Karl was the closest thing to a manager she had, and at some point he needed to know. Just not right now.

"Did I mention Bay is pregnant?"

Lexi's eyes widened. "Your new dog is pregnant?"

"Yes. Significantly so. I'm going to make an appointment to take her to the vet to get her checked out." She frowned. "Thor's been neutered, so he can't be the father. I wonder who it was. Regardless, we'll have puppies soon."

"You're pregnant. You haven't told your mom or Karl, but you now have a dog who's going to have puppies?"

Lexi's voice was filled with incredulity and shock, which didn't make any sense.

"Why are you saying it like that? What does one have to do with the other?"

"You're going to have a baby," Lexi said forcefully. "Your life is going to change in ways you can't begin to understand. The last thing you need is puppies in the house."

Stacey disagreed. Puppies were exactly what she needed. Being around Bay would allow her to observe motherhood in a safe and nonjudgmental environment. She planned to learn from the dog and use those lessons to help herself feel more connected to her own child.

"I think Bay and her puppies will be good for me," she said.

"You're the boss." Lexi stood. "I'm going to finish proofing your article, then email it back to you. In the meantime, if you have any questions, remember I've had three. I know it all."

"Thank you."

Stacey planned to call on her assistant when the time came. It would be good to have an extra resource for those questions she couldn't ask her mother or sister.

Too much of the literature she'd read mentioned hormones and instinct kicking in when the baby was born. While Stacey appreciated the power of innate intelligence, she was concerned she was somehow lacking vital pieces—especially when it came to being a mother. She'd never been normal before—why would that change now?

Becca walked slowly up the front steps to Mischief Bay High School when what she wanted to do was run or skip or even dance. Spring Break was over. Finally! She glanced around, wondering if anyone else was thinking the same thing, then sighed. Of course they weren't. Everyone else had gone away for Spring Break or had fun with their friends. Everyone else had plans. She'd been the only one counting the days until she could get back to something close to a life.

She sat on the stone bench to the side of the huge open double doors and faked looking for something in her backpack. She needed a second to remember how to pretend all the things she was supposed to pretend. That she didn't miss Kaylee every second of every day. Her best friend had moved to Boston at the end of last summer. After swearing she would never have another friend as amazing as Becca, after crying for weeks about how she would never fit in, Kaylee had settled into life in Boston easily and happily.

Between Instagram and Snapchat, Becca had a clear idea

of exactly how perfect Kaylee's new life was. She even had a boyfriend. Just like Jordan, Becca's second-best friend. Becca, on the other hand, hadn't even been kissed, not unless you counted a couple of stupid birthday parties with kissing games, which she didn't.

She knew it was wrong to be jealous of Kaylee learning to sail and dating the younger brother of a naval cadet, and in a way, she wasn't. She *wanted* Kaylee to be happy—it was just she also wanted to be missed as much as she was missing her friend. But the texts were getting less frequent and less personal. These days it seemed as if Kaylee was texting her grandmother rather than her friend.

As for Jordan… Becca shook her head. She had no idea what to do there. Jordan and her family had gone to Mexico for Spring Break. Back in November, Jordan had begged Becca to go with her. If she didn't have her best friend along, she would *die*. Then, over Christmas, Jordan and Nathan had started dating and in the end, Jordan had taken Nathan instead.

There were other friends—she was part of a group, just like pretty much every other girl in high school. But those were just regular friends. Becca had never been good at being close with a crowd. She preferred one or two people in her life, which made her weird and left her sitting alone on this stupid bench, freakishly excited about school starting in twenty minutes.

She looked around at everyone talking about their vacations, listened to the laughing and teasing and felt…sad. No, she thought. Not sad, exactly. Small. She was so small and everyone else was big and sometimes she felt as if she were getting smaller and smaller and one day she would just disappear.

Her phone chirped.

Where RU? omg I need to cu now

Becca smiled as Jordan's drama played out in text, even as she heard her friend's voice in her head.

Muinoup, she texted back, abbreviating "meet you in our usual place."

She started toward the science building where she and Jordan would meet up in the girls' bathroom. No one hung out here before school started, which meant the bathrooms were usually empty, allowing plenty of privacy for whatever revelation Jordan might want to share.

Becca wanted to hear all about her friend's vacation. Jordan had been oddly quiet during her trip, only posting a handful of Snapchat videos and three Instagram pics. Once Jordan was finished—because Jordan *always* had to go first—Becca wanted to talk about her new dog and her dad and his upcoming wedding that her mom still knew nothing about.

And the car. At some point Becca was going to have to come clean about the car.

She wondered how her mom would react when she found out her ex-husband was getting married. Would she be mad or would she cry? Becca didn't know what she was supposed to say. She wasn't happy about it, either. Her dad already pretty much ignored her. He'd promised to take her driving over Spring Break and that had never happened—not even on the long drive to Grass Valley. She needed her fifty supervised hours. Her mom always said she was too busy, and now her dad kept flaking out on her.

She ran up the steps to the science building, pushed open the door and turned into the girls' bathroom. Jordan was already there, texting. She smiled when she saw Becca.

"Finally! My God, I've been waiting and waiting. Where were you?"

Becca automatically started checking stalls to make sure they were alone. Jordan shook her head.

"I did that already. You'll never guess. Try. You won't, but try."

Becca looked at her friend. Jordan was one of those people who had been born beautiful. She had dark skin and hair, and big brown eyes. She was tall, thin and always knew what she was supposed to wear.

Becca and Kaylee had been friends since kindergarten. It had always been the two of them until junior high when they'd met Jordan. Then it had been the three of them. Kaylee had always been the pretty friend, but when Jordan came along, Kaylee had to give up her crown. As for Becca, well, she was funny and smart. As if that mattered.

"How was your vacation?" Becca asked.

"Perfect. Amazing. Life changing." Jordan spun in a circle, then grinned. "Do I look different? I feel different. More mature, you know?"

Becca studied her. Jordan wore skinny jeans and a cute, cropped sweater. Her hair was long, hanging down to the middle of her back. She had about a dozen bangles on her wrists, one ear cuff and a tiny diamond nose stud.

"You look great," Becca offered.

Jordan grabbed her arm and pulled her close. "You can't tell *anyone*. You have to *swear*."

"I never tell. You know that. What? Tell me." But as she asked, she got a sinking feeling she already knew.

Jordan released her, then sucked in a breath. "Nathan and I had sex. Not just fooling around. We did it. All the way." She paused. "He actually put it in!"

Becca didn't know what to say. Sure, she'd known this could happen eventually. Jordan and Nathan had been together for a while now and they had other friends who were hooking up, but still. Sex? Yet one more way Becca was being left behind.

She felt stupid and ugly and unwanted. Like aliens had come to school and abducted everyone but her because why would she be interesting to experiment on?

Jordan looked expectant. Becca tried to think of the right question. She and Jordan had talked about what it would be like to do that of course. More since Jordan and Nathan got serious, but to have done it…

"What was it like? Where did you do it? Do your parents know?"

Jordan exhaled slowly, then smiled. "It was nice. I liked it better when we were just, you know, fooling around, but it was good, too. I feel so different." She looked at herself in the mirror. "I keep waiting for my mom to figure it out but that would mean she noticed I was alive." Jordan rolled her eyes. "You know how she is."

Jordan's mother was a successful lawyer and her dad was a judge. They both adored and ignored their only daughter.

"Anyway, on Tuesday night Nathan sneaked into my room. We were fooling around, and then he got really serious." Jordan's eyes filled with tears. "He said he loved me and I said I loved him, and then it just happened."

How did something like that just happen? "Did it hurt?"

"Yes, but not for long. He was so sweet. He stayed the night." Jordan turned back to her. "I hope you find somebody, Becca. A *good* guy who wants to have sex with you."

Because the only ones lining up were bad guys?

Jordan smiled at her. "I want you to know that I'm still going to be friends with you. That you matter to me. Even though we're in different places in our lives now." The smile gentled and became annoying like a mom's. "You'll catch up eventually."

Jordan glanced at her phone. "Okay, we have a few minutes and I know you want all the details. Some are kind of personal, but still…"

Irritation flared. "I had a Spring Break, too, Jordan. It wouldn't kill you to ask about it."

"All you did was stay home." Jordan sighed. "Don't be jealous, Becca. I'm not going to be sorry that I have Nathan and you don't have anybody. You're my best friend and he's my boyfriend. You're going to have to find a way to get along."

"Why do I have to get along with him? Why doesn't he have to get along with me?" Becca shook her head. "And that's not the point. Nathan and I are fine together. This isn't even about that."

"You're not making any sense. Are you mad at me because everything is so great for me?"

"No. Of course not. I'm sorry."

The words were automatic, then annoying. Becca couldn't figure out what she was thinking or why she was apologizing. Why did Jordan get to be so selfish and Becca was the bad guy? What was going on with everyone?

She picked up her backpack. "We should go. It's time for class."

Jordan walked to the door, then glanced back at her. "I wish you could trust me not to leave you behind, Becca."

Becca thought longingly of the instruction book Great-Aunt Cheryl had left her. Maybe there was a command that would make Jazz bite Jordan. Not hard. Just enough to have her friend realize she was being the biggest bitch on the planet.

Chapter Five

HARPER COULDN'T SHAKE THE FEELING OF BEING watched—probably because she was. Even though Thor and Jazz were lying down on huge beds that nearly filled her tiny office, their eyes were open and firmly fixed on her. As if waiting for something. She supposed some of her unease came from the fact that they were huge, muscular dogs trained to do God knew what. For all she knew, they were assessing her and if she showed weakness, they would simply kill her and hide the body, then pretend nothing had happened.

"I can't believe I'm dog sitting," she muttered, as she moved the picture around on her computer screen. She had a one-off job to provide online content for a new boutique by the boardwalk. The owner had called in a panic after realizing that just because her twelve-year-old could design a slick website, he wasn't necessarily prepared to develop content. Harper was hoping the owner would be happy enough to keep her on to-do monthly updates.

She forced herself to concentrate, despite the sense of foreboding the two dogs engendered. She'd been expecting to have to deal with Jazz, but then Lucas had told her he was adding dog sitting to her duties. She would have refused only she not only needed the money—Jazz ate more than the average grizzly, and the food Great-Aunt Cheryl recommended cost as much as dinner for five at a decent restaurant—but she thought the two dogs might keep each other company, thereby freeing her from having to entertain Jazz.

She settled on a location for the pictures, cut and pasted the text, then studied the effect of the page. She'd added a section for featured clothes and had made the "style of the week" section bigger. Fifteen minutes of brainstorming over coffee had given her a list of suggestions she planned to share with the owner. One of them—a shop-your-closet feature—could give clients a reason to either come to the website or read the newsletter without feeling they were being sold to at every turn.

She got up to pour herself more coffee. Both Jazz and Thor raised their heads to watch her. She couldn't tell if they were curious, still confused about their new location or assessing her viability. She paused to lightly pet each of them before going into the kitchen. Clicking nails told her she was not alone. So far the dogs had followed her from room to room, including trying to get into the bathroom with her. She'd insisted they wait in the hall, telling them that she wouldn't watch them go and in return they couldn't watch her.

Now she poured her coffee, then turned and saw they were both standing there, staring.

"I know you want something, I just have no idea what," she admitted. "Do you want to go out?"

They both glanced at the back door, then at her. She sighed. She'd been very clear with Great-Aunt Cheryl. The last thing Harper wanted was one more life-form to take care of. She had enough on her plate—but had the woman listened? Okay, sure, technically, but not really. At the end of the day, Harper was still going to be a pet parent, whether she liked it or not. Becca had taken care of Jazz over the weekend, but the dog was still new to her. How long until her daughter was too busy or wasn't home to handle things?

Harper's cell rang. She pushed the button on her Bluetooth headset. "This is Harper."

"Harper, it's Cathy. Do you have a sec?"

"Sure."

She carried her coffee back to her office, then quickly found Cathy's file. The event planner used Harper to fill in when she needed an extra pair of creative hands. Harper could address two hundred envelopes in decorative calligraphy or paint a pin-the-tail-on-the-elephant poster or make custom napkin rings for a high-end dinner party.

"Okay, I talked to my clients, the ones hosting a fiftieth anniversary party for the parents. They've chosen the gift bag they want."

"Great." Harper sorted through the pictures she'd taken and slipped into the file. Next to each were the supplies needed, along with what they would cost and how long it took to assemble each bag.

She'd created three custom gift bags—not what went in them, just the bags themselves. Cathy had wanted them to be special, so they were all unique and not easy to put together.

"I have my information right here," Harper said.

"They've picked number three. Now you said it was going to be twenty dollars a bag, but we both know that's ridiculous. I told them I could get it for five dollars. I hope you're okay with that."

Harper stared at the picture, then scanned her notes. The bag was rose gold with a raffia handle. She'd applied delicate

printed paper from France to the front of the bag, then edged
it in tiny beads. After making by hand a flower done in shades
of gold, she'd stenciled on the couple's name and the date of
their wedding, fifty years ago.

The price she'd quoted wasn't just all the paper and trim, it
was the time. Her heart sank. Cathy frequently tried to undercut Harper's prices and most of the time Harper went along
with it, but there was no way she could do the bag for that.

"The supplies cost more than five dollars," Harper said,
trying to sound firm. "It will take me thirty minutes to complete each one."

"Can't you work faster? My God, it's a gift bag. Seriously,
Harper, no one is going to pay twenty dollars for that."

"Then they should pick one of the other ones."

"They want the one they want."

Harper's stomach tightened. Irritation mingled with fear.
She needed the work, but refused to take a loss. "The paper
is imported…there are multiple layers. If you want something unique and handmade, that is the cost. I'm sorry, but
my price is firm."

"I'm sorry, too. I hate to lose you as a resource, but if you're
not going to work with me, then I don't know if we can keep
doing business together."

The threat was like a kick to the stomach. Harper didn't
think she made any noise, but suddenly Jazz and Thor were
both standing next to her, looking intent. Thor glanced toward the doorway and growled low in his throat.

She couldn't remember the last time anyone had stood up
for her like that. The unexpected support brought tears to her
eyes, which was completely insane. She swallowed and petted
both of them before clearing her throat.

For a second, she wondered if she could somehow buy the

supplies cheaper. Maybe on eBay. No, she told herself. There was no time to search them out.

"I'm sorry, Cathy. That's my price."

"Then goodbye."

The other woman hung up. Harper did her best to ignore the knot in her stomach. She drew in a breath. "I might have just lost a client. No problem for you, Thor. Your owner has plenty of money."

She wasn't exactly sure how Lucas had so much cash to throw around. He drove a very expensive two-seater Mercedes convertible and she didn't think detectives made that much. Still, she wasn't going to ask too many questions. He paid his monthly bill the same day he received it—she knew because she paid his bills for him and why, yes, she did pay herself first. It was one of the very few perks of her work.

She returned her attention to the boutique website and continued to add pictures and text until she was happy with the layout. She saved everything, then sent a note and the link to the owner, asking for feedback.

"That's done," she told the dogs, who were still watching her. She swiveled in her chair to face them. "This would be a lot easier if you'd just tell me what you need."

Before they could answer, her phone rang again.

"This is Harper."

"It's Cathy. You're being ridiculous, so you know, but you do good work and I want to see if we can find a point of compromise. How about ten dollars a bag and I'll need them in three days?"

Harper held in a groan. There were forty bags, at about thirty minutes each, plus she had to go to three different stores to buy the supplies. That was twenty hours of work plus all the running around, for a grand total of four hundred dollars.

She didn't dare do the math to figure out the pitiful sum she would be making by the hour, but if she stayed up most of tonight and tomorrow night, she could meet the deadline.

"Harper?"

"Fine. Ten dollars a bag."

"Great. I'll let them know and I'll be by Thursday morning to pick them up. You're the best, Harper. Thanks."

Cathy hung up before Harper could say anything. Harper returned her attention to the dogs.

"I know what you're thinking," she muttered. "I'm letting her take advantage of me. That I'm probably making two dollars an hour on this job. Well, it's not this job, is it? It's all the other work she brings me."

Jazz's steady gaze never wavered. Harper sighed.

"You're right. I let her take advantage of me and that doesn't make any sense. I should be firm. I should tell her my price and stick to it. I'm training her to always undercut me. I get that."

She was sure the dog had more to say, but before they could continue the conversation, the doorbell rang. Thor and Jazz immediately rose. Jazz looked at Thor, who gave a low warning bark.

"Yes," Harper said, pushing past them. "I heard it, too, but thanks for mentioning it."

The dogs kept pace with her, but didn't walk ahead of her or run. When they reached the front door, they both sat and waited.

"I really need to read that instruction book Becca got," Harper told them as she opened the door. "Yes? Can I help you?"

A tall, gangly twentysomething guy stood on her porch. He was blond and wore board shorts, a T-shirt and athletic shoes. The T-shirt had a drawing of a cartoon version of him on it, along with the phrase Leader of the Pack.

"Harper Szymanski?" the guy asked.

"Yes."

"I'm Dwayne. I'm here to walk your dogs." He pulled a piece of paper out of his pocket and glanced at it. "Thor and Jazz. It's a daily service, which means Monday through Friday. I drive them to the beach and we walk along the boardwalk. It'll take about ninety minutes." Dwayne flashed her a smile. "Your husband paid for the top dog package. He must really like your dogs."

Harper didn't know what to say beyond, "He's not my husband." Because there was only one person who would have thought to arrange a dog-walking service. She would guess Lucas had done it for Thor, then added on Jazz. Damn the man for being thoughtful, good-looking and only interested in gorgeous bubbleheads in their twenties.

She held open the door for Dwayne to come inside. He saw Thor and Jazz and grinned.

"Oh, wow. Dobies. You guys are beautiful." He held out his hand so they could sniff his fingers, then he squatted in front of them and said, "Shake."

They both obliged.

"Lucas said you two were the bomb. He's right. Super great manners." He stood and looked at her. "I need their leashes."

Harper got them from the bottom drawer in the table by the front door. She handed over a new roll of poop bags, hoping the dogs would do their thing somewhere other than her backyard.

"Thanks," Dwayne said, snapping on the leashes. "We'll be back in an hour and a half. Do you want me to run them?"

"That would be great."

"Right? A tired dog is a happy dog. See ya." He looked at the dogs. "Thor, Jazz, heel."

The dogs stood and moved to his left side, Jazz taking the inside position. Dwayne walked them down the steps and out to his battered pickup. It was only after he'd driven away that Harper realized she probably should have checked with Lucas first. Just in case.

She quickly texted him, not sure when she would hear a response. Sometimes he was available, but a lot of the time, his phone was off. She supposed that came from being on the job catching bad guys or whatever it was he did in his day.

This time he answered her in a matter of seconds.

Are you concerned that someone cooked up an elaborate scheme to steal the dogs by pretending to be a dog walker?

Her lips twitched as she realized he kind of had a point.

I hadn't thought of it that way. Thank you for including Jazz on the walk. I'm sure she'll appreciate it. I know I do.

Happy to help. You can deal with your guilt by baking me something.

You know I will.

That I do.

She was still smiling as she walked into her pantry and studied the shelf that held her baking supplies. Not cookies, she thought. They were too ordinary. Tarts. She would bake Lucas chocolate tarts. But first she would go get the supplies she needed for the gift bags, then drop off the T-shirts she was shipping to her comedian client, Misty, then swing by the post office to mail Lucas's bills. *Then* she would bake tarts and tonight, while the world slept, she would make gift bags and curse her inability to stand up for herself when she knew she absolutely should.

Becca sat on the front porch step, her arm around Jazz. The dog was leaning heavily on her, her body providing comforting warmth.

"Are you still confused?" Becca asked the dog. "It's been a few days now and we have a routine. I'm sorry I have to be gone for school, but you have Thor, right? I could talk to Aunt Stacey about Bay. Maybe you three could have a playdate."

Jazz stretched out on the porch and rested her head on her paws, but even as she shifted positions, she still stayed close. Becca kept her arm around the dog, figuring they both needed the comfort.

Jazz wasn't the only one confused—Becca was starting to think she would never know everything going on, even in her own life. She missed Kaylee so much—more so now that Jordan had gone totally drama queen about Nathan. Kaylee would have called her on her crap and told her to stop talking about herself. Kaylee would have made a joke and smiled at Becca and asked about Jazz because that was what Kaylee had always done. She'd been a buffer against darker forces.

But there wasn't anything between Becca and Jordan, so Becca spent her day hearing about how amazing Nathan was and how he loved Jordan so much. Theirs was the greatest love ever and boyfriend-less Becca couldn't possibly understand. Worse, Jordan chided her about being bitter and angry, which wasn't true. Okay, not the bitter part. She didn't care that Jordan had Nathan, but she was starting to get pissed about her friend's attitude.

"Bay would never act like that to you," Becca told the dog. "You have better taste in friends."

For a second, she wished she could talk to her mom and tell her what was happening. Her mom could be dorky, but sometimes she had really good advice. Even if she didn't, she used to always make Becca feel better. They would bake something or do a craft project.

Not anymore, she thought grimly. Even if she was willing to do something so childish, her mom wasn't available. She was always too busy with her VA business.

Becca leaned over and kissed the top of Jazz's head, then straightened. She was about to pull out her phone and check the time when it buzzed with a text. She looked at the screen, then caught her breath when she read the message.

I'm tied up at work, kiddo. Sorry. Let's reschedule for some time next week.

Tears burned in her eyes. Becca blinked them away, telling herself to get over it. She knew she couldn't depend on her dad and she was stupid if she thought he would ever change. He always had something else he had to be doing. As for getting tied up at work—that was a complete lie. He was a podiatrist, which meant scheduled appointments. He wasn't a real doctor who had actual emergencies.

She shoved her phone back in her pocket and wiped her cheeks, just in case. Before she could scramble to her feet and escape to her room, Lucas pulled up and parked in front of her house.

He walked up the path and sat next to Jazz on the stairs, then patted the dog and smiled at her.

"Hey, kid."

His words were way too close to what her dad called her. "I have a name," she snapped.

"Yes, you do." She waited for him to call her on her attitude, but instead he asked, "What's wrong?"

"Nothing. I'm fine. You're here early."

"I was in court for most of the day. It's boring, but it's a shorter day. You didn't answer my question."

"I said nothing was wrong."

"You also lied. What is it?"

She stared at the top of Jazz's head. "It's just…" She swallowed against the tightness in her throat. "My dad blew me off again. I need fifty supervised hours to get my license. Mom's too busy and my dad swore he would help, but he never shows up." She rolled her eyes. "He said he was stuck at work. With what? An ingrown toenail? He doesn't care about me anymore. I don't think he ever did. He just walked out like I didn't matter and now he won't teach me to drive."

It was so much more than she'd wanted to say, but there was no way to call back the words. She folded her arms across her chest and did her best to hold in the pain.

"Interesting," Lucas said casually. "It's a drag about your dad, but there's time. It's not like you need your license right away."

She rocked forward and dropped her gaze to her Keds. "Yeah, well, Great-Aunt Cheryl didn't just leave me the dogs. There's a car." She glanced at him and started talking quickly. "It's a really good car. Ramon, her boyfriend, said it was in great condition and they'd always taken care of it. It's safe and has air bags, and it's not like my dad's going to buy me a car and Mom sure can't afford it."

She sucked in a breath. "I don't think Dad remembered to tell Mom because he was sick and she hasn't said anything. The car is paid for. I know there's going to be insurance and gas and stuff and I don't know how I'm going to deal with that, but right now I need my license."

Lucas nodded his head. "That's a lot."

"I know, right?"

He stood and called to Jazz, sent the dog in the house, then looked at Becca. "Okay, let's go."

"Where are we going?"

"To practice your driving."

"My mom's not here."

"I'm not taking you on the freeway, kid, I'm taking you to an empty parking lot to see what you know how to do and how we get along. If it goes well, I'll talk to your mom when we get back."

She stared at him. "Then what am I going to…" She spun to face the sleek, white Mercedes convertible. She didn't know much about cars, but she knew that one cost a lot. Maybe as much as their house.

"No way."

He shrugged. "It's insured. You'll be fine. Do you have your temporary license?"

"Let me get it."

She raced inside and dug her wristlet out of her backpack, then hurried back outside. Lucas stood by his car, the driver's door open.

"The car's not going to drive itself," he called.

Excitement and hope fluttered in her stomach. If Lucas would really help her get her hours, then she wouldn't have to depend on her dad or bug her mom. She vowed to do the best she could on their mini lesson so he would want to teach her more.

She joined him and got in the driver's side. He sat next to her and explained how to set the seat and the mirrors.

"The car sits really low to the ground," he told her. "It's going to feel different than your mom's SUV or your dad's sedan. Also, it has a more powerful engine, so be careful when you hit the gas."

She nodded, then wiped her suddenly damp palms on her jeans.

"Drive to the high school. Classes are out and there will be plenty of room to practice in the parking lot." He winked. "Okay, start her up."

She absolutely could not believe he was going to let her drive his car. Her mother had practically had a seizure the only time they'd practiced together.

She pushed the start button, then tried not to jump as the engine roared to life. She kept her foot on the brake as she shifted to Drive, then checked the mirrors four times before slowly pulling out onto the quiet street.

Mischief Bay High School was less than a mile away, but it took Becca nearly ten minutes to drive there. She stayed well under the twenty-five mile per hour speed limit and came to a full, lingering stop at every sign. By the time she pulled into the parking lot, she felt a little sick to her stomach.

"I don't know if I can do this," she admitted.

"Are you scared about driving or the car?" Lucas asked.

"Both."

"Driving gets easier with practice. Right now you have to think about everything you're doing. Once a few things become automatic, you'll be more comfortable. As for my car, like I said, it's insured. Okay, let's start with the basics. Drive to the end of the parking lot, do a three-point turn, drive back and pull into that parking space."

Becca tasted bile. "That's your idea of the basics?"

He flashed her a grin. "I've seen *Clueless*, kid. At least we're not going on the freeway."

"I'm never going on the freeway."

Thirty minutes later, Becca confidently circled the parking lot, making neat figure eights. She made a sharp turn ten feet in front of the flagpole and carefully backed into a parking space before turning to Lucas and laughing.

"I did it."

"You did good. I'm impressed."

"Thanks. This car is great. It drives so easily and I'm in love with the backup camera. Thank you for helping me. I really had fun."

"Me, too. Want to continue with the lessons?"

"Of course."

Lucas had been calm the whole time. When she'd messed up, he'd had her stop so they could talk about what had gone wrong. She was still nervous about driving, but less so than she had been.

"I'll talk to your mom," he said. "If she agrees, then we'll keep going. Oh, how are your grades?"

Becca felt herself flush. "They're, um, okay."

He looked at her without speaking.

She ducked her head. "I'm getting a couple of Cs and a few Bs."

"I thought you were a good student."

"I am." Or she had been. Lately she hadn't been that interested in school. What was the point? No one paid attention or cared how she was doing.

"I know you're smart," Lucas told her. "Something's going on. If you want me to help you get your driving hours, you're going to have to get your grades where they should be. A car is a lot of responsibility. If you can't be bothered to take care of business at school, then you can't be trusted with a car."

No one had talked to her like that in forever. Becca was both thrilled and annoyed, which felt really good.

"You're not the boss of me," she said automatically.

"In this case, I am. It's my time so it's my rules. If you want my help, then you will get Bs or better in all your classes."

"No problem."

"I want proof."

"What? You don't trust me?"

"There's an old saying. Trust but verify. From now until you get your license, you will show me all your test scores. Understood?"

"Yes. I promise."

"Good. Now let's go home."

Becca made the return trip in half the time. She stayed at the speed limit, stopped at the stop signs for a quick count of one-two, then pulled up in front of her house just as her mom drove into the driveway.

They all got out at the same time. Harper turned toward them, then nearly dropped her purse. "What are you doing? Did you *drive* that car? You didn't. Oh my God! Becca, no. Do you know what a car like that costs? Lucas, I swear, what were you thinking? No one asked me. Where's your father? Weren't you supposed to be practicing with him? I feel sick."

Lucas shook his head. "She gets real wound up."

"She does. I worry about her."

"You should." Lucas walked toward the SUV. "It's fine, Harper. Terence couldn't make it so I took Becca out for a practice session. Everything was fine and if it's all right with you, I'm going to help her get in her practice hours."

"Not in that car. There is absolutely no way."

"I have insurance."

"And a deductible!"

She started to say something else, but her phone rang. She touched her Bluetooth earpiece and said brightly, "This is Harper."

Becca sighed. There was no talking to her mother now. Not when she was on with a client—and she was always on with a client.

Chapter Six

HARPER POURED ANOTHER CUP OF COFFEE. IT WAS ONLY seven in the morning and she was already exhausted. Of course a lot of that could be because she hadn't slept much the previous night. She'd been up finishing the gift bags. Honest to God, she needed to grow a pair and stand up to that woman.

"Mom, we have to talk about my driving lessons."

Harper drank more coffee as she turned to look at her daughter. Becca sat at the table, a faithful Jazz at her side. The dog had sure figured out who loved her the most. If Becca was home, Jazz was right there with her.

Driving! How was that possible? Becca was supposed to still be seven. Only she wasn't. She was turning seventeen in the summer and talking about college. Harper swore silently. Her daughter was going to be heading off to college in less than eighteen months and she was making what, two dollars an hour on stupid gift bags?

The weight of failure threatened to make her topple over. It wasn't supposed to be like this. She was supposed to have it all together. Had going into business for herself been a mistake? She didn't think so, but if it wasn't the job, then she was the problem and she sure didn't want to hear that.

"Mom?"

Harper did her best to keep her tone even. "I know we do, honey. And we will. This weekend, okay? We'll sit down and come up with a plan."

Her daughter sighed. "Sure."

"What does that mean?"

"You always say we'll talk about something, but then we never do. You're too busy with work."

Harper didn't like the sound of that. "I don't. We will talk this weekend. You'll see."

Before she could think of a more convincing argument, the back door opened and Bunny walked in. Her hair was perfectly styled, her makeup in place and her clothes looked freshly laundered.

Harper was instantly aware of the fact that she hadn't showered in maybe two days and she couldn't remember the last time she'd put on makeup. She'd always worn her wavy hair in layers, but who had the time or money for that kind of maintenance? Lately she'd taken to simply pulling her hair back in a ponytail, which looked great on her beautiful sister but made her look like what she was—a woman of a certain age who had obviously given up.

"Morning," she said as cheerfully as she could.

"Morning." Her mother smiled at Becca, then frowned. "What are you eating?"

"Cereal."

Harper reached for more coffee.

"Cereal?" Bunny shrieked. "Where's your hot breakfast?" She turned to her daughter. "Harper Wray Szymanski, what is wrong with you? Your only child deserves a hot breakfast. As her mother, it's the least you can do."

"Grandma, cereal is fine. It's a nice change."

Bunny ignored that. "What's next? Store-bought cookies? Fast food for dinner? Taking care of your family is your most important job."

"You're right, Mom," Harper snapped. "Right now that means keeping food on the table. To pay for that, I have to work, so forgive me if I don't have time to make waffles from scratch every single morning."

"I always found the time."

"You didn't have a job."

Becca quickly finished her cereal, then put the bowl on the floor for Jazz to lap up the milk. When the dog was done, she set the bowl in the sink and escaped. Harper wished she could run off with her.

"I didn't have a job because I managed to keep my husband happy," Bunny said in a huff. "Perhaps if you'd treated Terence a little better, he wouldn't have left."

The low blow connected right in her stomach.

"Mom, you don't know anything about what went wrong in my marriage. It's my business and you don't have the right to judge me."

"I'm not. I'm simply pointing out that if you—"

Harper's cell phone rang. She grabbed it gratefully. "Mom, this is a client."

"But it's barely seven."

"Yes, I know." She pushed the button to accept the call. "This is Harper."

"It's Cathy. How are the bags coming?"

"They'll be ready on time." No way Harper was going to tell her they were already finished. Cathy would assume

Harper had been exaggerating the time needed. Explaining she'd literally stayed up all night to finish them wouldn't help, either.

"I'm glad to hear that. I have another job for you."

"I was talking to you," Bunny said between clenched teeth. "Tell her you'll call her back."

Harper turned her back on her mother, something she knew she was going to pay for. And speaking of paying. "Cathy, I'm happy to talk to you about more work, but I want to be clear. My rate is twenty-five dollars an hour, plus the cost of supplies. That is the price."

"That's ridiculous. My clients aren't going to pay that."

"Then I'm sorry but I can't help you."

"But you've always been willing to drop your price for me." Her voice became softer. "Harper, I know you need the work. I'm doing you a favor."

"What I need are jobs that pay me a reasonable amount. It's your call, Cathy. I won't be negotiating any more discounts."

"That is totally unacceptable. Goodbye, Harper." The phone went dead.

Harper turned back to her mother. Bunny raised her eyebrows. "With an attitude like that, it's surprising you have any clients. Twenty-five dollars an hour for what you do? That's ridiculous."

"Thanks for the support, Mom."

"What? I'm being honest."

"Right now I would rather you weren't. That's me being honest."

Before she could say any more, she heard a quick knock on the front door, then Thor raced into the house followed by Lucas calling out, "It's me."

The hundred-and-ten-pound dog bounced up to Harper

and woofed. Jazz joined him and they greeted each other with a quick sniff before tearing off into the living room. Lucas appeared with Persimmon at his side.

"Good morning," the young woman said, sounding way too cheerful. "Thor and Jazz are so sweet together. Hi, Harper. Hi, Bunny."

The gorgeous redhead wore a cute little dress and heels, which only made Harper feel even more frumpy and tired. Lucas walked over to the coffeepot and poured himself a mug.

"How's it going?" he asked.

"You don't want to know."

"There's no hot breakfast," Bunny announced. "Harper has more important things to do with her time." She looked at Lucas. "Would you like me to make you an omelet? I'm sure there's something in the refrigerator, unless my daughter has stopped going to the grocery store."

Lucas shot Harper a look. She wasn't sure if it was questioning, filled with pity or both. Regardless, she waved him toward the table, figuring Persimmon would join him. While Bunny was distracted, Harper escaped to her small office. She would hide out there until everyone was gone. Maybe then she could get a couple of hours of sleep.

Her phone rang again. She put in her earpiece, then hit the button.

"This is Harper."

"It's Misty. Is it too early? I'm sorry to be calling, but I had to tell you."

Her comedian client sounded breathless, but in a happy way.

"It's not too early. What's up?"

"You aren't going to believe it. I don't believe it. Oh, Harper, I'm going to be on an HBO special! It's called Rising Stars or something like that. I can't remember because I'm still in shock. It's taping in a few weeks and then I'm going on tour."

"Misty, that's so fabulous. Congratulations. You've worked hard for this big break. How can I help?"

"I want new T-shirts. Something fun. Oh, and let's be wild and get the ones that are the nicer material."

Harper was already taking notes. "I'll call the vendor as soon as we hang up and have her rush us samples. How many do you think you want?" Because there were price breaks at different levels.

"Let me think about that and get back to you. Once the special airs, I should be able to sell more. Oh, and I need to get you the tour info so you can ship me the T-shirts as I go."

"And care packages?" Harper asked.

"Please. They save me."

When Misty went on the road, she was gone for several weeks at a time. Harper shipped her snacks and toiletries so Misty didn't have to worry about any of that. She also shipped T-shirts to each hotel, saving Misty from having to haul them from town to town.

Harper continued to make notes. "I'm so happy for you. This is the best news I've had all week."

"I'm so excited. Thanks, Harper. I can relax knowing you're going to handle things for me."

"Absolutely. My job is to make your life easier."

Which was true. Now if only someone would do that for her.

Stacey came to a stop at the corner. Bay did the same, then sat down, her shoulders and right ear lined up with Stacey's leg.

"Good girl," Stacey told the dog, then lightly petted her head. The instruction manual that had accompanied the dog had been impressive, as was the list of commands Bay had mastered. There were the usual *come, sit,* along with some interesting specialized commands. Bay could distinguish between different types of weapons and toxic gases. She was also comfortable working aboard a ship. Stacey didn't know if that meant cargo or military. The notes had ended midsentence, as if the remaining information had simply been ripped away.

No doubt it was classified, Stacey thought as they crossed the street.

Bay had settled easily into their home. She ate well and was perfectly friendly. Whatever training she'd been given was more about purpose than affecting her personality. Not that Stacey was surprised. She'd only met Great-Aunt Cheryl once but the woman had been a sensible sort. Not someone to leave dangerous animals to a sixteen-year-old.

Kit had taken Bay to the vet the previous Monday to confirm her pregnancy and get an approximate due date. The dog had been pronounced healthy. Per the records, Bay had given birth before, so the vet had been confident the dog would know what to do. Her records indicated she was up-to-date on all her vaccinations.

Stacey had already started researching the canine birthing process so she could be ready when the time came. Although it was very likely that Bay would have her puppies while Stacey was at work. Still, being prepared was always preferable.

She and Bay reached the corner drugstore that doubled as an Amazon drop box. She loosely tied the dog's leash to the bike rack, then had her sit.

"Bay," she said in a firm voice. The dog immediately met her gaze. "Bay, stay." She paused. "No strangers."

The dog's nostrils flared slightly, but otherwise she didn't move. According to the book, Bay would stay where she was told for at least two days. None of the dogs had been tested beyond that. In addition, the "no strangers" command meant she wouldn't leave with anyone else. Should someone try, Bay would immediately start barking to alert Stacey.

"I won't be very long," she added, not sure Bay could understand her. Still, it was polite to let her know.

She walked into the drugstore and went to the back, where several dozen lockers of various sizes stood along one wall. After scanning the barcode on the email she'd received, she punched in the code and a locker opened. She retrieved the box.

It was the last of the items she'd ordered for Ashton's visit. His room was ready with a new bed, linens and a desk. Kit had moved in a TV they rarely used. Stacey had added a few framed prints for color, then had gone online for a back-to-school bundle box. Ashton only had a couple of classes to finish, but she didn't know if he would think to bring things like pens, paper and Post-it notes. Besides, who didn't love school supplies?

She carefully tucked the box into her backpack so as not to strain her body. Carrying the baby had thrown her body out of alignment. Her prenatal yoga helped her strength and balance, but she wanted to make sure she didn't pull a muscle.

Once the backpack was in place, she walked out and untied Bay.

"Good girl," she told the dog as she crouched down and hugged her. Bay licked her cheek.

Stacey rose and started back to the house. She liked having Bay around. The dog was easy to take care of and good company. What she didn't want to admit but couldn't avoid was the fact that the dog was also a distraction from her own pregnancy.

The same with Ashton. Kit was a perfect husband and had never once mentioned the irony of her interest in getting Ashton's room ready while refusing to do anything about their baby's space. Every morning he tore another sheet off the calendar, gently reminding her that there was an inevitable end to what she was going through.

Sometimes Stacey wished the baby was already here so she wouldn't be worrying about what was going to happen. She would already know if she could fake being a decent mother or not.

If only she was more like Harper, she thought. Talented and loving, with great mothering skills. But Stacey wasn't. She and her sister had always been close but oh so different. One of her earliest Christmas memories was of opening an Easy-Bake Oven from Santa. She'd immediately started mixing together ingredients—not to bake a cake, but to get a chemical reaction.

Bunny had never understood and Stacey's dad hadn't much cared. He'd regretted not having sons instead of daughters. But Grandpa Wray had been there for her. He'd wanted to talk about things like jet propulsion and living on Mars, and she'd wanted to listen.

He'd been the one to show her how to use a telescope and a microscope. When girls her age had been playing with dolls, she'd been trying to find a science club and building computers. With Grandpa Wray's help, she'd gotten to go to Space Camp when she was nine. The following summer, while the rest of the family had been at Disney World, she and Grandpa Wray had visited Cape Canaveral and been taken on a private tour.

"Grandpa Wray wanted me to be an astronaut," she told Bay as they turned onto their street. "I would have been interested if there had been a Mars mission on the horizon, but that's still so many years away. I went into medical research instead." She smiled at the dog. "He was a great man. You would have liked him."

Bay's stubby tail wagged as she listened attentively.

"I always fit with Grandpa Wray," she continued. "He didn't care that I was smart or awkward or that I couldn't make piecrust by the time I was eight." Unlike her mother, who had cared about all those things. Bunny had always resented her youngest being more interested in how the world worked than how to knit, sew or decoupage. How many times had Harper stood up for her, defending her when Bunny went on the attack?

Stacey undid Bay's leash as they entered the house, then lowered her backpack onto a chair. She checked on the Crock-Pot chili Kit had started that morning before walking into the bedroom to change out of her work clothes.

French doors led to their fenced backyard. Although they were only a mile or two from the ocean, they didn't have a view. Stacey had never understood paying for something as silly as the ability to see something in nature. The brain responded to inputs that were essential for survival. Everything else faded into the background. She knew that she would cease to see a view within a matter of weeks, so why pay for it?

She'd already bought the house when she met Kit. The first time he'd come over, she'd told him her theory about views. He'd responded by telling her she was about the sexiest woman he'd ever met.

The news had surprised her. Stacey knew she was relatively attractive and she kept herself fit. There had always been men in her life—no one all that special, but she'd had boyfriends. Still, she'd frequently had the sense that they were more inter-

ested in her body than in her brain. Kit was the first romantic partner who made her feel safe and loved for who she was.

She changed into yoga pants and a T-shirt, then walked
barefoot to the living room. Bay trailed along with her. Once
the DVD was in the machine, Bay curled up in her bed by the
sofa. She glanced at the door before putting her head down.

"Kit will be back in an hour," Stacey told her. "He goes
to a support group for stay-at-home dads." Something he'd
started when they'd learned she was pregnant.

"Kit's like that. He asks for help. He solicits advice. He's
extremely well-adjusted." All things she admired about him,
probably because none of those characteristics described her.
He'd suggested she look for a support group for working moms
but so far she hadn't been interested.

There's something wrong with you! You're not a normal girl.

The memory echoed unexpectedly in her mind, as vivid
and uncomfortable as it had been when the words had first
been screamed at her.

She'd been thirteen and eager to talk to her mother. Stacey
had secretly scheduled a meeting with one of the high school
counselors to talk about an accelerated program so she could
go to college early. She'd already decided to focus on medical
research—especially diseases of the central nervous system—
so why wait to get started?

With the information in hand, Stacey was determined to
convince her mother to let her start the process in the fall.
Bunny had wanted to talk about the fact that a boy had called
for Stacey.

Looking back, Stacey realized they'd talked at cross purposes for nearly ten minutes before figuring out what the
other was saying. Stacey had dismissed the call while Bunny

had refused to discuss Stacey starting high school in the fall and finishing in two years.

"No man wants a woman who's that smart," her mother had told her. "Accept who you are."

"This *is* who I am," she'd yelled back. "I want to go to college. I don't want to talk to some stupid boy on the phone, okay?"

"There's something wrong with you. You're not a normal girl."

She'd brushed off the assessment, raced to her room and had immediately called her Grandpa Wray. He and Bunny had fought for days, while Stacey's father had ignored whatever was going on at home and Harper had offered Stacey sisterly support. In the end, the outcome was inevitable. Bunny might not like it, but she could never say no to her father. He was, after all, a man.

As Stacey stood with her feet shoulder-width apart and began to concentrate on her breathing, she acknowledged yet more irony in her life. Bunny wanted her daughters to be exactly like her and she resented that Stacey refused to cooperate. That Stacey had been able to go to college when she was barely sixteen had happened because a man had intervened. She'd achieved her escape and her success in part because of her mother's anachronistic worldview.

She should find humor in that, only she couldn't. Instead she pressed her right hand against her growing belly and wondered if it was possible her mother was right. And if there was something wrong with her, how would that play out for Baby Joule?

Chapter Seven

HARPER HAD ALL THE GIFT BAGS STACKED TOGETHER IN boxes. Cathy had texted to say she wouldn't be picking them up until tomorrow, after all, which left Harper nearly frothing. She could have had an extra two days to maybe get some sleep instead of staying up for two nights to get them done. She didn't know if she was angrier at Cathy for playing her or herself for being played.

She heard a knock at the front door, then Lucas walked in. Thor immediately raced toward him. Lucas bent over and greeted the dog before calling out, "It's me."

Harper set the last box in place by the sofa and looked at her client/friend. Despite having worked all day, Lucas looked as fresh and handsome as he had that morning. His shirt was barely wrinkled, he was rested and tanned, while she was a hot mess. No, she thought, thinking of her mom jeans and stained T-shirt. Even her messiness wasn't the least bit hot. She was a cold mess.

"Hi. Catch any bad guys?"

"A couple."

"Want to stay to dinner?"

The invitation was automatic. She wasn't sure when or how it had started, but Lucas ate dinner with them at least three nights a week. Thanks to Bunny's skillful tutelage and years of training, Harper chronically overbought and overcooked, so there was always plenty for unexpected company. Lucas was funny, charming and a lovely distraction when things with her mother got too intense or moments with her daughter got too quiet.

Harper already had a salad made. She'd prepared vegetables for steaming and had Chicken Piccata ready to brown and simmer. The drama of this evening's meal would be the—wait for it—store-bought pasta.

"I'd love to," he said. "Thank you."

"I bought the noodles. Bunny's going to have a fit. Just so you're warned."

"Unarmed drama doesn't faze me."

They walked into the study together. Lucas crossed to the wall safe that had come with the house. It was a silly thing, really, but kind of sweet—whenever he came to dinner from work, he locked up his gun. She'd tried to explain it was unlikely that either Becca or her mother were going to lunge for it, and if they did, she was sure he could take them, but he insisted.

"What if I had a breakdown during the meal?" she asked. "I know the combination. I could take out everyone."

He put the gun in the otherwise-empty safe and turned the lock to secure it. "It's a plain black gun, Harper. You couldn't possibly use it without gussying it up in some way first. I'd have time to subdue you while the glue set."

Even as she chuckled, she wondered if there was an uncomfortable truth in his words.

They returned to the living room to find Jazz waiting for them. She ran over to get her greeting from Lucas. When he'd finished rubbing her face, he grabbed one of the rope toys the dogs loved and got on the floor with the two of them. There was much growling, yipping and wrestling as man and dogs vied for the precious toy. Harper retreated to the kitchen to continue prepping the meal. Per the rules of the universe, or maybe just per her mother, the salad plates should be set on the table at precisely six-thirty.

To that end, she got out a small mixing bowl, along with the ingredients for her Smokey Paprika dressing. She poured it into a dressing-size crystal pitcher, then whipped up the sauce for the chicken.

Lucas wandered into the kitchen and went to the sink to wash his hands. "Those dogs are smart. I have to up my game."

Harper nodded at them feverishly drinking from their bowls. "If it makes you feel any better, they're saying the same thing about you."

He dried his hands, then leaned against the counter. "I saw the gift bags. They're impressive."

"Thanks. It's a fiftieth wedding anniversary party. I'm sure it's going to be lovely."

Lucas's gaze settled on her face. For a second, she was terrified that he was going to ask her how long they'd taken or had she been paid enough. He was always ready with the unexpected question. Thankfully he only said, "You're busy these days."

"I am."

She walked into the dining room and studied the table. They were still celebrating spring, so the tablecloth was a pale mint color. She'd already stacked plates, patterned napkins and place mats on one end of the table. Now she just had to deal with the rest of it.

"Misty is going to be on an HBO special," she said, as she headed for the craft room.

Lucas followed her. "That's great."

"I know. She's so sweet. I love working with her."

"If you say she's your favorite, I'll be crushed."

Harper grinned. "She is, but I won't say it."

"Thank you. Let me know when the special's on. I'll want to watch."

"Some of the humor is fairly subtle. I'm not sure Persimmon will get it."

"Persimmon and I are reaching the end of our time together."

"Because she's turning twenty-three?"

"Something like that."

Harper flipped on the lights to her craft room. She kept her dining room supplies at one end. She pointed to several clear, plastic drawers.

"Napkin rings. Pink, rose or silver. You pick," she said as she studied her collection of vases and bowls, wondering what would be the easiest to put on the table.

Lucas held up four ribbed silver napkin rings. "These okay?"

"They're great."

She grabbed small, silver tone boxes in various heights and thrust them at Lucas, then chose flameless candles that would fit inside. Before turning away from the wall of crap she kept just because she was expected to decorate her table every single night for dinner, she flashed on her small, cramped office space and realized that, as always, Lucas was right.

"Oh no," she said. "I've been doing this all wrong."

"Your table?" her mother asked, appearing at the craft room door. "I've been telling you that for years. You need to layer your linens. Really, Harper, a tablecloth, place mats and napkins?

A monkey could be more creative. At least make shorter, contrasting runners to drape widthwise. It will add visual interest."

Harper found herself automatically considering her mother's idea. In that nanosecond, she thought about the fabric she kept on hand and how easy it would be to pull out her sewing machine and—

"No!" She literally took a step back and shook her head. "No, Mom. Stop, please. I'm not looking for more ways to waste time decorating the table for dinner."

"Waste time? It's dinner with your family. What could be more important?"

Lucas took the supplies she'd given him and left. Harper put the flameless candles down and put her hands on her hips. "Mom, I'm serious. I can't keep doing this. I have work I need to be doing. I have another order for gift bags, Misty needs new T-shirt designs. I heard back from the city and they want me to get going on the summer mailer. Once I design it and get it printed, I have to put on all the labels myself."

Lucas returned and collected the candles. "Hire someone to do the grunt work."

"What?" Harper and Bunny said together.

Bunny glared at him. "Lucas, I know you're trying to help, but be serious. It's bad enough Harper is taking time from raising Becca to do this, but to hire an assistant? If she's going to work, she should be doing it all herself."

Which was exactly what Harper had been thinking, only hearing her mother say it put the sentiment in a totally different light.

"Why?" she asked.

Bunny stared at her. "Why what?"

"Why can't I hire someone? Why is that so awful? Mom, I'm drowning here. My job is how I feed my family. I'm struggling every single month. Your rent money helps and I appreciate it, but it doesn't come close to covering the mortgage, let alone the expenses. I have no idea if Terence is going to keep his promise about paying for half Becca's college, so I have to deal with that, as well."

Bunny sniffed. "Becca's a beautiful young woman. Why does she need to go to college? She'll marry a nice boy who will take care of her."

Harper did her best not to shriek. "Mom, no. Just no. Becca is going to get an education so she has choices and can take care of herself. I thought I'd have a man to take care of me and look where that got me. I will not put my daughter in this position. It worked out for you but it doesn't work out that way for everyone. I want Becca to be strong and independent, like Stacey. She's smart and capable. We need to encourage her to be her best self."

"You're being ridiculous."

"I'm being honest. I'm nearly forty-two, Mom, and I'm struggling. It's my fault—I get that. I should have finished college. I should have gone to work when Becca started school, but I didn't. I'm doing the best I can with the choices I made." She squared her shoulders. "I didn't have time to make pasta. I bought some from the store. You're going to have to deal with that."

Bunny glared at her, then turned on her heel and marched out of the room. It was only then Harper saw her daughter and Jazz standing in the doorway.

"Your grandmother thinks I should layer more linens when I set the table."

Becca rubbed Jazz's head. "Going crossways? I can see how that would be pretty. You're not going to do it, are you?"

"No."

Becca smiled. "Mom, store-bought pasta is okay with me. The same with bread and cookies and anything else you don't want to make. I've had it all before at my friends' houses and it's not horrible."

"Thank you. I knew I couldn't trust those other mothers. They always said they were feeding you homemade but they were lying."

Becca giggled. Harper allowed herself to smile.

"Grandma loves the drama," Becca told her. "It makes her feel special."

An unexpected insight. "Thank you for that."

"You're welcome." Her daughter sighed. "Thor ate the raw chicken."

"What?"

Becca grinned. "I'm kidding, Mom."

Harper pressed her hand to her chest. "Don't do that. I'm getting old and I could very possibly have a heart condition."

Becca tried to summon some enthusiasm as she lay sprawled on the comfortable sofa. She had a feeling that Lucas hadn't been kidding about her keeping up her grades in exchange for him helping her get in her driving hours. She was doing okay in English, Spanish and geometry. It was European History where she was getting Cs. History was so boring. The whole second half of the class focused on World War II, which was, like, a million years ago. Why did anyone care about that kind of stuff?

"You're not listening," Jordan complained.

"I was thinking about the homework I have to do. I need to write a paper for European History and we have that chem test next week. I can't believe how much math there is in that class."

"I know. I thought we'd be doing more fun stuff in the lab, but nooo. There's equations." Jordan flipped her long hair over her shoulder. "I wonder when Nathan will get here. He had a meeting after swim practice. You know he got a scholarship to UCLA to play water polo, right?"

"Uh-huh." No point in mentioning that Jordan had already told her eight times. Yes, Nathan was a water polo god and the world stood in awe of his talent.

Which was something she could have joked about, but not anymore. Jordan was convinced that Becca couldn't get past her jealousy when it came to her friend's new sex life, and Becca couldn't figure out how to convince her otherwise. Possibly because she really didn't know how she felt.

Yes, she would like a boyfriend, someone who thought she was special, but sex? There was so much going on already, and to be honest, the thought of it was both exciting and scary. Most of the time, though, scary won.

There was a knock at the front door. Jordan flew across the family room to the foyer and disappeared from view. Becca sat up, uneasy at the thought of reclining with Nathan around. Not that she could say why, but sometimes he made her uncomfortable.

She told herself he wasn't the problem, she was. Maybe Jordan was right and she was jealous of the whole sex thing, although she really didn't think it was that.

She heard the happy couple murmur something. They stepped into view as Nathan pulled Jordan close and kissed her like they were halfway to doing it right there.

Becca looked away, but not before she saw Nathan's hand settle on her friend's ass. He squeezed really hard. Becca tried not to shudder. Whatever they were doing, it should be, you know, special, or at least in private.

She unzipped her backpack and pretended to be looking for something as the kiss went on and on. When they finally drew apart, she looked up. Nathan, six feet two inches of blond, blue-eyed handsomeness, winked at her.

"Hey, Becca."

"Hey."

Jordan wrapped her arms around Nathan's narrow waist for a second, then jumped back. "Okay, I'm going to go upstairs and put on more lip gloss. Becca, get out some snacks from the freezer and put them in the oven. I'll be right back."

Becca got up and walked into the kitchen. The giant Sub-Zero refrigerator nearly filled one wall. The freezer was filled with all kinds of prepared foods—mostly from Whole Foods or Trader Joe's, but still. Becca's grandmother would have a fit if she ever saw them.

She reviewed the selection, picking mini quiches that were always good. She set the temperature on the oven, then put the quiches on a cookie sheet. In the refrigerator she found prepared ranch dip and a plate of cut-up vegetables. There were chips in the pantry.

Nathan leaned against the bar-height counter and watched her work. "You know your way around Jordan's kitchen," he said.

"We've been friends a long time and I'm here a lot. Her mom always makes sure there's plenty of food for us."

She had the need to keep moving, although she couldn't say why. She'd been in the same room with Nathan dozens of times. He was perfectly fine. In fact, he mostly ignored her, which sometimes she preferred. But today he seemed to be watching her.

"Jordan tell you about Mexico?" he asked.

"That you went with her family?"

He moved toward her. "No, Becca. The other part."

Somehow she found herself backed against a corner of the counter. Nathan stood in front of her and there was nowhere to move. He put his hands on her waist and leaned close. For one horrifying second, she thought he was going to kiss her, but instead he whispered, "I can do that for you, too, if you want."

He smelled faintly of chlorine and too much cologne and she didn't like the way his fingers squeezed ever so slightly.

"I d–don't know what that means," she whispered, wishing he would move back and give her more room.

He kissed the side of her neck. "The virgin thing. I'm good with virgins. I take things slow and easy. You'll like it."

She shoved him hard and glared at him. "What are you talking about? You didn't just say that. Jordan's your girlfriend. You're supposed to be in love with her."

"I *told* her I loved her," he said with a shrug. "There's a difference."

What? That didn't make any— She felt her eyes widen. "You lied? You lied to get her to sleep with you? That's disgusting."

"Whatever gets the job done. So what about you?"

He started toward her again. She had no idea what he was going to do, but she was sure she didn't want any part of it. She shoved him again, as hard as she could, then pushed past him. She grabbed her backpack, then raced out the front door. She was still running when she reached the end of the block.

Halfway home, she slowed enough to catch her breath. Her whole body hurt, her head felt funny and her stomach was a mess. She tried to slow her breathing only to have to turn toward some bushes and throw up. She vomited until there was nothing left, then started to cry.

What had just happened? Why had Nathan acted like that?

Becca couldn't think, couldn't breathe. She started running again, not stopping until she made it to her house.

Her mom was on the phone with a client. Becca hurried past her mom's office, toward her own room. When she got there, she collapsed on the bed and gave in to more tears. She was scared and confused and sick.

A few minutes later, she felt a weight on the bed. She raised her head. "Oh, Mom…" But it wasn't her mother. Jazz had come into the room and jumped up on her bed. Thor stood close by, as if standing guard. Becca threw her arms around her dog and hung on. Jazz snuggled close.

"It was so horrible," Becca whispered. "He scared me. I didn't think he was going to do anything bad, but what he said… I thought he and Jordan were in love."

Jazz watched her attentively. Thor lay down on the floor, but kept his attention on her. Becca swallowed. "He's her boyfriend. What is he thinking?"

She had a bad feeling he was thinking that he could use Jordan's friends the way he used Jordan.

Her phone chirped. She reached for it and saw a text from Jordan.

Nathan says ur mom told u to get home but I know the truth. U have 2 get over it, B. Don't be jealous of me. Ur my friend.

Becca stared at her phone, then tossed it on the floor and rolled onto her back. She had no idea what to do or think or say. All she knew for sure was that Nathan was a jerk, Jordan was blind and none of this was going to end well.

Chapter Eight

THE LANDSCAPING COMPANY PUSHED HARPER OVER the edge. She'd been prepared to do all the work herself, to stay up nights and give up sleep, but an unexpected call from a landscaper who needed her to do the billing for him was one job too far.

The money was good and the work relatively easy. There was an existing database. All Harper had to do was enter the amount for the month, print out the invoices, stuff them in envelopes and pop them in the mail. Easy-peasy—except for the fact that there were nearly five hundred clients and the invoicing had to be done in less than two days.

Between that new job, her regular clients, the additional brochure work she had for the city and a flower shop client who wanted a "spruce" on content for her website, Harper was slammed. She'd been forced to hire help.

Rather than go through the trouble of placing an ad online or interviewing people, she heard about Morgan Wolfenbarger, a friend of a friend, who was looking for part-time work.

In the "oh goody" column, Morgan showed up right on

time. She was tall and curvy, with long, curly dark hair. Under items that would be considered less fortunate, Morgan was a talker.

"Your house is really nice," she said as Harper showed her to the small office where she would input the information on Harper's only computer. Note to self—if she was going to continue to use extra help, she would need a second computer.

"We need to remodel our kitchen," Morgan continued, as she settled in the chair. "It's a disaster, but with the kids and everything, when would we find the time? And what would we do while it was torn up? I guess I could freeze a bunch of meals, but who wants to do that? Trust me, after running Supper's in the Bag all those years, the last thing I want to do is prep meals."

Harper remembered the cute storefront in town. "Was that your company? I heard good things about it." Not that she would ever have used the service. Supper's in the Bag provided ingredients and recipes for easy meals. You went in and prepped a handful of meals, then took them home and cooked them when you needed them. A time saver for the busy mom—or at least one who wasn't expected to make every single thing from scratch.

"My husband bought the franchise for me. We both thought it was a great idea, but then it turned out to be way more work than I expected. I lost my best employee." Morgan rolled her eyes. "Don't ever hire family. It's a disaster. Anyway, after that, I had to put in more hours, which was a mess and in the end, we sold the franchise." She sighed. "I'd really rather stay home, but Brent says I need to bring in some money for the kids' college funds. Oh, speaking of money, you're going to pay me under the table, right?"

"What? No. I'll be reporting your income." If she didn't,

Harper wouldn't be able to claim the deduction, which she needed to reduce her own taxes. Oh, yeah, and it was illegal.

"I thought you said you would." Morgan's mouth formed a pout. "You said I would have to be contract labor, so what does that mean? I have to keep track of my own income and report it and stuff?"

"Yes, that's what it means. I don't want to hire you as an employee until we both know this is going to work out."

"That sucks." Morgan turned back to the computer and sighed. "Fine. What do you want me to do?"

Harper showed her how to pull up the individual landscaping invoices and enter the amount to be billed.

"I get it, I get it," she grumbled halfway through the explanation. "I was hoping the work would be more interesting. I told Brent getting a job like this was going to be a drag. Maybe I should try something in sales."

"Until then," Harper murmured, trying not to snap at the other woman. If Morgan worked as hard as she complained, everything would be fine. She left her to do the billing and went into her craft room to start on the next set of bags she had to make for Cathy.

Four hours later, Harper thought longingly of the book of instructions Great-Aunt Cheryl had left. Maybe there was a command that would have the dogs stalking Morgan without actually hurting her. Her so-called helper had been anything but helpful. Morgan had found twenty excuses to stop billing and start talking. She'd taken three breaks, had spent time on her cell phone, both talking and texting. At the end of her scheduled time, she'd hadn't entered even a quarter of the invoices.

"I know I said I could come tomorrow," Morgan said as

she walked to the front door. "But I just don't know. Can I text you later?"

Harper gritted her teeth. "Sure. Let me know." Because as annoying and inefficient as Morgan had been, Harper needed help.

"Okay, and you'll pay me on Friday?"

Harper wanted to ask, "Pay you for what?" but instead forced herself to smile and said, "Of course."

"Great. It was fun today. Bye."

Morgan drove away. Harper went into the living room and screamed out loud. Both dogs stared at her as if concerned about the state of her being.

"I'm fine," she told them before sinking onto the sofa and covering her face with her hands.

"That doesn't bode well," Lucas said as he let himself into the house and bent down to pet an enthused Thor. "What happened?"

She raised her head. "I hired someone."

"Good for you."

"She was a disaster."

"Did you check her references?"

Lucas looked good, as he always did. Jeans, boots, long-sleeved shirt and blazer. There was an air of competence about him. He was a gentleman who knew how to handle himself. He turned to Jazz and greeted her before sitting across from the sofa.

Harper groaned. "I didn't ask for references. She's a friend of a friend and I was desperate. I thought it would be fine, but it wasn't. She never shut up. When she wasn't talking to me, she was on the phone. She took three breaks in four hours and she wanted to be paid under the table. She barely did any work, so I'll be up late tonight finishing the invoices."

She held up her hand. "Don't say it. I know. I'm the boss. I should have told her to shut up and do the work." Only that wasn't her style. She didn't want to have to manage her help—she wanted them to show up and do their job for the time paid.

She waited, but Lucas didn't speak. Finally she groaned. "What? Just say it."

"You told me not to say it."

"I take it back."

"Your business isn't going to be what you want it to be until you take it seriously and treat it with respect. You're only playing at being a business owner, Harper, and it shows."

She winced. "That's harsh."

"What do you want from all this? You're more than capable. Set some goals, then follow through. Until then, you're only five minutes away from everything crashing down on you."

She'd thought she was closer to ten minutes from disaster, but his point was a good one. Brutal but honest. Maybe it was time to listen to what she already knew was true.

Stacey found herself wanting to bounce in her seat as they drove to the airport. She didn't know why she was so excited to see Ashton again, but she was. A voice in her head whispered it might be because he would be a distraction from worrying about the impending baby, but she ignored that. She enjoyed spending time with Kit's nephew.

"What are you thinking?" her husband asked as they headed north on Pacific Coast Highway.

"That I hope Ashton enjoys his time with us."

"I do, too. He's been through a lot."

He had, dealing with his mother and getting moved around

so much. "I'm glad he's going to be with us until he heads to college." She looked at Kit. "He's going to need a car to drive. Instead of trading in yours for the SUV you want, let's keep it and he can use it. Do you think he'll need a car when he goes to MIT? Maybe we could keep it here for him to use on break."

Kit had been researching the safest SUVs so they could have it before the baby was born. Yet one more area where she was woefully unprepared to be a parent—she hadn't even thought about things like safe cars or babyproofing the house. Ashton would be easier. He could mostly take care of himself.

Kit glanced at her again and shook his head. "You won't mind?"

She struggled to figure out what he was talking about. Her being a bad mother was unlikely to be the topic at hand.

"Mind what?"

"Not trading in my car? It's worth about six or seven grand."

"We can afford a new car without it. Don't you want Ashton to have a car?"

"Yes, I want him to have a car. I just don't want you to think I'm spoiling him or..." He drew in a breath. "He's my problem, Stacey, not yours."

"I thought he was *our* family. Was I wrong?"

Kit grabbed her hand and kissed her knuckles. "You're not wrong and I'm one lucky guy."

She was grateful he thought that. From her perspective, she was riddled with flaws and the good fortune was all hers.

"Then it's settled," she told him. "You'll go get the SUV in the next week or so and Ashton will drive your Escort. I'll keep the Accord. Everyone is happy."

"Everyone is."

Before they could pull into the cell phone lot, Ashton texted that he had his bag and would be waiting for them on the lower level. Stacey watched for him, then waved when she spotted him.

"Over there."

Kit maneuvered through the crush of cars. Stacey jumped out when he came to a stop.

"You're here," she said, hugging him. "How was your trip?"

"Good. Both flights were on time. I had an aisle seat and the flight attendant gave me extra peanuts."

He grinned as he spoke, which made her chest tighten just a little. Ashton had Kit's smile. The continuity between the generations gave her an odd sense of comfort. Unlike his uncle, Ashton had hazel eyes that were almost gray. Ashton's hair was a little darker, and as much in need of a cut as Kit's. He was about six feet tall and still had the lanky build of a growing teen.

Kit got out of the car and approached. "Good to see you."

"Hey, Kit."

They grasped hands, then did that kind of semihug, back-slap that men seemed to favor these days. Ashton tossed his battered suitcase in the trunk and grabbed his backpack before sliding into the back seat.

"The baby still a secret?" Ashton asked as they drove toward the exit. "In case I see Bunny."

"Oh, you'll see her," Kit said cheerfully. "Stacey, honey, want to share the good news?"

Stacey glanced back at Ashton. "My mother still doesn't know."

"Okay, how far along are you?"

"One hundred and ninety-seven days."

"That's precise."

"We have a calendar," she murmured. "It makes it easy

to remember when the baby is due." They'd had the option to buy a calendar that counted up or counted down. At least theirs didn't directly remind her of how few days there were left to tell her mother.

"We got a dog," she added, mostly to change the topic. "Bay is also pregnant and everyone knows. She's a Doberman and very well trained. She used to work for the government."

"So don't mess with her," Kit added. "Not only can she kill you, I'm pretty sure she would know how to hide the body."

"Bay is very sweet." Stacey shook her head. "I don't want Ashton to be worried about our dog."

"I get along with dogs," Ashton assured her. "Puppies will be fun."

"I've been studying what's involved with the canine birthing process. The vet thinks since Bay had puppies before, she'll be an excellent mother." Stacey was hoping the dog could teach her a thing or two. It would be nice to expand her knowledge on the subject, which was, to date, virtually nonexistent. All she knew about being a mother was that she didn't want to be like hers. She never wanted her daughter to feel about her the way she felt about Bunny. Not exactly the role model for a well-rounded upbringing.

The return trip was quick. Kit pulled into the driveway. While Ashton collected his luggage, Stacey went inside to remind Bay they were adding to the pack. Technically dogs didn't think of their family members as being part of a pack. Dogs were more loyal than that, so the family unit was more like a gang where allegiance was sworn and members protected each other to the death. But when she'd tried to explain that to Kit, he'd told her that talking about their pack was going to be easier for everyone. And when it came to things like social niceties, she trusted Kit implicitly.

"Bay, sit," Stacey said as Ashton walked into the living room. The Doberman's ears went up, but she stayed in place.

Ashton dropped his bags and slowly approached the dog. "Hey, Bay. I'm Ashton. You're beautiful."

"Bay, greet," Stacey said.

Bay rose and stepped toward Ashton. She sniffed his hand, then his shoes before turning her attention to Stacey.

"Good girl. Ashton is going to be living with us now. He's part of the pack."

Bay looked between them before walking closer to Ashton. He dropped to one knee and rubbed the side of her face. Her stubby tail wiggled furiously as she swiped his cheek with her tongue. Ashton winked.

"Told you. Dogs love me." He grinned. "As do the ladies."

"Let's see if you love your room," Kit said, carrying his nephew's bags.

They all went down the hall and into Ashton's room. Stacey hovered in the doorway, anxious about his reaction.

"If I forgot anything, just let me know. There are school supplies in the desk and toiletries in the bathroom."

Ashton turned in a slow circle, then faced her. "Stacey, it's perfect. Thank you for letting me stay here."

"We're happy to have you."

She hesitated, wanting to say more. It seemed as if Ashton needed something, but she had no idea what. Should she ask about his mother? The friends he was leaving behind? Did he want the house Wi-Fi code?

Uncertainty made her uneasy and she looked to her husband, who appeared perfectly relaxed. Harper would know, she thought regretfully. Bunny, even Becca. She was the only one who was forever scrambling to be just like everyone else.

"This is Harper."

"What the hell, Harper? Is this how you treat all your clients? What's wrong with you? You're not just fired. I swear, if I had time, I would sue you."

Harper went cold as her stomach clenched into a knot. She stared at the phone number on the screen, but didn't recognize it.

"I'm sorry," she said as calmly as she could. "Who am I speaking with?"

"Stan over at Mischief Bay Landscaping. You messed up my billing. From what I've been able to figure out, nearly a quarter of my customers were billed wrong. Wrong amount, wrong invoice—you name it, you screwed it up. I'm going to tell everyone I know what a shitty job you did. Mischief Bay is a small town and I'm going to do my best to see you never get another job in it again."

There was a click, then silence. Harper thought she might throw up, only there wasn't time. She raced into her office, Thor and Jazz on her heels. She flipped open her laptop and clicked on the landscaping billing program, then grabbed the stack of invoices that were to be entered.

The first three or four were fine, but as she got deeper into the stack, she saw that Stan had been right. The amounts were transposed or the wrong services had been entered. Two lawn service clients had been billed the right amount but the column for pool service had been checked.

It went on like that through the first quarter of the stack. After that, the billing was correct.

Harper sank onto her chair and moaned. No, no, no. It

couldn't be this bad. It couldn't. But it was, and she only had herself to blame.

She'd known Morgan wasn't paying attention to her work, but she'd been too wimpy to call her on it and too busy to check her work. Now she was going to pay big-time.

Stan wasn't kidding. Mischief Bay might be smack in the middle of Los Angeles County, but it was still a small town where nearly everyone knew everyone else. If he started telling people how she'd screwed up, she was done for.

Bile rose in her throat. She swallowed it back and told herself not to panic. She had to figure out how to fix the problem. She couldn't undo the mistakes in the billing and Stan was mad. Even more important, his customers were pissed at him and he could easily lose business from the mistake. So she had to make it right.

She tugged off her headset and raced to the kitchen where she grabbed her handbag.

"I'll be back in a bit," she told the dogs. They had a doggie door should they need to go to the bathroom and they'd already been on their walk with Dwayne, so they should be tired.

She hurried to her car and drove directly to Stan's office. With luck he was still there, plotting his revenge. She burst into the small building and found the older man sitting at his messy desk. He glared at her.

"What do you want, Harper?"

She'd done her best to plan her response on the way over, but faced with in-person fury, she found her mind going blank. For a second she thought her stomach was going to make good on its earlier threats, then she drew in a breath and told herself she had to get a grip. There was no one else around to fix this particular mess.

"I wanted to apologize in person," she told him. "You are right about everything you said. The invoices were wrong and that is inexcusable. I didn't do my job correctly. Worse, I made a mess for you to clean up when all you wanted to do was get one thing off your already-full plate."

His stern expression didn't relax. "So? You're sorry. You said it. Now go."

"I will in a second. First I would like the chance to fix what I did. By five this afternoon I will have compared every invoice with your original paperwork. I'll make a complete list of which are correct and which aren't. Over the next two days I will personally call every customer who received an incorrect invoice and explain it was my fault, not yours. I will send out corrected invoices." She swallowed. "I would also like to do next month's invoicing for free. After that, you can be rid of me."

"Are you kidding me? That's ridiculous. Do you know how much money you're going to lose?"

"No, but that doesn't matter. You relied on me and I let you down."

Stan glared at her. "It wasn't your mistake, was it?"

She raised her chin. "It's my company and my responsibility. That's what matters here."

"You're killing me, Harper, you know that? Fine. Fix the invoice and call the clients. You can do next month's billing for the amount we agreed on, but if there's even one mistake, we're through. Got it?"

"Yes. I'll get you the report by five today. Thank you for allowing me to fix this."

He waved to the door. "You have a lot of work to do. Get out of my office."

She did as she was told and escaped. Once she was in her

car, the shaking started. That was followed by waves of cold, then her old friend nausea returned. When she was able to hold her phone without dropping it, she texted Morgan and told her she was fired. Perhaps not the most professional of reactions but Harper figured she had earned the right to be pissy. Now all she had to do was clean up the Stan mess, which meant finding an extra twenty or thirty hours in every day.

Chapter Nine

MEETINGS TO UPDATE A RESEARCH PROGRAM COULD BE exciting or frustrating. Breakthroughs tended to come in clusters, which meant long periods when there was little to report beyond what hadn't worked. Stacey firmly believed that failure was as useful as success—not as satisfying, but just as important. Each failure brought the team closer to their ultimate victory.

Her job was to direct, inspire and innovate, as well as manage her team. She enjoyed the variety in her day, although her favorite times were when she was working in the lab. But that was not today. She sat in the conference room with the rest of the team leaders as they brought each other up-to-date. There were six team leaders and their assistants. She and Lexi were the only women.

Karl ran the meetings. While she technically reported to him, he had no control over her research or her results. Those were managed independently to avoid any potential conflict of interest. Four years ago a large bribery scandal had rocked the company when it was discovered that researchers were being paid to consider options that weren't viable for the general population, but might help a handful of patients. Patients who had access to lots of money.

The researchers involved were fired and Stacey was brought on to take over the MS program. She'd cleaned up her department, reworked the team and was very pleased with their progress. While others sought to find a way to prevent MS from ever happening in the first place, Stacey's group wanted to improve the lives of those already afflicted with the disease. Lesions in the myelin—the coating that surrounded every nerve—prevented normal communication with the nerves and caused the symptoms. The more lesions, the less communication, the greater the impact on the patient.

That was her area of research: looking at ways to repair or regenerate the myelin. Once the nerves were damaged, the regeneration wouldn't help, but for those patients with functioning nerves, reducing the lesions would allow motor function to be restored.

Some progress had been made. New medications and treatments were being developed, but Stacey wanted more. Stopping the process wasn't enough—she wanted to reverse the damage done.

Karl, a big bear of a man, dropped his reading glasses onto the table. "About the travel schedule for the second half of the year. Stacey, you're in demand as a speaker as always. I want to balance your work schedule with your travel schedule. We're so close to a breakthrough with your team's work that I'm concerned about you being gone. Having said that, there's a symposium in Orlando in July I think you should consider attending."

Stacey involuntarily glanced at Lexi. Her assistant attended the meetings to take notes and document what was discussed.

More of the company's mandate to be transparent about the research.

Lexi smiled encouragingly at her, as if pointing out that the opportunity to tell Karl about the baby wouldn't get much better than this.

Stacey cleared her throat. "I won't be able to attend," she said firmly. "I'm taking three weeks off in late June. I've already cleared it with HR."

She paused. Lexi mouthed, "Go on."

"I'm going to be out on maternity leave."

"You're adopting a child?" Karl asked. "You never mentioned it."

"I'm not adopting. I'm pregnant."

Everyone but Lexi stared at her. Most of them looked down, as if wanting to confirm her growing belly. Something she'd done her best to conceal.

"You're having a baby?" Max, one of the other team leaders, asked. "In June?"

She nodded, not wanting to say exactly how many days she was pregnant.

"You're forty," Karl said, then winced as if he wanted to recall the words.

"I'm aware of the risks of an older mother's pregnancy," she told him. "Gestational diabetes, preeclampsia, miscarriage and preterm delivery. As of now, I am perfectly healthy. There's no reason to assume that will change. I'm going to work up until delivery. I have discussed all this with HR," she added, in case they hadn't heard her the first time.

The men looked at each other. Max leaned toward her. "What about after the baby is born? You'll only be on maternity leave for three weeks?"

"Yes. Kit is going to stay home with the baby. The school year ends in early June, so that works out nicely."

"Kit's going to be a stay-at-home dad?" Karl asked. "What about breastfeeding, Stacey?"

She bristled. "That is not an appropriate question, Karl. I don't ask you if you use Viagra. What decisions my husband and I choose to make about our child are our business. What you need to know is that I will be gone for three weeks and nothing else. I've already proven I am more than capable of doing my job while pregnant, which is all that matters for the purposes of our discussion." She paused and glanced around the table. "If there's nothing else, can we get back to our meeting?"

Karl glanced down at his notes, then reached for his glasses. "Of course. Ah, congratulations, Stacey. Max, you're next in line for the symposium. Do you have any scheduling conflicts?"

Stacey looked at Lexi. Her assistant grinned and gave her a thumbs-up. Stacey tried to take comfort in that, but there was little to be had. She was shaking and wasn't sure what had upset her. She was used to standing up for herself in all sorts of ways. Being a woman in her field of work wasn't usually an issue, but she'd dealt with it before and not been the least bit bothered.

She wondered if this time was different because she was pregnant. Did she feel vulnerable because of her condition and her biological need to protect her unborn child? She wanted to say no but she knew for a fact that hormones were powerful and the body's need to pass on its DNA would not be denied.

She told herself she would work on the problem later, then turned her attention back to the meeting. As she listened to Max and Karl talk about the symposium, she tried not to notice the furtive glances from her male colleagues. Even if they were looking at her differently, it wasn't her problem—it was theirs.

Calligraphy was one of those weird things that was both simple and difficult at the same time. It was just writing different letters, something Harper had been doing since she was maybe five or six. But there was an element of precision that always made her a little nervous.

She'd already created the name cards, taking a plain white stock and lightly painting it with watercolors that matched the wedding's colors. After writing all the names, she would glue on tiny fabric hearts in the upper left-hand corner.

The guest list was one hundred and ninety-seven people. Harper had been torn about taking the job. It would require a lot of time and effort and most people didn't want to cough up the money for something as disposable as a place card. Paula, a far more reasonable party planner than Cathy, had asked her to charge whatever seemed fair. Harper had done a practice card, multiplied by one hundred and ninety-seven, then had added a buffer for fatigue. She'd said she would have to charge five dollars a name card, plus the cost of supplies. Shockingly, the bride had agreed, leaving Harper with yet more work, although this time she was making well above her goal of twenty-five dollars an hour.

She sat at the big desk in her craft room, the wedding guest list on her left, the stack of painted cards on her right. She was up to the Fs when she noticed Becca hovering in the doorway, Jazz at her side.

Harper put down her pen and opened and closed her hand, flexing her sore fingers. "What is it, Becca?" she asked, turning to face her daughter.

Becca pressed her lips together. "Do you, um, want me to help?"

An unexpected offer. "Not with the calligraphy, but maybe later with the gluing. That would be nice. Thank you." She paused. "Was there something else?"

Becca hesitated, then shook her head. "No. That's all."

"Okay. I need to get back to this."

Harper continued writing out names. She used a ruler to keep track of where she was on the list and checked the spelling both before and after she wrote the card. No one wanted a misspelled place card.

Movement caught her attention. Becca and Jazz were back. She capped her pen and stood. "What is it, honey?"

Her daughter shifted her weight from foot to foot. Never a good sign. Harper ran through the possibilities in her head. Something with school, something with a friend, something with Terence. As far as she knew, Becca was doing fine in her classes. Her last quarter grades had been a little lower than usual, but Becca had a heavy load, academically. Jordan was around plenty, so the friendship should be fine. There hadn't been a boy that she knew of...

Harper thought about how busy she'd been lately. She was always scrambling to get her work done. Was that the problem? Was she ignoring Becca?

"Come on," she said with a smile. "I need more coffee. Let's go raid the kitchen."

"Okay."

Harper poured herself coffee while Becca carried the cookie jar over to the island. They settled on stools next to each other. Becca opened the cookie jar and looked inside.

"Frosted sugar cookies, peanut butter, snickerdoodles and oatmeal raisin with chocolate chips."

In an effort to both help and shame her daughter, Bunny regularly brought over batches of cookies she made in her apartment.

"Oatmeal raisin," Harper said. "That way I can say I'm getting my whole grains."

"Cookies don't count, Mom."

"Says who?" She took a bite and sighed as the flavors settled on her tongue. Bunny might have unrealistic expectations for Harper, but the woman could bake like nobody's business.

She sipped her coffee and waited for the combination of sugar and caffeine to heal her. Then she turned to her daughter and said, "Okay, I'm braced. What's up?"

Becca had picked a peanut butter and a frosted sugar cookie. She put them on a napkin. "Great-Aunt Cheryl left me her car." She looked up. "It's in really great shape. Ramon said she'd taken good care of it and the tires are new. I know it's a big deal, Mom, but I'm sixteen. Now you don't have to worry about buying me a car."

"I wasn't planning on buying you one," Harper said automatically as she tried to process the information. A car? A car!

A thousand thoughts crowded her head. Everything from "Really, you couldn't have mentioned this before?" to wanting to yell at her ex-husband for not mentioning it when he and Becca got back from Grass Valley. A car? There would be insurance and upkeep and—

"You don't even have a license yet."

"I'm working on it. I've passed my class at school and I have my learner's permit. I only need the practice hours. Lucas is helping with that. He's a cop, Mom. You can trust him."

"Detective," she corrected automatically. "Do you know what the insurance is going to cost? And gas?"

"I'm going to help with that, I swear. I'll get a job. You'll see, Mom. It will be great. You won't have to drive me any-where."

A job? Becca was too young for all this to be happening. Only she wasn't. She was, as she'd pointed out, sixteen, al-most seventeen. She would be a senior in the fall and then she would be off to college. But a car.

Harper thought about her monthly budget and nearly began to cry. Putting Becca on her insurance policy would save a little, but still, how was she going to pay for insurance? Even if her daughter did get a job, it wouldn't be enough. She would have to talk to Terence about him kicking in something. Becca was his daughter, too.

Becca's phone chirped. She glanced at it, then back at her mom. "That's the delivery service. They're here."

Harper nearly fell off the stool. "The car is here now?"

Becca raced to the front door, Jazz at her heels. "Uh-huh. Come see."

No wonder her daughter had been hovering, Harper thought grimly. She'd been trying to figure out how to break the news. Harper supposed she should be pleased that Becca hadn't simply had the guy park it in the driveway and waited for her mother to notice.

A large car carrier was parked in the middle of the street. A man was unchaining a pale blue Toyota Corolla. As she watched, he got in and backed it down the ramp before pull-ing it into the driveway, where Becca danced impatiently.

"Isn't it beautiful?" her daughter asked, laughing as she spoke. "Ramon said all the paperwork is in the trunk. It just had an oil change a couple of weeks ago, so I won't have to worry about that for a while."

Ramon, Great-Aunt Cheryl's longtime boyfriend, had obviously done his best to make the car ready for Becca. If only he'd thought to call Harper and give her a heads-up.

"What's going on?" Bunny asked as she came around the side of the house. "What's that? Did you sell your car?"

"No. Great-Aunt Cheryl left this to Becca. It was just delivered."

Bunny looked delighted. "Dogs and a car. What did she leave you, dear? Nothing?"

Harper refused to engage. No matter what Great-Aunt Cheryl had left or not left her, they had been friends and Harper would always treasure that.

The man handed Becca the keys, then walked over to Harper. "You need to sign for delivery."

She scrawled her name. Becca opened the driver's door and got behind the wheel, then jumped out and spun in a circle.

"This is the best! I can't wait to get my license and go driving." She wrapped her arms around Jazz. "You'll be my first passenger."

"Too bad Great-Aunt Cheryl didn't think to leave money to pay for insurance," Bunny said.

"It will be fine," Harper assured her. "At least this way I don't have to worry about buying her a car."

Becca opened the trunk and pulled out a box. "Mom, this is for you. Ramon said there were a couple of things Great-Aunt Cheryl wanted you to have."

Harper did her best not to look smug as she took the good-sized box from her daughter.

"What is it?" Bunny demanded.

"I have no idea." She turned to Becca. "You are not allowed to move that car one inch until it's insured. Understood?"

"I swear, Mom. I won't drive it until you say it's okay." She continued to dance around the car, her phone in hand, taking pictures from every angle.

Harper sighed, then went inside. Her mother followed.

She set the box on the kitchen table and opened it. Inside were several smaller boxes, including one that got her heart beating faster.

Bunny moved closer. "Is that…"

"An Hermès Birkin bag? Yes, it is." Not black. Great-Aunt Cheryl would never waste her time with a boring black bag. No, this one was orange. Harper read the card inside.

"It's a Togo Birkin bag," she said, wondering if she sounded smug. "And still in beautiful condition."

Label-conscious Bunny looked as if she'd eaten a lemon. "That's ridiculous. You have nothing to wear with that."

"I know. Even so, I plan to use it with everything." She opened a smaller box and found three blue boxes with the magical phrase *Tiffany & Co.* on top. Her heart pounded a little faster.

The first box contained a peach enamel and diamond bracelet. Bunny moved close and gasped. "That's a Schlumberger bangle! Do you know what those cost?"

"I have no idea."

"A lot!"

The second box held a sea horse broach, also Schlumberger, according to a miffed Bunny. The last box revealed simple diamond studs, each the size of an M&M candy.

While Bunny fingered the pin, Harper slipped on the bangle. It was heavy and unyielding and looked fabulous. She decided to wait on the earrings until she could see herself in a mirror.

She picked up the last box. It was unmarked and flat. Inside were dozens of photographs, mostly of Great-Aunt Cheryl.

They ranged from her nursing days during World War II to just a few years ago. Harper's chest tightened as she looked through them. The bag and the jewelry were amazing, but these were the best gift of all.

She would sort through them and make an album, she thought. Something special that—

She found a handwritten note at the bottom of the box.

Dear Harper,
We all knew this day would come and here it is. I want you to
have these things because I have always loved you. Remember
to be brave, strong and happy. That's what life is all about.
And don't you dare waste a second putting the old pictures in
an album. You have better things to do with your time.

Harper laughed, then felt her eyes burn with tears.

"What did she say?" Bunny demanded, snatching the letter from her. She scanned the words, then handed the sheet back. "That car is going to be a problem."

"I don't care. I'm letting her keep it." Because that was what Great-Aunt Cheryl would have wanted.

"I'm nearly forty-two," Harper said as she sat on the sofa in Stacey's living room. "When am I going to stop being manipulated by Mom?"

Stacey wasn't sure her sister wanted an answer, but decided to provide one anyway. "When you stop caring about what she thinks of you."

"You care, but you don't let it interfere with your life. Not that I wouldn't have let Becca keep the car, but I would have at least thought about it a little longer. Instead I reacted to

Mom being bitchy about what Great-Aunt Cheryl left me. I can't figure out if every family is twisted or just ours."

"I'm sure it's all of them."

Harper laughed. "I hope you're right. Okay, how's it going with Ashton?"

"Fine. He's settling in nicely. It's only been two days, but we have a routine. He has two classes to finish and he's going to get a part-time job."

Her sister nodded. "Didn't you say he'd been in foster care or living with a friend or something before he moved here?"

"Foster care. Kit's sister wouldn't let him live with us, so we had to wait until he was eighteen and aged out of the system. We flew him out the next day."

"Does he have enough stuff?"

"What do you mean?"

Harper shrugged. "I don't know much about foster families. On TV they're usually awful. Does he have clothes and shoes and whatever else he needs?"

"I asked and he said he was fine."

Harper's expression turned pitying. "And you believed him?"

"He has no reason to lie to me."

Her sister stood. "Pride, Stacey. Guilt. Shame. He's a kid."

"He's eighteen."

"He's a kid."

Harper got up suddenly and walked down the hall before tapping on Ashton's half-open door.

"Come in."

She went inside. Stacey followed, not sure what she was going to do.

"Hey, Ashton. I'm about to pry, so brace yourself. Can I see your suitcase?"

He glanced from Harper to Stacey, then walked over to his closet and pulled out his ratty suitcase. As Stacey stared at it, she realized it was ridiculously small and it had contained everything he had in the world. She glanced at the battered computer on his desk. A computer that had to be at least four years old. The phrase *her heart sank* suddenly made too much sense.

"Do you have paper?" Harper asked.

He looked more intrigued than confused as he opened a desk drawer and pulled out a pad of paper. "Stacey got me a bunch of school supplies, so I'm good."

"Uh-huh." Harper sat on the chair and started writing. "Underwear, socks." She paused to glance at his feet. "Athletic shoes, sandals, jeans, shorts, T-shirts. Do you have a lightweight jacket? June can be cool and foggy by the beach."

Ashton tensed. "I'm good. I don't need anything."

"So that's a no." She continued writing. "Deodorant, sunscreen." She glanced at his face. "Razors or an electric shaver?"

"I use disposable razors."

Harper turned to Stacey. "Let's get him one of those nice shavers all the kids love. He can go scruffy and be irresistible to the girls."

Ashton flushed. "Aunt Harper, I'm fine."

"Just Harper, please, and don't even try. I can be so bossy. I get it from my mother." She put down her pen. "I'm thinking the mall first. Old Navy and Macy's for clothes, then Target for toiletries." She grinned. "I haven't been shopping for a while, so I'm excited. Let's go."

Ashton looked more uncomfortable than pleased. Stacey was right there with him. How could she not have noticed he needed pretty much everything and why hadn't he told her when she asked if he was all right?

Chapter Ten

ONE TRIP TO THE MALL LATER, ASHTON HAD EVERYTHING a man his age could possibly need to get him through the summer and into the fall. Harper had been her usual thorough, maternal self. The shopping had gone quickly and easily and within a few minutes of them arriving at the first store, Ashton had been joking around with her and seemed at ease. Stacey knew that she should be grateful to her sister for her help, and she was. Her internal discomfort came more from a gnawing sense of inadequacy.

How had Harper known Ashton hadn't been forthcoming about his needs? How had she been able to figure out the situation so quickly and how had she known what to buy him? It wasn't as if she had male children.

Once again she heard her mother's words in her head—the ones telling her she wasn't normal. She glanced at the calendar counting up to the birth and tried to tell herself everything would be fine. The problem was, she knew it wouldn't be fine at all. It would be a disaster. She was never meant to be a mother.

She'd tried to tell Kit that—explaining how she loved her work so much and she'd never felt the need to be like everyone else. But he'd only laughed and kissed her, then he'd taken her to bed where she could experience normal in the best way possible.

Kit would be a good father, she thought as she brewed herbal tea. Maybe that would be enough. He would be the main parent and she would be little more than a shadow figure. She could accept not being important in her daughter's life—what terrified her was somehow hurting Joule the way she'd been hurt as a child.

Ashton walked into the kitchen. She pointed to the teapot. "I'm making tea. It's not the best drink in the world, but it's not awful."

He flashed her a smile. "Now I have to try some."

"Harper brought over cookies. My mother made them."

He got a mug from the cupboard and joined her at the counter. "I remember your mother's cookies. I'm all in."

He would probably inhale the entire plate of them before she had a chance to finish one, but that was okay. She enjoyed having Ashton around. They were friends, or so she'd thought.

She waited until they were seated at the kitchen table, then forced herself to look at him.

"Why didn't you tell me you needed clothes and toiletries? I asked because I was concerned. It wasn't an empty question, Ashton. You live here now. We want you to be comfortable."

He flushed. "I didn't want to be a bother. Stacey, you guys have taken me in, you're paying for a lot of my college. That's more than anyone has ever done for me. I don't need new clothes or anything else."

"Yes, you do." She thought about his ancient computer, then decided this wasn't the time to bring that up. "We want you to have what you need. We're very fortunate financially." She hesitated, not completely sure how much she could discuss without crossing the invisible and ever-moving lines of social correctness. If only Kit were here. He would know what to say.

"I'm going to get a job," Ashton told her. "Then I can pay for more things."

She gripped her mug. "It's not about money. It's about taking care of you. We want to take care of you. We want you to feel safe here, and welcome."

He blinked several times, then cleared his throat. "Thanks. I do feel that."

"Good. If you need something, tell me. I'm not like my sister. I'm never going to be able to guess what's going on."

"You and Harper are really different, huh?"

"I know. She's so maternal. She always knows the right thing to say or bake or how to decorate. She takes after our mom."

He reached for one of the cookies. "Your mom sure can bake."

"She's a big believer in home and family being the most important things in the world. Everything else takes a distant second." She looked at him. "Do you know about my Grandpa Wray?"

"No. Who is he?"

"In the 1960s, thirteen men walked on the moon. Graham Wray was one of them. He was a fighter pilot and an astronaut."

"No way. Why didn't I know this?"

"I have no idea. I thought I'd told you, but maybe not." She sipped her tea. "Back then, being an astronaut was like being…" She searched for an analogy.

"Being in a boy band?" he offered with a grin.

"Maybe. Grandpa Wray was famous, as was his family. When he got back from the moon, they all went on a world tour."

"Cool."

"I think so but my mom hated it. She was only fifteen and thought her dad should stay home with her. The space program is demanding and he'd missed birthdays and Christmases all her life, and she never got over it." She reached for a frosted sugar cookie. "Psychology is not my area of expertise, but from what I can piece together, Bunny decided that she was going to only focus on family. That nothing else mattered. She passed her entire skill set on to my sister, but when it came to me, I was a disaster."

"You took after Grandpa Wray."

"I did. He was wonderful. When the family went to Florida, they all went to Disney World, but I went to Cape Canaveral to see the space program with my grandfather. Everyone knew him and respected him." She smiled at the memories. "They treated him like visiting royalty. I got to be a part of that. He was always bragging about how smart I was. He was the one who paid for my college. He wanted me to study astrophysics, but when I went into medical research, he teased that it was so I could help him live forever."

"You miss him."

"I do. He was a great man. It's just, as far as my mother's concerned, being like him isn't a good thing. Like I said, I'm not like Harper, so there's no way I can anticipate what's wrong or guess when you need something."

"I promise to tell you when I'm out of socks."

"Thank you."

They looked at each other, then away. Stacey had the sense she was missing something vital. Did Ashton want her to hug him? Did they have that kind of relationship? Harper would

know, she thought with a sigh. Harper would be the perfect
surrogate mother, just like she'd been the perfect parent to
Becca, while Stacey was unclear on what it meant to have a
baby beyond being the vessel.

Harper ran the numbers one more time. One of the advantages of all her Virtual Assistant training was she could put
together a spreadsheet on a moment's notice. The disadvan-
tage was she could no longer hide from the sad reality that
was her monthly budget.

Cathy's stupid gift bags had cost her. Not only had the supplies turned out to be more than she'd expected, leaving her
earning even less, but adding shopping time to the assembly
time and including delivery, which Cathy had insisted on at
the last minute, had made the project take much longer than
she'd estimated. She had realized all of a dollar twenty-five
an hour. All told, it had taken her nearly twenty-seven hours.
That was almost half a week's work.

She could have spent the time doing something that actually
paid—like those calligraphy name cards. That was the frustrating part—she was short on money but she had plenty of work,
which meant she was doing something seriously wrong. She
had to get smarter about her business, and she had to figure
out a way to get the money to pay for Becca's car insurance.

She'd spent a couple of hours on eBay, looking at Schlumberger pieces for sale. Either the pin or the bangle would be
enough to bail her out of her current financial mess. But then
what? She would have given up something precious from
Great-Aunt Cheryl all because she was an idiot.

Harper glanced at the clock, then picked up her phone and
pressed a few buttons to connect with Terence's private line at

work. She knew when he took his lunch. With luck he would pick up rather than let the call go through to—

"Hello?"

"It's Harper," she said, not assuming that after nearly sixteen years of marriage he would still remember the sound of her voice.

"Hello, Harper. How is everything?"

He always sounded so calm and rational when they spoke. Not the least bit concerned that she might get emotional or accuse him of things. He'd always been like that—totally in control of his feelings. He'd been calm when he'd proposed, unruffled when she'd told him she was pregnant, serene when he'd confessed to his affair and deadpan when he'd told her he was leaving and that he wanted a divorce. The most agitated she'd ever seen him had been when he'd been in the middle of the allergy attack from being in the same car with three dogs. Even that had been the result of a medical emergency rather than actual emotion.

"Did you want to mention the car your aunt left Becca?" she asked, knowing neither of them really cared about small talk.

"Damn. I'm sorry. I forgot to tell you, didn't I? I guess I wasn't thinking about anything that day except trying to breathe. Did it arrive?"

"It did."

"Good. At least you don't have to worry about buying her a car now."

Really? Because that would only be her responsibility? She didn't know how he did it, but Terence had an uncanny ability to piss her off.

"Before *we* would have to deal with any car purchase, she would need to get her license, wouldn't she? Terence, you're supposed to be helping her get her hours in."

"I know. I've explained to her that I've been busy. Why aren't you doing it?"

"Because I'm doing everything else when it comes to our daughter. She asked you, Terence. Becca rarely asks you for anything. Can't you at least get off your ass and show up every now and then? You're supposed to see her every other weekend."

"I'm the one who drove to Grass Valley with her. That was four days together."

"Oh, wow. You're right. Then your parenting responsibilities are done for the year."

"Fine. You're right. I'll get some times on my calendar."

He was going to put his daughter on his calendar. Wasn't that special? She nearly said that out loud, but figured she'd already gone far enough with her sarcasm for one conversation.

"You also need to pay for half the insurance," she said.

"Of course. Get me an invoice and I'll send a check."

Because that was how Terence rolled. God forbid he should simply pay for something. Nope, he needed to be billed. He'd actually had the balls to ask her once whether if he paid the bill in ten days, he would get a discount. She'd hung up on him because unlike her ex-husband, she did run on emotion.

"I'll get an email out to you today."

"Thank you. Anything else?"

Anything else? After all this time and having a child together, was there really nothing they could talk about? She knew the marriage was over and after the shock of trying to figure out how to make it on her own, she had to say she wasn't sorry. They hadn't been happy together for years, but still. Wouldn't it be nice if he had a few regrets?

"No, that's all. Goodbye, Terence."

"Goodbye, Harper."

★ ★ ★

Becca supposed she should be annoyed by a duty visit to a relative she'd never met, but to be honest she was kind of intrigued by the thought of meeting her uncle Kit's nephew. Becca's dad was an only child and Aunt Stacey hadn't had her baby yet, so not only didn't Becca have siblings, there weren't any cousins, either. Unless Ashton counted. She wasn't sure.

Normally on a half day of school, she and Jordan would have made plans, but Becca was doing her best to avoid her and their usual group of friends, mostly so she didn't have to see Nathan. She had no idea what to do about him or who to tell. It wasn't as if he'd done anything bad, right? He hadn't hurt her or forced her, he'd just…suggested.

Thinking about that made her stomach hurt, so she concentrated on how well Jazz walked beside her. The Doberman kept close and was alert, but never barked or chased other dogs.

They turned onto Stacey's street. Becca tried to remember how many times Ashton had been to visit. Two maybe, or three. Bunny had taken her and her mom to Hawaii the first time he'd come to see his aunt and uncle. It had been right after the divorce and the trip was supposed to make everyone feel better. It hadn't worked.

The second time Ashton had visited, she'd been away with her sophomore government class. They'd gone to Sacramento to study state government. It had been interesting, but kind of lame, too. So every time he'd been around, she'd been gone, until now.

She knew he was eighteen and going to MIT in the fall. She imagined some short, glasses-wearing nerdy guy who stuttered or only talked about quasars. She smiled at the thought, then told herself she would deal because he was family.

She climbed the couple of steps to the porch and knocked

on the front door. When it opened, she felt her jaw drop and her skin flush. For a second her vision reduced to a pinpoint before expanding to include the most beautiful boy she'd ever seen in her life.

He was tall, maybe six feet, with hazel-gray eyes. His skin was pale, his hair shaggy. He wore jeans and a T-shirt and athletic shoes. Nothing out of the ordinary, yet he looked like he could be doing a photo shoot for *Seventeen* magazine, or *GQ*.

He smiled. "Hi, you must be Becca. Nice to finally meet you. I'm Ashton."

She couldn't speak, mostly because she couldn't breathe. Why hadn't someone warned her? Why hadn't her mother or aunt casually mentioned that Ashton was incredibly hot and that she might want to take an extra thirty seconds with her appearance? As it was she'd pulled her hair back in a ponytail, hadn't even put on lip gloss and she was pretty sure her T-shirt had a stain on the front.

Bay nosed past Ashton to greet Jazz. Becca released the leash, giving Jazz permission to race into the house with her friend.

Stacey appeared next to Ashton. "Hello, Becca. I'm glad you made it before I have to leave for my doctor's appointment." She sighed. "Despite my excellent health, regular checkups are required so we can keep track of the baby's growth."

Becca managed to step past Ashton into the house. "How are you feeling?" Because talking about her aunt's pregnancy seemed to be the only topic she could think of while in the presence of such an unexpected man.

"I'm perfectly fine. Thank you for asking. You haven't met Ashton before, have you? I think there were timing issues on his previous visits. As I told you, he's with us until he leaves for MIT. I'm hoping you two will be friends." She smiled. "After all, you have me in common."

As jokes went, it was pretty lame, but Aunt Stacey tried, so Becca laughed, as did Ashton.

Stacey collected her handbag. "I'll be back later this afternoon. What are you two going to do?"

Kiss, Becca thought dreamily. It would be so great if Ashton kissed her. On the lips and as if he really meant it. Soft at first, but then with more intensity as he was swept away by—

"I thought we'd take the dogs for a walk," he said. "On the boardwalk."

"Don't forget poop bags," Stacey said as she headed for the garage. "Have fun."

"Because nothing says a good time like carrying around dog poop," Becca said before she could stop herself.

Ashton chuckled. "If your dog is anything like Stacey's we need to bring a couple of bags."

"I know, right?"

There was a moment of awkward silence, then he held out his hand. "I think our introduction got interrupted. I'm Ashton."

She braced herself before shaking hands with him. Yup, there it was. Warm boy skin and tingles. "Becca. Nice to meet you."

He opened the door on a small cabinet and pulled out a leash. "Shall we?"

The afternoon was warm and sunny but not as hot as it would be in the summer. Becca was aware of him next to her. Every now and then their arms brushed. The light contact messed with her head and made it difficult to think of anything to say.

"Aunt Stacey said you moved here from Tennessee."

"I did. My mom's in rehab and I ran out of places to stay, so I got stuck in foster care. I aged out when I turned eighteen, which was a good thing. Kit and Stacey had been trying to get me out to live with them for a while but Mom kept saying no."

The info dump left Becca more speechless than before, but this time it had nothing to do with how cute he was. Instead she had to process the information. No one she knew ever said anything that honest. Not right away. Even if they did, she had no experience with foster care or rehab or any of that. Mischief Bay was a stupid little town where the worst thing that happened was your parents divorced and everyone forgot about you. But when compared with what Ashton had been through, how could that possibly matter?

"I'm sorry," she managed.

"It's okay." He glanced at her. "I didn't know how much Stacey had told you already. I didn't mean to dump all that on you."

"She probably explained everything to my mom and my mom didn't want to upset me or something. She thinks I'm still nine."

"That's not a bad thing, Becca. Your mom cares about you. That's nice."

What was she supposed to say to that? Of course her mom cared about her—that was what moms did. They loved so much, they were annoying. Only Ashton's mother was in rehab and she hadn't wanted Ashton to live with his uncle, even if that was better for him. So maybe for him, a nice mom was something special.

The concrete boardwalk cut through the sand, running parallel to the ocean in front of them. To the south, in the distance, were the high hills of Palos Verdes, to the north, the pier and the park.

"That's the Pacific Ocean Park, or POP as we call it. It used to be the old Santa Monica Pier. When it was torn down, parts of it were brought here." She paused, hoping she didn't sound too stupid. "When I was little, my mom used to take me to ride on the carousel nearly every day. It was my favorite thing."

"We should go sometime. See if it's still as good as you remember."

W-was he asking her out? No, he was just being friendly and polite. She would be a fool to read anything else into his words.

"Um, sure. That would be great."

"Stacey said you're a junior in high school?"

"Uh-huh. And you're going to MIT in the fall. Are you excited?"

"Mostly nervous, but don't tell Stacey. She's all about how great college is going to be."

"From what I've heard, she was kind of too smart for high school and she left early," Becca said. "I don't think she fit in very well." Something Becca was experiencing herself these days, but for different reasons.

For a second she wondered if Ashton would have an opinion on what had happened with Nathan. Maybe a guy would know what to do. Only she didn't know him well enough to ask his advice and she was afraid the story would make her sound even younger and more inexperienced than she was.

"When you go to college, everyone in your class will be new," she said instead. "You'll all have that in common."

"That's what I try to tell myself." He reached down to pet Bay. "How you feeling, little girl? Doing all right?"

The dog licked his hand and wagged her tail.

Becca glanced at her belly. "She's getting really pregnant."

"I know. The puppies are going to be great." He smiled at her. "You're going to have to come over and help me socialize them so they can be adopted."

"That sounds like fun. I'll bring Jazz so she can learn to be an aunt."

Jazz wagged her tail at the mention of her name.

Ashton stopped and looked at her. "I know you're busy with school and your friends, but if you have any free time, I'd like to hang out. Stacey and Kit are great but they're…"

Becca's heart fluttered, although she did her best to look totally normal and not as if she was going to squeal. "Adults?" she offered.

Ashton laughed. "That's the word I looking for." He paused.

She realized he was waiting for her to respond to what he'd said. The hanging out part. She cleared her throat and sucked in a breath. "We can hang out."

"Good. You can tell me about your friends and school and if I get the job I applied for at Backyard Bounty—the daily farmers' market—I'll fill you in on the exciting world of produce stocking."

"I hear there's an art to stacking apples."

"Man, now I'm already feeling pressure."

Becca laughed and relaxed just a little. Yes, Ashton was very nice to look at, but there was a real person inside. One who was funny and sweet and nothing like gross and disgusting Nathan, and wasn't that just the best?

Chapter Eleven

HARPER MADE THE CALLS SHE'D PROMISED STAN THE landscaper. Most of the customers had been disinterested in her apology, one had yelled at her for being stupid and two had congratulated her on being so conscientious. She tried to hang on to those good feelings as she looked at her to-do list.

There were new T-shirt designs to email to Misty, a handful of website updates, a meeting with the city manager to discuss more work. Cathy, the evil party planner, had been bugging her for a while, but Harper was going to ignore her messages, at least for now. Paula, the good party planner, had hired her to create a custom Pin the Curls on the Beautiful Six-year-old game, which was both sweet and creepy. There was the usual assortment of chores for Lucas, and she had to figure out what she was going to wear when the handsome, charming, private jet salesman, Blake, breezed into town in a couple of days. He was taking her out for a cocktail, something he did when he was in town.

Aside from that, her day looked completely open. Maybe

she should schedule a massage. At least she didn't have to walk the dogs. They were out for their daily fun time with Dwayne.

Harper spent five minutes figuring out the order in which to do her work. The meeting couldn't be moved, so everything else had to fit around it. She reviewed the latest T-shirt designs one more time, then sent them to Misty before pulling up the digital picture of the little birthday girl and wondering how on earth to turn her ringlets into a game. Before she could decide, the doorbell rang.

She walked to the front of the house and found Morgan on the porch.

"What are you doing here?"

Morgan rolled her eyes. "You owe me money. You said I could pick up my check today. Did you forget?"

Why yes, she had, Harper thought resentfully, what with having to redo all of Morgan's work, then fix her mistakes. She didn't dare calculate how much money she'd lost or she would start keening.

"Let me go write it up. It will just take a second."

She desperately wanted to close the door in Morgan's face and let her wait outside, but that would be rude, so Harper stepped back to allow the other woman into her living room.

She raced back to her office, quickly calculated the few hours Morgan had worked, then wrote out the check. When she returned to hand it over, she said, "It's well under the legal reporting minimum so I won't be sending you a 1099."

While Harper would expense the payment, it was up to Morgan to declare it or not.

Morgan waved the check. "You're making a mistake, you know. Firing me. You need the help. What's the deal? You have to do everything yourself? That's really stupid."

Harper felt as if she'd stepped into some alternate universe. "Are you asking for your job back?"

"I don't know. Maybe. It wasn't awful working here. Maybe if the work was less boring I'd be interested."

For one horrible second, Harper found herself actually tempted. She was genuinely overwhelmed by what she had to get done. She couldn't seem to get her arms around all of it or get organized enough to avoid a constant scramble. Just when she managed to get her finances on track, something happened like the great gift bag debacle or Morgan's screwup, and then she tumbled into the abyss again.

Having someone to help could change everything. She could take on bigger projects and leave the small stuff to her assistant. Yes, there would be an awkward transition, but once that was over...

No! Harper heard the voice scream in her head and knew she had to listen. She did need help, but not the Morgan kind.

"I only have boring work," she forced herself to say as calmly as she could.

Morgan sighed. "I guess I could do that."

Harper realized she was in no way trained to hire and fire. She didn't know how to do it. Texting had been so much easier than this face-to-face crap, yet she couldn't possibly hire Morgan back.

"No, you couldn't," Harper said as firmly as she could. "You barely got through a quarter of the invoices when you should have finished all of them. Worse, nearly every invoice you entered had a mistake. The amount, the customer's name, the service—all wrong. I lost that account because of you. I was fired, Morgan, and I was counting on that income. To make things right with the client, I had to go back through all your work, call each client and explain what had gone wrong. Next month, I'll be doing the client's billing for free, as my way of apologizing for your screwup. So as much as I'd like to say sure, welcome back, I simply can't afford to have you work for me."

They stared at each other. Harper wondered if she was as wide-eyed as she felt. She'd only meant to say "Thanks but no thanks," but the rest of it had spilled out. She felt lighter somehow. Relieved and more than a little smug. Right up until Morgan's cheeks flushed and her mouth curled back in what could easily be described as a snarl.

"You are a total bitch. My God, why didn't I see that before? No wonder you can't get someone to work for you. You can forget it, lady. I wouldn't work for you ever, no matter how much you beg. Go to hell, you hear me?"

With that she turned on her heel and stomped out the door.

Harper stood in the center of the living room trying to ignore the sudden shaking that swept through her. That had been five kinds of awful. She really had to get better at dealing with people.

"I've told you and told you. Starting your own business was a mistake."

Harper spun and saw Bunny standing at the kitchen door. Her mother shook her head.

"Family is your first priority, Harper. Take care of your husband and your daughter. But you wouldn't listen and now look at where you are."

Anger and frustration joined the trembling. "You're not helping, Mom," she said as she pushed past her and headed for the coffeepot. "I'm going to ask you not to lecture me right now. I can't deal with it. I have a lot to do today and I need to focus."

"Becca should be your focus."

Harper slammed her mug on the counter and faced her mother. As always, Bunny was perfectly dressed, with flattering makeup and coordinated jewelry. Harper had yet to shower, something else she would have to squeeze in before her meeting.

"This is how I pay the bills," Harper said, trying not to grind her teeth. It couldn't be good for her and she honestly couldn't afford any dental work right now. "This isn't some feel-good movie where I win the lottery and all our problems are solved. This is real life. I *am* thinking about my family when I work. I really need you to understand that and if you can't, at least stop lecturing me."

Bunny's eyes filled with tears. "I can't believe how you're talking to me. I'm your mother. You apologize right now." She planted her hands on her hips as if she were prepared to wait forever. Harper couldn't figure out how her entire life had gone to hell so quickly.

"I'm sorry if your feelings are hurt," she began, "but I won't apologize for how I feel. You're not supporting me, Mom. Telling me I'm doing everything wrong doesn't help."

The tears spilled over. "You are a horrible daughter," her mother said, then pressed a hand to her mouth and hurried out the back door.

Harper closed her eyes and told herself when she opened them, everything would be better. Seconds later, she discovered she'd been wrong. Everything was still the same. Her list, the drama with her mother.

She knew the drill. Bunny would sulk for several days, then they would have a meaningless conversation designed to smooth things over. It was what they did. For whatever reason, Bunny couldn't accept Harper's situation and refused to believe that a job was required to provide income. Maybe it was because her mother had never held a job in her life. Maybe it was generational. Maybe the powers that be simply found her life to be an endless source of amusement.

The doorbell rang. Again.

Harper marched to the front door prepared to do battle with whomever was there to screw with her. She'd taken all she could take for a single day. She was hungry, she was tired and she hadn't had nearly enough coffee that morning.

She pulled open the door. "What?"

The teenage boy on her porch jumped back. His eyes widened and he looked terrified.

"Um, Mrs. Szymanski?"

"Yes."

"I'm, um, here to, ah, clean up your yard?"

The sentence was more question than statement. Harper looked more closely at the kid, then dropped her gaze to his T-shirt, which advertised a dog poop scooper service. You Poop, We Scoop.

All her anger, frustration, fear and uncertainty faded, leaving her feeling weak and just a little like crying.

"You're going to clean up the dog poop?" she asked, her voice trembling. "Really?"

The kid looked more scared. "Um, yes? Every week?"

Lucas, she thought with gratitude. The man was incredible. He might have an affinity for twentysomethings, but the man had hired someone to scoop dog poop. What could be better than that?

"What's your name?" she asked.

"B-Brandon?"

She smiled. "I'm sorry I snapped at you, Brandon. I just had a fight with my mom."

The kid relaxed. "Oh. Those are the worst."

"Tell me about it."

Becca sat on the front porch, waiting. She'd left Jazz inside with Thor. Once she got her license, she would take her dog with her, but not during a lesson.

She was both excited and nervous—Lucas had said he would be over at four, but what if something came up at work? She knew his hours varied. If he was in the middle of a case, he would be late, or if he didn't want to bother, like her dad.

Thinking about her dad made her uncomfortable, and then weirdly, she remembered what had happened with Nathan, which made her stomach hurt.

She didn't want to think about that so she thought about Ashton, who had texted her that morning. Just a quick hello, but still. It was nice. He was nice. She couldn't believe how easy things had been between them and hoped he'd liked her, too. Although why would he? He was this cool, good-looking guy who was going to college and she was just some dumb girl who—

Lucas pulled up in his Mercedes. Becca jumped to her feet and danced toward him.

"You came!"

"Hey, kid, I said I'd be here." He nodded at the car in the driveway. "I heard about your new wheels."

"Isn't she beautiful? I love the color. I'm thinking I'm going to have to give her a name, but I can't think of one I really like. Plus, I don't know if it's silly or not."

"If you want it, then it's not silly." He reached into his pocket and handed her a bottle of nail polish. "For Jazz."

"What?" She studied the label, then started to laugh. The *pawlish* was Fire Hydrant Red. "OMG, do you think she'll let me paint her nails? That would be the best. Thanks, Lucas. I love it."

She put the polish in her bag, then hurried to her car. "I can't wait to go driving. Mom's super busy. She took me out for an hour, but that's it. I'm still not comfortable driving my car, but I know I'll get better with practice."

She opened the driver's side door and got into the seat. Instead of joining her on the passenger side, Lucas strolled over and looked at her.

"Not so fast."

"What?"

"First we're going to talk about the car."

"What about it?"

"What kind is it?"

Becca had no idea what he meant. "It's a blue Toyota Corolla."

"What year?"

Her stomach sank like it did when there was a pop quiz in history. "I don't know."

"How many miles does it have on it?"

She stared at him.

"How often does it need an oil change? What *is* an oil change? What's the right pressure for the tires? How do you know how much tread you have left on your tires? Is the car front wheel or rear wheel drive? What does that mean? Does this car drive okay in the rain?"

The sick feeling grew. Becca told herself there was no way she was going to cry. This was Lucas. He wasn't trying to hurt her, he was making a point. One she should probably listen to.

"You're saying I have a car now and I need to know something about it. If it's my car, it's my responsibility."

"Bingo."

She smiled. "You know, only old people say *bingo*."

"I'm down with that."

She laughed. "You're right. I wasn't thinking. A car is a big deal." She might not know anything about tire pressure, but she'd looked in the glove compartment and knew there was a manual. "I'll study up for our next lesson."

"That's my girl," he said and closed her door.

They drove around the city for nearly an hour. Lucas had her practice on narrow residential streets as well as on the busy Pacific Coast Highway. He didn't make her go on the freeway, but she had to make three left turns, two without an arrow.

They drove to his place where he set up his trash can and recycling can along the curb. Becca stared at the tiny space in between.

"I can't fit in there."

"It's at least double the length of your car. This is just the starting point, kid. Next time, the cans will be closer together." He tapped the trash can. "Bumper of the car in front." He pointed to the recycling can. "Bumper of the car behind. The goal is to not hit either one."

"I'm going to throw up."

"The lawn is over there."

He got behind the wheel and showed her how to line up with the car in front, then turn the wheel sharply to the left.

"When you start to crank the steering wheel, make sure that part of the door is lined up with the rear bumper. See what I'm doing?"

She looked out the passenger window and nodded. "Yeah, I do. Oh, I get it. The car will go back and then you just have to straighten it out." She turned back to him. "It looks easy when you describe it but I have a feeling it won't be so easy when I do it."

"Maybe not the first time, but you'll get it."

She practiced pulling in and out. The third time she totally ran into the recycling can, which was humiliating, but Lucas didn't even laugh. After a few more tries, they put the cans where they belonged and started back to her house.

They were nearly there when Becca impulsively pulled over by the elementary school. The kids were long gone and the street was quiet. She looked at Lucas.

"I need to ask you a question," she said.

He shifted so he was leaning against the passenger door. "Shoot."

"But you can't tell. I mean that. Not even my mom."

His green eyes narrowed. "That's a big thing to ask."

"I know." She bit her lower lip. "I'm not in trouble and I didn't break the law. I just don't know what to do about something that happened and you're the only one I can ask."

"I promise not to tell anyone," he said, then swore softly. "Which I suspect I'm going to regret. Talk."

She drew in a breath. "Jordan has a new boyfriend. His name is Nathan. They've been going out for a while and over Spring Break they did it."

She spoke quickly, talking about how Jordan always went on and on, saying Nathan loved her and blah, blah, blah. She stared at the steering wheel as she haltingly explained what had happened at Jordan's house.

"I didn't know what to do," she said, swallowing against the tightness in her throat. "I wasn't scared. I mean I was, but I didn't think he was going to hurt me or anything. It was just gross and icky and I don't want him to do that again. Plus, how can Jordan be with him, and why does he tell her he loves her when he doesn't? Is it because he's mean or is it sex? What is it with men and sex? My dad, you, Nathan. I don't understand."

"What's his last name?" Lucas asked.

Becca was so startled, she nearly blurted it out. "Why?"

"I'm going to find him and arrange to have him killed."

She stared at him. "You're kidding, right?" His face was a mask—she had no idea what he was thinking. Maybe he wasn't kidding.

"I can't decide." He sucked in a breath and looked at her. "Let's be clear. Nathan's a total asshole. He's the kind of person who uses others to get what he wants and he doesn't care who gets hurt. You did nothing wrong. Later, I'm going to show you how to nail a guy in the nuts, so if he ever tries anything you can get away."

She felt herself flush. "I guess I need to know that, huh?"

"I'm sorry, Becca. You shouldn't have to go through anything like that. For what it's worth, I think you should talk to your mom."

"No way. She wouldn't understand. Besides, she's way too busy for me." It had been like that for a while now. Before the divorce her mom always had time for her, but not anymore. The business came first.

Lucas muttered something under his breath. "You're going to make me have this conversation then, aren't you?"

"What conversation?"

He rubbed his face with his hands, then shook his head. "Honestly, I'd rather be shot again. Okay, here goes. Don't have sex with anyone until you know it's the right thing for you. Only you. I know everyone is doing it and it seems cool, but it's not. Your first time is going to change you and you can't undo it. Boys are desperate to get laid and they will say or do anything to get into your pants. Wait until you're sure, then wait some more."

She felt herself flushing. Oh. My. God. This was so much worse than the awkward "where babies come from" conversation she'd had with her mom. Okay, maybe not that bad because Lucas was obviously suffering and that was a little bit fun. Plus, she knew he cared about her.

"You're saying wait until I'm in love."

"Exactly."

"But you have sex with lots of women and you're not in love with any of them."

He closed his eyes and groaned. "Kill me now."

"You know, Lucas, those women you date are only a few years older than me. That's not right."

He opened his eyes and glared at her. "We're not talking about me."

"I'm just saying. They're somebody's daughter, too. Why don't you have to be in love or why don't they have to be in love?"

"It's different. They're…experienced. You're…" His expression softened. "Becca, you're right where you should be. You're smart and funny and you have so much to offer. Don't sell yourself short. Don't let some little shit take anything from you. You deserve to be as much as you can and guys like Nathan only want to make you less."

Tears burned in her eyes. She blinked them away. "Thank you," she whispered, wanting him to know how much that meant.

"You're welcome. What's your plan when it comes to Nathan?"

The question was unexpected but as she thought about it, she realized Lucas was right. She needed to have an idea of how to deal with him. Jordan was her friend and where she went, Nathan was sure to follow.

"I won't be alone with him," she began. "Ever. I'll keep my distance. Are you really going to teach me how to kick him in the balls?"

"You know it."

"Then if I get scared, I'll do that."

"Are you going to tell Jordan what happened?"

"What? No. She would never believe me. She'd say I was jealous." And then she wouldn't have any friends. "I can't."

"Okay."

She glared at him. "I know what you're thinking. You want me to tell her because if she was really my friend she should know what her boyfriend is doing behind her back. Only it's not that simple."

He held up both hands. "You're doing all the talking here, kid."

She sighed. "Why did you have to bring that up? Now I'll be wondering what to do for like weeks."

"Yeah, I can be real pain." He winked. "How are your grades?"

She grabbed the steering wheel with both hands and screamed. "Don't you think you've tortured me enough today?"

He didn't say anything.

"Fine," she told him. "I'm working on them."

"Work harder. Ready to go home?"

She sagged back in her seat. "Sure."

As she started the car, she realized she wasn't as upset with Lucas as she pretended. In fact, she wasn't mad at him at all. He'd been there for her. He'd listened and given her good advice—except for telling Jordan about Nathan—and he made her feel like he was on her side. She liked that.

She checked the road before pulling out and starting toward the stop sign. If only it were like this with her dad. If only he would listen and show up when he said. But he didn't, and despite his promises, she had a bad feeling he was never going to change.

Chapter Twelve

HARPER WOULD NORMALLY HAVE GONE TO HER MOTHER for fashion advice and a jewelry loan, but as they weren't speaking, that wasn't possible. She was on her own as she got ready for her "date" for drinks with Blake.

This would be the third time they had gotten together, and while she would love to believe the evenings were a high spot in his month, she had her doubts. She was his lowly virtual assistant while he was a world-traveling private jet salesman who looked like Daniel Craig and had a smile that could serve as an alternative form of energy.

She studied herself in the mirror. She'd chosen a simple black faux wrap dress with three-quarter sleeves, although the word *chosen* was a little strong. It wasn't as if she had fifteen dresses and, hey, this one spoke to her. She had two and Blake had seen the other one last time.

She'd debated wearing her new diamond earrings, but they seemed a little fancy, so she'd put on simple gold hoops and her new peach Schlumberger bangle. The bangle from Great-Aunt Cheryl reminded her to be brave. Or so she hoped.

She slipped on her kitten heel pumps that she'd gotten on sale about three years ago and walked to the kitchen. Becca was curled up on the family room sofa, flanked by Thor and Jazz, and reading her car's owner's manual. Her daughter had taken Lucas's instructions to heart, Harper thought, both pleased and annoyed. On the bright side, at least someone could get through to Becca. On the annoying side, it wasn't her.

Becca looked up and smiled. "You look nice."

"Thank you. It's my quarterly drink with Blake. I shouldn't be late, but I won't be back by dinnertime. I've left food in the refrigerator, along with instructions."

Becca put down the manual. "Grandma won't be over?"

"No." She hesitated. "It's complicated."

Her daughter studied her for a second before saying, "Okay. Stacey texted about me coming over there for dinner, so I might do that instead. I'll text you."

Harper wanted to complain that Becca should have at least pretended to ask, only she would then be totally in the wrong. First, it wasn't as if she was going to be home herself. Second, going to Stacey's was perfectly allowed. Her sister lived only a handful of blocks away. Becca had been going over there by herself since Stacey had bought the house. Third, if Ashton was the real reason her daughter wanted to hang out with her aunt, who was Harper to stand in the way of her becoming friends with her new cousin?

"Thanks, Becca. Have fun whatever you decide."

"I will. You, too, Mom."

Harper drove to Olives—a martini bar-slash-restaurant. It wasn't the sort of place she went very often, or ever. She'd married relatively young and had never been the bar type

before that. Still, she did her best to fake confidence as she
walked in and looked around.

The space was open and upscale with only a handful of
olive-based pictures on the wall. The customers were a comfortable blend of local business types and tourists. Harper saw
an empty table and headed for it, only to be stopped when
Blake walked over and smiled at her.

The man was good-looking, she thought, as she smiled
back. Polished, tan, with blond hair and blue eyes. She would
guess his suit had a designer label, his tie was silk and that his
shoes had cost as much as her annual food budget. He was
the kind of man she could imagine surprising his significant
other with tickets to New York for a long weekend, where
they would eat at places she read about in *People* magazine and
stay at a fancy hotel by the park.

"Harper, so nice to see you." He lightly held her upper
arm as he leaned close and kissed her on the cheek. "You look
lovely. How is everything?"

"Good. How was your flight?"

"Uneventful, which is how I like them."

As he spoke, he steered her toward a small table by the
window. A server appeared, as if he'd been waiting for them.

"Welcome to Olives. What looks good?"

Blake ordered twelve-year-old Scotch while she got a very
boring glass of red wine. She wanted to be wild and order
some exotic martini, but that was a lot of alcohol and she still
had to drive home. Plus, it wasn't as if she had much in the
way of tolerance when it came to liquor. She almost never
drank. Honestly, her life was boring even to her.

"How's work?" she asked when their server left.

"Busy. The King of El Bahar just ordered a new plane.
That's going to be fun."

"Lots of gold leaf and pictures of himself?" she asked.

"Actually he's really down-to-earth and his wife has excellent taste." He winked. "The fun part for me is the unlimited budget. As a guy who works on commission, I appreciate that. Speaking of appreciation, the gift basket you put together for my mom's birthday was inspired. She loved everything. Thank you for that."

"It's why I'm here. To take care of the details."

Their drinks arrived and they touched glasses. He asked about work and life in Mischief Bay. They were twenty minutes in when she realized they had nothing in common. Absolutely nada.

Was it her? Should she get out more or watch more news shows on television? Should she be reading celebrity gossip magazines so she could talk about the Kardashians?

Blake being Blake, and the consummate salesman, picked up the slack conversationwise and kept her entertained with stories about things that had gone wrong with deliveries and the strange things the rich and famous wanted in their private jets. Fifty minutes after she'd sat down, he flagged the waiter and asked for their check.

"It's always good to see you," he said as he signed the credit card receipt. "Thank you, Harper. I hope we can do this again, soon."

"Sure," she murmured when what she was really thinking was *why*? They had no chemistry and she had to admit that for some reason she couldn't explain, her fantasies about Blake had all fizzled. Yes, he was handsome and had a killer smile, but she wasn't disappointed to be leaving and going home. Which meant she officially had no one to daydream about for the three minutes it took her to almost dry her hair every morning, and how sad was that.

Maybe a movie star, she thought as she drove home. If he was a movie star, she wouldn't care that he was married or secretly or not so secretly a jerk. She'd always liked Matt Damon, who was involved in that water charity and seemed to really love his wife and kids. Or she could go totally age inappropriate and use her blow-dryer time to lust after Liam Hemsworth, although she was about as far from sexually liberated and totally self-possessed Miley Cyrus as it was possible to get, so maybe not. The last thing she needed was a fantasy guy who judged her.

She was still working on the nonproblem when she pulled into her driveway, only to have a familiar Mercedes convertible park at her curb.

Lucas got out and walked toward her. "How was the date?"

She wrinkled her nose. "Not a date. Just a polite glass of wine with a client."

"But you were with the James Bond–like Blake. I thought simply being in his presence was the stuff of dreams."

"I never said any of that to you," she began, then groaned. "Stop talking to my daughter when you give her driving lessons."

"She's sixteen, Harper. Not talking isn't an option. I do my best to control the topics, otherwise we end up places I don't want to go." He shuddered. "Yes, chunky heels could make a comeback but do we have to talk about it?"

She laughed. "That sounds like my girl." She glanced at her watch. "You just getting off work?"

"Yeah. We had some excitement at a bank today that took a little longer. I'll pick up Thor and get out of your way."

"Do you want to stay for dinner?"

"Sure you don't need the alone time to relive Blake's charming conversation?"

She put her hands on her hips. "Hey, do I mock you about your girlfriends?"

"Most of the time."

"Oh, right. I forgot. Okay, then I take it back. And no, I don't need any alone time. It turns out Blake and I don't have much in the way of chemistry. I need a new fantasy boyfriend."

"They're making lifelike sex robots these days."

"Don't make me regret asking you to dinner."

He winked.

They went inside. Harper excused herself to go change. She returned to the kitchen in jeans and a T-shirt. Her feet were bare and she'd left on the bangle because it made her happy. Lucas sat at the kitchen table, petting his dog. Jazz lay in her bed.

Harper opened the refrigerator. "All right, let's check out the leftovers."

"Or we could order pizza."

She turned and stared at him. "Oh. My. God. Seriously? Order in food? Do you know what would happen?"

Lucas raised his eyebrows. "The heavens would open and rain toads?"

"Maybe." Still, the thought was tempting. "Becca would be really mad. I never let her order pizza. I make it myself, of course, but she says that's not the same."

"It's not and she doesn't have to know. The Slice Is Right delivers. I'll take home the leftovers, including the box. It can be our guilty secret."

She was incredibly tempted. Guilty secrets had been noticeably absent in her life lately and it wasn't as if she was doing anything really bad. Most people would consider delivered pizza an ordinary occurrence. Plus, Bunny was out with friends, so she wouldn't be around to judge.

He pulled out his phone. "I'll let you pick the kind of pizza as long as you don't get one that's gluten-free, or vegetarian."

"I wouldn't do that."

He looked at her.

She sighed. "All right. I might try to go healthy in an effort to alleviate my guilt, but I won't."

They agreed on barbecue chicken with extra cheese. Lucas placed the order using an app while she set the table. She looked through her pitiful collection of wine before choosing a bottle.

"I'm going to stop bringing flowers and start bringing you liquor," he muttered as he opened the drawer containing the corkscrew.

"You don't have to bring me anything."

"I do if you feed me."

"You already got me a guy who will scoop dog poop. That's about the best gift there is."

"You're welcome."

He'd taken off his blazer and gun holster. She would guess he'd already put his weapon in the safe, as he did whenever he came directly from work. He'd rolled up his shirtsleeves to his elbows.

He was good-looking in a different way than Blake. He had more edges and less polish, but there was a solidness about him that always made her feel as if he could handle whatever happened. She supposed that came from a career in law enforcement. He'd had to learn how to deal with a crisis. He was a detective now, but he must have started as a rookie and worked his way up.

She fed the dogs, then joined Lucas in the family room while they waited for the pizza to arrive.

"How old were you when you joined the LAPD?" she asked, settling on the sectional. Lucas sat in the recliner.

"I was a kid, still in my twenties. I got my AA in criminal justice from Mischief Bay Community College. When I graduated, I applied and was accepted."

"Did you always want to be a police officer?"

He looked at her. "Asking about my past?"

"I guess I am. You know way too much about me and I know almost nothing about you." She raised a shoulder. "Excluding your despicable taste in young women."

"*Despicable* seems harsh."

"I suppose, although it's wildly accurate."

One corner of his mouth turned up. "Point taken. All right, I didn't always want to be a cop. That happened over time." He paused, as if trying to figure out what he wanted to say. "My father's family had money. Not a huge fortune, but enough that if he was careful, he would never have to work for a living. My dad took advantage of that. He bought a modest house here in Mischief Bay and lived a pretty good life, hanging out with his friends, surfing, going from girlfriend to girlfriend. One day one of those girlfriends showed up with a ten-year-old kid. She said she was done with him and took off. That kid was me."

Harper honestly didn't know what to say. Lucas had been abandoned by his mother? Left? It was one thing to give a baby up for adoption—a lot of times that was to give the child a better future, and it wasn't as if the baby would remember. But a ten-year-old?

"You must have been devastated," she whispered. "Oh, Lucas."

He held up a hand. "Water under the bridge. Yeah, I wasn't

happy, but it wasn't as if she qualified for mother of the year. I barely noticed she was gone."

A total lie, she thought. It didn't matter how bad his mother had been—she'd been his mother. The one person he'd believed loved him and cared about him. Her walking away would have changed everything.

"My dad surprised the hell out of me," Lucas continued. "He took one look at me, said I looked just like *his* father and that was that. I was in."

"How was it, living with him?"

"Decent, I guess. He didn't see any reason to change his lifestyle. There were plenty of parties and women around. My dad didn't believe in discipline or making me go to school or anything like that. By the time I was twelve, I was starting to get into trouble. By thirteen, I'd been arrested."

Harper felt her eyes widen. "You have a record?"

"Calm down. I was arrested. There's a difference."

"My daughter is being taught to drive by a criminal."

He chuckled. "Way to find that silver lining. Do you want to hear this or not?"

"I definitely want to hear about how you turned your life around after years in the pokey."

"Crazy lady."

The doorbell rang. Both dogs ran to the front of the house and took their positions. Harper assumed they were prepared to take down anyone who threatened the pack, but they would wait for a command, or possibly a scream.

Lucas collected the pizza while she carried their drinks to the kitchen table. She set out plates, then waited while he opened the box.

The delicious smell assaulted her, leaving her mouth watering and her stomach growling. Guilt threatened, but she pushed it away. Lucas would take home the evidence of her decadent dinner. No one was ever going to know.

She slid a slice onto her plate. "Keep talking. You were in jail and…"

"I was arrested," he corrected. "One of the cops brought me into an interrogation room. I kind of recognized him, but I wasn't sure. It turns out he lived down the street from my dad and knew exactly who I was. He gave me a pretty serious talk about where I was heading and told me I either did what he said or I served hard time." He grinned. "Andy scared the crap out of me, so I showed up at his house when he said to."

"What did he make you do?"

"Mow his lawn and weed the garden. That turned into hanging out with him and his family. The kids were one and three, so way younger than me, but they were so great. Within a few months, I'd pretty much moved in with Andy and his family. My old man didn't notice, or if he did, it didn't matter to him."

Harper wasn't sure what to make of that information. She'd long suspected Lucas had an interesting past, but nothing like this. She picked up her wine.

"Andy taught me how to be a man. He showed me what it meant to work hard and be honorable. By the time I was seventeen, I was an honor student at the high school, was on the baseball team and had a part-time job so I could pay for a car. All I wanted after graduation was to join the LAPD. Andy made me promise to get my AA first. I was involved in a couple of police charities and avoiding my old man as much as I could. Then one day, Andy didn't come home. He had a heart attack at his desk and died seconds later."

Harper set down her pizza slice as the little she'd eaten turned to rock in her stomach. "He died?"

Lucas nodded. "We were all in shock. Andy's wife wanted to move back to San Francisco to be with her family and I packed up my stuff to go live with my old man. I had no idea if he'd take me in or not and I was scared of both outcomes. What if I forgot everything Andy had taught me? What if I didn't turn out the way he'd expected? I didn't want to disappoint him, but I was afraid."

Harper desperately wanted to run around the table and hug him, which was weird. She told herself it was just a mom thing, but even so, why would she be hugging Lucas?

"What happened?" she asked instead.

"One of the guys from the station showed up and told me I was going to live with him until I graduated from high school." He looked away and cleared his throat. "I wasn't a relative or anything, still, the guys took care of me. While I was in high school and through community college, there was always a place for me. When I graduated with my AA, I applied to the police academy."

His smile returned. "I had so many letters of recommendation, they had no choice but to take me."

She felt her eyes tear up and had to blink several times. "That's the nicest story you've ever told me."

"Every word of it is true."

"What happened with your dad?"

"Not much. We stayed in touch. I saw him maybe twice a year. When he died, he left me the family money. There was still a good chunk of it left."

She thought about the expensive car sitting in front of her house. "That's how you afford the things you do. I'd wondered."

"I live on my salary, but use the other money for the odd toy."

Which spoke highly of him, she thought. He could have

been like his father, not working at all. Instead he chose to put his life on the line every single day. She sipped more wine. She was feeling relaxed and comfortable.

"Do you ever get scared? You know, at work?"

"Sometimes. I have a good partner."

"Who let you get shot!"

"Not his fault."

She didn't know the exact details of Lucas's injury the previous year, but she knew he'd been in the hospital, and then had spent over a month recovering.

"That didn't make you want to retire?" she asked.

"No way. Being a detective is cool." He winked. "The ladies love danger."

"Oh dear God. Seriously? You risk your life to get laid?"

His raised his eyebrows.

She glanced at her wineglass and saw it was empty. Perhaps the second glass of the evening had gone to her head.

"I'm sure you could find someone to date you even if you weren't Mr. Danger Pants."

"Mr. Danger Pants? I chase down bad guys so you can safely walk the city streets and you call me Mr. Danger Pants?"

She reached for the bottle of wine and poured herself another glass. She might regret it in the morning, but right now more wine seemed like an excellent idea.

"Technically I live in Mischief Bay and we have our own police department, so while I appreciate your effort, it's not on my behalf." She took a sip. "Do you think your mom leaving is the reason you like younger women?"

He stared at her. "We're not having that conversation."

She waved away his words. "I mean it. I'm really curious. Is it a commitment thing? Oh, did your dad date younger women?"

His expression turned wary. "Maybe."

"Huh. So you learned that from him and having your mom do what she did—by the way, that was a total jerk move. What a bitch. I hate her."

"Good to know."

"Anyway, maybe you're afraid of commitment or you're afraid of being left." She paused to reflect. "Or maybe you're just afraid of saggy boobs. It's hard to know."

Lucas's mouth twitched. "You are so going to regret this in the morning."

"Maybe. Still, it's been fun." She frowned. "I think this is the first time it's only been you and me at dinner. I'm having a good time." She held up her hand. "Please take that in the spirit it's meant."

"You're not coming on to me?" he asked, sounding amused.

"Oh, please. I'm going to be forty-two. That's probably a hundred and twenty-seven in Lucas girlfriend years."

He laughed and pushed the pizza box toward her. "Eat up before Becca gets home and you're exposed as the hypocrite you've become."

"It's not my fault," she said cheerfully, taking another slice. "I'm going to be totally immature and put the blame squarely on my mother."

"That's my girl."

Chapter Thirteen

STACEY ARRIVED AT THE RESTAURANT FIRST. LUNCH WITH her sister was a relatively rare event, but one she looked forward to the few times a year they got together. When Stacey's all-day meeting was canceled, she'd put a call in to Harper and suggested they meet at Let's Do Tea.

At street level there was a retail store with a take-out counter while upstairs was the actual restaurant. All things British and tea related were represented. While she supposed there were those would wouldn't appreciate all the frilly touches, Stacey liked the attention to detail. It comforted her, maybe because it was so different from her house.

She and Kit shared a similar sense of style—they liked clean lines and minimal clutter. While she could admire a shelf filled with vintage teapots, silver boxes and bone china, she didn't want it in her house. How much was a baby going to change that? How much was a baby going to change everything?

She glanced down at her growing belly and wished... She sighed, not sure what she would wish for. Not that it would matter. Wishes were an exercise in futility. Wishing did nothing but waste time and disappoint the soul. She couldn't wish the baby away or wish that she was going to be a halfway decent mother.

When she and Kit had first started dating, he'd mentioned how much he wanted children. She'd surprised herself by saying she would like a baby, as well. Not that she'd been lying, but until that moment she'd never really thought about having a child. She hadn't been sure how much of that was because of her work or her social awkwardness or not being with the right man.

Even before she and Kit got married, they'd discussed the logistics of having a family. She hadn't wanted a family to interfere with work and he'd been more than willing to stay home with their baby, solving both their problems at once. Only what sounded so right when it was just the two of them often produced stares and disapproval from others.

Harper walked into the dining room, spotted her and smiled. "Hey, you."

They hugged. Harper stepped back and stared at Stacey's stomach.

"You're finally starting to show."

"I know."

"I showed in the first fifteen minutes. You're so lucky, except now you're *really* going to have to tell Mom."

"Can you do it for me?" Stacey was only half kidding with her request.

"I would except we're not currently speaking."

"Lucky you."

They sat down. There was no need to look at the menu— the two of them frequently chose this restaurant for their lunches.

"How are you feeling?" Harper asked. "What does the

doctor say? You're over six months, so you're getting close. Are you still sleeping?" She shook her head. "Wow. I just got that. It really is over six months. It's nearly seven. You're due at the end of June. Stacey, honey, you've got to get your act together."

Stacey thought about the debacle with Ashton—how she hadn't realized what he needed but Harper had figured it out in less than a minute. She thought of the empty baby room, the looks on her coworkers' faces when she'd told them and found herself wanting to cry. A ridiculous response that wouldn't help anyone, least of all her.

"Having you tell me that isn't helpful," she said instead.

"Sorry. I went into problem-solving mode and you probably just need me to be a sister." Harper touched her hand. "What can I do to help?"

Before Stacey could form an answer—not that she had one—their waitress appeared. They each ordered the royal lunch—a combination with finger sandwiches, a small salad and scones. Perhaps not the most balanced of meals, but it was delicious and Stacey would have a vegetable-based smoothie later, along with a protein bar.

The server, an older woman with a sympathetic smile, glanced at Stacey's belly. "I've got just the tea to fix you right up. I give it to all my expectant mums. Back in a flash, dearies."

Harper waited until she was gone to lean forward. "I never asked and I should have. Do you want a shower? I'm happy to put one together for you."

Stacey stared at her. Why would Harper want to put together— "You mean a baby shower? No, thank you. I'd rather not."

Harper pressed her lips together. "Stacey, you've got to accept you're having a baby."

"I have. I see the doctor regularly. I exercise with my prenatal yoga video daily. We've picked out a name."

"A first name," Harper corrected gently. "Have you figured out the last name?"

Stacey hadn't taken Kit's last name when they'd married, mostly for professional reasons. He didn't seem to mind, but it did create a problem when it came to their offspring.

"We're thinking of hyphenating."

"Bloom-Poenisch? There's a mouthful. Have you started your birthing class yet?"

"It's too soon."

"And the nursery?"

Stacey felt familiar tension creep into her body. "Why are you pressuring me?"

"I'm trying to illustrate that maybe you're not taking this baby thing as seriously as you should. I don't want to upset you. I love you. You're my very favorite sister."

Stacey smiled at the familiar joke. "I'm your only sister."

"That's just a detail." Harper smiled at her. "Okay, I'm officially letting the whole baby thing go."

"For how long?"

"Just the rest of the day."

"Thank you."

Stacey knew she had to handle the details of what was going to happen when they brought their daughter home, but every time she tried, she got so caught up in feeling inadequate that she could barely breathe. It was so much easier to pretend she would be a vessel forever instead.

Their waitress returned with a big pot of tea, two cups and saucers and a plate of little sandwiches.

Harper poured them each a cup of tea, then asked, "How's work?"

Stacey laughed. "I assume you want me to say it's fine rather than give you any specific details."

"You can talk specifics. I'll tune it out but I'll nod enthusiastically."

Which was more than most people did, Stacey thought fondly. Harper had always been there for her, being the big sister, standing between Stacey's oddness and their mother's frustration that her youngest had no interest in crafts, baking or otherwise taking care of the home.

"Work is fine," Stacey told her. "Are you still busy?"

"Swamped. I mean it's good. I need the income, but I'm constantly scrambling to get everything done. I keep feeling as if I'm not as organized as I could be. Plus, if I could get an extra six hours in each day, that would help."

"You need to hire someone."

Harper winced. "This is payback for talking about the baby, isn't it?"

"No, it's because you told me about Morgan."

"She was a disaster, and my own fault for hiring her without knowing anything about her. I need to do a better job at that." She reached for a sandwich.

Stacey pulled a single sheet of paper out of her tote. "I brought a résumé for you to look at. His name is Dean and he's a stay-at-home dad with twins. He's looking for part-time work that still allows him time with his kids." She smiled at Harper. "Kit met him at his stay-at-home father support group. Dean goes, too."

Harper stared at her. "You brought me a résumé? I'm not sure I've ever seen a résumé, which is pathetic, right? Thank you. I appreciate your…" She glanced down at the paper, then back at Stacey. Her eyes were wide. "He was a movie set de-signer? Are you crazy? I run a virtual assistant business from my home, Stacey. I'm small-time. I couldn't possibly… I'm looking for someone to put postage on postcards and enter dates on my computer. He would never want to work for me."

Her sister's reaction made no sense. "You can't possibly know what he wants without speaking to him. According to Kit, your assistant job is exactly what Dean described. Kit says he's funny, smart and creative. Why wouldn't you want someone like that helping you?"

"Because he's going to be too important."

"He's a stay-at-home parent."

"Now!"

"I'm genuinely confused," she admitted. "You need help and you've admitted you're not comfortable with the hiring process. I've brought you an appropriate résumé, but you won't consider the applicant. Are you afraid you'll get it wrong again, like you did with Morgan?"

"Ouch, and maybe."

So many people had that fear, she thought. It must be part of the human condition and yet it was as wasteful as wishing.

"When we're trying to solve a problem in the lab, we ex-pect literally thousands of failures before we find the solution. If we discover an answer quickly, we're highly suspicious of it working over time simply because it doesn't happen very often. Every failure brings us closer to our ultimate success."

Harper groaned. "You're not going to tell me the Thomas Edison and the lightbulb story again, are you?"

"Not now that I know you've remembered it." Stacey leaned forward. "You might know how to be a good mother, but I know how to solve a problem. Keep trying until you get to the correct solution. Morgan didn't work out. That means the right person still has to be found." She tapped the résumé. "Here is your next opportunity to fail."

"Oh, joy."

Stacey picked up a sandwich and grinned. "Mom would tell you that sarcasm isn't pretty on anyone."

"Yes, she would, and how nice of you to remind me."

They looked at each other and both started to laugh.

"Tire pressure is really important," Becca said as she and Jordan spread their notebooks and papers on the kitchen table. "Having under or overinflated tires means the car doesn't handle right. It can be dangerous and affect gas mileage."

Jordan shook her head. "I can't believe Lucas is making you learn all about your car."

"I was mad at first," Becca admitted, "but now I don't mind. It's been kind of interesting. He taught me how to change a tire."

Jordan flipped her hair over her shoulder. "Don't you have some phone number you can call so they send someone out to change it for you?"

"Yes, but I want to know how to do it myself."

She liked the feeling of independence, she thought. Something she never would have guessed. Plus, Ashton had been impressed when she'd told him.

She still couldn't believe he wanted to hang out with her. He was so gorgeous and mature and, well, everything. But he did. They texted a lot and they'd watched movies at Aunt Stacey's. Becca was hoping he would want to take her out somewhere, just the two of them. Like a date.

She held in a sigh. Yes, that was really old-fashioned but the thought of being alone with him and maybe holding hands or kissing was exciting. Scary, too, but in a fun way.

"Earth to Becca," Jordan said. "You okay?"

"I'm just thinking about Ashton."

"Isn't he your cousin?"

"No." She considered the question. "Maybe, but not, you know, biologically. Stacey's my mom's sister and Kit is her husband. Ashton is his nephew."

"That's confusing, but okay." Jordan moved her chair closer and lowered her voice, even though they were alone in the house. "So you like him?"

"Yeah, I do. He's really sweet and funny and smart. He's going to MIT in the fall."

"So you'll be dating a college guy. That's great."

Becca smiled. "We're not dating."

"But you could be."

This was the Jordan Becca wanted to hang out with. She'd missed her friend and wondered if she should say that. Before she could decide, Jordan spoke.

"Let's get Nathan and Ashton to take us out to dinner."

Becca's stomach flipped and she felt a shiver slip down her spine. The last thing she wanted was to be around Nathan.

"I think it's too soon," she hedged. "I don't want Ashton to think I'm assuming anything."

"He won't. We'll keep it totally casual. Being around another couple will give him ideas."

Becca wasn't sure that being around Nathan would give him any good ones. Not that she thought Ashton would ever act the way Nathan did with a girl, although how could she be sure? She would never have assumed Nathan could be so...scary.

Jordan stared at her. "Is that a yes?"

"I need to think about it."

"Oh. My. God. What is wrong with you? Becca, you're the worst. When you told me about Ashton, I thought you were over it, but you're not, are you?" Jordan's mouth tightened into a straight line. "I know he's hot and all that, but get over it."

Becca had no idea what she was— "Wait. You think I'm interested in Nathan?" She tasted bile in the back of her throat. "That's not it, I swear. There is no way I would ever—" She bit her lower lip. Nope, she couldn't go there. Talk about a conversation she didn't want to have.

"You're right," she said by way of distraction. "We should have dinner or something." Maybe Ashton would be busy with his new job and have to back out. That could buy them some time.

"What?" Jordan demanded. "What aren't you saying?" Her eyes narrowed. "Tell me."

"Nothing. It's all good."

"Tell me. What do you know about Nathan?"

What did she know? Not much, but all of it was scary and gross and not anything she wanted to think about or share with the person who was supposed to be her best friend now that Kaylee had moved on.

"Nothing."

"Tell. Me."

Becca wished she was a better liar—then she could come up with something that would convince Jordan that everything was fine. If only she'd heard about some award or scholarship he was up for. Or that he'd been asked to star in a teen movie over the summer. But she couldn't, which only left the truth.

"I have to go," she said as she gathered up her books.

"Oh no, you don't." Jordan stood. "You are not leaving this house until you tell me whatever it is you're hiding. Do you hear me?"

"You sound like your mom."

"Whatever works."

Tears burned. Becca blinked them away. There was no way this was going to go well. She only had the truth and there was no way Jordan would believe her. They would fight and not be friends and then what? But if she didn't tell her, Jordan would hound her until she had no choice but to...

"Becca, I mean it. What's going on?"

Becca finished putting her books and notebook into her backpack, then looked at her friend. "Nathan said he was willing to sleep with me so I didn't have to be a virgin anymore."

For one second, nothing about Jordan changed. She was still beautiful and Becca's friend. Then her eyes widened, her mouth dropped open and she started screaming.

"You bitch! You fucking bitch! You made a play for him, didn't you? You tried to sleep with my boyfriend."

Becca flinched. "I didn't. I swear. I would never do that. Jordan, you know me. I don't do that."

"Because no one wants you. Because you're ugly and disgusting and everyone thinks you're stupid. I hate you." Tears slid down her face. "Kaylee was right. You're awful and she's lucky not to have to see you ever again. I hope you die."

Becca was already moving toward the door. Her chest was tight, her heart pounding and the nausea had returned.

"I will always hate you," Jordan screamed after her. "We're all laughing at you, Becca. Nathan especially. Stupid, ugly Becca, who thinks she can get a boyfriend. Nobody wants you. Not even if you're giving it away."

There was probably more, but Becca was outside and couldn't hear it. She started walking toward her house, then running. She made it all the way home without throwing up, then raced into the house.

Luckily, her mom wasn't home so she didn't have to worry about answering any questions. Jazz and Thor greeted her, both dogs circling her happily, wanting attention. She gave them each a pat as she headed for her bedroom.

Once inside, she dropped her backpack on the floor and crawled into bed. Only then did the tears come.

She hurt everywhere, as if Jordan had beaten her with more than words. She couldn't breathe very well and sobs racked her body. She pulled her knees to her chest and tried to make herself as small as possible. Then the bed shifted. Both Jazz and Thor jumped on. Thor stretched out against her back and Jazz settled in front of her. She stuck her nose under Becca's arm until she could lick her face, then inched closer until Becca had to roll onto her back to give her room.

She stared at the ceiling, tears running down into her hair. Thor and Jazz stayed close, their bodies warming her.

She told herself that Jordan had been mad and scared and reacting to that as much as what Becca had told her. She told herself that Jordan hadn't meant all the horrible things she'd said, only she wasn't sure if she was telling the truth. Because that was her greatest fear—that for once, someone had been totally and brutally honest. And then what?

Harper made notes as Valerie talked. The city of Mischief Bay was a dream client. The work was interesting, there was no drama and rarely any rush work. Things were organized, planned in advance and she never had to follow up to get paid.

Harper looked over the hand-sketched postcard Valerie had given her. "Okay, that's very doable. I'll have a couple of options to you by Monday."

She'd been hired to design their summer mailer. It went to all residents and highlighted various city-sponsored events. After Harper had design approval, she would get the postcards printed, apply the labels and get them in the mail.

"I can always count on you," Valerie said with a smile. "I wish my other vendors were as efficient."

"Maybe I should hold a class," Harper joked.

"If only you would." Valerie flipped through the papers on her desk. "Okay, here's the other project. We're just playing with this one, so I'm not totally sure what I want. And isn't that ridiculous?"

"Not at all." A lie, but for the right client, Harper would say almost anything. "Tell me what it is and I'll figure out a way to make it work."

"It's for the website. We want some short, snappy videos showing different parts of Mischief Bay. You know, to attract tourists. Eventually we might work them into a TV campaign, but that's way down the road."

Harper had never worked with a video camera in her life, and the only actual videos she'd ever recorded had been with her phone and of her daughter.

"For television quality, you're going to need a professional," she said, trying not to sound reluctant. Yes, she would work her butt off to satisfy a client, but there was no way she could set herself up to fail by overpromising something she couldn't begin to deliver.

"See, this is why I love working with you," Valerie told her. "You tell me the truth. You're right, for TV we would hire a video company, but for the website, let's see what happens. Want to give it a try?"

She would have to buy a decent camera. With the price of electronics dropping, that might not be too much. Becca knew how to work one—she'd taken that class last summer through the city park's department. In fact...

"Absolutely. Let me shoot two or three short videos and you can have a look at them. If you like them, we'll figure out exactly what you want and I'll do them. If you hate them, no harm." Not counting the expense of the camera, but the city account was worth the investment.

"We have a plan. Yay."

They chatted for a few more minutes, then Harper left. By the time she got home, she figured out what she thought was a workable plan.

She spotted a plate of cookies on the center island and couldn't help smiling. She and Bunny were speaking again, albeit in short sentences. But the leaving of food signaled the frost was over. Yes, when in doubt, bake.

Harper went into Becca's bedroom and saw her daughter was on her computer at her desk and the dogs were on her bed.

"Hi, honey," she said, shooing Jazz and Thor to the floor. "How was school?"

Becca didn't bother looking up. "Fine."

Harper wasn't convinced. Had her daughter been crying? Tension joined hands with anxiety. Dealing with one more thing was not her idea of a good time, but if Becca needed her... She sat on the bed.

"Are you okay?"

Becca hesitated, then turned in her chair. "Just thinking about stuff. I still don't know what I'm going to study in college."

Thank God. College was easy. "You're not going to be applying until the fall, sweetie. It's okay to change your mind between now and then and even after you apply. You can take a lot of your general ed classes at first. Most freshmen do."

"I guess. Ashton is studying mechanical engineering. I guess I wish I was that sure of stuff."

"You will be." Ashton had been through a difficult time with his mother and living situation. No doubt that had matured him. Not that she was going to say that to Becca. "I have something that might be a fun distraction and solve a problem all at once."

Becca barely smiled. "Sure. What is it?"

Harper explained how the city wanted short videos for the website. "You took that media class last summer and really liked it. Do you think you could help me out by shooting the videos and editing them?"

There was a beat, then Becca smiled for real. "That would be cool. I could do the carousel and the beach, of course, but maybe something about all the parks. Especially the dog park, The Barkwalk. I could even download some music. There's plenty in the public domain and then if the city wants something better, they can license it." Becca's expression turned serious. "You don't ever want to just copy a song without licensing it. That's stealing."

"Good to know. So here's the thing. I'll pay you for the time you're working and we'll put the money toward your half of the car insurance."

Her daughter's eyes widened. "Really? You'd do that? Thanks, Mom."

Becca got out of her chair and threw herself at Harper. She hugged her daughter and was surprised at how the teen hung on.

Finally Becca stepped back and took her seat. "Okay, let me get the specifics. You'll want them short. Maybe twenty or thirty seconds. Any longer than that and people lose interest. I might try them with a host. Ashton could talk about the town and what's fun. I wonder if he's relaxed in front of the camera." She glanced at her mother. "Some people freeze up and it's not pretty."

Harper nodded, but what she was thinking was that at some point, when she hadn't been paying attention, her little girl had gone and grown up.

Chapter Fourteen

LEXI HOVERED AT STACEY'S SHOULDER. "YOU HAVE YOUR meeting with Karl," she said, reminding Stacey for the third time in as many minutes.

Reluctantly, Stacey pulled her attention away from her computer. She was in the lab all week, a rarity for her these days, and she hated to have that time interrupted for something as ridiculous as a meeting. But Karl had insisted.

"I'm going," she said, slipping off her lab coat and reaching for her blazer. "Don't let anyone touch anything. I have a system working here."

Lexi grinned. "No one would dare touch anything, not even me, and you know I like to rearrange your desk for sport."

Stacey walked down the hall. Her back hurt a little, no doubt from her center of gravity shifting as the baby grew. There were other changes. Her feet were starting to swell a little and she was having trouble concealing her condition. Kit was more delighted by the day, while she continued to wrestle with ambivalence.

When she reached Karl's office, she was shown in by his assistant. He waved her to a chair.

"Good morning, Stacey. How are you feeling?"

Not a question he would have asked before she'd told him about her condition, she thought, trying not to be irritated. "Fine. Are you feeling well?"

He appeared slightly startled, before he answered. "Yes. Ah, thanks for asking."

She offered a tight smile, then shifted in her chair, wishing they were already done. She had important work to do—something he was aware of, so she didn't bother pointing out the obvious.

Karl pushed up his glasses, leaned back in his chair, then shifted forward. "I want to bring in someone to help you," he said. "You have a lot of responsibility and with everything happening, that might not be a good thing. It wouldn't be permanent, of course. Just for a couple of months while you're dealing with…" His voice trailed off as he waved at her midsection.

"My pregnancy?" she asked, just to be clear.

He nodded without looking at her.

She slid to the front of her seat and squared her shoulders.

"What an interesting idea, Karl," she said, careful to keep her voice low and controlled. "Confusing, of course, but interesting. After all, I'm ahead of schedule, my team is the most productive in my division and per my employment contract, I can't be removed from my position, except for cause." She paused. "Unless you're telling me that pregnancy qualifies as cause."

Karl stiffened, and then went pale. "No. No, of course not. I never said…"

"Good, because I know an excellent employment attorney

and while I'm sure she would appreciate the business, neither of us want to take it that far, do we?"

"No," he said, his voice slightly strangled.

"Let me be clear. If you take away any part of my project, I will sue you. If you demote me, I will sue you. Not just the company, Karl. You personally. And then I will go to the media. One of the reasons I was brought in was because I have an excellent reputation and the company had gone through some difficult times. Did you know it's already a problem to find and hire women here? With the Federal contracts requiring diversification, do you really want the world to know you're the kind of person who assumes a woman can't do her job simply because she's pregnant?"

"I didn't say—"

"You didn't have to."

"But your maternity leave will be—"

"Three weeks. Judd took off that long to go to Europe last year and you were fine with it. So Europe is okay, but pregnancy is a problem? Oh, and while we're discussing parity, I believe Ron took three weeks of paternity leave when he and his wife adopted their baby and you didn't have a problem with that, either."

She rose and stared down at him. "If I ever don't perform my job at my current level, we should absolutely have this conversation, but until then, don't ever bring it up again with me or any other woman in the company. Is that clear?"

She didn't wait for an answer. Instead she swept out of his office and into the hall. Once she got there, she realized she was shaking and could barely stand. She managed to get back to her lab, where she collapsed in the closest chair.

Damn him, she thought as she did her best to slow her breathing. *Damn him for acting like this*. Karl wasn't her manager but she still had to work with him. While they'd never exactly been friends, she'd assumed he respected her and her abilities. She'd assumed he saw her as an important member of the team. She'd never once thought the word *woman* in any way defined her.

She pressed her hands against her belly. Everyone tried to warn her that the baby would change everything. That having a child meant being different, but she hadn't listened. She'd gone on as if she were nothing but the vessel, believing that if she saw herself as the same, so would everyone else. But she'd been wrong about all of it. And that wasn't the worst of it. The worst was she still had to tell her mother.

Becca did her best to stay calm, at least on the outside. Calm and casual, because the last thing she wanted was for her mom to figure out she had a thing for Ashton. She didn't think her mom would mind her going out with a boy—Becca was sixteen and considered responsible. No, her bigger concern was what her mother would say. Out loud!

Even though her mom was always busy with work, every now and then she noticed stuff and when she noticed, she spoke out. Sometimes it was funny, but when the subject was Ashton, Becca didn't want to take a chance.

So she hovered by the front door and saw when he drove up. She had the door open before he'd climbed the porch steps. Jazz immediately came to investigate. Ashton let her sniff his fingers, then rubbed her ears, but his gaze was on Becca.

"Hey," he said.

"Hey, back." She smiled, hoping it was a cool smile and not some goofy grin like she'd just been introduced to Ed Sheeran.

He walked with her into the family room and took a seat.

"I got the job," he told her as they sat on opposite ends of the sofa. "At the farmers' market. I stock produce."

"Good for you." She knew he wanted to save as much money as he could for college. Not to pay for tuition or board—he had a partial scholarship and Stacey and Kit would cover the rest—but for his own spending. He'd talked about not wanting to be a burden for them. A concept she'd had trouble with, but then she wasn't depending on anyone but her parents and she was their responsibility.

Thinking about how different their lives were was a nice distraction from his hazel-gray eyes and handsome face. Just looking at him for too long was like staring up at the sky. She got dizzy and couldn't keep her thoughts straight.

"I start at five in the morning," he added.

She winced. "That's no fun. At least it's close."

"Less than a five-minute drive. I figure I can shower the night before, sleep until four-thirty and eat a protein bar on the way."

She laughed. "That is one serious plan."

"Planning is the key to success." His voice was teasing as he spoke.

"I have news, too," she said, suddenly not sure where to put her hands. On her lap? They seemed too weird just resting on the sofa. Inspiration struck and she patted the cushion so Jazz jumped up and snuggled next to her.

"My mom wants my help with some videos for the city. Promotional stuff, you know, to remind people what they can do for free and maybe to attract tourists. They'll be posted on the city's website."

He angled toward her, his eyes wide with interest. "You know how to do that? I can take a video on my phone, but they're not website worthy."

"I was in a summer program last year that focused on different kinds of media. We learned about filming and editing, so yeah, I can do something easy like a twenty-second video. Mom's going to buy me a camera and I'll take it from there."

"Impressive."

"Thanks. I was wondering if maybe you'd like to, um, help."

She forced herself to keep looking at him when she really wanted to duck her head. But her aunt Stacey was always talking about how it was important for women to ask for what they wanted, otherwise they weren't going to get it.

"Sure. What do you need? Me to carry your equipment and help you set up?"

"I thought maybe you'd be willing to host." She swallowed. "I'd write up a whole script. You'd only have to memorize a few lines, but easy stuff about the POP or the dog park or whatever."

His expression turned quizzical. "Me?"

She felt her cheeks burn. "I think you'd do well on camera."

Her mom walked into the kitchen, saw them and came to a stop.

"Ashton, did I know you were stopping by?"

Becca did her best not to roll her eyes. "I told you this morning, Mom. Remember?"

"Oh, right. For the videos. I hope you're willing to help Becca. I've seen her work from last summer and she's really good. The city is one of my bigger clients, so the work's important."

Becca felt a flash of pride at her mom's words. The flash was quickly followed by hurt and annoyance. Yes, she was being trusted with something that mattered, but shouldn't she matter as much as a job? Why was her mom always too busy to talk to her? She still didn't know about Jordan and the fight, not that Becca would tell her because that would mean explaining about Nathan and she didn't want to go there, but still!

Ashton met Becca's gaze. "I'm happy to help out, Mrs. S. Becca just has to tell me when and where and I'll be there."

"Oh, good. All right, you two, have fun figuring it all out. I have T-shirts to ship to Misty and gift bags to put together. Why aren't the days longer?"

She filled her water bottle and hurried out of the room. Becca waited until she was gone to say, "Are you sure you want to be in the videos?"

"Are you kidding? This is LA, baby. Everyone wants to be in the movies."

She laughed. "You've been here long enough to know that's not true. Can you see Aunt Stacey in a movie?"

"Only if she got to play a scientist." He looked at her. "Want to start this weekend? Are you going to be around or do you spend the weekends with your dad?"

An innocent question that had her stomach tying itself in knots that had nothing to do with the beauty of Ashton's eyes.

"Nah," she said, trying to sound casual. "He's really busy. He's getting married in a few weeks and he always has stuff to do with Alicia."

He frowned. "He is? Stacey hasn't said anything."

The knots doubled in size. "I don't know if he's told my mom," she admitted. "He said he would but the way she's acting, I'm not sure she knows."

"Do you think she'll be upset? Is she still in love with him?"

"What? No. She's not." At least Becca didn't think so. Sometimes she had no idea what her mother was thinking. "The divorce was really hard on both of us, but she's gotten it together since then."

"Is she dating?"

"No!"

Ashton's expression turned quizzical. "Why do you say it like that? Your dad's getting married again. Why wouldn't your mom be dating?"

"Because she's my mom." Becca knew how childish that sounded…but honestly, her mom?

"You don't think she wants to find someone and fall in love?"

"Can we please not talk about this?"

Her mom barely paid any attention to her now. What would it be like if there was a new boyfriend hanging out? Plus, if they had sex… She closed her eyes and groaned. She absolutely could not deal with that!

"Your mom is a person, too," he said gently.

"Okay, then, that's a no." She looked at Ashton. "You are not as nice as you look."

He laughed. "You're right. I'll stop." He stood and held out his hand.

She wasn't sure what to do, so she put hers in his and he gently pulled her to her feet.

"I should go," he said, still holding her fingers. They were standing close. Really close, and she had to look up to meet his gaze. Her chest was tight and her heart felt all fluttery.

"W-why?"

"You have homework. You said Lucas was demanding good grades. Plus, you need to do well in school for yourself. So you can get into a good college. Life is all about having choices and taking advantage of opportunities."

Because of what he'd been through, she thought, feeling young and small. He knew stuff, had experienced things, and she'd only ever lived in Mischief Bay.

Fear and sadness mingled with a sense of never exactly fitting in. She wanted to be happy and a part of something, but lately all that happened was she didn't know where she belonged. First with Jordan and now with…

She didn't get to finish the thought because without warning, Ashton leaned down and kissed her. He lightly brushed his mouth against hers before straightening.

She stared at him, not quite sure what had just happened. Had he really done that? Kissed her? Like a boy kissing a girl?

She'd had a few awkward kisses before—all at parties and as part of stupid games. But never had a guy stood in front of her like this and deliberately kissed her.

"You're so beautiful," he murmured before cupping her face in his free hand and kissing her again.

This time she was slightly more prepared. She didn't know exactly how to stand or what to do, so she stayed still and tried not to act stupid.

His mouth was warm—not soft, exactly, but not hard, either. Tingles exploded everywhere in her body, like her entire bloodstream was suddenly carbonated. She thought she might be able to float, only she didn't want to do anything to interfere with the moment.

She could hear the loud ticking of the clock on the wall and smell soap and something like maybe verbena on Ashton. She hoped her breath was okay and wished she knew what to do with her hands. The one holding his seemed lame and the other one just kind of trembled.

He released her fingers and put both his hands on top of hers. He raised her arms until they were at his waist, then went back to cupping her face. He tilted her head slightly and pressed a little harder on her mouth.

There were too many sensations. The way his T-shirt felt against her skin, the heat of his body beneath, his lips moving against hers, her body melting and shaking until she wasn't sure she could stand or breathe or survive what was happening.

His tongue lightly stroked her bottom lip. Becca knew what that meant. She'd read about French kissing and talked about it and had seen it in movies, but she'd never had it happen. Oh, God, she was so dumb and ridiculous. A twelve-year-old would do better than her.

"Relax," Ashton whispered.

Relax? Relax! He knew! He knew she was a pathetic, inexperienced virgin who—

She opened her mouth to tell him she had to go, or maybe scream out that the earth had to swallow her up right that second, or...

But it didn't matter. None of it. Because at that exact second, Ashton brushed his tongue with hers and everything suddenly made a whole lot more sense.

She hadn't known, she thought as every part of her turned around to pay attention to what was happening. She hadn't known it could feel so good. No, so *great*. She'd had no idea that kissing anyone could be like touching stars.

Without thinking, she raised her hands to his shoulders and leaned into to him. He wrapped his arms around her and hung on as if he would never let go. He deepened the kiss and she reveled in the sensations sweeping her body.

She wasn't sure how long they stood there, kissing and kissing until she'd learned every inch of his mouth only to discover she wanted to start at the beginning and do it all again forever. When he drew back and rested his forehead against hers, they were both breathing hard.

He gave her a smile. "I knew it would be like that with you."

"You did?"

"Uh-huh." He straightened and kissed her forehead. "You need to do homework and I need to spend some time thinking about anything but kissing you." He grabbed her hand and kissed her palm. "See you soon?"

She nodded because she couldn't speak, or maybe she didn't want to. Far better to be quiet and allow the wonderful memories to sink into her brain so she could hold on to them forever.

She walked Ashton to the door. He kissed her again, lightly this time, then walked out of the house.

Becca had no idea how she got to her bedroom. Maybe she floated. Jazz joined her on the bed, where Becca snuggled close to her dog and sighed.

"I think I'm in love."

Chapter Fifteen

STACEY NODDED AS THE SERVER CLEARED HER PLATE. She'd been in the mood for pasta, and Pescadores had the best clam linguini in town, but she'd already eaten too many carbs that day and needed more protein, so she'd ordered tilapia and vegetables. Mostly she didn't mind being a vessel but every now and then she missed having the ability to simply indulge as she wanted.

Kit leaned close. "You should have had the pasta."

Because he always wanted her to be happy. He'd insisted on celebrating after she'd told him about her run-in with Karl, and the next morning at breakfast he'd worn his I'm with the Beautiful Scientist T-shirt. He was so supportive and loving. While she wasn't a big believer in luck—from her perspective, it was little more than awareness, preparation and a willingness to take a chance—she had to admit when it came to her husband, she'd been the victim of good fortune.

Harper sipped her iced tea. "I hope you appreciate how I support your pregnancy by not ordering wine with dinner."

"I do, and while it's very kind of you, it's not necessary."

Her sister glanced at Kit. "Oh, I think it's nice to be on the team."

It was perhaps the second or third time Harper and Kit had exchanged a look. She had a vague sense of something going on with them, which made her uncomfortable, only she wasn't sure why. She trusted each of them implicitly. Besides, she was hardly one to see emotional subtleties.

Kit paid the bill. Harper tried to give him money for her dinner, but he refused. Stacey let him handle her sister—she knew that pointing out that their combined salary far exceeded hers would only lead to conflict. They got up from the table and headed for the door.

"Stacey," Harper said when they were outside, "Kit and I want to take you shopping. It's past time and you need to get going on some of your decisions."

They were walking as she was talking and it wasn't until they stopped in front of a baby store that Stacey realized the evening had been a setup and that she hadn't imagined those looks between her sister and her husband.

She turned to Kit, who looked uncomfortable but determined. "I'm sorry," he said before she could speak. "I've tried to get you to go look at baby furniture for weeks now and you won't commit to a day or time. Telling your mom is your business, Stacey. I get that and I'm fine with waiting however long you want. But us getting ready for Joule is something else. There's a lot to consider, a lot to buy. What if you end up on bed rest for the last couple of weeks, or she's early? I'm not having our child sleep in a dresser drawer because we couldn't get our act together."

Kit almost never spoke forcefully but tonight his tone was firm. Hurt circled her heart and tightened, making her want to lash out at him, but the logical side of her brain pointed out he wasn't completely wrong. Or wrong at all. She *had* been avoiding anything to do with the baby. Unless it involved taking care of herself.

Harper touched her arm. "I love you, Stace. You know that, but come on. It's way past time. Suck it up and pick some furniture. Choose a color scheme. Make a decision on diapers."

Stacey wasn't sure she could speak without yelling or crying, so she nodded and led the way into the store.

It was big and bright with a wide center aisle and upbeat music playing in the background. On the left were mock rooms set up with all kinds of furniture. On the right were aisles and aisles of clothes, toys, diaper bags, strollers and a thousand items she couldn't begin to identify.

"See," Harper said, standing next to her. "It's not so bad. We'll start with the big stuff. If worse comes to worst, Kit and I can pick out things like baby monitors and blankets. But you need to have a say in what the baby's room looks like."

They walked toward the displays. Kit and Harper headed for rooms of white furniture while Stacey decided to walk through to the back, then go more slowly on her return trip. But each setup made her feel more and more uncomfortable. There were too many choices—wallpaper, comforters, rugs, stuffed animals. One bookshelf had dozens of picture frames, each of them showing a handsome couple holding a beautiful baby, a mother and her child or a father and his baby. She supposed she should have an opinion about whether she wanted silver frames or wood or some cute animal theme, but she found herself more concerned about the photos themselves. Yes, the people were models, but they represented a reality that made her uncomfortable.

She picked up a yellow painted frame showing a man holding an infant. A girl, she would guess, based on the frilly blanket and ribbons on the baby's hat. The man's expression was loving, as if he couldn't imagine anything more perfect than his daughter. A sweet image, she told herself, and one that terrified her more than anything.

She set the photo back in place, but couldn't look away. How much would Kit love their baby? A normal amount? More than most? Would he love their daughter more than he loved her?

She didn't want to think about that, but she couldn't avoid the possibility. Kit was all she had—he understood her and no other man ever had. If he didn't love her anymore, or if he loved someone else more, where would that leave her? Before she'd been loved by Kit, she wouldn't have minded because she wouldn't have known what she was losing, but now she did know. Now he was everything to her. What if she lost their relationship and never got it back?

She tried to tell herself that her fears were normal and she should simply talk to Kit about them. Only she couldn't get past the shame. She was so afraid he wouldn't understand, that he would think she was weak or broken or unlovable. What if by asking, she created the very scenario she wanted desperately to avoid? What if he took their baby and left her?

"Stacey?" Kit walked over, grinning at her. "Okay, this is totally crazy, but they have some nursery furniture with a midcentury modern feel, and you know how we both love that. They're calling it antique white, but it's more of a dark cream, which means we can do anything with the decorating. Plus, there's a piece called a chifforobe that we have to have. It has both drawers and shelves and is the cutest thing ever."

He tugged her up toward the front, where Harper was on the floor, shaking the base of the dresser.

"It's solid," she said as she looked up. "You want to make

sure the pieces don't fall over. Some you can attach to the wall, but with others, it's just not practical." She pointed to the crib. "It's a little pricey, but it converts to a toddler bed. Later, when Joule is older, you can use the back and front of the crib as a head and footboard, so you'll certainly get your money's worth out of it, assuming you're not all sick of it in eight years."

She stood and walked over to the changing table. "There's a lot of storage. I prefer open shelves for diapers and supplies, but you could get some kind of shelving unit or Kit could install a floating shelf. Trust me, you don't want to be dealing with drawers every time you have to pull out new diapers, wipes, or whatever else you'll need."

Kit nodded as Harper spoke. "The color is really neutral. I think it will work well in the space."

He sounded so hopeful, she thought, trying not to let her panic show. Furniture? They were already buying furniture? Shouldn't they wait until…

Even she couldn't finish that sentence. Wait until when? She'd given birth? Their daughter was ten? Despite her fears, she had to accept the fact that there was going to be a baby.

She forced herself to smile. "I like it a lot," she said, thinking she neither liked nor disliked the furniture. What bothered her the most was what it represented.

Kit hugged her. "I knew you would. Great. Let's place the order. I hope they have everything in stock."

"Me, too," Stacey said faintly, hoping her husband didn't figure out how much she was lying.

"Happy birthday to me," Harper sang softly as she lay in bed, telling herself she really had to get up. It was nearly six and just because she'd officially turned forty-two, the world didn't actually stop turning and the work didn't do itself.

She briefly wondered what Terence was doing for and with his girlfriend today and tried to avoid the irony of her ex's girlfriend turning all of twenty-eight while she was one year closer to fifty.

She sat up and told herself she didn't actually mind getting older, only to stop and realize that was total crap. No one wanted to get older, but she thought maybe if she had something of a personal life, she might not mind as much. Not that she had time to mind at all these days.

She glanced at the dresser, but there was no wrapped present waiting for her. Something Terence had always done. He'd had his flaws and getting a vasectomy without telling her was probably the biggest one—except for the affair, of course—but if she ignored those two rather sizable disasters, they'd had a relatively happy marriage. Okay, not *happy* exactly, but average. And while she in no way wanted him back, she wouldn't mind having someone in her life. A man she could care about who would care about her. And while she was wishing for the moon, a few extra thousand dollars in her bank account would be nice, too.

She showered and dressed, then went directly to her tiny office, where she finished the last of the free billing for her landscaper. Her to-do list was endless and just looking at it exhausted her.

The sound of rustling in the kitchen had her turning in that direction. She knew that her mother would have arrived plenty early and started cooking a special birthday breakfast, because that was what one did for one's daughter, regardless of the state of the relationship.

It wasn't that she and Bunny weren't speaking—they were. But there was tension between them. Tension born of Bunny being Bunny. It was a generational thing or a situational thing or a personality thing or maybe all three. Regardless, the unease would continue until one of them sucked it up and made things right, and the odds of her mother doing that were, well, nonexistent.

"Happy birthday to me," Harper murmured, saving the billing file before leaving her office.

She found her mother at the stove, frying bacon. A very attentive Jazz sat at a polite distance away—not crowding or even whining, just gently reminding Bunny that she was there and bacon was her favorite.

"Good morning," Harper said cheerfully.

Bunny turned and smiled. "Good morning, Harper. Happy birthday."

"Thanks, Mom. You didn't have to go to all this trouble."

"I wanted to."

The kitchen table was set with festive birthday dishware. Yes, plates and mugs and bowls covered with birthday hats, tiny banners proclaiming Happy Birthday and little presents. Happy Birthday confetti, the same colors as the floral centerpiece, decorated the table. A pitcher of fresh-squeezed orange juice sat on one side of the table, next to a bowl of fresh fruit.

Homemade croissants sat in a bread basket warmed by a terra-cotta stone that would have been preheated in the oven. She would guess that her favorite blueberry French toast casserole was finishing up in said oven at this very moment. Bunny might not be willing to move with the times, but she made a heck of a birthday breakfast.

Harper walked over to the stove and hugged her mother. "Thank you. This is wonderful. I feel very pampered."

"I'm glad."

Harper told herself to suck it up and just get it over with. "Mom, I'm sorry we fought before. I didn't mean to upset you and it made me feel bad that you were unhappy."

A bit of a weaselly apology, what with her not admitting what she said was wrong, mostly because it wasn't and she wasn't going to give up that ground unless she had to, but as it was her birthday, maybe Bunny would cut her a break.

Her mother smiled at her. "Thank you, Harper. I appreciate that."

Harper waited to see if there was more. When her mother added, "Now, go get my granddaughter so we can eat breakfast," the last of her concern faded. All was forgiven. Nothing was resolved, of course, but hey, with every family came a bit of dysfunction. Normal was so last year.

A half hour later, breakfast was finished. Everyone had celebrated, even Jazz, who'd been given two strips of bacon. Bunny had tucked a check for five hundred dollars into a card. Harper had appreciated the generosity more than any present. Right now paying her bills was a lot more fun than going to the mall.

"Thanks, Mom."

"You're welcome."

They shared a smile. Harper picked up the small package her daughter had put at her plate and briefly wondered when Terence had taken his daughter shopping. When she pulled back the wrapping paper, she realized he hadn't, but that was perfectly fine.

The gift was a small booklet, created by hand and bound at one end. Inside were a dozen coupons, all made by Becca. Her daughter watched anxiously as she flipped through them.

Good for one: *Send me to my room when I'm pouting.*
Good for one: *No, we're not having this discussion again.*
Good for one: *Clean up my room.*

The coupons were all variations on a theme—silly things she and Becca fought about in the course of their lives. The thoughtfulness of the gift touched her nearly as much as how much time her daughter had put into making it. Harper felt unexpected tears fill her eyes.

"Thank you," she said, smiling at Becca. "This is so wonderful."

"I'm glad you like it."

Harper reached for her and hung on to her child. She had the brief thought that they never hugged anymore, never touched. Everything was moving so fast that she barely had time to breathe, but still. Was she losing touch with her daughter? When Becca had been little, they'd always hung out together. How had she let that slip away?

Before she could figure out an answer, Becca grinned and stood. "Are you ready?"

"I'm stuffed," Harper said with a laugh, "but yes."

Because in the Szymanski household, every birthday breakfast ended with cake.

Becca brought it out from the pantry and set it on the table. The small cake was frosted in white and decorated with only a few ribbons of pink. A single deep pink candle in the shape of a lotus flower sat in one corner.

"I found the candle online," Becca said, her eyes bright with anticipation. "Grandma watched the video with me." She smiled at Bunny. "You light it, Grandma."

"No, dear. You do the honors."

While Harper watched, her daughter pulled matches out of the junk drawer. She lit the candle and stepped back.

For a second nothing happened, then the flame grew thicker and higher. Jazz gave a low growl in her throat as if warning of impending danger.

"It's okay," Becca told her as she scratched her ears. "You'll see. It's like magic."

The flames were steady, then suddenly died. The flower fell open and morphed into nearly a dozen tiny lit candles spinning slowly in the morning light.

"How did they do that?" Harper asked, as she stared in wonder. "I love it. I want a candle like that at breakfast every morning."

Bunny and Becca shared a high five, then her mother started to cut the cake. "The internet is a magical place, Harper. Everybody knows that."

Full on breakfast and cake, Harper got down to the reality of keeping her business afloat. By ten she'd made serious inroads on her to-do list and had set up an appointment to meet with Dean, Kit's stay-at-home dad friend, about him working for her. A couple of minutes past the hour, she was interrupted by someone ringing her doorbell. It was too early for Dwayne, she thought, walking to the front of the house, an alert Jazz at her side. She opened the door to find three women holding buckets, mops, large tote bags and a vacuum.

"Harper Szymanski?" the shortest of the three asked.

"Yes."

She handed Harper a card that read,

Happy birthday, Harper. I know this will make you crazy, but just go with it.

There was a scrawled signature underneath she recognized as Lucas's.

"I don't understand," she said faintly, even though she understood fully. Understanding wasn't the problem. Her issue was grasping.

"We're here to clean your house."

"But I..." Someone else cleaning her place? Her mother would have a heart attack. You weren't supposed to farm out work like that. A woman took care of her house herself. It was... It was...

What was wrong with her? Someone had bought her house-cleaning for her birthday. Next to Becca's coupon book, it was the best gift she'd received in the last five years.

"Thank you," she said with a smile. "Come on in!"

Chapter Sixteen

"YOU'RE A VERY GOOD GIRL," STACEY TOLD BAY AS SHE clipped the dog's nails. The Doberman lay on the floor, patiently enduring what Stacey suspected was less than professional level grooming.

She'd never considered herself much of a pet person before, but Bay made it easy. The dog was attentive, smart and had excellent communication skills. She spent a couple of days a week over at Harper's house, hanging out with her friends. Stacey wasn't sure how that would change when the puppies were born.

"You'll be busy with your own family," she told the dog. "Then when I have Joule, Kit will be home with you all day and I think you'll like that."

Bay's brown eyes locked on her face, as if the dog didn't want to miss a word.

"The vet says you're doing really well with your pregnancy," Stacey continued. She glanced over her shoulder to make sure they were alone in the family room, then lowered her voice. "I'm expecting to learn a lot from you on the baby front. Not so much the actual giving birth part, but after. How you take care of them. I'm still not feeling any kind of connection with Joule and I don't know when that's supposed to happen."

She had more to discuss with the dog, but stopped talking when she heard footsteps in the hall. Ashton walked into the family room and sat on the large sectional. He was pale and looked uneasy.

"Do you have a second?" he asked, avoiding her gaze.

"Of course. What's wrong?"

"I heard from my mom. They let her call me, which means she's doing better in rehab." He laced his fingers together, then pulled them apart and jumped to his feet. He paced to the window, then turned back.

"She wants me to ask Kit for money, and then send it to her. I'm not supposed to tell him it's going to her because he would never send her any. Not after all those other times, but she says he won't refuse me."

He was right, Stacey thought. Kit had been dealing with his sister's drug problem for decades. He'd spoken to drug counselors enough to know that he couldn't participate in her cycle of destruction. But while he wouldn't give his sister a penny, he would definitely give Ashton whatever he needed. Hence the problem.

Stacey finished with Bay and carefully collected all the clippings on a paper towel before moving to the sectional. What was she supposed to say? She didn't know Ashton's mother or what he wanted to do. She felt as if there were hidden questions or concerns in what he was saying. Should she ask? Make assumptions, although that never went well. Not when it came to interpersonal situations. If only Harper were here. She would know what to say.

But Harper wasn't here, and Stacey knew she couldn't

ask Ashton to put his feelings on hold until someone better equipped was around to help him deal.

"You know the situation with your mother isn't your fault," she began.

He nodded. "I know. Whatever makes her do drugs happened long before I was born." He joined her on the sofa and angled toward her. "But it's still hard, you know? She's my mom."

"Because while you can say it's not your fault you still feel guilty?" she asked, hoping she was going in the right direction.

His mouth twisted. "Something like that."

She touched her stomach. "I get that. I'm the one who's pregnant but in my heart, I think of this baby as Kit's."

The words came out with no warning. She blinked several times, not able to believe she'd said that out loud.

Ashton gave her a slight smile. "Not surprising, Stacey. You can't even tell your mom you're pregnant. You should really get on that."

"I know." She sighed. "Okay, so we've established we're both bad at this. How can I help?"

He hesitated. "Just listening helps."

A total lie, she thought. If he was comfortable making a decision on his own, he wouldn't have come to her. He wanted her to make the decision for him. But which one?

"All right," she said slowly. "How about this? You can't have the money. I'm going to tell Kit what's going on, so he won't give it to you and I won't give it to you, either."

Ashton shocked her by completely relaxing. All the worry and tension left his body and he sagged against the back of the sofa.

"Thanks, Stacey. I really appreciate that."

She'd guessed right? She was still trying to absorb that when he upped the shock factor by adding, "I shouldn't be surprised. You always know what to say to me."

"I do?"

"Sure." He grinned. "Kit was lucky to find you. I remember when we first met. He told me who you were before I came to visit. I looked you up online and read a couple of your papers." He chuckled. "Okay, I tried to read them but couldn't. Still, I was really interested in what you were doing. I started thinking about studying science in college, which is how I found my way to engineering."

"I didn't know that," she admitted, not sure what else to say. She hadn't thought she could influence someone in her family. Mostly everyone didn't have a clue as to what she was doing, and if they did, they weren't very interested. Not Kit, of course, but he was different.

Ashton leaned toward her, his hands loosely laced between his open knees. "Thanks again for letting me stay here with you. Mischief Bay is great. I like my job, and you and Kit are easy to be with." He grinned. "And there's Becca, of course."

"Of course," she echoed automatically, before the truth of that statement settled in her brain. "Oh my God, you're dating!"

"What?" He straightened. "No, we're hanging out. Just friends." He hesitated, then flushed. "I mean I like her and all, but we're..."

Stacey waited.

His lips moved, but he didn't speak. Finally, he drew in a breath and looked at her. "I'm sorry. I don't know why I tried to keep that from you. Habit, I guess. It's always easier if my foster family or my mom don't know anything about my personal life. It's different here and sometimes I forget. Yes, Becca and I are dating."

Stacey wanted to bolt, or scream, or both. "Does Harper know?"

"I have no idea. We haven't been keeping it a secret or anything."

Stacey tried to work the problem. Becca was sixteen, nearly seventeen. She would be a senior in high school next year. Having a boyfriend was completely normal, and Ashton was a conscientious, age-appropriate teenage boy.

"I'm comfortable with you dating my niece," she said. "But I do have expectations I need you to meet."

Ashton looked more curious than concerned. "Sure. What?"

"You need to be sexually responsible."

He stood so abruptly, Bay got on her feet and began looking for danger. Stacey wondered if he would be the one bolting now. He glanced at the door, then sank back on the sofa. Stacey called the Doberman over and had her snuggle with her on the couch.

"We're not having sex," he mumbled, avoiding her gaze. "Jeez, Stacey, I thought you were going to say to call when I said I was going to or something."

"That, too, but the sexual component can have lasting consequences for both of you. I expect you to use a condom when you have sexual intercourse with Becca."

"We're not having sex," he repeated.

"Not yet, but you're young and healthy and hormones are very powerful. We've actually looked at them in my work, but they didn't help with…" She sighed. "Not the point. As I was saying, I expect you to—"

She looked at him. "Has anyone ever talked to you about sex?"

He groaned. "I know what goes where."

Which was the least of it. Who would have explained things to him? Not his mother. She doubted any of the foster families got close enough to have any kind of discussion with him.

If he and Kit had ever discussed sex, Kit would have mentioned it to her.

"All right," she began slowly as she organized her thoughts. "I will mention a few key points, and then we'll be done. First, use a condom every time. If you give me the name of your preferred brand, I'll make sure they are always available in your bathroom. If you don't want to choose, I'll do some research and pick for you."

He buried his face in his hands. "Is there more?"

"Yes, there is. Don't push. It's more than no means no. If the girl is reluctant, then stop. Go home and masturbate. It's not like you don't know how. Studies have shown that sexual release can be very therapeutic."

Ashton made a strangled sound deep in his throat, but otherwise didn't speak.

"Girls are not whores or there for your amusement. I can't see you participating in some gang rape, but even a girl who's drunk and saying yes shouldn't be considered an available partner." She softened her tone. "Be a good guy, Ashton. Like your uncle. Always aim for the decision that makes you proud of yourself."

She paused, wondering what else she should mention. "Are you familiar with the female clitoris and how to stimulate it so that your partner has an orgasm? Oral sex can be very helpful with this. I can direct you to a few articles if you want to—"

He stood and glared at her. "Are we done?"

"You don't want to discuss how to please a woman sexually?"

"Not with you."

"All right. Then I guess we're done. You can ask your uncle any follow-up questions if that would be easier."

"It would."

"Then thank you for listening."

Ashton shook his head, started to speak, threw up his hands, then stalked away. Stacey watched him go before turning back to Bay.

"I think that went very well. What do you think?"

Bay gave her a low yip of approval.

Harper carefully stirred the mixture. Kettle corn could be difficult and if she had the heat even a couple of degrees too high, then the sugar would burn and she would have to start over. Because life was nothing if not exciting.

Stacey walked into the kitchen.

"You must be excited," her sister said.

"I am. Misty's always been a fun client and it's great to see her get a break like this, and on HBO." Harper poured the kettle corn into three large serving bowls and started to hand one to her sister, only to set it down.

"Jeez, Stacey, you're seriously starting to show. You've got to tell Mom."

Her sister flushed. "I know. I was going to do it tonight, but Becca said she's not coming."

"She's out with her friends. Marg just announced she's moving into a retirement community and Bunny wants to talk her out of it." Because her mother was always very free with her opinion.

"That sounds like our mother." Stacey leaned against the counter. "I don't know how to ask this, so I'm just going to say it. Do you know that Becca and Ashton are seeing each other?"

What? Of course she knew. They were right outside in her living room, waiting for the HBO special to start. They were friends, nothing more. Becca was too young to— Okay, not too young, but she wasn't going to—

"No," she admitted in a whisper. "Are you sure?"

"Ashton told me."

Her daughter had a boyfriend and she hadn't said anything to her?

Her chest tightened as her throat seemed to swell shut. She felt the telltale burning in her eyes and knew she was seconds from an emotional meltdown.

"She never said anything. Not a word. He's been over a few times, but I thought it was like a family thing."

"You know they're not related, don't you?"

"Yes," Harper snapped, then held up a hand. "Sorry. I'm not mad at you. I'm not mad. It's just…" How could Becca not have said anything? A boyfriend? A first boyfriend? Had they really stopped talking that much?

She thrust two of the popcorn bowls at her sister. "Take those out. I need a second, okay?"

Stacey hesitated, then nodded.

Harper waited until she was alone to sink into one of the kitchen chairs. She told herself she would cry for one minute, and then she would get over it. Whatever was wrong with her relationship with Becca could be fixed. Look at the great birthday present her daughter had given her.

Words that should have made her happy but didn't. She couldn't shake the feeling she'd lost her little girl.

"What's wrong?"

She looked up and saw Lucas standing in the entrance to the kitchen. She quickly wiped her face and faked a smile. "Nothing. I'm good. Is Misty on yet?"

"No. There's some guy who isn't that funny." He crossed to the table and sat down. "Tell me what's going on."

She shook her head. "It's nothing. Silly things. Too bad Pomegranate couldn't make it tonight."

"Her name is Persimmon, which you know, and I'm not seeing her anymore. Harper, tell me."

She drew in a breath. "Apparently Becca and Ashton are more than just friends and she didn't tell me." She held up a hand. "It's fine. She's nearly seventeen and it's not like I'm her closest friend. It's just, I thought we could share the moment, you know."

His green eyes locked with hers. "You're hurt."

"Yes. Hurt and disappointed and wondering when I became a bad mother."

"You're not a bad mother."

"My daughter wouldn't agree with you." She squared her shoulders. "Enough about me. Let's go watch Misty kill it."

Lucas didn't budge. "She loves you. I hope you know that."

"I do. And I love her, so we have that in common. I'll be okay, I promise. I just need a little time."

Before he could respond, Becca flew into the kitchen. "Mom, Lucas, come quick. Misty just came on stage." She did a little dance. "Mom, she's wearing that bracelet I braided for her. Can you believe it? It's like a shout-out to us. Hurry!"

They stood. Lucas moved close and murmured, "Not exactly the words of a daughter who hates you."

Harper knew he was right. *Hate* was too strong a word. But somewhere along the way, they'd lost the closeness she'd always taken for granted. And she couldn't help thinking that at the end of the day, it was going to be because of something she'd done. Or worse, something she hadn't.

"Becca, I need to speak to you for a moment."

Not words any student wanted to hear from a teacher, Becca thought, as she nodded while collecting her notes.

Most of the other kids had already left the classroom, darting out as the bell rang. Becca had taken to lingering so no one would see her leaving by herself and realize she'd become the unwanted loner.

With Jordan's defection, nearly everyone else had followed. Becca now ate lunch alone, walked to class alone and spoke to no one. Okay, sure, there were the odd greetings and a couple of the weird kids had smiled at her, but that was it. She remembered learning a word when she'd been little and liking it so much she'd tried to use it all the time, but it had been difficult. Now she was the very definition of *pariah*.

She walked to the front of the classroom. Mrs. Nemecek peered at her over her half-glasses, then shook her head.

"I expected better of you, Becca. You barely earned a C on your last test, your homework has been haphazard at best. What's going on?"

A lot, Becca thought. European History was her least favorite class this semester. The class emphasized World War II and she'd discovered that nothing very nice had happened during that time period. All the talk of war and death and concentration camps was gross. When she was pushed for time, history homework came in last. But telling Mrs. Nemecek that she was getting As and Bs in her other classes wouldn't be much help.

"I'm sorry," she said instead, then hesitated, wondering if she could talk about her personal life and get some sympathy. There was her dad getting remarried and what had happened with Nathan, but she wasn't sure her history teacher would want to know or if she would care.

Still bad grades weren't an option. Lucas made her show him her grades online and if she was doing badly, he would stop showing up for their driving time and she desperately wanted her license. Besides, she'd always been a pretty decent student.

"Becca?" Mrs. Nemecek sounded impatient.

She opened her mouth to make up some lie, then mentally swerved at the last second and instead said, "You're right, Mrs. Nemecek. I've been phoning it in. To be honest, I don't like the subject matter. It's all so grim and sad and people are dying. I can't believe there were concentration camps. I mean I know there were, but who would do that? Who would kill other people just because of where they were born or what they believed? It's wrong."

Her teacher's stern expression never softened. "It is wrong, but that is beside the point. Becca, I enjoy having you in class, but let me be clear. You earn your grade from me. It's not a gift. If you don't do the work, you will fail. If you do bad work, your grade will reflect that. Liking or not liking the subject matter is immaterial."

Becca wanted to stomp her foot at the unfairness of that. Why did she need to learn history anyway? It was over and done and no one really cared about it. But that wasn't information that was going to sway her teacher and she really had to get a good grade in the class.

"I want to earn extra credit," she said quickly. "Please, give me a project. Or I'll come up with one. Make it icky. I'll do the work. I want to do better."

"Better can't be measured." Her teacher shook her head. "I don't know, Becca. I appreciate your honesty, but I'm still disappointed in your attitude."

"You should be," Becca said, thinking this was exactly like talking to her mom.

"That's refreshing. All right, I want a fifteen-page paper on some aspect of the war between Russia and Germany. You pick the topic. I want more than facts and if I find even a single sentence copied from another source, you'll get an F.

Make me feel something, Becca. Show me you understand what was happening."

Fifteen pages? Was she kidding? Wasn't that about as long as a book? Most papers were three pages or five. Fifteen was totally unfair and—

"I'll do it," she said.

"You have until the Friday before finals. There will be no extensions."

"I won't need one. Thank you, Mrs. Nemecek."

Becca grabbed her backpack and left the classroom.

School was over for the day and most of the students were already gone. No friends lingered for her and there was no one around she wanted to talk to.

Sadness threatened, but Becca pushed it away. She was going to get a good grade for sure, which meant she had to plan out the paper. Fifteen pages would take at least a couple of weeks.

She hurried home and found Jazz waiting by the front door. Her dog stared at her expectantly. Becca skidded to a stop as she realized that she needed to make time for Jazz. She'd promised to take care of the dog and that meant more than feeding her and letting Dwayne take her for a daily walk.

"I know," Becca said, dropping to her knees and hugging the dog. "We need to go outside and play. You've just been hanging out, huh? Let me put my stuff away and we'll figure out something."

Then she had to do homework and start researching her paper. Plus, she had to spend a little more time with her car's owner's manual because she had another driving session with Lucas.

She'd barely put her backpack down when her mom walked into her room.

"Hi, sweetie. When did you get home from school?"

"Just now."

"Have you thought any about the videos? I want to be able to get back to Valerie with a delivery date."

Becca felt herself tensing. "I don't know, Mom. Let me figure out what I'm going to do when. I have finals coming up and a big paper for European History. There's a lot."

Her mother's smile faded. "Is it too much? Do you want me to find someone else to do the videos?"

"No." The single word came out more sharply than Becca intended. She tried again. "I mean, of course not. I want to do them. Things are really complicated right now. Give me a day, okay?"

"If you're sure. I don't want to make things more difficult."

"You're not. I really want to do the videos." They would be fun and she needed the money.

"All right. We'll talk tomorrow. Why don't I go make you a snack? You can't study if you're hungry."

"Thanks, Mom."

Becca sank onto the floor. Jazz settled next to her and leaned close.

"I've got to figure this out," Becca told the dog, even as she reached for the phone. She sent off a quick text to Kaylee, but there was no response. Of course. Kaylee was too busy having fun.

Becca scrambled to her feet and started making a list of everything she had to get done. It was way too long and she was left with the sense of being trapped in some kind of cage with no escape. By five, she'd figured out there wasn't an interesting part of World War II that didn't involve a lot of people being dead, Kaylee still hadn't answered, she'd totally screwed up her math homework, she had no friends to talk to and the usually well-behaved Jazz had chewed one of her cat slippers.

"Jazz, no!" she yelled, picking up one ear and a bit of tail—all that was left of the fuzzy slippers. "These are mine. You have your own toys."

Her dog simply looked at her.

Becca didn't know if she should cry, scream or run away. Her phone chirped with a text from Ashton.

Hey. Thinking of u.

Becca looked at the chewed-up slippers, the bored dog, the notes on a paper she still hadn't figured out, her unfinished math homework. She thought about the fight with Jordan and how Kaylee had well and truly forgotten all about her.

Her life was a disaster and she didn't know how to fix it, but she did know one thing. Having a guy in her life would change everything. And there was only one way to make sure that happened for real.

She was going to have sex with Ashton. Then everything would be fine.

Chapter Seventeen

DEAN PRYOR LOOKED EXACTLY LIKE THE CHEER CAPTAIN at an LA college. He was handsome in a very chiseled way, tall and lean, with dark hair and eyes. He wore pressed khakis, a white polo shirt and an honest-to-God sweater over his shoulders. By comparison, Harper felt unwashed, disheveled and decidedly uninspired.

He shook her hand, made friends with the dog and exuded charm and confidence.

"I was so glad to get your call," he told her as he followed her into the dining room, where she'd decided to conduct their interview. Although the thought of her interviewing anyone made her want to both giggle and throw up. She wasn't in business, not really. What did she know about hiring an employee?

But she'd dutifully read a few articles online and had taken notes. She was hoping not to embarrass herself too badly.

"I've wanted to get back to work, but the movie business so isn't going to be it. Those hours are impossible and I don't want to travel."

He settled across from her and gave her a conspiratorial smile. "It's those damn kids. I hate to be away from them." He pulled out his phone and showed her a couple of pictures of adorable twin girls. "Mandy and Miranda. They are so beautiful. We call them Tater and Tot and I have no idea how *that* started. Lance, my husband, says I need to get out of the house or I'll start crocheting clothes for the dog, and then he'll be forced to lock me in a closet." Dean grinned. "And honey, I'm way past coming out of the closet."

Harper laughed involuntarily. "I'm all for moving forward, but I'm a little worried this job isn't going to be interesting enough for you. I don't know how much Kit told you, but I operate a home-based virtual assistant business." She paused. "Although a few of my clients don't get the concept of *virtual*." She made air quotes.

"I know that one." He leaned toward her. "I'm not looking for excitement. I want a little creative challenge and some income and to get out of the house." He handed her a slim folder. "Here's my résumé and some references. My hours are flexible. As long as I can be home in time to pick up my kids, I'm good. I'm happy to work from here or from my house. Why don't you tell me what you need help with?"

Harper explained about her clients, without mentioning names. "Some of the work is steady, some is hit-and-miss."

"Especially with party planners," he said with a knowing nod. "They're busy, you're busy. They're quiet and there's nothing. That makes it tough."

"Tell me about it. I have two sets of gift bags I need done by Tuesday, some envelopes to calligraph and that's just this week."

"You know calligraphy?" He sounded impressed. "I don't

have the patience." He winked. "Is this where I tell you there are computer programs for that?"

"I've mentioned it to my party planners, but some people still want the real thing."

"Oh, we all want the real thing. The trick is finding it." He looked around. "Where do you work?"

"I have a home office. It's small."

They went into the back bedroom. Dean looked around and tsked.

"You're overwhelmed with clutter and it's not your fault. You need supplies, but where do you put them? I don't suppose you have a bonus room, do you? I'm a big believer in making a space work."

Harper hesitated.

"What? You're hiding something. I can tell."

Rather than say anything, she waved him forward and together they walked into her craft room.

Dean turned in a slow circle before putting his hands on his hips. "You are crazy. You know that, right? This needs to be your office. Working in that tiny bedroom has to be depressing. How can you get anything done with the walls closing in? This space is bright and happy. What's going on?"

An excellent question. She looked at all the shelves, the giant flat work surfaces, the closets and wondered why on earth she'd been so resistant to change. Her business brought in money. The craft room was just...

"It's my before life," she said, unable to stop herself from speaking. "Before the divorce, before I started my business, before I was a mess."

"We're all a mess, Harper. Some of us are just better at faking it." He untied his sweater and let it drop over the back of a chair. "Are you ready to let the past go or do you need to hang on to it longer?"

"I'm ready."

"Then let's get to it."

"What do you mean?"

"I say let's move your office here and your crafts into the small room. We'll talk while we work and get to know each other. By the time we're done, I'll bet we'll know if we want to work together or not."

"But it's going to take hours."

"Tater and Tot have Mandarin class today, so I'm yours until four." He rolled his eyes. "Lance and I are such a cliché. Yes, we have enrolled our girls into Mandarin class, and gymnastics and fencing, if you can believe it. I'm turning into my mother, and let me tell you, we can't decide who that makes more uncomfortable, me or her."

Harper began to laugh. She'd known for a while that she had to switch her office with the craft room, but she'd never had the time or energy. Maybe she'd been waiting for Dean to come along to inspire her.

"Let's do it," she said.

By the time Dean had to leave to collect his girls, Harper knew she'd found someone she could work with. Dean had been organized, efficient and funny. The move had happened more easily than she would have thought possible. They'd gone through her crafts, pulling out ridiculous things she would never use but had held on to because she had the room. Now she had a huge pile to take over to the local women's shelter for them to use for crafts for the kids.

Dean had left with the supplies for the first of the bag projects. He would have them back to her by Monday. They'd

agreed on an hourly wage for him and an approximate schedule. Her work life, it seemed, had taken a turn for the better. Now all that was left was figuring out how to reconnect
with her daughter.

Still flush with her successful conversation with Ashton,
Stacey decided to take her relationship-confidence on a test
drive and finally tell her mother about her pregnancy.

Sunday morning she and Kit drove over to Harper's, where
Kit would wait with his sister-in-law. They'd talked it over
and agreed that Stacey would literally come screaming out of
her mother's apartment if things went very badly. Should that
not happen, Kit would join her after twenty minutes.

Stacey had a vision of herself running down the stairs, yelling at the top of her lungs, while the neighbors on both sides
called 911 and reported an insane intruder. Of course that
would be a distraction from what was sure to be her mother's
disapproval.

"Maybe she'll understand," Stacey said, more to herself than
Kit. "She loves babies and she's getting another granddaughter. We're actually doubling the pool number."

"That could happen."

Stacey glanced at her husband, more than a little convinced
he might be humoring her rather than expressing his opinion.
Not that telling her the conversation was going to end with
her screaming would make her feel any better.

They arrived far too quickly. Rather than go into Harper's
and put off the inevitable, Stacey went directly upstairs and
knocked on her mother's bright blue front door.

Bunny answered seconds later. "Stacey! Did I know you
were stopping by?"

"No, sorry, Mom. Kit and I were in the neighborhood and I decided to come see you. Do you have a second?"

"Of course."

Bunny's apartment was above the oversize, detached three-story garage. Huge west-facing windows offered a perfect view of the Pacific Ocean.

Bunny waved her toward the overstuffed sofa, then hurried to the kitchen to no doubt prepare refreshments.

"I'm okay, Mom," Stacey said, following her into the small kitchen. "You don't have to—"

But it was too late. Bunny had pulled cookies out of a large pink handbag-shaped cookie jar. She got grapes and a small cheese plate from the refrigerator, then poured lemonade into crystal glasses.

Stacey tried to remember the contents of her refrigerator. If there was lemonade, it would be in a carton and she knew there wasn't a cheese plate. She might be able to find a few grapes—she wasn't sure.

In less than five minutes they were seated at the small, round dining table. In addition to food, Bunny had put out lace place mats with matching napkins, flatware, all the serving pieces, crystal snack-size plates that were the same pattern as the glasses, along with a floral centerpiece.

Part of her wondered how it was possible to always be so prepared for company. The rest of her calculated the production hours lost to such a ridiculous pursuit. But then Bunny would tell her she was missing the point, and maybe she was.

Bunny poured her a glass of lemonade, then smiled. "This is lovely. You don't stop by very often, do you? I rarely see you without Kit along. Not that he isn't a very nice man, but I do enjoy spending time with my little girl."

Stacey didn't bother pointing out she was forty and hadn't been little for decades.

"I should do this more often," she admitted, sliding a few slices of cheese onto her plate. "I did want to talk to you about something, Mom."

Bunny's gaze locked on her. "What is it? Are you changing jobs? Don't tell me you're moving away. You only came home a few years ago. Kit has a good teaching position and I thought you were happy with your work."

"We're not moving. We're staying right there, in Mischief Bay."

"Oh, then what?"

Her mother looked expectant. Stacey swallowed against her suddenly dry throat, then told herself she hadn't done anything wrong. Or at least not very wrong. Besides, it was her body and if she didn't want to—

"Stacey Wray Bloom, tell me what you came to say."

"I'm pregnant."

Her mother stared at her for several seconds, then her face crumbled as tears filled her eyes. "Oh, Stacey, that's wonderful."

Stacey found herself being hugged fiercely as Bunny sniffed and tried to speak.

"I'm so happy for you. Another grandchild." She returned to her seat and pulled an embroidered hankie out of some hidden pocket before lightly dabbing her eyes. "I'd hoped of course, but I never thought it would happen. You're forty. Have you talked to your doctor? You know you have to take care of yourself. There are concerns when you're over thirty-five. I don't know exactly what they are, but still." She smiled. "A baby."

So far, so good, Stacey thought with cautious optimism. "I've talked to my doctor. She specializes in high-risk pregnancies and I'm doing very well. I've been taking care of myself and I have excellent genetics."

"You get those from me." Her mother laughed. "All right, and maybe from your father. What are you going to do about work? Are you going to resign or just take a long maternity leave? Not that I can see you quitting that job you love so much. So what will you do for day care?"

"I'm taking off three weeks after the birth and Kit will stay home with the baby."

Bunny's mouth dropped open. "What? Three weeks? That's absurd. You can't take off three weeks. You have to breast-feed. You have to take care of your child. That's what a mother does, Stacey. This isn't some project you can assign to someone else. You are responsible for your own children."

Something Stacey was very clear on. It was being responsible that made her so uneasy.

"I won't be breast-feeding, Mom," she said as gently as she could. "It's not practical. I love my work and I want to get back to it as quickly as possible."

"That's totally ridiculous. There is no way Kit can be a stay-at-home father."

"Why not? He's far more nurturing than me. Mom, we've talked about this and it's what we want to do. I make way more money than Kit. I have excellent benefits. Why shouldn't I be the one to support the family?"

"But he's a man!" Her mother looked appalled and uncomfortable. "Everything about it is wrong."

"The world is changing. Kit's in a support group for men just like him. There are more out there than you would think." She tried not to get defensive. After consciously lowering her voice, she smiled and touched her mother's arm.

"It's a brave, new world, as they say. Men are doing all kinds of things we never thought they could do."

"Don't try to be funny," her mother snapped. "I can't believe it. This is a nightmare. It was bad enough when you wouldn't take his last name, but now this? What am I supposed to tell my friends? That my son-in-law is staying home with the baby?"

"It's the truth." Stacey held in a sigh. "Kit and I decided on this before we even got married. We wanted to try to have a baby and we knew that it made more sense for him to stay home. He'll work through the end of the semester, then resign. His principal already knows. It's going to be great."

Bunny frowned. "Why would he stop working so soon? When are you due? Around Christmas?" Her expression softened. "A Christmas baby would be so nice."

Uh-oh. Crap and double crap. There was no easy way around her due date. Kit had warned her waiting would be bad. She'd known in her head, but the thought of telling her mother had been impossible to imagine, let alone get done.

"I'm due at the end of June."

Her mother's mouth dropped open as her eyes widened. "What?" she asked, her voice a shriek. "In June?"

"I'm sorry. I wanted to tell you sooner, but time got away from me. Kit and I agreed to wait until I was past the three-month mark. Given my age and possibility of miscarriage, that seemed the best thing. Then that came and went and we got busy and I didn't mean to keep it from you, Mom. It just sort of happened."

Her mother stared at Stacey's midsection, then threw up her hands and sprang to her feet.

"How could you?" she demanded. "You kept this from me, which is just like you. You're due in less than two months and

I'm just now finding out?" Tears filled her eyes. "What kind of daughter does that make you? Or are you going to make this all about me? Once again, I've failed you. Well, not this time, missy. You should have told me!"

Bunny grabbed the back of the chair on the opposite side of the table and glared. "You are a constant disappointment, Stacey. I'm your mother. Why are you punishing me?"

For the first time since getting pregnant, Stacey felt as if she were going to throw up. She was cold, nauseous and light-headed. Her mother's anger and hurt assaulted her, making her feel small and unsure, just like when she was a kid.

Somewhere in the distance, she thought she heard a door open and close, but she wasn't sure. Maybe she was simply imagining there was an escape.

"Don't you have anything to say for yourself?" Bunny asked. "This is so like you, punishing me for something I never did."

"Stop it."

The firm, male voice had them both turning. Stacey raced over to Kit, who put his arm around her. Bunny glared at them both.

"You're in this together," she announced. "I don't know why you take such pleasure in deceiving me, but be assured, I'm never going to forgive this."

"Stacey wasn't ready to share the news," Kit told her. "That's all it is, Bunny. You can try to make it more, but that's on you, not her. She's told you now and I hope you can be happy for us, but if you can't, then the loss is totally yours. As for how we're going to raise our daughter, again, it was our decision to make and we've made it."

He smiled at Stacey, then turned back to Bunny. "You've raised an amazing daughter and she's going to have a baby. I wish you could be happy for us. I thought you would be. I guess I overestimated you."

With that, he led Stacey away. She made it to the bottom of the stairs before bursting into tears. Kit hugged her tight and promised everything would be fine, but she knew he couldn't be more wrong.

Chapter Eighteen

"MOM, I NEED TO TELL YOU SOMETHING," BECCA SAID on Monday morning.

Harper sat at the breakfast table, her tablet in front of her, her third cup of coffee in her hand. She was trying a new organization program with a phone and tablet app that allowed her to sync her devices, but she was having trouble getting the hang of it. She had the feeling it was going to be worth the effort, but until then, she wasn't sure what she was supposed to be doing when.

She was about to tell Becca this wasn't a good time when she remembered about Ashton, her daughter's first boyfriend. Thank God, Becca was finally going to reveal all.

"Sure," she said brightly, closing her tablet and smiling at her daughter. "What's up, honey?"

Becca shuffled from foot to foot before sitting down and looking at Harper.

"It's about Dad."

"Dad? I thought…" She cleared her throat. "Okay, tell me about Dad."

Becca looked down, back at her, then squeezed her eyes tightly shut before blurting, "He's getting married at the end of the month." She opened her eyes. "I wanted to tell you before but I thought you'd be mad or upset or something and I'm really sorry but I have to go. I'm in the wedding. Alicia doesn't want me to be but Dad made her and I have to wear a stupid dress and it's gross and I'm scared and I really want you to come with me. Please?"

Harper hadn't seen her mother since Stacey had dropped the baby bomb on her yesterday. After getting the recap from her sister, she'd gone to check on Bunny, but her mother had gone out and hadn't returned until late in the evening. Harper had tried to imagine how shocked and upset she might be, but she knew she hadn't come close. Until now.

Terence was getting married? Married! Not that she wanted him back, but WTF? The bastard couldn't be bothered to tell her himself? And to make Becca be in the wedding? And he was getting married again?

She wanted to throw something. Or scream. Or both. Instead she had to suck it up because that was what she always did—suck it up for the greater good—and talk like a normal person so as not to terrify her daughter.

"Your dad hasn't said anything to me," she said, doing her best not to sound shrill. "If you don't want to be in the wedding, tell him. Or I'll tell him."

"I know, but it's just easier to do it and then it's over. I know he doesn't really care if I'm there or not. He just wants to say I was there."

"Becca, your dad loves you."

"I hear that a lot, but he sure doesn't act like it. He never listens. No one listens."

All Harper's mother-senses went on alert. She recognized

that quiet, resigned, unhappy tone. It was way worse than talking back or sarcasm or anything annoying. It was filled with sadness and resignation. As if the worst had occurred and couldn't be mended or undone.

"What do you mean?" she asked. "I listen."

Becca rolled her eyes. "Oh, please. Mom, you never listen. Not anymore. You're busy with work all the time. Everything is more important than me. If a client calls, the entire world has to come to a halt. I could be lying on the kitchen floor, shot, and you would still take a client call."

Harper felt the words as if they were physical blows. She wanted to duck and weave, to protect herself from the assault, but she was too shocked to speak.

Her daughter stood and glared at her. "You don't know me anymore. You don't know what happened with Kaylee or Jordan or Nathan. You don't know *anything!*"

Becca grabbed her backpack and stormed out of the kitchen. Harper rose and stared after her, not sure what to do. She glanced at the clock and realized school would be starting in half an hour. No doubt Becca had timed the conversation about her father so that she had an excuse to bolt, but Harper doubted she'd expected the conversation to go so badly.

She tried to breathe and couldn't, then collapsed back in her chair. Her daughter's words continued to echo—that Harper didn't know anything about her life. She tried to tell herself it wasn't true, but look at how wrong she'd been about Ashton. And she had no idea what Becca meant about Jordan, Kaylee and some other kid.

It wasn't her fault, she told herself as she fought against tears. She was trying to keep them afloat financially. Things were difficult and she had to focus on keeping food on the table and—

Had she really lost touch with Becca? Had she really screwed up that badly? Was this just teenage craziness or had her daughter been telling the truth? And if she was, didn't that make Harper the worst mother alive?

Bunny walked in the back door and slammed it behind her.

"I assume you heard what happened with Stacey?"

Harper wanted to cover her face with her hands and have it all go away. "Mom, I really can't talk about this right now."

"You don't have a choice. Can you believe it? Your sister is a piece of work. I'm so angry." Bunny's lower lip trembled. "She was awful to me and the things Kit said… I can't ever forget them. But the worst part is the baby. She's going to have a baby in a few weeks and I didn't know."

Harper nodded, wishing there was a way to distract her mother so she could run and hide until she stopped hurting so much.

"We need a plan," her mother said firmly. "Some way to show them they were wrong."

Harper shook her head. "I'm not going to help you punish Stacey. She's dealing with enough. Think about it, Mom. This can't be easy for her. Stacey's incredibly brilliant but she's hardly maternal. She didn't want to tell you. I know that makes you feel bad, but for once consider the fact she wasn't trying to hurt you. She was trying to protect herself. There's a difference."

Bunny stared at her. "You *knew*! You knew all this time and didn't tell me. Why didn't you tell me?"

Harper thought longingly of the blissful relief of banging her head against a hard surface. Maybe she would give herself amnesia, and then she wouldn't have to deal with her family at all.

Bunny's eyes filled with tears that slipped down her cheeks. "How could you do that to me? I'm your mother."

"And Stacey's my sister. Mom, I'm really sorry. She asked me not to tell, so I didn't. I kept her secret."

"I'm your mother. I thought you loved me. I thought my daughters loved me. It's always been the two of you against me. This is just like when you were little. You *always* defended her. You always took her side. What about me? Why don't I matter?"

"Knock, knock!"

Harper heard Dean's voice as he let himself into the house and held in a groan. Timing was not on her side this morning.

He walked into the kitchen. "Good morning. How are we do—"

He looked from her to Bunny and immediately started backing out of the room.

"I'll be in the office," he mouthed silently.

Lucky him. He got to escape.

Harper turned back to her mother, who was already halfway across the kitchen.

"Mom, wait. Please. We have to talk."

"There's nothing to say," her mother told her. "You both betrayed me. I have to deal with that and what I thought was our relationship. Obviously you two are still much closer to each other than to me. I don't matter at all. I'm just... Well, I don't know what. Goodbye, Harper."

She slammed the door behind her.

Harper honest to God didn't know what to do. Go after her mother? Chase down Becca? Hire someone to beat the shit out of Terence?

The front door opened again. Seconds later she heard the familiar scramble of dog nails on her tile floors. Jazz came flying down the stairs and went to greet her friend. Harper returned to the kitchen table and reached for her coffee just as Lucas walked in.

"Morning," he said, then frowned. "What?"

"Oh, you really don't want to know."

He sat across from her with an expectant look.

"Don't say I didn't warn you," she grumbled. "Fine, you want me to tell you? Fine! In no particular order, my daughter has a boyfriend. I knew she and Ashton were dating, but now it's serious. And before you can ask, I don't object. From all I've heard, he's a really good kid. It's not the boy I mind, it's that once again, she didn't tell me."

She gripped her cup more tightly. "She said we never talk anymore because I don't have time to listen. She said I don't care about her." She felt tears and just let them fall. "I do care. She's my kid, my world. But I've totally screwed up and that sucks."

She cleared her throat. "Stacey finally told Bunny about the baby. That was a disaster, as you can imagine, but right after Becca dumped on me, Bunny figured out I'd known all along. Now I'm the other bad daughter. So I'm fighting with my daughter and my mother and I'm the common denominator, so what if it's my fault? Also, Terence is marrying the bimbo at the end of the month. The bastard never told me and while I don't care, he should have said something. Becca has to go to the wedding and she's upset and wants me to go with her. Although if I'm such a shitty mother, I'm not sure why, but hey, I'll go because even though she doesn't believe me, I do love her and would walk through fire for her, so I have to go to the wedding and I suppose the only good thing is the bimbo will be upset. Although I'm not really the kind of person who wants to upset a bride on her wedding day, even her, so where does that leave me and aren't you sorry you asked?"

Lucas's gaze was steady, his green eyes unreadable. "Do you need a hug?"

The question was so unexpected, she started to laugh, which oddly made her cry harder. Then the most unexpected thing happened. Lucas walked around the table, pulled her to her feet and, well, hugged her.

It wasn't romantic or sexy. Instead it was solid and encompassing and even after a minute, he didn't let go. He just hugged her, despite her crying into his crisp, white shirt.

He held on until she could breathe again and the tears had subsided. Then, only then, did he release her.

She wiped her face. "Thank you, Lucas. I guess I did need a hug."

One shoulder rose and fell. "Happy to help." He pulled an index card from his shirt pocket and handed it to her. "A new client. He wants custom baskets delivered to the staff of a specialized nursing facility every week. His daughter is in a coma and he wants to thank the staff for taking such good care of her."

"Thanks." She glanced at the card. "That's not going to be cheap."

"He has money."

"Not a cop?"

"No, he's a former drug kingpin who turned his life around." Lucas waved away any questions. "Don't ask. He's someone I know, but not a friend. But when he mentioned what he needed, I thought of you. If the idea of working with him makes you uncomfortable, don't call him. I didn't give him your name."

"I don't know what to say."

"Think about it. I have to get to work." He hesitated. "You okay?"

"No, but I will be."

"You know how to reach me if you need anything."

"Like another hug?" she asked, hoping she sounded teasing rather than pathetic.

"Whatever. Just text me."

She nodded and he left. Seconds later Dean appeared and snatched the card from her hand.

"We so have to work for this guy. I wonder if we'll meet him. Wouldn't that be interesting?"

"He used to be a drug dealer, so no."

Dean raised his eyebrows. "Not a lowly drug dealer, he was a drug kingpin."

"How is that different?"

"He was in management."

Despite everything, Harper started to laugh. "There's something seriously wrong with you."

"Lance says that all the time but the truth is I have an adventurous spirit and he doesn't. Speaking of adventures, you told me this job was going to be boring. You were so wrong."

She groaned. "You heard?"

"Oh, honey, the neighbors heard." His expression turned concerned. "Are you all right?"

"Like I said before, no, but I will be."

"You need a date for your ex's wedding. Showing up by yourself will make you feel awful. I'd offer to go, but Lance is traveling the rest of the month so if I'm not here, I'm with the twins." He glanced toward the front door. "What about Lucas? He's very handsome and I'm sure he knows how to behave. You could ask him to bring his gun and shoot the groom." He winked. "Or the bride. Your choice."

"No one is getting shot and he would never go with me." She laughed at the thought. "Lucas's idea of a good time is a woman between the ages of twenty and twenty-two. It would be like hanging out with his mother."

"I'm not talking about a date. You need an escort." His eyes widened. "Oh, I have friends who are professional escorts and part-time models. Want me to call one of them?"

"No." She poked him in the chest. "I mean that, Dean. No escorts. No boyfriends, no guns. I will go with Becca, assuming she still wants me to, and I will be fine."

"If you say so, but I still think you should ask Lucas." He tapped the index card against his palm. "I really want this new client. Say no if you disagree."

"Go for it," she told him. "Let's add a former drug kingpin to the stable."

Stacey continued to experience the fallout of her Bunny encounter for several days. The vague sense of impending disaster never fully went away—not that anything bad was going to happen. She knew that. It was just fighting with her mother had never ended well, at least not for her. Bunny seemed blessed with an ability to skate through life without an emotional scratch.

While Kit told her about his day, she found herself barely able to listen. She didn't want to eat or do much of anything. The most appealing thought for the evening was to simply curl up in her bed and wait for the icky feelings to go away.

A ridiculous idea, she told herself. There were several ways to change a mood, and many of them were safe during her pregnancy. Exercise, for example. Or she and Kit could watch a funny movie. Many studies showed that—

"There's something wrong with Bay," Kit said as he tossed

down his napkin and stood. He circled the table to crouch by the dog, who was standing by the back door.

"What do you mean?"

"She's been pacing for a couple of hours. I've let her out, but she doesn't want to leave the house. She didn't eat her dinner." He stroked her head. "What's going on, little girl?"

The dog looked at him and whined, then started walking around the living room. Stacey watched and saw that he was right. She did seem agitated, almost uncomfortable.

"She's in labor." Stacey sprang to her feet, prepared to go into birthing mode. Not that there was anything for her to do. "We should take her temperature. If it's dropped, then she'll go into labor in the next twenty-four hours." She studied the pacing dog. "Maybe it's too late for that."

They'd already set up a comfortable canine maternity ward in Kit's office. He'd sectioned off about a quarter of the room, putting up a low wall that Bay could easily step over while the puppies would be contained. There was a large, thick, mattress-style dog bed with a plastic cover. Old sheets were on top of that. Clean newsprint covered the floor.

"Bay, do you want to go get settled?" she asked, patting her leg and leading the way to the office.

Bay followed. She'd seen the birthing area before, had sniffed it all, but hadn't wanted to stretch out on the bed. Now she stepped inside, then went back out and back in again. She sniffed it all before lying down on the mattress and locking her gaze with Stacey's.

The message was clear. *Don't leave me.*

"I'll be right here," Stacey promised. "I'm going to stay for as long as it takes."

Kit brought in lots of pillows along with a low beach backrest, so Stacey could get comfortable. They put on classical music and offered Bay water, which she refused. She got up and tore a few of the papers into shreds, then went back to the bed.

"I'm scared," Stacey admitted, squeezing Kit's hand. "What if something goes wrong?"

"What if something doesn't?" he asked. "She's done this before. The vet says she'll know what to do and we have the information for the emergency vet clinic programmed into our phones. If it gets bad, we'll throw her in the car and take her with us."

Ashton got home about eight and joined them. Bay wagged her stubby little tail when she saw him, then closed her eyes as her breathing changed.

"Females go through a lot," he said, shaking his head. "I sure wouldn't do that."

Stacey thought about the baby she was carrying. She wasn't overly concerned about giving birth. She understood the process and had already discussed pain management with her doctor. It was what came after that had her terrified. How was she supposed to know what to do? She was less than two months from her due date and she still didn't feel a connection or any sense of bonding.

By nine o'clock, the first of the puppies had been born. Bay licked the puppy clean, then allowed Kit to tie off the umbilical cord with a bit of dental floss. Two more puppies were born right after each other. Within the hour, they were all nursing and Bay had fallen asleep. Kit and Ashton cleaned up the dirty newspaper and laid down fresh.

The vet had said to wait a few hours before offering her food, then only small, frequent meals until she was ready for more. Kit and Ashton worked out a schedule that excluded her, despite Stacey's willingness to get up and feed Bay.

"You need to rest," her husband told her. "We'll handle this."

But after everyone had gone to bed, Stacey returned to sit with Bay. The Doberman opened her eyes and wagged her tail, but otherwise didn't move. The three tiny puppies were curled up against her, asleep.

"You were great," she told the new mother. "You handled it all perfectly. You were brave and so smart. You knew exactly what to do."

Stacey pressed her hand to her belly and willed herself to feel something. Anticipation, hope, anything but the ongoing sense of terror and disconnection.

"I don't think I can do it," she whispered to the dog. "I don't know how to be a mother. I've never wanted to learn. I'm not that interested in people and I've never enjoyed being around children. I don't understand them. Babies are even more confusing. That level of dependency doesn't make me comfortable."

She thought about all that had happened. Her fight with her mother, how Harper and Kit had tricked her into going shopping because they couldn't just ask her without her refusing.

"I'm not going to be a good mother," she told Bay. "I don't have it in me. My mom always said there was something wrong with me and now I know she was right." Her eyes burned with tears. "What if I can't love my baby? Worse, what if she knows? I'm not like you, Bay. I don't have instincts. I just have my brain and every now and then I have to admit it does me absolutely no good. This is one of those times. I can't think myself into loving my baby. I'm going to mess her up and I don't know how to make it better. Kit is going to be disappointed in me and I don't think I can survive that."

She curled up on the floor and cried until there were no

tears left. She got cold and her back hurt, but she stayed where she was until she heard Kit walk into his office. He settled next to her, then gently drew her into a sitting position and wrapped his arms around her.

"What's wrong?"

"I don't know how to be a good mother. I'm afraid Joule is going to hate me." She was mostly afraid she would lose him to their daughter, but there was no way to tell him that.

He put his hand under her chin, forcing her to look at him. "Has it occurred to you that of all the women I could have married, I chose you, Stacey? You're the one I want to spend my life with. You're the one I want to have our daughter with. I want this to happen with you. Just you."

She nodded and leaned close so he could kiss her. That would make him think she understood and that everything was fine. Even though it wasn't at all.

Chapter Nineteen

HARPER DROVE UP HER STREET, SLOWING AS SHE SAW a moving truck backed into her driveway. All her senses went on alert. Was this one of those scams she'd seen on the news? Was she being robbed?

She hit the gas and skidded to a stop in front of her house, only to see her mother directing the three men loading the truck. What on earth?

"Mom? What's going on?"

Harper hurried around the side of the house in time to see her mother's dresser being carried down the stairs.

Bunny sniffed and folded her arms across her chest. "Isn't it obvious? I'm leaving."

"I don't understand."

"What isn't clear? I refuse to stay where I'm not wanted. An apartment opened up at the old folks' home, so I'm going to live there and wait to die. With my heart broken, it shouldn't take long."

"You're leaving because Stacey didn't tell you about the baby?"

"That's really the least of it," her mother told her. "What about you not telling me?"

"It wasn't my secret to tell." Harper did her best to say calm.

"I'm your mother! You always take her side and now you're doing it again. Well, fine. It can just be the two of you, the way you've always wanted it. I won't be in the way anymore."

"Mom, please don't ask me to pick sides. I know you're upset and I totally get why." She offered what she hoped was a sympathetic smile. "You're hurt and you feel cut off from what was happening."

"Don't try to placate me. *Cut off* doesn't begin to describe what I'm feeling. You think you know everything, but you're wrong. All you care about is your business, as if making money is the most important thing in the world. Well, it's not! Family matters more, but you can't seem to remember that. You and your sister. You're exactly alike. Selfish and thoughtless, and I'm too old to have to deal with you right now."

With that, she turned and went back up the stairs, into her apartment. Harper walked into her house and texted her sister. Stacey called right away.

"I'm sorry," her sister said over the phone. "This is my fault."

"It's not. She's being dramatic. I just feel bad."

"Me, too, and you have to deal with it."

Harper watched the movers load more furniture. "Not for long. At the rate they're hustling, they'll be done within the hour."

"Want me to come over?"

"No. I'll handle it. I just wanted you to know."

When they'd hung up, Harper tried to figure out what she felt. Concern, sadness, irritation and more than a little fear at the loss of the thousand dollars a month her mother had been paying her for the apartment.

Her mother walked into the house a couple of hours later. "I wrote down my new address. I doubt you or your sister care, but my granddaughter might want to come see me."

"Mom—" Harper started, only to have Bunny hold up her hand.

"No. We've said all there is to say. I'm leaving. I put you down as my emergency contact. I'm sure one of the staff will call you when I die."

Harper took the card and stared at it. The upscale retirement community was less than three miles from the house. "Mom, I honestly don't know what to say to you. I'm sorry you're mad at me. I'm sorry I disappoint you every single day and I hope you'll be happy in your new apartment."

Her mother glared at her before handing over the apartment keys. "How dare you." Then she walked to her car and drove away.

Harper set the card on the counter. She had no idea what to do or say or think about any of it. She threw herself on the sofa. Thor and Jazz jumped up and sat on either side of her. She put her arms around both of them and tried to figure out exactly when her life had gone to shit.

She didn't know how long she sat there. Dean was working from home and Becca was still at school. She was well and truly by herself. The dogs were oddly comforting. Maybe she should close her eyes and take a nap or something. But before she could decide, there was a knock at the front door, followed by a familiar voice calling, "Harper?"

Thor jumped off the sofa and raced down the hall.

"In the family room." She waited until Lucas and Thor

walked in to say, "It's the middle of the day. What are you doing here?"

"I was in court and we just wrapped up early. Bunny texted to tell me there was a crisis. What's wrong?"

"My mother has your number?"

"I gave it to her in case there was an emergency."

"My mother?"

"What's going on?"

Talk about the question of the hour, she thought, deciding she probably shouldn't start laughing. If she did, she might never stop and that would freak him out. Was it too early to drink? Lucas had brought over a bunch of wine the other day. If she started now, she could probably get through at least two bottles by dinnertime. No doubt it would make her sick, but that might not be such a bad thing. Throwing up would be a distraction.

He sat in one of the club chairs and rested his ankle on his opposite knee. Thor lay down next to him.

"I have all day," Lucas told her.

"You haven't put your gun away."

"I might need it."

That made her smile. "I think the only person worthy of being shot is me, so I'd prefer you didn't."

He didn't respond. Instead he watched her as if trying to illustrate his "I have all day" point.

"Fine," she grumbled. "My mother has moved out. She's gone to the old folks' home, as she calls it, where she plans to wait to die. I feel guilty for hurting her and I'm worried about making up the income the apartment brought in, which makes me a bad person." She sighed. "There's my ex's wedding, my daughter." She paused. "Dean's working out, so that's good."

She had more to say, but suddenly couldn't speak as the

bitch that was reality slapped her. "I can't believe I'm going to say this, but I think I miss my mom."

Lucas shook his head. "There's no reason to and your problems are all easily fixed."

Seriously? "Enlighten me."

"Was that sarcasm I heard in your voice?"

"Yes. How is any of this easily fixed?"

"How much did your mom pay in rent?"

"A thousand dollars."

He swore. "Harper, the apartment has a perfect ocean view."

"I know. We always joked about the fact that there's no view from the house but the garage apartment has..." She felt her mouth drop open. "It has an ocean view. And a private entrance and parking. Oh my God! I could get double what she paid."

"Or triple."

Triple? Three thousand dollars a month? That would cover her mortgage, utilities and insurance.

"I'm not that lucky," she said, "but it's nice to dream."

"I'll check out anyone you're considering renting to." He lowered his foot to the floor. "Next, your mother." One shoulder rose up and down. "Give her some time. She needs to get over what happened with Stacey. If it helps with the guilt, I'll bet she was feeling a little lonely. Maybe a change of scene will give her the chance to meddle in other people's lives."

"I wish it were that easy. I still feel guilty."

"That I can't help with. Now, Becca."

"You're not going to be able to pretend to fix that one, at all. I have to think about what she said. I have been busy with work but I never thought..." She cleared her throat. "I'll figure that one out."

For a second she thought he was going to say something, but he only nodded.

"The wedding."

She grinned. "Please don't tell me you know someone who could take out the bride. I might not be happy about the way Terence has acted, but I don't want to do her harm."

"Fair enough. What if I take you to the wedding instead? I'd be a buffer between you and the ex, and you wouldn't have to sit by yourself while Becca's off doing her thing."

Harper thought about Dean's suggestion and wondered if the two men had spoken. *No*, she told herself. *Dean wouldn't do that.* But why on earth would Lucas volunteer for that kind of duty?

"You can't be serious. You don't want to go to a wedding with me. I mean it's sweet of you to offer and I'd have to run it by Terence…"

Telling her ex that she was Becca's plus one but wanted to bring a plus one of her own *would* be kind of thrilling, but no. She couldn't.

She smiled at him. "Thank you for offering, but it's not practical. We're friends and I don't want to make things awkward. I mean, what if people thought I was your date? You couldn't handle that."

"Why not?"

"I'm forty-two."

"I know."

"That's nearly double Pomegranate's age."

"Persimmon, and I told you, we're not dating anymore."

"You were never dating. You were sleeping with her. Lucas, you're being so nice to me and I appreciate it, but I'm not sure you could handle being in the presence of an age-appropriate woman for that long. I'm afraid you'd shrivel up and blow away."

"I'm over here all the time."

"Yes, and no one knows."

"You're making fun of me."

"You're kind of an easy target." She laughed. "Okay, I'll stop because you're being so nice to me."

He didn't smile back. "I'm taking you to the wedding."

"As if."

"I mean it." He looked plenty serious.

She thought about what it would be like to sit alone while Becca was in the ceremony. Later she would have to deal with mutual friends and the bride's family. She doubted ducking out early was going to be an option. Which meant she would have a hideous evening. Going with someone would help and it wasn't as if Lucas was someone she had to worry about. He was funny and confident and she would bet he looked really good in a suit. Plus, she would get to dump on Terence about not telling her about the wedding himself and the fact that she was bringing a date. No need for him to know it was all for show.

"You're sure?" she asked.

"More than sure."

"Then I'm going to say yes, and thank you."

"Anything else about oil pressure?" Lucas asked.

Becca was torn between pride and wanting to roll her eyes. "Sometimes people experience low oil pressure at different times of the year. Less of an issue here because we have relatively consistent temperatures, but in other places, like Minnesota, it could be a real problem."

"And?"

"And if that happens you need to pay attention to the type of oil you're using. A high viscosity oil works in the summer because it's really thick and the heat kind of dilutes it. In super cold temperatures, it's too thick and causes problems with the engine. It works in reverse, too. A low viscosity oil in hot weather isn't going to work because it's too loose."

"You're looking smug," he told her. "Do you know what any of that means?"

"Of course. If you live where it's really cold, change your oil with the seasons. Even a place like Phoenix, where it doesn't get really cold, it gets really hot, so you might need a special oil there."

He grinned. "Well done."

She opened the driver's door of her car and slid inside. "I was kind of mad at you," she admitted as she checked her seat position and mirrors. Every now and then Lucas broke into her car before their lessons and changed everything. The man took his teaching job seriously.

"About?"

"Making me learn all about my car. Other kids don't have to. But now that I know everything, it's kind of interesting. Plus, if there's a problem, I can talk to the mechanic." She glanced at him. "I'm thinking of taking auto shop for my elective next fall."

"Does your mom know?"

She laughed. "No, and you can't tell her. I want to see if it works in my schedule."

"It's good to know a few things." He pointed down the street. "Head to Pacific Coast Highway. From PCH, take Torrance to Hawthorne. Go south on the 405 to the Long Beach freeway, then PCH back."

Her stomach tightened. She'd been on the freeway before,

but not for that long and she'd never gone from one freeway to another. She generally got on at one exit and off two exits later.

"You can do it," he told her.

She nodded, checked her mirrors again, then pulled into the street.

"Did you hear about Grandma leaving?" she asked, more to distract herself from her nerves than because she wanted to talk about her family. "She was really mad about Aunt Stacey not telling her about the baby. I don't get it. Why didn't she say something before? Grandma would be happy to have another grandchild."

"It's complicated for Stacey."

"Because she cares about her career more than making sure the napkins match the tablecloth. I think Aunt Stacey is great. She's helping people with MS. That's more important than remembering it's national ice cream day."

She turned onto Torrance Boulevard and got over as quickly as she could. She would be turning left onto Hawthorne, but with a green arrow, so that was okay. She still didn't like turning left in front of oncoming traffic. She was never sure how much space she should leave and usually left so much that the car behind her started honking. Sometimes it was easier to just make three right turns instead.

"Are you dissing your mom?" Lucas asked, his tone sharp. "She takes really good care of you, Becca. She cares about you. You have no idea what it's like to live with an indifferent parent."

"You're wrong," she told him, careful to keep her attention on the road. "She doesn't care about me. She's too busy with work."

"Huh. I wonder why that's so important to her. Could it be that you like eating?"

She really wanted to glare at him, but didn't. Instead she sighed heavily before saying, "It's not my fault my parents got divorced and it's not my fault she kept the house. Do you think I like knowing I'm the reason my mom is struggling? I'm going to be gone in a couple of years and then what? Why couldn't she have sold the house, and then everything would be fine."

"How do you figure?"

"Because my dad pays her alimony and child support."

"You know the child support goes right into your college fund, don't you?"

Um, no. She didn't. Becca felt herself flush. "How do you know?"

"She told me. She'd probably tell you, if you asked."

"But there's alimony."

"Right. You know your dad. Do you think he's paying her very much? And it's going to run out in a couple of years, but sure, she should wait to try to support herself and you because you need attention."

"That's mean."

"That's honest. I'm not saying your mom isn't busy. I'm sure she is. She could probably listen more, but you know what? You could ask her to make time. You could tell her you have something important going on."

"Why does it always have to be me?" she yelled. "Why do I have to be the one to do the right thing?"

She turned onto Hawthorne, got in the right lane, then risked a glance. Lucas's expression was incredulous.

"What?" she demanded.

"Seriously? You're going to pull that crap on me? Like you give in even half the time? Like you're some saint who never pouts or screws up or lies or doesn't do what you're supposed to. Sure. It's all your mom."

"I'm not saying it's all her. Just that it doesn't always have to be me. She's the mom."

"Yeah, she is. One quick question. When is it you?"

"What do you mean?"

"You said you didn't want it always to be you. So I'm asking, when do you take care of stuff for her? When do you get up early to make breakfast or do her laundry, or clean the house, or take her shopping or make sure she's okay? Have you ever once walked in and said, 'Mom, I know you've been working really hard. How can I help?' Just one example, Becca."

She pulled into a strip mall parking lot and drove into a spot, then turned off her car.

"Why are you doing this? Why are you being mean and taking her side?"

His expression was unreadable. "I'm saying that when you diss your mom for no reason, it's not fair and it doesn't speak well of you. You're a good kid, Becca, but you're also selfish and entitled. You expect to be taken care of but you don't offer very much in return." He waved his hand, pointing at her dashboard. "Like this. What do I get out of helping you get in your driving hours? You're not doing anything for me in return. I'm not a relative. You and I don't hang out. So why would I bother?"

He leaned toward her. "I don't expect an answer. My point is, you don't even ask the question. We should all live to serve you."

"It's not like that. I'm not that person."

"Really? When was the last time you cleaned up after Jazz in the yard?"

"I... There's a service."

"Uh-huh. And what else do you do for that dog? You feed her but do you ever stop to think she needs more than just sitting around waiting for you to get home? What about your grandmother? Have you been to see her since she left? Are you keeping up your grades? That was part of our deal—or do you have an excuse?"

"Stop it!" She got out of the car and tried to catch her breath. "I'm not horrible. Stop saying I am."

"Then don't trash your mother."

They glared at each other. Lucas looked way more calm than she felt. She wanted to scream at him to go away, but she couldn't. Not only were they several miles from the house, she thought maybe he was right. Not about everything, but about the driving, for sure. Why *was* he helping her? He didn't have to. Her own dad couldn't be bothered and Becca had never had the heart to ask her mom. Even she could see how her mom was struggling to hold it all together.

He got out of the car and stared at her across the roof. "Get your shit together, Becca. Figure it out because no one is going to do it for you. I see a lot of potential in you, but potential is meaningless until you do something worthwhile. The world is filled with sad people who had potential. Now either get in and finish the route or head back home. It doesn't much matter to me which."

She met his gaze and saw the truth there. He hadn't said anything, but she had a feeling that if she took him home, that would be the end of her lessons with him.

"You really like her, huh?" she asked.

"I respect her, Becca, and so should you."

She waited for a second, then got in the car and started the engine. When she pulled out of the parking lot, she turned right and headed for the freeway.

Chapter Twenty

STACEY READ THE LETTER TWICE, THEN DROPPED IT IN her tote. The written apology from Karl would go in her permanent file, and she'd been given a raise. Her team was doing well. Their latest experiments were moving to the human trial stage, which was always exciting. At her last checkup, her doctor had said the baby was developing nicely. Things could not be better.

She just wished *she* felt better or even okay, but she didn't. She was restless and sad and emotionally uncomfortable every second of every day. The only place she felt at peace was with Bay and her rapidly growing puppies.

She got home at her usual time and called out a greeting to Kit, then retreated to their bedroom to change her clothes. Once she was in yoga pants and a T-shirt, she went to check on the new family.

Bay waggled her tail as Stacey approached and stretched out her head for a quick rub.

"Hi, sweet girl. How are you feeling? Your babies look good. Are you happy?"

Kit walked into his office and joined her on the floor. "Both my new moms are glowing," he said, leaning in and giving her a kiss. "How was work?"

"Fine. I have a written apology from Karl."

"Good. I didn't want to have to beat him up, but I would have done it for you."

Kind words, loving words. He was such a good husband and she was a complete and total mess.

"What?" he asked gently. "Stacey, what's going on? You haven't been yourself for a while now."

She stroked the small puppies. They still had their eyes closed, but they were starting to develop personalities. Bay licked her puppy and Stacey's hand, always the vigilant mother.

"She knows what to do," Stacey said. "The way she handled the birth and now. She's amazing."

Her husband watched her without speaking.

"It's instinct," she continued. "It's very powerful. There are hormones and chemicals at work. Some studies suggest that when animal mothers reject their offspring the hormones aren't present. Scientists are looking for ways to create them synthetically but I think it's going to be a long time until that happens."

"Interesting." His tone was noncommittal, as if he knew there was more.

She felt their daughter move. While she was happy to know that all was well and to have the regular reminders that Joule was growing stronger every day, she didn't feel anything else. No connection, no anticipation. If Kit told her he'd changed his mind and wanted them to give up their baby for adoption, she wasn't sure she would mind very much. Or at all.

A truth that would shock him and probably change how he saw her, she thought sadly.

"Stacey, please. Tell me what you're thinking."

What was the line from that movie? *You can't handle the truth.* But she had to say something.

She kept her gaze on the puppies as she said, "When I was growing up my mom always said there was something wrong with me, that I wasn't like other children. I never cared about that before, but I do now."

She looked at him. "Bunny was right. I'm not normal. I'm not like everyone else."

He surprised her by smiling. "Is that all? Honey, we're all broken. Some of us just show it in different ways. It's okay that you're scared about how you're going to deal with Joule. You're not a kid person and you've never been around babies. It may take a while but I'm confident you'll bond with her and love her. You're going to be a great mom."

"What if you're wrong?"

"I'm not."

Hardly a helpful statement. "It's easy for you. You like everyone and everyone likes you. You're a really good guy."

"And just as broken as everyone else."

"I don't believe you."

"Remember when I told you about being married to Geena?"

His first wife? She nodded.

"She'd had cancer when she a teenager and as a result of that, she couldn't have children. I told her I was fine with it and we got married. At first everything was okay, but after a couple of years, I started to resent not being able to have kids. I wanted to talk about adoption, but she wasn't interested. I loved her, but I wasn't happy and I couldn't bring myself to tell her."

"Because it would be like blaming her for having cancer?"

He nodded. "Exactly that. There was an unwritten rule that we were never supposed to talk about her being anything but whole. Just when I finally grew a pair and was going to insist we talk about the problem, her cancer came back."

He touched her face. "Look at my sister. What she's been through. I grew up with her high, looking to get high, coming down from being high and generally spiraling out of control. None of us is exactly how we want to be. The goal is to be the best person we can be, given our flaws."

She knew what he was trying to say and she appreciated the effort, only he was talking about a normal level of brokenness while she was wrestling with the possibility of being so far from everyone else that she couldn't ever find her way back.

"You're going to be a great mom."

Something she knew not to be true, but she loved Kit and she didn't want him to worry so she kissed him and smiled. "You're right. It might take a while, but I'll get there."

Becca hadn't known what to think about Lucas's lecture. She wanted to tell herself he was wrong about everything, but she couldn't seem to convince herself. She missed her friends, she missed talking to her mom and she didn't know how to stop feeling so uncomfortable with herself.

The only two good things she could count on were Jazz and Ashton. Both were there for her. Jazz was always waiting, just like Lucas had said. And Ashton, well, he was funny and kind and every time she thought about him, her heart beat faster.

They'd shared a couple more kisses, so she was getting better at that. She still thought that sleeping with him would change her enough that everything would be okay, only she didn't know how to tell him she wanted to do that. What did you say? Just blurting it out seemed really impossible, but it wasn't as if she could bring it up in a text.

From everything she'd heard and read and seen in the movies, guys just naturally tried to take things further and further, but so far Ashton hadn't done anything other than kiss her. What was up with that?

"Ready?" her mother asked.

Becca collected Jazz's leash and nodded. "Thanks for dropping me off," she said. "It's kind of far to walk both ways."

"You sure you're going to be able to get home all right?"

Becca smiled. "I know how to cross the street."

Her mother laughed. "Okay, okay, you're right. I can't help it. No matter how grown-up you are, you'll always be my little girl. Have fun, sweetie."

"I will. Thanks, Mom."

Her mother waved and drove off. Becca watched her go and thought about all that Lucas had said to her about what her mother did for her. She was still kind of mad at him, but she couldn't stop thinking about his words. Was it possible he was right? Not anything she wanted to deal with so she turned and studied the complex in front of her.

There had to be at least a dozen three- and four-story buildings. Signs pointed every which way, showing where she could find The Clubhouse and Memory Care. She knew her grandmother was in an apartment building called The Beach House, so she followed the signs to that one. Only when she came to two different paths, there was no little arrow showing her where to go.

She chose right and entered one of the apartment buildings. Sliding doors closed behind her, giving her the sensation of being trapped. Jazz stayed close, her ears forward, her head held high as she checked out the situation.

"It's okay," Becca told her, gently petting her, even though she wasn't sure it was.

The foyer opened up onto a big, airy common room with lots of seating and several televisions on the wall. They were all tuned to HGTV, where a cheerful couple explored homes in Spain. Several old people sat in wheelchairs or on sofas. A couple had IVs attached to their arms and one man was slumped over in his wheelchair.

Becca felt herself start to panic. Why was her grandmother living here? She wasn't old—at least not as old as these people—and she wasn't sick. Why had she left to come here?

A woman in a bright purple nurse's uniform walked over and smiled. "Hi. Can I help you?"

"I'm looking for my grandmother." Becca looked around the room. "I don't think she's here."

"This is one of two skilled nursing facilities. The memory unit is next door." Her tone gentled. "Did she come in from the hospital?"

"What? No! She's fine. She just moved out and I..."

The woman touched her arm. "It's all right. I know this can seem a little scary, but it's not. Do you know the name of her building?"

"The Beach House."

The nurse chuckled. "That's where our wild seniors live. Let me take you to the path and I'll point the way. I know the campus is big and can be really confusing, but once you get to know your way around, it's pretty easy to navigate."

Before they could turn toward the door, a white-haired lady using a walker made her way over. Her attention was focused on Jazz.

"I had a dog just like that one when I was a little girl. I called her Roxie. She and I would play all day long."

The woman reached out for Jazz to sniff her hand, then leaned forward to pet her. But she was short and the walker was wide and she couldn't quite reach. Jazz glanced at Becca, who motioned her forward. Jazz immediately walked around to the woman's side and sat next to her.

"Oh, what a good girl you are," the woman said as she stroked Jazz's face. "Just seeing you makes my day." She smiled at Becca. "You're a very lucky girl to have such a beautiful dog."

"I know. Thank you."

The nurse led Becca out to the main path and pointed the way.

"Turn left at the three palm trees," she said. "The signs will lead you the rest of the way." She hesitated. "Have you thought about training your dog to be a therapy animal? She's so gentle and sweet and I know my residents would love to have her visit."

"I don't know anything about that," Becca admitted. Train Jazz to hang out with old people? Why would she want to do that?

"It's not that hard to get a dog certified. They have to be trained, but you already have a leg up with her. It would be nice for them and I think your dog might enjoy it, too. Something to consider anyway."

Becca nodded. "Thanks for the directions."

She found Bunny's building and walked inside. The main open area was set up like a big living room, with lots of sofas and chairs. There was a stage at one end and what looked like a very complicated karaoke setup next to it. A woman at the front desk smiled at her.

"You must be Becca. Bunny told us you were going to stop by. She's on the third floor, apartment 318. You can go on up.

There's an elevator behind me or stairs at each end of the hall."
She pointed to her right. "That staircase gets you the closest."

"Thank you."

They walked down a wide hallway. There were a couple of classrooms, a computer lab, a huge movie theater–style room and gym. As she walked by she saw a yoga class in session.

She and Jazz took the stairs to the third floor, then found their way to Bunny's apartment. Her grandmother answered quickly.

"Becca! You came." Bunny let her in and petted Jazz. "I've missed you so much."

The warm hug was familiar and comforting. When her grandmother stepped back and led her into the apartment, Becca saw it was about the same size as the one she'd left at their house and all her grandmother's furniture was in place.

"How are you?" Bunny asked when they were seated, with Jazz lying on the carpet by Becca's feet. "Tell me everything. I'm so on my own here. It's not like I ever see your mother."

"Mom said she's stopped by to see you twice already and you're always too busy for her."

Bunny busied herself pouring lemonade into glasses. "Yes, well, I might have a few things going on, but that's beside the point. I should come first."

Two weeks ago, Becca would have enjoyed the bitchfest about her mother, but Lucas's stupid words were stuck in her head.

"I don't understand," she admitted. "You left with no warning. You didn't talk to Mom at all about your decision—you were just gone. She's come by to see you, even though you never got in touch with her, and she's the one in trouble?"

Bunny pressed her lips together. "Why, that's not at all what

I said. How's school? How are your grades? You only have a few weeks left."

Becca accepted the change in subject, mostly because she doubted her grandmother would tell her the truth. "I'm doing okay. Better in some classes than in others. Grandma, what's a memory care unit? Is it for people with Alzheimer's?"

"Why would you ask?"

"Jazz and I got turned around and ended up there. The lady at the front desk was really nice. One of the residents wanted to pet Jazz. It must be sad not to remember things."

"I'm sure it is. Getting old isn't easy or fun, so enjoy being young. Now tell me, what else is going on with you?"

"Just school and stuff. I'm nearly done with my driving hours so I'll be taking my driving test soon. Oh, I've got Dad's wedding coming up." She wrinkled her nose. "I don't know how I feel about that. It's going to be weird."

"I don't think I knew that he was getting remarried. Your mother never tells me anything. Well, it's her own fault she lost Terence. If she'd taken better care of him, they would still be married."

The tirade was familiar. Becca had heard her mother and grandmother fighting about it more than once, but it had never been said directly to her and she wasn't sure how she felt about it. A familiar knot formed in her stomach as she instinctively started petting Jazz. Her dog looked at her anxiously, as if sensing the tension.

"Grandma, please don't talk about that with me. It's not right. She's my mom."

"Since when did you get so delicate? You have to be very upset with the way she's changed, working all the time. Her clients matter far more than her family. It's a disgrace."

"She's taking care of me. Do you think my dad cares? He

doesn't. He's too busy with Alicia and getting married. He
hasn't helped with my driving even once. He never shows up
when he says he will. He doesn't bother to come on the weekends anymore. I never see him. But Mom is always there. Yes,
she's busy, but that's so she can take care of me. You're being
unfair, and I can't listen to it anymore."

She stood and hurried to the door. Jazz was at her side the
whole way. Together they ran down the stairs and out of the
building. It took Becca a second to get her bearings, then she
started for home.

Anger and confusion battled. She didn't want to take her
mom's side, but she couldn't help herself. Her grandmother
was wrong and always finding fault. That couldn't feel good
and to have Bunny so close, always judging...

Her phone chimed. She pulled it out of her pocket and read
the text from Ashton.

Talked to Stacey about the wedding weekend. Want to come
over after the fun and stay here? There's an old show called
Mystery Science 3000 that's pretty cool and lame at the same
time. One of the cable channels is having an all-night marathon. Stacey and Kit are in and it would be fun if you'd be
here, too.

Her heart bounced so hard, it lodged in her throat. A
sleepover with Ashton? Technically it was an all-night TV
marathon, but she doubted a very pregnant Stacey would last
much past midnight and Kit wouldn't stay up without her,
which meant Becca and Ashton would be alone. For. The.
Night! Who knew what could happen. If they slept together,
then maybe the rest of her life would start to make sense. At

least she would have something in common with Jordan again. Not that Jordan was speaking to her, but still.

Love to. I have to check with my mom. Can Jazz come?

Let me know and sure. Miss you.

Her heart dropped back in place as her breathing stuttered to a stop. He missed her? He missed her? Wasn't that really close to him liking her? As in "You're my girlfriend and I really like you?"

Hope burned so hot and bright, she had to close her eyes against the brilliance, then she began to run. Jazz kept up easily, watching her closely as if wanting to know what was going on.

"It's just Ashton," she told the dog, even though it was so much more.

Back at the house, she found her mother in her office with Dean. They both looked up at her, then her mother said, "You're back early." Her smile faded. "What happened?"

"Nothing much. She had stuff to do."

"For a woman who went to an old folks' home to die, your mother has quite the social calendar," Dean said before heading for the door. "I'll go busy myself in the craft room for a few minutes."

Harper waved Becca into his chair. "Tell me what happened. Did she upset you?"

"She didn't. Mom, it's okay." There was no way to talk about all the horrible things her grandmother had said. "I wanted to talk to you about after the wedding. Can I go over to Aunt Stacey's house? There's a TV marathon I want to watch."

"With Ashton?"

Becca felt herself flush. "Yes. He'll be there, but so will Aunt Stacey and Uncle Kit."

Her mother's gaze was steady. "You're seeing a lot of him."

"We're hanging out. He's nice." She ducked her head. "It's not exactly dating, but it's kind of close."

"Do you like him?"

Becca nodded, then looked at her mom. She smiled. "Have you seen him? He's so…"

"Hot?" Her mom laughed. "Can I say that? Does it make me sound old?"

"You can say *hot*."

"Those eyes and his smile. Stacey says he's a really good guy." Her mother's expression turned serious. "You know he's going to college in September, right? At MIT, which means he'll be all the way across the country."

"I know. But until then, he's here. So is Saturday okay?"

"Sure. Don't forget to pack a change of clothes. There's no way you'll want to spend the night in your bridesmaid dress."

Becca groaned. "No one should have to wear anything with that much pink tulle. I'll bring yoga pants and a T-shirt." Anything else would cause suspicion. But she would have on her best bra and matching panties and she'd shave and, well, she didn't know what else to do to prepare. Maybe she should look that up online.

The sex thing was complicated, she thought as she and Jazz went into her room. Maybe it would be easier when she got the hang of it, but even if it wasn't, she was going to sleep with Ashton, and then everything would be better.

Chapter Twenty-One

DRESSING FOR AN EX'S WEDDING WAS A BITCH. WHILE Harper was technically speaking to her mother, she didn't want to ask her for advice or accessories. The subject of Terence's marriage would open a verbal can of worms she simply didn't want to deal with. That left her in the unfortunate position of having to get ready on her own, with her very limited wardrobe and fashion sense.

She figured her black dress was somewhat inappropriate, which left her sleeveless floral print. There was no way she was going to shop for a new dress—if she was going to spend hard-earned money on clothes, it would be for a happier occasion than Terence's nuptials.

In a charming coincidence, the dress—mostly white with swirls of black and a scattering of peach flowers—went perfectly with the very expensive, very beautiful enamel and diamond bracelet Great-Aunt Cheryl had left her. She also put on the big-ass diamond studs. Terence wouldn't notice either, or care, but the bride would and that was good enough for Harper. She finished up her outfit with a pair of strappy black sandals that would be killing her by the end of the evening, but looked good enough to be worth the pain. She'd used hot rollers to get a little curl action and plenty of spray to keep it in place. She went a little heavier than usual on her makeup and called it a day.

After transferring her cell, her driver's license and a credit card to a small clutch, she went to check on her daughter. She'd already done Becca's hair in a fancy braid that she'd wrapped around her head and had helped her apply the perfect cat's eye liner. Becca stood in the pale pink sheath that went under the ballet inspired tulle skirt the bridesmaids were wearing. She sighed when she saw her mom.

"It's pretty hideous," she said. "I feel like I'm five and dressing up for a dance party."

"Imagine what the bride's friends feel like. At least you're young enough to pull it off. They'll just look weird."

"You're not going to say her name, are you?"

"The bride's? No, I don't really see the point. After today I can refer to her as your father's current wife."

Becca grinned.

Harper helped her daughter into the tulle skirt, then fastened the buttons in the back and tied the wide sash. She'd brought along a sewing kit so she could tack the bow into place. Otherwise it would be coming undone every fifteen minutes. Her gaze settled on the backpack by the door. The one Becca would take to the wedding so she would have a change of clothes for tonight.

Harper felt a slight twinge and wondered if she should talk to Stacey about Ashton and Becca. Just to make sure they weren't left alone at three in the morning. Only Stacey was still upset about Bunny's freak-out and Harper was concerned her sister would feel that Harper didn't trust her.

Still, Becca and Ashton not having sex was kind of important, so she decided to send a text, which made her a total and complete coward. Of course a text was also how she'd dealt with Terence and the issue of her bringing Lucas to the wedding. Terence's terse, Do you really have to? along with her saying she did, had been the extent of their communication on the subject.

Families, she decided. What a mess.

"You're beautiful," she told her daughter. "Everyone in the wedding party is going to be so jealous."

Becca surprised her with a hug. "Thanks for helping me today, Mom. And for coming. I know you really don't want to go to Dad's wedding."

"Not really, but then he doesn't want me there, either, so it's kind of a win-win. I get to support you *and* annoy him. What's not to like?"

Becca laughed. "You have style—you know that?"

The compliment shocked her, but she tried not to show it. "Thank you. As do you."

They walked out to the living room. Lucas arrived right on time. He wore a medium gray suit with a shirt and tie the same gray color. The shade brought out the deep green of his eyes and looked sophisticated. The man was a looker, Harper thought, reminding herself that he was only doing her a favor. They were friends, nothing more. In Lucas girlfriend years, she was about a thousand and fifty-seven.

"Are we ready?" he asked, holding out his hand.

"We are."

Harper passed over her car key. His convertible only had two seats, so they would be taking her car.

Thirty minutes later they were pulling in to the Ritz-Carlton in Marina Del Rey. A valet handed over a ticket, which Lucas tucked in his jacket pocket, and they walked inside.

They made their way to the ballroom where the wedding and reception would be held. The huge space was divided in two, with the far end opening on an outdoor area for the ceremony and the reception side spilling out onto a massive deck overlooking the marina. Lucas said he would take care of himself while Harper got Becca settled.

It only took a few minutes to find the bride's room. One of the bride's cousins, a girl about Becca's age, took charge and showed Becca where they were waiting.

"We're junior bridesmaids," the teen said as she rolled her eyes. "It's humiliating."

Becca flashed Harper a smile. "I'll be okay, Mom. I know where to find you and Lucas."

"Yes, we'll be with the unwanted guests."

Becca laughed. "Save me a seat."

Harper left her and found Lucas on a balcony overlooking the marina.

"She okay?" he asked.

"Yes. She's made a friend. Apparently there are junior bridesmaids. I know she thinks she's only in the wedding because of her dad."

"Isn't that true?"

"Yes, but I'm sorry she had to figure it out. I don't want her hurt."

She looked at the huge gazebo covered in flowers and the rows of chairs, then back at the marina view.

"What are you thinking?" Lucas asked.

"Terence and I got married in my parents' backyard. My mom and I made all the food ourselves. We cooked for days.

I'm guessing our whole wedding cost less than the champagne they'll be serving today."

"Is that a problem?"

"No. More of an observation. A big, expensive wedding wouldn't have saved our marriage. What about you?" she asked, mostly teasing. "What was your wedding like?"

A silly question, because Lucas had never been married—had he? She realized she'd never asked. He didn't talk about his romantic past very much, or at all.

His face was unreadable. She stared at him.

"OMG, you *were* married before! Tell me everything."

"OMG?"

"I have a teenage daughter. I'm allowed to say things like that. So, am I right?"

"Yes."

A server carrying a tray of filled champagne glasses paused by them and smiled. "Here with the wedding?"

"We are," Lucas said and took two glasses.

She accepted the one he handed her and stared expectantly. "You have to tell me something."

"I got married when I was in my early twenties. Her name was Lynette, and for me it was love at first sight."

Which meant the story wasn't going to end well, Harper thought as she leaned against the railing. "You don't have to talk about this if you don't want to."

"It was a long time ago." He stood in front of her, looking over her shoulder. She doubted he was actually seeing the docked boats.

"She was beautiful. Bright, funny, charming. We had a big wedding with a reception at a local restaurant. I used most of my inheritance to buy us a great house. I'd never been happier."

Harper started to get tense. "I'm sorry. I was only teasing before. I didn't mean to make you remember all this."

"It's okay. You should probably know what happened. We agreed to start a family and she kept putting it off. One day I confronted her and she admitted that she really didn't want to be married to me, but when she'd moved to LA to start her acting career, she'd realized it was going to be harder than she thought to get things moving. So she found some poor sucker to support her until she could get a decent part in a movie."

Harper moaned. "No. That didn't happen."

"It did. We fought. She left. Two days later she was on a plane to Thailand for some movie role. I filed for divorce that same morning. I'd been smart enough to keep my inheritance separate and the house was only in my name, so I got all that back when I sold the place. Stuck the money in the bank and vowed not to be stupid again."

"Hence the bimbos? They're easy and you'll never fall in love with one of them?"

"Something like that."

"I'm sorry."

"It happens."

"What about her career?"

"She had some minor fame, never made it big. I don't know what happened to her." He glanced around. "People are heading in. Let's go get good seats. I want the bride to see you when she walks up the aisle."

"That's just mean."

He winked. "I know. Pretty great, huh?"

Becca stood quietly through the relatively quick ceremony, but her mind wasn't on the wedding. She'd had a good time with Michelle, Alicia's younger cousin. She'd missed having

friends in her life. But despite the fun, she couldn't stop thinking about Ashton and their night together. At least she hoped
it was going to be their night.

She had to admit, if only to herself, that she was feeling a little sick to her stomach about the whole thing. While she knew
what would happen, she was less sure about how and where. No
guy had even seen her naked. What if he thought she was gross?
And she wasn't sure how she felt about touching a penis. What
did it feel like and did guys know it was kind of funny looking?

Maybe she should wait, she thought, only to berate herself
for being a coward. She wanted to fit in—she wanted to be like
everyone else—and that meant it was time for her to have sex.

Ashton texted a few minutes after the ceremony ended, asking when he could come get her. She told him she was ready
anytime, then went to tell her mom she would be taking off.
She found her with Lucas out by the marina.

"You were lovely," her mom said, giving her a hug. "Are
you having fun?"

Becca shook her head. "It's weird. Alicia's pretty much ignoring me and Dad's busy with his buddies. Can I please go
hang out at Aunt Stacey's now?"

Harper hesitated. "Is there a head table where you're supposed to sit?"

"No. Did you see our table? It's in the very back. The place
cards say 'Becca plus one' and 'Plus two.' She didn't even use
your name."

"I don't actually use hers, so I suppose it's fair." Her mom
hugged her, then lowered her voice. "You have to make sure
it's okay with your father, then sure. Run while you can."

Becca nodded, sucked in a breath, then said as casually as she
could, "You remember I'm spending the night." She turned
to Lucas. "There's a *Mystery Science 3000* marathon."

"I remember that show," he said, watching her more closely than she would have liked. As if he'd guessed what she was going to try to do, although there was no way he could, could he?

Becca waved at them and hurried to find her dad. He was with Alicia, talking to a bunch of people. Her new stepmother glared at her for a second before getting Becca's dad's attention. Alicia whispered something in his ear.

He moved toward her, his expression impatient. "What's up, Becca? I've got some guests I need to talk to."

For a second, she told herself the person he was annoyed with was Alicia, not her, but she knew that wasn't true. Sometime in the past year or so, she'd become the forgettable person in his life. The daughter who didn't matter to him anymore. The realization caught her off guard, as did the bleak coldness that followed. He was supposed to love her forever, she thought. He was supposed to take care of her.

"Becca? What is it?"

She swallowed against the tightness in her throat and said, "I wanted to make sure it was okay for me to leave a little early. You're so busy and I, um, have schoolwork."

"Sure. That's fine. Just stay through dinner, and then you can head out whenever." He kissed her cheek. "I'll call you when Alicia and I are back from our honeymoon."

No, you won't. But she only thought the words, she didn't say them. Instead she waved and walked back into the crowd, as if she was going to join her mother, then she turned and ducked out of the ballroom.

She found her tote bag where she'd left it and ran to the hotel lobby. Ashton was just pulling up. She raced to the car and slid into the passenger side before he could get out and open the door.

"Hi," she said, both excited and nervous. "Thanks for coming to get me."

Ashton stared at her. "You're beautiful."

"Oh." Her cheeks heated. "Thank you. It's my bridesmaid dress. There's a lot of tulle."

He frowned. "What's that?"

"The skirt material. It's called tulle. I think it's French. Anyway, people use it a lot at weddings and stuff."

"If you say so." He pulled out of the hotel and headed south toward Mischief Bay. "How was the wedding?"

"Good, I guess. I didn't really want a stepmother and Alicia doesn't like me very much, but I'm trying to deal. I don't think it's going to get better now that they're married. I mean, if she has a baby I won't exist."

"Family is hard."

There was something about the way he said the words that had her studying him. For the first time she noticed that he seemed tense and he wasn't smiling as much as he usually did.

"What's the matter?"

"Nothing." He shook his head. "Okay, something. I talked to Kit. He…" He glanced at her, then back at the road. "This is his car. He's buying a new SUV for the baby. Instead of trading this in, he wants me to have it. He says I can take it to MIT if I think I'll need it there. Otherwise, I can keep it here for when I come back on break."

Becca tried to figure out why that would be a problem. "That's great, isn't it? Don't you want a car? Now you don't have to walk to work." Plus, if they were dating and she thought they were, then they could go places more easily.

"They're already doing so much. Taking me in, helping me pay for college. They're starting their own family. I'm not even related to Stacey. They're just supportive all the time."

She had no idea what they were talking about. "That's what grown-ups do, especially if they're family. I know Aunt Stacey makes a lot of money and Uncle Kit has a good job." Although he would be quitting when the baby came. Still, they could afford to help.

He stopped at a red light and looked at her. "Is that what it's like for you? You need something and it happens? Get in trouble and you go to your mom?"

"Not all the time." Her happy mood shifted to something slightly darker. "It's not like that. I'm not a kid," she added defensively. "I don't expect to snap my fingers and get everything I want. Why would you ask that? It's just…"

He reached across the console and covered her hand with his. "Sorry. It's me, not you. I've forgotten what it's like to be part of a normal family. I'm dealing with stuff and I shouldn't take it out on you. Forgive me?"

He was so direct, so clear on what he was thinking. She didn't know guys could be like that. "I understand."

"Thank you. So what do you know about *Mystery Science Theater 3000*?"

"I read about it online. It sounds like fun."

"I've seen a few episodes before. It's lame and funny at the same time. Stacey swears she's going to stay up with us, but she's been tired lately, so it's just going to be you, me and Kit, I think."

"That sounds good," she murmured, wondering how late Kit would stay up and if, after he went to bed, Ashton would try to have sex with her. It was what she wanted, she reminded herself, even as her stomach began to writhe at the thought.

The wedding had been lovely. Harper did her best not to be bitter or angry. Lucas's story about his failed marriage had started her thinking about her own failed marriage and everything that had gone wrong with her relationship with Terence. There were some key moments that explained a lot and sadly many of them were her fault.

"We should go," she said after Becca left to meet Ashton.

"No way. We're staying through dinner. The food is paid for and it will be fun. Plus, we wouldn't want to not use the Becca plus one and plus two place settings."

She looked at the huge crowd of strangers, the stunning bride and Terence carefully avoiding looking in her direction. "I'm not sure *fun* really describes it."

Servers began to file out with huge trays of salads. Lucas grabbed her hand and pulled her toward their back corner table.

It turned out that Becca wasn't the only one to cut and run. Of the eight place settings at the table, only one other couple showed up, and they sat on the opposite side so conversation with them was impossible.

Lucas smiled. "See, it's fine. There will be plenty of food. Come on. We'll have a good time."

"You're insisting on looking at the bright side. Why is that?"

"I have a sunny nature."

She laughed, then settled in the chair he held out. "All right. I suppose Terence owes me a good meal or two."

"Was he a jerk during the divorce?"

Lucas angled toward her, as if he were really interested in the answer to the question. A server came by and filled their wineglasses before moving on. She picked up the glass of red and took a sip.

"It's very nice. You should try it."

"I will when you answer the question."

"Fine. He wasn't a total jerk during the divorce—no more

than the average man trying to get free of a marriage and pay the least he could." She glanced toward the head table and watched as Terence picked up his bride's hand and kissed her palm.

"I worked to put him through podiatry school," she said, turning her attention back to Lucas. "We were married and I was really sure we would be the perfect couple, but a lot of people in my life more than hinted he was using me to pay for his education and that he would dump me when he got a good job."

"Including your mother?"

"Are you kidding? My mother was *thrilled* that I was marrying a doctor. I was young and scared and instead of talking to him about marriage and my concerns, I panicked."

Lucas picked up Becca's place card. "You got pregnant."

"That I did. I don't know if Terence figured it out or what. We'd agreed to wait to start our family until he was settled in his practice but instead there was a surprise. Becca was born and I stayed home with her and started turning into my mother. I thought everything was fine."

She tried to remember the last time she'd told this story. Obviously her sister knew the truth and Harper had shared the bare bones with her mother, but no one else. It was too shameful, too humiliating.

"I wonder if that's where our marriage started to fall apart," she murmured. "With that deception. When I was ready to have another baby, I couldn't get pregnant. When I told Terence I wanted us to see a specialist, he admitted he'd had a vasectomy...without telling me."

She willed herself not to think about anything but the words themselves. If she got caught up in the meaning, if she remembered how shocked and betrayed she'd felt, she would cry or scream or do something that wouldn't look good at a wedding.

Lucas stared at her. "He's a dick."

She laughed. "Thanks for that. I was devastated. We went into counseling and tried to put the pieces back together. It worked for a while."

Servers came by with their entrées. Lucas ignored his as he continued to study her. "Did he cheat? Is that what ended things?"

"He did. I want to tell you that I was strong and together and kicked him out, but I didn't. I crumbled, and then he left." She picked up her fork, then put it down. "I was a mess. I hadn't ever really worked, not since Becca was born. I was in no way prepared to be on my own. That's what I hated the most. Being so helpless and dependent. I wanted to be stronger than that."

She grimaced. "I don't expect you to get that. You've taken care of yourself your whole life, but it wasn't like that for me. I was raised to be so damned traditional."

"At least you can blame your mother for that part of it."

She laughed. "One of my few victories."

"Speaking of which, how are things with Bunny?"

She appreciated the change in subject. "Even though she would rather die than admit it, I think she's doing really well. I've dropped by a couple of times. She's always too busy for me and does her best to make me feel guilty. It's a great combination for her."

"You have to admire her consistency."

The lights dimmed as the bride and groom got up to dance.

Lucas leaned close and lowered her voice. "You've got it together now. You're successful with your business and you have your first employee."

"Dean is amazing. He's so creative and we work well together." She smiled at him. "Don't worry. I promise not to be sad and introspective. I know that I've been very lucky and I'm grateful for that." She held up her hand before he could speak. "I know there was hard work involved, as well. I've learned from my mistakes and I've done my best to do better each time."

"If the rest of you would like to join the bride and groom on the dance floor…"

The voice came over the loudspeakers. Harper was prepared to go on about how she was taking advantage of her opportunities, mostly so Lucas wouldn't start to feel sorry for her, but before she could say anything, he stunned her by standing and holding out his hand.

"Shall we?"

"Shall we what?"

His smiled was oddly sexy and appealing. "Dance."

She glanced over her shoulder, half expecting to see a twenty-two-year-old standing behind her. "With me? You do realize I just turned forty-two, right? I'm already taking calcium supplements. In twenty-three years I'll be eligible for Social Security."

"Shut up," he said conversationally, and pulled her to her feet.

They walked to the dance floor, where he drew her against him. Somehow one of her hands was locked with his while her fingers rested on his shoulder. His other hand settled on her waist. Even more stunning, they were standing incredibly close together.

"This is so confusing," she admitted. "Although I'm not going to complain. It's the most action I've had in years."

She half expected him to recoil at her words. Instead he laughed and eased just a little closer until they were touching.

What? No. What? She wondered if she'd had more wine or champagne than she'd realized. Was she drunk? Was Lucas actually dancing with her, their bodies swaying together?

"Are you on any medication?" she asked before she could stop herself.

"You're not a restful person. I never noticed that before."

"Oh, please. I'm an adult woman. That's what you can't get over."

He looked into her eyes, then shocked the crap out of her by leaning close and lightly brushing her mouth with his. Under any other circumstances, she would have sworn he'd just kissed her. But he couldn't have. This was Lucas. He liked them young and fresh and malleable and she was none of those things.

"Did you just..."

"Yes." His green eyes were bright with amusement.

"On purpose? You didn't slip?"

"I didn't slip."

"I'm surprised and wary."

He tilted his head back and laughed. The sound made her happy, so she smiled at him, then rested her head on his shoulder as they swayed together for the rest of the dance.

Chapter Twenty-Two

KIT LASTED UNTIL NEARLY TWO IN THE MORNING. Finally, he stood and stretched, then glanced at Becca and Ashton, who were stretched out together on the sectional.

"I'm exhausted," he admitted, then hesitated, as if actually seeing them. His expression sharpened. "And you two are going to stay up all night."

Becca could see him working out the situation and had a bad feeling that he knew exactly what she was hoping would happen. Okay, not *hoping* exactly. Or wishing. The thought of taking things that far terrified her, but she also knew that if she did it, then she and Jordan could be friends again and she would fit in.

Even as she thought all that, she heard a voice in her head laughing, asking "Really?" in a super sarcastic tone.

Ashton scrambled to his feet and faced his uncle.

"Nothing's going to happen," he told Kit. "You have my word."

Becca felt herself blushing. She couldn't believe what he'd said. Nothing was going to happen? What was up with that?

Why did everything she read or saw in the movies talk about how guys were only after one thing? What was wrong with her? Why didn't he want to do that with her? Was she too ugly? Did he know she was a virgin and think she was stupid or figure it would be so bad as to not be worth it?

Her eyes burned with tears as Ashton offered his uncle his hand. The two men shook, then Kit called out, "Good night," before heading for the bedroom he shared with Stacey.

Ashton turned back to face her. "You're probably wondering why I said that."

"I don't have to wonder." She stood and shoved her feet into her shoes. "I need to get home. It's really late and I don't want to stay over." Not with someone who didn't want her. Didn't want to do that. He'd... He'd...

The world went blurry and she realized she was crying, which only made things worse. Now he would know she was completely desperate and awful and she just wanted to die and—

Ashton pulled her close and held her tight. "You're a lot of things, Becca, but easy isn't one of them."

"Let me go."

"Not until we talk. Please look at me."

She sniffed and raised her head. He groaned before wiping away her tears, then kissing her.

"I don't want you to leave and I figured Kit was about five seconds from taking you home." He gave her a lopsided smile. "He's a very responsible adult."

"So you were lying?" Did she sound too hopeful?

"Sorry, no. I wouldn't do that. The thing is..." He brushed her hair back and kissed her. "The thing is, we're not ready. We're still getting to know each other. I like that we're taking it slow. Don't you?"

"Yes, but guys are supposed to want that, no matter what. Why don't you want me?"

His hazel-gray eyes darkened with emotion. "Is that what you think?"

She nodded without speaking. It was all too humiliating.

"Becca, I know what it's like to make a mistake. I know what it's like to have regrets. I don't want that for you. I like you a lot. I want us to keep seeing each other. You're the best girlfriend I've ever had. This is amazing, so I don't want to screw it up. Please believe me."

Girlfriend? He said she was his girlfriend?

All the tension left her body and she sagged against him. "So we're like a couple?"

"Is that what you got from what I said?"

"It's the most important part."

He chuckled. "Okay, we're a couple, if you want us to be."

"I do want that."

"Me, too." He kissed her. "I want you. You have no idea, and yes, that is all guys think about. But you're worth more than that. When we do make love, I want it to be special and amazing and because we're both ready. Agreed?"

"Agreed."

He released her and dropped to the sofa, then pulled her down next to him. She snuggled close and breathed in the scent of him. Her anxiety was gone, as was her fear. No matter what, Ashton would take care of her. Always.

Harper let herself enjoy the wine-and-champagne-induced buzz. Tomorrow she would be responsible and run around like a crazy person, but for tonight it was so nice to relax in her car and let someone else take charge.

She and Lucas had stayed through the cake cutting. They'd

danced several more times, although he hadn't kissed her again, which was fine with her. One brief almost-kiss was plenty. Later she would fantasize that he'd wanted her desperately but was too overwhelmed to act, or whatever, but for this night, the conversation, the laughter and the dancing had been wonderful.

He pulled into her driveway and turned off the engine. "Here you are. Safe and sound."

"Thanks for driving," she said as she got out of her SUV. "I really enjoyed that second glass of wine."

"And the third?"

She grinned. "That was good, too."

He walked her to her front door. Lucas used her keys to let them in. She walked into the silent, dark house. Becca was at Stacey's, her mother was gone, so there was only going to be her in the house tonight.

"Only one plate at the table," she murmured, petting Jazz and Thor as they came to greet them. That was what it would be when Becca left for college. Just her rattling around in this big house.

"What are you talking about?" Lucas asked as he flipped on the hall lights. Thor walked over to him and gave his hand a quick lick before he and Jazz retreated back to the living room.

"Things always change." Harper waved at him. "Ignore me. I'm fine. Really." She took the keys and tossed them on the entryway table, then dropped her small clutch next to them.

She was going to get into her pj's, wash her face and sleep very, very late tomorrow, she told herself. She turned back to Lucas.

"Thank you again for keeping me company tonight. I had a good time."

He studied her intently. She wasn't sure what he was thinking—probably that she looked old in the harsh overhead light. Or maybe he was wishing football season would start. With guys, you just never knew.

What she didn't expect was for him to take a step toward her, hold her upper arms in his large hands and kiss her. Really kiss her. With lips and tongue and an intensity that made her toes curl in her incredibly painful sandals.

She was so shocked she almost didn't notice the heat that kiss generated. Then tingles exploded along with longing and need and swelling and—

She drew back and stared at him. "What on earth are you doing?"

"I would have thought that was obvious."

"Yes, you were kissing me, but why?"

"You have to ask?"

"Apparently." She did a fast rewind of their evening. "Is this about my marriage ending and everything I told you? Is this a mercy kiss, because honestly, I just can't take that."

He glared at her. "Next time you ask me why I date women in their early twenties, remember this moment. It perfectly illustrates why."

He was so close and so good-looking, she thought hazily. The lingering effects of his kiss were making it hard to concentrate on anything but the way her breasts ached. She hadn't had sex in so long, she was pretty sure she was practically a virgin—wouldn't it be nice to have a penis again? Even if it was just for the night?

"I really have to start dating," she muttered. She looked at Lucas. "Men like younger women, right? I mean look at you. So what? A guy in his sixties." She shuddered. "I should probably go visit my mother more. Imagine how sexy I'll look to the men around there. It's just so depressing to think about, though."

She started to step out of her shoes. Before she could finish the job, Lucas put his hand on her arm.

"No," he said firmly. "You're not having sex with a man in his sixties—you're having sex with me." He shrugged. "If you want to."

She nearly fell over. "You can't be serious. No. There is no way. My God, I've had a child. Do you know what that does to a woman's body? Plus, those girls you date are perfect and I'm not. No, thanks. I don't need that kind of judgment in my—"

He drew her close and kissed her again. Against her will, okay not really, she melted into him. Her body just kind of found his and leaned in. His arms came around her, his tongue invaded her mouth and she let herself *feel*. That was it—just feelings, of his lips and his hands. After a couple of seconds, she realized there was more. Much more.

She jumped back and dropped her gaze. "Holy crap, you have an erection."

His expression was pained. "You really haven't been dating since the divorce, have you?"

"OMG, you want to have sex with me."

Yes, there were complications, yes, this could be a huge mistake, but honestly, who cared? She grabbed his hand and started for her bedroom, only to come to a stop and spin toward him.

"I don't have condoms."

"I do."

"I haven't washed the sheets in three days."

"Shocking but I'll recover."

She bit her lower lip. "I'm not sure I remember how."

One corner of his mouth turned up. "I'm happy to reac-quaint you with everything you need to know."

They had sex. Twice!

Harper lay awake at five in the morning, reliving what had happened and trying not to sigh like a schoolgirl.

They'd gone into her bedroom and they'd done it. Twice! Lucas had been a skillful, slow-handed lover, who had made her body sing with pleasure, then he'd filled her until she'd had no choice but to come again.

They'd gotten up for snacks and in her kitchen, he'd told her to sit on her countertop and she had. Right there, her bare ass exactly where she rolled out her cookie dough, he'd gone down on her until she'd screamed loud enough to wake, well, anyone. Then they'd gone back to bed and he'd made love to her until she'd thought she would cry from the wonder of it.

Now she lay in the dark, grinning like a fool. Happy, content and not the least bit concerned about what would happen in the morning. She knew. They would get up, make small talk, and then he would leave. Before he walked out, she would tell him while she'd enjoyed the action, she had no illusions about her place in his life. She appreciated their night and expected nothing more.

She was going to be mature, sophisticated and unaffected. She would cherish the experience even as she returned to her regularly scheduled life with no Lucas-based illusions and she had to admit, she was damned proud of herself for her attitude.

Stacey watched her sister carefully write out place cards for a bridal shower. Once she'd finished with the names, she applied a spray of tiny oblong glass beads to look like a flower, then dusted the whole thing with glitter.

Stacey understood the concept of the shower even if she'd never attended one in her life. She'd been living out of state when Harper had had hers. The friends, the party, all made sense, but the place cards.

"You're judging," her sister said as she smiled without looking up from her work. "I don't get it, either, but hey, they pay me and that's what counts."

Stacey sat across from her at the kitchen table. "Can I do anything to help?"

Harper passed her a blank card. "See if you can put the flower on that. If you can, then sure. Use tweezers," she added. "Otherwise the glue gets on your fingers, then gets on the card and I'll have to start over. That eats into my slim profit margin."

Stacey pulled the tray of glass beads close and studied the sample card before picking up a bead with the tweezers and putting a dot of glue on the back. She carefully put it in place before reaching for a second bead.

Although she was happy to help her sister, she would rather be home. But that wasn't an option today. Kit and Ashton were painting the baby's room. Even though the paint was supposed to be low fume and very safe, Kit had insisted she leave, so she'd driven Becca home and had asked Harper if she could stay for a few hours. Stacey supposed she could have gone into the lab, but it was a Sunday morning and going into work would seem sad. One of the things she liked about her marriage was spending time with Kit. She liked how they were as a couple and worried the baby would change that more than she wanted.

Harper glanced over her shoulder, then looked at her sister. "Tell Kit thanks for talking to Ashton about the sex thing," she said quietly. "I got a text from Becca about three-thirty saying she knew I would worry, but that Ashton was bunking on the sofa and she was in his room, by herself." Harper smiled. "Apparently Kit was fairly stern and Ashton gave his word that nothing would happen."

"Oh," Stacey said, trying not to sound surprised. Kit hadn't mentioned that to her at all. "You know he's good with kids."

"He is. All that training will be very helpful when he's a stay-at-home dad. Kit's a great guy." Her smile returned, along with some color in her cheeks. "It was difficult having her, ah, gone last night, but probably good practice. College isn't that far away."

Because Harper would miss her daughter. Stacey got the concept and wondered if she would ever bond with Joule enough to miss her when she was gone.

"Does Becca have any idea—"

There was a single knock at the back door. Harper jumped and turned, her expression almost guilty, which didn't make any sense. Then the door opened and Bunny stepped into the kitchen.

"Good morning," her mother said, sounding more determined than cheerful.

Harper blinked a couple of times, as if confused by the visit. Or had she been expecting someone else? Stacey didn't always read the social cues correctly.

"Mom?" Harper rose and hugged her. "What are you doing here? Did I know you were coming by?"

"Can't a mother visit her daughters when she wants to?" She turned to Stacey. "Aren't you going to say something?"

"Hi, Mom." She got up and hugged her, then straightened.

Bunny carried a large tote to the counter and began unloading containers of food and baked goods.

"How are you feeling?" she asked Stacey, eyeing her belly.

"I see you're showing. Not that you wouldn't be, as far along as you are. I assume you're seeing your doctor regularly. And eating right. There's a baby to think of."

Harper lightly touched Stacey's arm. "Mom, stop. Stacey knows what she's doing. She's eating what she should, doing prenatal yoga and following all the rules. You don't have to worry."

"We're talking about my second granddaughter. It's my right to worry."

Stacey looked from her mother to the food and back. As her sister seemed surprised to see Bunny, as well, this wasn't a planned visit. Which meant there was a reason.

"How did you know I was here?" she asked, then shook her head as she figured out what had happened. "Never mind. Kit called you."

"He did," her mother confirmed. "He said it was time for us to be a family again. He said a few things, and well, I realized he was right."

Harper leaned close and murmured, "You know, because a *man* said it, it must be true."

"Harper Wray," her mother snapped.

"Sorry, Mom."

"You don't sound sorry."

Harper grinned. "I can't help that. I'm just so happy to see you."

Bunny studied her for a second, as if assessing the truth of that statement. "You girls have always been a handful. Mark my words, Stacey. You're going to find out what that means sooner rather than later."

Harper moved to the island and started sorting through the food. "You brought enough for an army."

"I thought we could have lunch together. Becca's home, isn't she?"

"She is, and I know she'll be happy to see you."

"Uh-huh." Bunny put her hands on her hips. "What is going on with you, Harper? You're smiling."

"I'm a happy person."

"No, something happened." Bunny's eyes narrowed. "You're keeping secrets."

"What about you, Mom? What secrets are you keeping?"

Stacey was stunned when Bunny flushed and turned away. "I have no idea what you're talking about."

"Hooking up with the cute guys at the retirement home?"

"I am your mother, young lady. You'll do well to remember that."

Harper's grin was unabashedly cheeky. "Oh, Mom, good for you."

Stacey couldn't tell if they were kidding or not. Was their mother dating? Or was Harper just teasing? She returned to the table and continued gluing glass beads onto place cards.

Bunny began emptying food containers into bowls and pots. She nodded at Stacey. "Wash your hands and set the table. Harper, where are your Memorial Day decorations? It's next week."

"I didn't put any out."

Bunny's eyes widened. "You can't be serious. Memorial Day is an important event to celebrate. What could be more important than that?"

"Working for a living." Harper sighed. "Mom, I love you, but no. I am focused on my work. Becca is fed and clothed and loved. As for the rest of it, I just don't have time."

Bunny muttered something under her breath, then turned to Stacey. "Despite the fact that you hurt my feelings and I'm not over it, I'm prepared to be the bigger person." She paused as if waiting for applause.

"All right," Stacey said cautiously.

"I have to admit, I expected a little more gratitude."

"Mom, she has no idea what you're talking about," Harper told her. "Neither do I."

"Oh. I suppose you're right. Fine, I've decided that despite what happened and how you treated me, you're still my daughter." She drew in a breath. "I will come stay with you for two weeks after the baby's born."

"Okay," Stacey said slowly, wondering if there was more or if that was it.

"You don't sound very pleased."

"It's a generous offer, but I'll be home with Kit and the baby for the first three weeks."

Harper shook her head. "Stacey, honey, I'm sure that sounds like enough, but it's a newborn. Mom drives me crazy way more than she bugs you, but in this case, I say accept the offer and stock up on her favorite coffee."

"Harper Wray!" Bunny glared at her. "I'm standing right here."

"I know, Mom. That's why I was as polite as I was."

"You're in a mood."

"Maybe I am. Maybe I'm feeling especially good today." Harper turned to her sister. "Newborns are wonderful and a little piece of hell. Trust me, you're going to want all the help you can get." She lowered her voice, as if trying to keep Bunny from hearing, although with their mother standing right there, of course she could. "Besides, I think this is a peace offering."

"Harper, I swear, if I believed in spanking, I would take you over my knee right now."

"Mom, I can so outrun you."

Stacey glanced between them. She had to admit, their mother was right. Something had happened with Harper, although Stacey had no idea what. Instead of trying to figure it out, she smiled at Bunny.

"Thanks, Mom. Kit and I both appreciate your generous offer."

Bunny sniffed again. "You're welcome. And Harper's right. You'll need to get some of my favorite coffee in the house. It's the least you can do."

Chapter Twenty-Three

AFTER THE SLIGHTLY AWKWARD BUT NONETHELESS heartening reconciliation between Stacey and Bunny, Harper finished her place cards, planned out her week, spoke to Misty, who was still flying high from the HBO success, and managed to not think about Lucas until she was safely alone in her room after watching *Game of Thrones* with Becca.

She stood in the center of her room and stared at her bed, where they'd done it. Yes, there were the other places, but the bed was somehow the most significant. Maybe because it was a bed that hadn't seen action in years.

She hadn't changed the sheets, which meant when she slipped into them, she could almost smell the scent of his body. A nice reminder, but not one that solved her most pressing dilemma. What now? How did she act the next time she saw him?

There'd been no morning-after awkwardness because Lucas had been called into work to deal with a guy who'd been arrested. Lucas had explained something about an open case he was trying to crack but honestly she'd been too caught up in her postcoital afterglow to do much more than smile and nod as he'd dressed, quickly kissed her, then left.

But time had passed and now they were going to be facing each other for the first time since their night of superhot sex and she had no idea how to behave.

She wanted to be cool and mature. Ah, emotionally mature, not old looking. She wanted to smile, greet him as if nothing had happened and move them quickly back to their normal relationship. Wishing for anything else was ridiculous and potentially pathetic. She didn't want that. So, no matter what, she would be totally calm and rational. The sophisticated woman who had had adult sex with an equally sophisticated man and now they were both fine. It would be great—she was sure of it.

Early the next morning, Harper found herself slightly less in control than she would have liked, and most of that was not her fault. The shipping company had lost Misty's new T-shirts, Paula had emailed that she needed to modify the place card order and while she would be paying for the new cards, Harper had just picked up six more hours of work, which was six more hours than she actually had. She was still on the phone with the shipping company when Becca came into the kitchen, Jazz at her heels.

"Mom, I finished the videos for the city. Do you want to see them?"

"I'm on the phone, but when I'm done threatening to kill people, I'd love to."

Becca glanced at the clock and shook her head. "I have to get to school, but tonight for sure?"

"I promise."

"Mrs. Szymanski?" the voice on the phone said. "I've located your order. It's in Albany."

Harper groaned. "As in New York?" Maybe she would get lucky and there was an Albany, Arkansas, because Misty and her show were in Little Rock.

"I'm afraid so. When does your client need the T-shirts?"

"Today. She needs them today." Misty had a show that night.

"Let me see what I can do."

Harper was slapped back on hold, where she did her best not to swear too loudly. Becca waved and mouthed goodbye. Harper tried to remember if she'd eaten breakfast or not, then told herself her daughter was of an age to take care of that herself. She always had spending money.

"Mrs. Szymanski? I have good news. I was wrong about the T-shirts. They're in Little Rock after all."

"That was fast," Harper muttered before she could stop herself.

"I read the code wrong. They're at another hotel only a few miles away. I'm going to put you on hold again and see if I can get one of the drivers to deliver them this morning."

"That would be great." She certainly didn't want to ask Misty to go pick them up, not that Misty would complain, but still. It was her job to make sure Misty's travel was as smooth and effortless as possible.

"All right, I've found someone. He's going to get them now and have them delivered by ten-thirty this morning."

Harper heard the front door open and close. Seconds later Thor burst into the kitchen and rushed to her. She juggled greeting him with taking down the information from the delivery people. Seconds later, Lucas strolled into the kitchen.

The man looked good. She felt her mouth go dry while other parts of her...did not. Her brain supplied perfect memories of what they'd done together, while her gut tied itself in knots and her heart fluttered.

"Morning," he said, then glanced at her headset. He lowered his voice. "I have to get going. I'll see you later."

With that, he was gone. Harper continued to scribble information. When the call ended, she dropped her headset onto the kitchen table and groaned.

Ten words. He'd said exactly ten words. How was she supposed to interpret that? Was he okay with what they'd done? Disgusted? Ready to pretend it had never happened and move on? There was too little information—how was she supposed to obsess over anything if she didn't know anything? Not that a lack of specifics ever got in her way, but still. It was frustrating.

Before she could really get into psychoanalyzing what had just happened, she glanced at the clock on the wall and shrieked. Dean would be here any second and she wasn't ready.

It took her ten minutes to slap on basic makeup and change into her professional *let's meet a client* outfit: black pants, a brightly patterned shell and a tailored black jacket. She slipped into her sensible pumps before racing by her office and grabbing her tote. Thank goodness she'd put everything in it yesterday, she thought as she dashed to the front of the house only to find Dean waiting by the front door.

"Hurry, hurry, hurry," he said with a smile. "We are a tiny bit behind."

"I know and I'm sorry. Misty's T-shirts didn't get delivered and I've been on the phone trying to find them."

"Where are they?" Dean asked as he backed out of her driveway.

"At first they told me Albany, but now it turns out they're just across town, so they'll be delivered this morning. Honestly, I don't know how to make the T-shirt delivery more foolproof. If we ship too early, the hotel loses the package. If we trust the shipping company, stuff like this happens."

"Sometimes you have to accept a flawed system."

"That's hard for me."

He chuckled. "I've noticed that."

They arrived at their destination four minutes before their meeting and went inside. The real estate office was large, with over twenty agents, most of whom were extremely successful. The Mischief Bay real estate market was booming, much like the LA market, and selling houses by the ocean was big business.

Tanya Elliot was an attractive brunette with a warm smile. She led them to a small conference room and offered them coffee. When they were settled, she got right to the point.

"I need help," she began. "I'm not interested in a full-time employee. It's too expensive and the paperwork for payroll would make me crazy. I simply don't have time. I'm at that wonderfully awkward place in my career where I've got more business than I can handle, but not so much that I need a full-time employee."

"Which is where we come in," Harper told her. "You mentioned help with designing flyers, keeping them stocked, along with entering the multiple listing information. Is that right?"

"That would be a huge help."

Dean pulled several flyers out of his briefcase. "These are samples of your flyers. Harper and I looked at several other agents' flyers in the area." He winked. "Including some with other firms."

"The enemy," Tanya said with a laugh. "I keep track of them, too."

The three of them went over the various designs and Harper explained a few modifications she and Dean had brainstormed.

Tanya seemed excited about their suggestions and used the video screen on the wall to pull up a map of her current listings.

"We all have our sweet spot," she explained. "The more you work in an area, the more people get to know your name and seek you out."

Dean walked over to the screen and traced a route. "It would be easy for us to check flyer inventory regularly. What are you thinking? Daily for the first week, then every other day for two weeks. Assuming the house isn't sold by then, we'd move to just Mondays, after the weekend rush?"

Tanya's eyes widened. "I hadn't thought of a schedule being that organized, but it makes sense. That would be great."

Harper made notes. Once they'd agreed on the statement of work, she would send Tanya a contract. "What else could we do to help you?"

"Ushering my listings through closings would be great, but you need training for that. Right now, handling printing and distributing the flyers and keeping the MLS up-to-date is plenty." She glanced between them. "I'm interested if you are."

"We are," Dean told her.

"I'll get you the contract today," Harper said as they rose and all shook hands. "We can start tomorrow if that works for you."

"That would be fantastic. Thank you."

Harper and Dean walked back to his car. She waited until they were driving away to say, "It's a great account. It could be a lot of hours, though."

"Too many?" he asked.

"I don't think so, but it's sending us in a new direction. Real estate is big business. Tanya can't be the only agent who needs this kind of help. The idea of ushering a listing through closing is interesting."

"Let me do some research on what's involved and how extensive the training is. Maybe it would be worth it to offer it as a service."

"That's what I was thinking!"

He grinned. "We share a great mind. It's nice when we both use it."

She laughed. "It is. If the escrow thing works out, we'd probably be looking at hiring more people to help with the other clients. Or we could have one person who focused on the closings."

"As long as one of us was trained, as well."

"Right. So we wouldn't get stuck if our person was away."

He held up his hand for a high five. "See, we're rocking and rolling now!"

The day passed in a blur of activity. Dean left around three to pick up the twins and Harper finished up the new place cards. While the work was slow and sometimes tedious, it paid well, she reminded herself as she got up from her craft table only to realize it was nearly six and she'd done absolutely nothing about dinner.

Becca met her in the hallway. "Hey, Mom. Can we talk about the videos now?"

Harper started to put her off, then realized she'd been doing that a lot these days. Too much, in fact. She saw Jazz hovering close by, as she always did.

"Where's Thor?"

"Lucas picked him up about an hour ago."

And he hadn't stopped by to see her? What did that mean? Was he upset? Avoiding her? What was she supposed to think or—

"Mom? The videos?"

Jazz whined in the back of her throat.

Harper told herself she was healthy, successful in the tiniest of ways and she'd had great sex in the past forty-eight hours. She should shut up and be grateful and deal with what mattered most.

"Did you feed Jazz?" she asked.

Becca rolled her eyes. "Of course I did. I feed her every day."

"Then you're a better mom than me because I totally forgot about dinner. Tell you what. Let's go get Chinese for dinner and while we're at the restaurant, you can show me what you've done."

Becca relaxed. "That would be great. I have the videos loaded on my laptop. Dean said they were good, but I don't know if they're exactly what you were thinking."

Dean had seen them? Harper held in a groan. Was everyone better at parenting than her? She would change that, she told herself as she went to collect her purse while her daughter tucked her laptop into her backpack. Starting right this second, she would figure out how to do it all or die trying. Okay, not die exactly, but close.

Becca sat in her usual place on the front steps with Jazz and Thor next to her. Lucas was due for another driving lesson and she was excited to get in the hours. She was *so* close to getting her license.

Lucas pulled up and waved at her, then got out of his car. "How's it going?" he asked as he approached. Both dogs raced over to greet him.

Becca grinned. "It's going great. I did the videos for my mom and she loved them. She's going to pay me for my time, which means I'm already saving for my car insurance."

She wanted to point out other ways she was being responsible, but wasn't sure how without sounding pathetic and needy. She also wanted to tell him that she was really trying, but he'd want proof. Lucas was like that. He was always there for her, but he sure had high expectations.

He looked at her. "Good to know you're planning on paying for your car insurance. What about your paper for history? Is that done?"

"No, but I'm working on it."

"So you don't have a B in that class?"

"Not right now."

"Okay, then we're done."

"What?"

"Shriek all you want," he told her as he whistled for Thor. "You know the rules. You broke them and now there are consequences."

"You can't do that."

Thor ran out. Lucas led him to the car. When Thor was buckled into the front seat, Lucas turned back to face Becca.

"I just did, kid. You think you aren't treated like an adult. Maybe if you acted like one, you wouldn't have that problem. Let me know when you turn in your paper and I'll take you driving. Until then, find someone else."

"I hate you," she yelled as he drove away. Lucas only waved.

Becca sank back on the step and put her head on her raised knees. "He's being totally unfair," she told her dog. "He's mean and selfish and I really do hate him."

Jazz's steady gaze seemed to make it clear that she knew Becca was lying.

Becca sighed. "Okay, maybe I don't *hate* him exactly, but why do I have to always do the right thing?"

She already knew the answer and shifted so she could hug

her dog. "Growing up sucks," she muttered. "Just so you know."

Jazz sighed in agreement.

The birthing class was the nightmare Stacey had expected. She'd tried to convince Kit that she didn't need to go. She'd read dozens of articles online, including several written by doctors and birthing professionals, and understood what was going to happen, but he insisted they needed to go to a class, just like other couples.

She'd endured a morning of lectures and videos. The afternoon would start with exercises on breathing and mindful relaxation to aid in the birthing process.

A boxed lunch was provided. Stacey picked up the sandwich made with whole grain bread and what she assumed was organic cheese and unprocessed sliced turkey. They sat at a table with another couple. Both of them were in their twenties, as were most of the women in the class. A handful were much younger, but there was no one Stacey's age.

Their instructor was a gray-haired Earth Mother type who wore a long flowing dress and spoke in what Stacey assumed was supposed to be a soothing tone. Everything about the class annoyed her, even the stupid sandwich. She tossed it down and wished she could simply leave.

Kit caught her gaze and winked. His moment of attention relaxed her enough so that she could pay attention to the conversation at their table. It wasn't anyone's fault that she was crabby, she told herself. She would endure the next three hours, and then she would never have to do this again.

"We're having a boy," one of the pregnant women said. Stacey knew she'd introduced herself, but there was no way she could remember her name.

"A girl for us," Kit said. "We're calling her Joule."

The woman frowned. "After the singer?"

"No." Stacey tried not to grind her teeth. "*J-O-U-L-E.* It's a measure of work or energy. It's the amount of force one newton…" She saw Kit shaking his head and sighed. "It's scientific."

"Oh. That's nice. A pretty name with a different spelling. A lot of people are doing that. We really like the name Brandon, but so many people are using that." She smiled at her husband. "We've been getting a lot of pressure to name him Fred, after his great-grandfather, but that is so not happening. Fred? Really?" The woman laughed.

Stacey glanced longingly toward the door.

When lunch was done, the couples returned to their large classroom. Tables and chairs had been pushed aside and thick mats were arranged in a circle. Stacey wanted to question the wisdom of feeding pregnant women, then asking them to get on the floor, but no one was interested in her opinion. She glanced at the clock. Two hours and forty-seven minutes.

"Let's get started with some breathing," Erin, their instructor, said. "Lean into your partner and feel your breath expanding in your lungs and down to your belly."

"Uh, Erin?" One of the youngest mothers-to-be raised her hand. "Does the breathing really help with the pain?"

"Of course it does."

"But if it's really bad, I can take something, can't I?"

Erin hesitated just long enough for everyone to get the subliminal message of how wrong that would be. "You can, but it's better for the baby if you don't."

The pregnant teenager looked crushed. "I'm just worried about being able to, you know, get through it."

"Women have been giving birth for thousands of years. You'll be fine."

The teen didn't look convinced. "But if I really need it…"

Erin's warm expression hardened. "If you go into the process with that attitude, it's not going to go well. You have to have faith."

"Oh, stop it," Stacey snapped before she could help herself. "Why do you do this? Why do you insist on women suffering, as if that in any way helps with the birthing process? Not every natural act is easy or comfortable. A heart attack is completely natural but no one wants one of those. Why on earth would you promote suffering when there are safe and easy solutions to the problem? *You* may not want to go in that direction, but you don't have the right to decide for everyone else."

Stacey turned to the teen. "With a spinal, the amount of chemical that gets into the bloodstream is incredibly small. Many studies suggest it's far better for the mother to be relaxed and comfortable when delivering her baby. Being exhausted, screaming in pain, doesn't help anyone. The chemicals secreted by the body from pain and fear are also delivered to the baby."

Erin's mouth fell open. "Who do you think you are, saying things like that? I'm the teacher here."

"I'm a scientist who works with human DNA to find a cure for neurological diseases, so don't try to convince me I don't know what I'm talking about."

Erin pressed her lips together. "I see," she said tightly, then glanced toward the teen. "I suppose if the pain is too much, it wouldn't be awful to take something."

The girl relaxed. "Thank you."

Behind her, Stacey felt Kit's chest moving. She turned and saw he was chuckling.

"You're not mad?"

He leaned in and kissed her. "Mad? Naw. I'm impressed. I think you just earned your first badge as a tiger mom. Joule's lucky to have you on her side."

Stacey kissed him back, then returned her attention to Erin's instruction. Maybe the class wasn't going to be so bad after all.

Chapter Twenty-Four

"I DID THE BACKGROUND CHECK ON YOUR POTENTIAL renter," Lucas said. "She's squeaky clean. No arrests, only two speeding tickets and neither of those are in the past five years. You did the credit check?"

Harper appreciated the information and the question, but really? Now?

Twenty minutes ago he'd shown up with no warning at ten o'clock on a weekday. He'd asked if Dean was around and when she'd said he was working from home, Lucas had started kissing her. Seriously kissing her, until she had no choice but to respond, then melt, then try not to squee as he led her into her bedroom.

The sex had been hot and fast and incredibly satisfying. Afterward, as she did her best to catch her breath, he wanted to talk about her soon-to-be renter?

"You need to work on your postcoital chitchat," she told him.

He rolled onto his side, supported his head with his hand

and grinned at her. "I would have thought three thousand a month in rent money would be pretty sexy."

God, he looked good. All tanned and chiseled and manly. She was still flush from her orgasm and feeling more than a little naughty, not to mention confused. Not that she didn't appreciate the unexpected delight, but what exactly was going on?

"I have to get up," she told him, thinking that any conversation that wasn't "take me, take me hard," should occur while she was dressed. "Close your eyes."

"Why?"

"Because I'm not sufficiently skilled at draping to get from here to the bathroom without something showing."

"I've seen you naked."

"You've seen me naked and lying down. There's a difference." Was he being dense on purpose? "I'm not twenty-two."

He leaned over her, lightly kissing her, then staring intently into her eyes. "You have to let the age thing go."

"You first."

He grinned. "Point taken." He flopped onto his back and closed his eyes. "Better?"

She grabbed her clothes and ran rather than answer. After tidying up, she dressed and returned to the bedroom where Lucas had pulled on his clothes. They stared at each other across the mussed bed.

"What are we doing?" she asked.

She thought he might tease her with a silly answer, but instead he said, "I haven't got a clue, but I like it. How about you?"

"I like it, too," she admitted. "But I'm nervous. You're used to dating girls named Bambi and Thumper. That's not me."

"I've never dated a girl named Thumper but I get your

point. You want to know where this is going. What are my expectations, which is completely fair. Can I ask what you'd like them to be?"

She held up both hands. "No way. You first. You're the scary one. I'm conventional."

"I like you," he said, meeting her gaze. "I'd like to continue spending time with you."

"Including sex."

He grinned. "Including sex."

"So dating…ish?"

"Dating-ish works." One corner of his mouth turned up. "Now tell me the rules."

Because there would be rules, she thought. *There would have to be.* "Becca can't know. She's dealing with a lot and I don't want to upset her. Plus you're here all the time already, so it's not like that will be different."

"Agreed."

She hesitated, then told herself to just say it. Blurt it out and deal with any consequences. Because if Lucas said no, she would be smart to walk away.

"I want exclusivity. I'm not expecting this to be much more than a fun, short-term thing, but you don't get to cheat. When you're done and ready to move on, say you're done. No showing up at my house with one of your women."

"I wouldn't do that."

She put her hands on her hips. "Was that agreement?"

"Assuming I'm the one who ends things—"

"Oh, please. Lunch meat has a longer shelf life than your relationships." She paused. "I mean that in a nicer way than it came out."

"Good to know. As I was saying, assuming I'm the one to

end things, I promise to tell you and not simply show up with one of my women."

Holy crap! They were doing this. They were figuring out a semirelationship. Was she ready? Was she sure? There were a thousand other questions, but Harper realized they didn't matter. She liked Lucas and she really liked having sex with him. She was going to go for it and figure out the rest of it later. Terence had always told her she needed to be more spontaneous. For once, she was going to listen to her ex.

"Then we're good," she said, glancing at the clock. "What time do you have to be back in court?"

"I've got a couple of hours."

"Want to get an early lunch?"

He pulled her close. "Not really."

"There's a delivery for you in the conference room," Lexi said.

Stacey looked up from the report she'd been reading. It took her a second to return to the ordinary world and to be honest, she found it disappointing. There was so much exciting research being done all over the world. Keeping track of it was nearly impossible and her reading time was precious. Something Lexi knew, which meant she wouldn't interrupt without a good reason.

"A delivery?" Stacey asked as she came to her feet. "What kind?"

"I'm not sure. Reception called and asked you to go check it out."

"That's incredibly odd."

Stacey went down the hall and pushed open the conference room door. The space was pitch-black and it took a second for her to realize she had to turn on the light to see anything. As soon as she did, over a dozen people yelled, "Surprise!"

There were Welcome Baby! banners taped to the wall, piles of presents and trays of food on the table. Even more startling, Kit was there, along with Harper and Bunny, Karl, Max, her team and some of their spouses. While she realized that she was being given a baby shower, she mostly couldn't believe it was happening.

"I know, I know," Lexi said as she ushered Stacey into the room. "I should have asked, but you would have said no. You're always the one telling me to seek forgiveness, not permission. I'm just taking your advice."

Kit came over and hugged her, as did Bunny and Harper. Stacey greeted all her coworkers and their significant others. She was confident she said and did the right things, all the while having the sense of an out-of-body experience. She was observing rather than participating.

"I was so happy when Lexi called," her sister told her. "I'd been thinking about throwing you a shower, but I knew you wouldn't want one. This way it's happening and you're not mad at me."

Stacey smiled at what she was sure was supposed to be a joke, then turned as Max introduced a pretty blonde woman.

"This is my wife, Karen. Karen, Stacey Bloom."

Karen shook her hand. "I'm so excited to meet you. Max talks about you all the time. You are the most together person I've ever met. I really admire how you've balanced your career and a relationship." She glanced over her shoulder, then lowered her voice. "Is your husband actually going to stay home with the baby?"

"Yes. More and more fathers are staying at home."

Karen smiled. "You're so brave. I would never trust Max

with our kids. For a few hours, sure, but not long-term. Who knows what kind of trouble he would get in and what he would teach them." She laughed as she spoke, as if telling a joke, but Stacey knew she wasn't kidding.

"Kit's very excited about staying home with the baby," she said, wishing someone would come and interrupt them.

"If you say so." Karen laughed.

Bunny walked up. "This is nice," she said, shaking hands with Karen, then turning to Stacey. "Maybe later you can show me around the lab."

"Are you sure?" Stacey asked before she could stop herself. "It's fairly scientific."

Her mother sniffed. "Are you saying I'm not smart enough to understand?"

Karen excused herself and quickly walked away.

"No. Of course not. I would be pleased to show you my work if you think you'd be interested."

"You're my daughter. Why wouldn't I be interested?"

Stacey felt as if she'd stepped into a Bunny-created mine-field and no matter where she stepped, she was going to get it wrong. Thankfully Harper appeared.

"I'll keep track of the presents," she said as she snagged a small sandwich from a nearby tray. "Make a note of who gave it to you and what it is. Also, pass me the cards and the gifts, so I can keep everything together."

Stacey eyed the stack of presents and wished she were any-where but here. Even that horrible birthing class had been less stressful.

"And that is so…" she began.

"You can write your thank-you notes," her mother said, sounding scandalized that Stacey would have to ask. "You have to get them out by this time next week, although within forty-eight hours is better."

Because she had nothing else to do with her day? But Stacey knew better than to say anything like that. She and her mother were finally speaking. She didn't want that to change. Despite their differences, Bunny was family and Stacey needed her in her life.

Lexi clapped her hands and got everyone's attention.

"All right, let's get started with the game," she said, and had the group find seats at the table.

She picked up two large grocery bags and turned them upside down in the center of the table. Dozens and dozens of small socks spilled out. Some were obviously for babies and others were for toddlers. Lexi held up her phone.

"You have three minutes. Whoever matches the most pairs of socks wins. Go!"

Stacey watched in amazement as everyone else dived into the pile. There was plenty of laughter and groans as people tried to put the socks into pairs.

"Those don't go," Bunny told Karl. "That's a sheep and that's a cow. They're not the same thing."

"Close enough," Karl muttered good-naturedly before splitting the pair he'd made and digging into the huge mound.

Kit rapidly sorted socks. When he saw Stacey looking at him, he winked. "I hope there's a prize," he told her. "I feel lucky."

Stacey snagged a few socks and realized right away they didn't match. As the pile diminished, she had an easier time collecting pairs, but before she had more than four, Lexi called time.

Kit won with twelve pairs. Sure enough, there was a prize of a ten-dollar Starbucks card. Max rubbed his hands together.

"Now that I know we're playing for real money I'm going to try harder."

Karen smiled at Stacey. "He's so competitive. I have to admit, at first I worried about him working with a woman, but you've really mellowed him."

"I'm not mellow," Max protested. "I'm still a tough guy."

"Of course you are," his wife told him.

Stacey's sense of being out of sync with everyone only increased. She had very little to do with Max on a daily basis. How could she have had any effect on his personality?

They played another game where they had to guess the contents of a sealed brown paper lunch bag by feel alone. The items were all baby-oriented, but some were still difficult to discern. Harper and Bunny tied for the Starbucks card, which Harper offered to her mother.

While everyone else ate, Stacey and Kit opened their gifts. She tried to get him to open all of them, but he insisted they alternate. There were onesies, bibs, little knit hats, a thermometer, boxes of diapers, sheets that coordinated with what they'd already bought, baby wipes, pacifiers, bath sets, lotions, stuffed animals and clothes.

Stacey held up tiny tights and shirts, frilly dresses and pink shoes with bows. Everything was so delicate and girlie, but more than that, it was small.

She knew that Joule would likely be less than ten pounds when she was born and that her body would be proportional to her weight, but still. The physical manifestation of the abstract that was the baby growing inside of her was not comfortable. She'd always feared she would be a terrible mother, that she would never bond with her child and always see her as an intrusion, and now that feeling grew.

Resignation joined terror as she looked at the smiling faces of the people watching her. Bunny was obviously thrilled, Harper was relaxed, and Kit... Well, Kit looked as if he'd finally been given everything he'd ever wanted. He fingered the dresses, the shoes, the stuffed animals and announced that he couldn't wait to be a father. That it was going to be the greatest experience of his life.

Lexi teared up at his words while Max put his arm around Karen. Bunny sniffed and Stacey wished she'd never gotten pregnant in the first place.

Harper tried not to wince as she handed over her credit card. Some of her pain came from the amount she was forced to pay but a good portion of it was left over from the waxing treatments she'd just endured.

Given how busy things were at work, the first and last month's rent, not to mention the security deposit her new tenant had given her and her surprisingly intimate relationship with Lucas, Harper had decided to treat herself to a little TLC. She'd gone to Epic Day Spa for a haircut and highlights, a brow wax and a modified bikini wax. The latter was a first-time thing for her and while she'd been (somewhat) prepared for the embarrassment based on what she'd read online, she had in no way been prepared for the pain.

The brow part had been a little uncomfortable, but when her technician had ripped off those little girl-part hairs, it had been all Harper could do to keep from screaming. She was still walking like a cowboy and hoped Lucas appreciated the effort.

After adding a generous tip to her credit card slip, she signed it and gingerly walked to her SUV. Once there, she checked her phone and saw she had two missed calls—one from Let's Do Tea, and the other she didn't recognize.

She called the tea shop first and spoke to Vera, the owner.

"We're in a pickle," the older woman said. "Our website needs a complete redo. It's old and dated and I just don't know what I'm supposed to say. We have delicious food and tea, come visit us? But I've been told that's not good enough."

Harper chuckled. "Customers can be annoying that way. Do you like the navigation as it is or do you want to change that, as well?" She was happy to update content but didn't have the skills to deal with the technical end of a professional website.

"Navigation?" Vera asked, sounding wary.

"Do you like where the links are and what they do when people click on them?"

"Oh, yes, that's totally fine and all works. It's what's on the pages I don't like. Plus, we're thinking we want to offer a coupon for Tuesday. That's our slowest day and I have no idea why. It's Tuesday—a great day for scones and tea."

"I agree completely. Let me get back to my office and look over the website, then put together a proposal on what I'd suggest. The basic information won't have to change—you still serve delicious food and tea—but with a few easy updates, we can probably make things look fresh and new."

"I'd like that a lot. We were so happy with that flyer you did for us, and the design for the holiday gift cards."

"I'm glad. I'll get you a proposal by tomorrow afternoon, say by three, so I can call after the lunch rush?"

"Perfect. You're a lifesaver, Harper. Thank you."

"You're welcome. I'll talk to you tomorrow, Vera."

Harper sent herself a reminder, then returned the second call to a woman named Phyllis.

"This is going to sound really strange, but my sister uses the landscaping company you did the billing for. The one where everything got messed up?"

Harper held in a groan. Why did mistakes always have a half-life? "That would be me."

"She was so impressed with how you handled yourself. She's friends with the owner and he told her the whole story—how you corrected everything and did a month's billing for free. It's a work ethic I can respect. I own a pool cleaning business. We have customers all over the South Bay area and the billing takes forever. Normally I do it, but I'm getting married and honestly, I want to cut back on my hours for the next few months. I don't want to hire someone just for the billing so my sister suggested I give you a try."

"I'd be happy to help you out," Harper said, more than a little surprised by the odd referral. Maybe Morgan screwing up had a bright side. "Let me call you when I'm back in the office and I have my schedule in front of me. I'd like to set up a time to come by and look at your program and discuss what you need more fully."

"Sounds great. I'll wait to hear from you."

Two jobs in a single morning, Harper thought happily as she drove home. She ran into the house and yelled for Dean.

"We have more clients!" she announced happily. "Let's Do Tea wants a website spruce and a pool service business wants us to do the billing."

Dean walked into the living room, then put his hands on his hips. "I knew it," he said as he circled her. "I knew it in my gut. Lance told me I was imagining things, but I'm not wrong, am I?"

Harper's elation shifted into caution. "I have no idea what you're talking about," she said primly, even though she could make a decent guess.

"Oh, you know. There's a *man*." He pointed at her. "Highlights *and* a brow wax. You've been extra happy. Getting laid happy. Who are you seeing and why haven't I met—" Dean's eyes widened. "Shut the F up. You're sleeping with Lucas."

"What? That's crazy. I'm too old for him. You've seen his girlfriends. I could be their mother."

"Uh-huh, while that all sounded convincing, you didn't deny it." Dean grinned. "He's very handsome and I like his style. I think you make a cute couple."

"No, we're not a couple. We're not." Harper wished she sounded a little more certain and a lot less whiny.

Dean patted her arm. "I get it. You're keeping things quiet because of Becca. Don't worry. I won't say a word." He linked arms with her and led her back to their office. "Now tell me all about the new clients and how much pretty money they're going to be paying us! And after you're done with that, I have a proposal."

"Which is?"

Dean had rearranged the big workspace so that their desks were pushed up against each other in the center of the room. That left the wall space available for cabinets, files and a long worktable for special projects. A big dry erase calendar showed what was due when and there was another progress list for big jobs that had to be done in stages.

Dean gestured. "We're going to need to hire someone to help with all we have going on." He held up a hand. "Before you tell me that getting another person in here freaks you out and that you're not sure how much of this work is permanent and you'd hate to find someone and train them, only to fire them in three months, I have a solution."

"We really do share a mind. That's exactly what I was thinking."

"Scary, huh?" He grinned. "Here's my suggestion." He paused for a second. "Becca."

"My daughter?"

"She's smart, she's responsible and those videos she did for the city were great. Summer's coming up and she's going to want to earn some money. Working here is the perfect solution, especially because she can work for me."

"What do you mean?"

"She'll be my employee, not yours. You and I will figure out what we need her to do and I'll pass on the assignments." He leaned back in his chair. "Trust me, I know all about mother-daughter dynamics. She's a great kid and you're tight and all, but you're her mother, not her boss. I think things will go more smoothly if I'm the one she reports to. The best part is, come September, she's back in school. At that point you and I can assess where we are. We'll have an idea of which clients are steady and which are one-offs. At that point, we can make a more informed hiring decision."

Once again Harper knew she had reason to be incredibly grateful to her sister for suggesting Dean. Everything he said made sense—especially the part about Becca working for him.

"I couldn't love you more right now," she said.

"I know." Dean sighed. "It's a curse, but one I live with. I'll talk to Becca when she gets home from school. Now tell me about our new clients."

"One of them is Let's Do Tea."

Dean groaned. "Do not get paid in scones. I would eat them all and explode."

"Don't worry. I'm not going to risk that for anything."

Chapter Twenty-Five

BECCA JOGGED ALONG THE BOARDWALK, JAZZ AT HER side. She was tired and her back hurt from her being hunched over her computer, but the report was done. She'd stayed up late three nights, had done more research than she ever had before and had rewritten two sections twice, which should have seriously pissed her off. Instead, she felt a weird sense of accomplishment. As if she'd done something really important.

She wanted to tell herself it was just a dumb report to get a decent grade so that Lucas would help her get the last of her driving hours, but something told her that wasn't really the case. She'd done a great job. She'd worked hard and she was proud of herself. It wasn't a feeling she was used to.

Maybe this was what Lucas had been talking about all along—how she had to step up and do the right thing, even if it was hard or boring or whatever. She still missed her friends, still wanted her mom to pay more attention to her, but other than that, she had to admit, she was pretty happy. Ashton was amazing and she loved spending time with him. He always listened and he totally got her. As for the sex thing, it was possible he'd been right. She liked what they were doing.

Beside her, Jazz kept up easily. They left the boardwalk and headed back toward the residential area. Becca slowed to a walk and Jazz did the same.

"We are busy, aren't we?" she said aloud. Jazz glanced at her, as if agreeing. "You're such a smart dog. We should do something with that."

They turned at the corner and Becca was surprised to find that she'd automatically walked toward Jordan's. She stood in front of the familiar two-story house for nearly a minute before marching up to the front door and ringing the bell. Jordan answered, then frowned.

"What do *you* want?"

"You were wrong," Becca told her. "I was your friend and I told you the truth because I care about you. I was protecting you from something bad and you punished me for that. Our friendship had value and you threw it away for a stupid guy. One day you're going to regret that."

She turned on her heel and walked away. Jazz kept pace. When they reached the corner, Becca began to run again.

Back home, she gave Jazz fresh water, then began researching online. The steps to getting Jazz certified as a therapy dog were straightforward. She had to pass the AKC Canine Good Citizen test and pass a Therapy Dog Temperament test. Becca found a local volunteer organization in Santa Monica that offered both kinds of tests.

"I'm pretty sure you're going to be able to pass easily," Becca told her dog. "Oh, look. I have to take a one-day class to be your handler." She grinned. "Wouldn't you know it? I'll have to go to classes more than you. Why am I not surprised?"

She thought about the old people where her grandmother

lived. It would be scary to go there, but they seemed to like Jazz and it would be something for her dog to look forward to.

Becca printed the application she had to fill out and noted the date of the next handler class before doing a search on dog agility. She watched a couple of videos on YouTube.

"You could so do that," she murmured. "Want to see?"

Jazz didn't raise her head.

"I get it. Dogs don't watch videos." She typed on her keyboard and found a local park class that taught basic agility. The registration fee made her swallow hard, but that was nothing when compared with what she found when she went looking for the equipment.

"Jazz, there's only one way this is going to work. You're going to have to get a job in television or as a model."

Stacey sat in her car for a second. She had to rally so she could walk the last ten feet from the garage to the house. For some reason, she'd been exhausted for a couple of days. Maybe Joule was having her prebirth growth spurt and that was using up all of Stacey's resources. Maybe it was her last-minute push to get as much work done as she could before she went into labor. Whatever the reason, all she wanted to do was crawl into bed and sleep for days. She was so tired she didn't even want to bother with dinner.

But she would, she thought as she got out of the car and walked into the house. Because her baby needed the nutrition and it was what she should be doing. If only her ankles weren't so swollen and her back didn't hurt.

She found Ashton on the family room floor with the puppies crawling all over him and Bay watching from a safe distance. The mother dog looked as tired as she felt. Having a baby, or raising puppies, wasn't easy.

"Hey," Ashton said, barely glancing up from the game. "How was your day?"

"Good. And yours?"

"Fine. Somebody called in sick, so I got a couple of extra hours today. Woohoo."

She smiled as she set down her backpack and pulled out her phone, then set it on the entry table. "Did you get your last assignment in?"

The question was more about conversation than concern—Ashton always did what he was supposed to. She only checked up on him because she wanted to make sure he knew she and Kit were interested in him and the articles she'd read said it was important. From her point of view, Ashton was more than capable of taking care of himself. She hoped that over the summer their relationship could evolve such that she was able to make him feel loved and welcome without having to ask stupid questions.

He didn't bother looking up from the television. "I'll do it later."

She was halfway to the kitchen, but came to a stop. "It's due this week. You said you'd have it done by now. You have to finish the class to graduate. If you don't graduate, you won't be able to go to MIT."

He looked at her. "Relax, Stace. I've got it handled."

She wanted to correct him. Having it handled would mean having it done. Unease joined exhaustion and she honestly didn't know what to say to him.

Bay glanced at her as if following the conversation. Stacey wanted to ask the dog for advice, but that was ridiculous. Ashton was a mature teenager and he would do the right thing. She was sure of it.

Only the unease followed her into the kitchen as she began

to prepare dinner. Kit had his support group that night. He'd made friends with several of the men and they met early to have dinner together. As always, he'd left her an easy dish that only had to be reheated.

She put the lasagna in the oven to warm and assembled a salad, then headed to her bedroom where she changed into maternity yoga pants and a T-shirt before walking back into the kitchen.

Bay joined her. After stroking the dog for several minutes, Stacey fixed her dinner and set her bowl in the corner of the eat-in kitchen. Bay began to eat.

One of her puppies trotted up and began sniffing at the food, then turned his attention to his mother's ankle and began to chew. Bay stopped eating long enough to make a low sound in her throat. The puppy ignored her and continued to chomp on her foot. Bay growled louder. The puppy immediately stopped and began to back away.

"That's telling him," Stacey said as she scooped up the puppy. "Did you hear that? You should listen to your mom. She knows what she's talking about."

The puppy licked her nose.

Stacey was about to set him on the ground, when she got what had just happened. The puppy had done something wrong. Bay had issued a warning, then a sterner instruction, and the puppy had listened. She and Ashton were completely different, but still… It might work.

She walked into the family room and turned off the television.

Ashton frowned. "Why'd you do that?"

"You told me you would finish your last assignment several days ago. You said you had less than thirty minutes of work to do. Dinner's going to take about that long. Please get it done now, before dinner."

His mouth straightened and his eyes narrowed. He stood and took a step toward her in an obvious attempt to intimidate her with his size. Honestly, the males of every species were just so predictable.

"You're telling me what to do? For real?"

She was tired, huge, swollen and only a couple of weeks away from giving birth. She didn't have the patience for any of this.

"No, Ashton. For fake. You told me you would do the work and you didn't, so I'm asking you to do it now. Unless you're comfortable lying to me and if that's the case, we have a bigger problem. Go finish the damn homework now so we can get on with our evening."

He hesitated as if considering his options. She had no idea what she would do if he flat-out refused to do his homework. If only Kit were here—he would have handled the situation so much better.

"Fine," Ashton grumbled. "I'll go do it now. Then can I watch the game while we have dinner?"

"Sure."

He started for his bedroom, then stopped and returned to her. After taking the puppy from her, he shocked her by pulling her into a hug.

"Sorry," he said as he released her. "You're right. I've been a butt. I really will go do it and finish out my class."

"Thank you."

Still carrying the puppy, he retreated to his room. She sank onto the sofa and covered her face with her hands. There was no way she was ever going to figure out parenting. It was hard and unpredictable and she just plain didn't want to. But based on the size of her belly, it was too late for second thoughts.

Harper moved her fingers as quickly as she could. The pattern was familiar and guilt fueled her speed.

"Mom, you're really intense."

"I know. I can't help it. I'm a terrible sister. Lightning is going to strike me for sure." She glanced at her daughter, then returned her attention to her knitting. "You might want to sit across the room in what would be considered the safety zone."

"You know Aunt Stacey doesn't care, right? She's not into all that baby stuff."

"Maybe not, but I have an obligation."

One that had gotten lost in the past couple of months. Her sister was due in less than two weeks and Harper hadn't made her anything. Yes, she'd been there for the shopping for the baby furniture and after Kit and Ashton had painted the room, she'd helped with the setup and she already had a week's worth of casseroles in the freezer to take over after the birth, but still.

"I ignored decorating for Memorial Day and now it's all going to hell."

"How's this?"

Becca held up a small cap done in a pale yellow. Harper had already crocheted most of the tiny flowers she would sew onto the cap. On the table were the completed pink tiger hat she'd made, along with a summer dress that would match Becca's cap. She was going to do a quick blanket and maybe a bunny hat and hope that was enough to keep her from a fiery end.

"It's perfect," Harper told her daughter. "Thank you so much for helping out."

"You're welcome."

Harper realized she couldn't remember the last time she

and her daughter had done something together other than eat. They didn't hang out much anymore. Or ever. Some of it was because Becca was older now and had more going on in her life and some of it was Harper being busy trying to keep her business and the family afloat.

She thought about all the time she and Becca had spent together over the years. Craft projects and afternoons making cookies or quick breads. How sad those opportunities had drifted away.

"How are your driving lessons coming?" she asked, hoping to start a conversation. "Lucas mentioned you were doing well."

Becca made a face. "I'm kind of mad at him right now."

Harper's heart froze at the horrifying possibility of her daughter knowing about her affair. Would Becca—

"But maybe he was right," her daughter continued, then looked at Harper and smiled. "I had to do a makeup paper for my history class and I wasn't done with it, so he wouldn't go driving with me the last time. I was so pissed, but then I kind of realized he was only trying to help me be more responsible and mature."

"That is so unfair," Harper said before she could stop herself. "If I'd done that to you, you wouldn't have spoken to me for a week!"

She immediately wanted to call back the words. Why was she screwing up a perfectly nice moment with the truth?

Becca stunned her by grinning and saying, "You're right. I would have been mad and pouted. But at least you have coupons you can use to make me behave."

Harper didn't know what to say to that so she cautiously asked, "Where are you on the report now?"

"It's done. I'm going to turn it in tomorrow. I spent a lot

of time on it and I'm really happy with how it came out." She made a face. "I thought history was boring so I didn't pay attention. Lucas told me that I can't just participate in the fun parts of life. He asked if I thought you enjoyed all the stuff you do for me, and while I want to say that you have to like it because I'm your kid, I guess cleaning the toilet is never fun."

"It's not my favorite," Harper admitted, wondering what else Lucas had discussed. Not that she didn't trust him, but talk about being close-lipped. The man had depths. It was kind of nice to know he was more than a pretty face who was good in bed.

"According to the emails I've gotten from your teachers, you're doing well in your other classes," Harper said.

"It's been a good semester. I'm supposed to focus on my precollege classes for next year, but I really don't know what I want to study or be. I don't know why we have to decide so early and college is expensive."

"Don't worry about the money. We'll figure it out." She'd been saving as much of the child support as she could and she would bully Terence into helping. Plus, with the new renter and the business growing, thanks to Dean, there was a little left over every month.

"It's hard to know what you want to do with your life at seventeen," she added. "These days, it seems like everyone has three or four careers."

"That makes my decision confusing," Becca admitted. "All the articles they make us read talk about using our passions as a guide, but I'm not sure I have any." She finished the last row on the hat and cut the yarn, then took a needle and wove the strand into the pattern so it was secure and undetectable.

"Mom, I want to get Jazz certified as a therapy dog and take her to where Grandma lives. There's a memory unit and a skilled nursing facility. I've talked to the manager there and once Jazz has passed her tests, she said I can bring her by. I promise it won't get in the way of my hours working for Dean. I'm going to need a senior project next year anyway and I thought it could be about working with old people." She wrinkled her nose. "I think Jazz would like it a lot and it's easier to get your project approved if it involves volunteering."

Harper stared at her daughter. "I think that's a great idea. What made you think of it?"

"When I went to see Grandma the first time, I got lost and ended up there. It was scary because they were old and some were really sick, but Jazz didn't mind."

Harper had the sense of having missed a big portion of her daughter growing up. When had Becca become so caring and thoughtful? She'd been that way as a little girl, but over time, she'd turned into a teenager. Was she morphing back into who she'd been?

"I'd like to come along when you go," Harper told her. "If that's okay."

"Sure. We can go see Grandma and stock up on cookies and brownies."

"Because she's still making them nearly every day."

Harper knew her mother would never admit it, but she was enjoying her new life at the retirement community. She'd made friends, there was lots to do, plus she got to complain about her children. What could be better? Stacey had pointed out there were lots of single men there, but despite joking about it before, Harper couldn't deal with the thought of her mother dating. Yes, Bunny was relatively young, and yes, Harper didn't feel that her mother had to live alone for the rest of her life, but honestly, she could not wrap her mind around her mother having sex. No doubt that was exactly how

Becca would feel if she knew about Lucas. Not that anyone was going to tell her.

"Dean suggested I make videos of my training with Jazz," Becca said, starting another hat. "When I have them edited, he said I should show them to the trainer to see if she wants to hire you guys to update her website."

"Dean's quite the idea man. Are you going to be okay working for him?"

Becca rolled her eyes. "Oh, Mom, you know I couldn't ever work for you. We'd fight all the time. You're so bossy."

"Hey!"

Her daughter grinned. "Well, you are, but it's okay. I'm very happy with my job. Thank you for letting Dean hire me. I promise to do my best."

"I know you will, honey." She finished the tiny flower she would sew onto the hat Becca had completed. "When we're done with this, want to go out for dinner?"

Her daughter's eyes widened. "You mean eat food someone else prepared? Are you sure that's okay?"

"Stop it. We can bring Ashton along, if you'd like." Harper did her best not to smirk. "I haven't spent much time with your new boyfriend. I'm sure there are a lot of questions I should be asking him."

"You wouldn't."

"I absolutely will, but I'll try very hard not to embarrass you...too much."

Becca groaned and reached for her phone. "Let me see if he's around," she said, already typing in the message. "But no pictures from when I was little. You have to swear."

"Cross my heart."

Becca was still smiling as she sent off her text. Harper watched her and felt her heart fill with more love than she could have ever imagined. This young woman was the best part of her. How could Terence have so little to do with her? Before the wedding, he'd never been around and once he got back from his honeymoon, she doubted things would get much better.

She was going to have to talk to him, again, and somehow convince him that his daughter was important and if he didn't think so, he had to see that she needed him. If that didn't work, she was pretty sure Lucas knew a guy willing to beat up Terence for a price.

Chapter Twenty-Six

BECCA SET THE FOLDER ON MRS. NEMECEK'S DESK. "I did it. The paper is longer than you requested. I added a couple of maps." She paused. "I thought about pictures, but that seemed like too much."

Her history teacher didn't pick up the folder or even acknowledge it. Instead she asked, "What did you write about?"

"Germany's decision to invade Russia. Why Hitler did it and what were the consequences."

"Such as?"

"He couldn't invade Russia and Great Britain at the same time. Even he didn't have the resources. From our perspective, going into Russia is suicide—the land mass is too big and there are too many people. But back then, it made sense. Germany had resources and a trained army. The Russians had to draft people to protect their country. They didn't know how to fight or have weapons."

Mrs. Nemecek looked skeptical. "I asked you to make me feel something, Becca. You're giving me information."

Becca shifted her weight from foot to foot. "It's in the paper.

The fighting was awful. The Russian commanders had orders to kill any deserters. There wasn't any food or weapons. Hundreds of thousands of people starved to death. In the Battle of Stalingrad, if you were a new private, you probably wouldn't last more than a day and they were like my age. I can't imagine what they went through and then they died and no one cared."

Mrs. Nemecek gave her a rare smile. "I look forward to reading your paper. I'll post your grade before the end of the semester."

"Thank you. I appreciate that you gave me this chance."

"You're welcome, Becca. Try to remember that while you won't enjoy every class you take, if you make an effort, you can always learn something."

Becca nodded and left. Ashton was waiting for her in the hall.

"How did it go?" he asked.

She shrugged. "I don't know. I hope she likes it." She was about to say it was because she wanted the good grade so Lucas would help her finish her driving hours, but she realized it was more than that. She wanted to get a good grade because she'd worked hard and had something to prove.

Ashton took her hand and led her out of the building. "You did your best, right?"

"Uh-huh."

"Then let it go. Feel the freedom of having turned in your last paper."

"I still have finals."

"But, for this afternoon, you're young, you're happy, you're with me."

She laughed. "I am with you."

"Next up, agility equipment for Jazz."

Becca's good mood evaporated. "Yeah, I don't think that's gonna happen. It's really expensive."

"That's why we're going to explore used. You have the address?"

Becca pulled a small piece of paper out of her back pocket. She'd found someone selling agility equipment online. It looked a bit battered in the picture, but was so much cheaper than anything new. Becca had her savings and she would be working for Dean, so she would have some money, but no way could she afford the lessons and the equipment unless she could get a good deal.

They drove to the Culver City address the seller had given her. A fortysomething black-haired woman greeted them at the door and led them around to the backyard.

"I only used it for a couple of years. Hero, my dog, had some trouble with his hips, so we had to let the training go. It's real good quality."

Becca didn't say anything. The ad had offered the equipment for five hundred dollars. She had two hundred in cash—it would clean her out, but be a really good start for Jazz. There were cheap kits online for less than that, but everything she'd read said not to waste her money. Jazz was too big, too strong and powerful and she would tear up the lightweight plastic in a few sessions.

As promised there were jumps, rings, weave poles, even a teeter-totter. The chute tunnel had a couple of tears, but otherwise was in good shape. But the price...

"How much?" Ashton asked.

"Five hundred and that's firm."

Becca's heart sank. Saving to get five hundred dollars seemed impossible, especially with her car expenses and the cost of the training classes.

Ashton walked over to the weave poles. "I could make these out of PVC pipe. That's the white plastic pipe. I could just cut it into poles and we'd stick them in the ground."

Becca studied the poles and realized he was right. "We could make a chute tunnel," she said slowly. "My mom can sew anything. I think she has special needles to work with plastic." She smiled. "She makes all our seasonal outdoor flags out of waterproof material."

Maybe she should look online for DIY instructions for making the rest of it. At least for now. Lucas would help, and Ashton. She was only going to be working about thirty hours a week. Even with Jazz's classes and visiting the memory unit, she would have time to—

"I knew it," the dark-haired women said. "You're trying to get me to reduce the price."

"I was hoping you would, but I only have two hundred dollars, so there's no way we can make this work. Thank you for your time."

Becca and Ashton started for his car.

"Wait!" The woman hurried after them. "Do you have it in cash?"

Becca pulled the bills out of her jeans front pocket. "Right here."

"Dammit."

The woman looked from the equipment to the cash, then sighed. "Fine. Just take it. I'm tired of looking at it anyway."

Becca handed over the bills. The woman counted them.

"I'd like a receipt," Becca told her.

"Of course you would. Fine. I'll go write it up while you load everything in the car."

Fifteen minutes later, they squeezed all the equipment in

the car. Becca had to share the passenger space with the weave poles and flattened chute tunnel, but she didn't mind.

"Mom and I never use the backyard anymore," Becca said, hoping she didn't sound too young in her excitement. "The patio sometimes, but never the grass. I can set all this up right away. Jazz is going to love it. She's really smart and athletic. She doesn't have a strong hunting drive like some breeds, but she's a working dog, so she'll do what she's supposed to because it makes her feel good."

Ashton grinned at her. "Someone's been doing her homework on the topic." Before she could decide if he liked or didn't like that about her, he added, "I always wanted a smart girlfriend and now I have one."

She laughed. "Let's wait and see what Mrs. Nemecek gives me on my paper before we say if I'm smart or not."

"I don't need your teacher to tell me, Becca. I already know."

Happy words that made her feel all squishy inside, she thought. Very happy words.

Harper knew it was a cliché, but she actually felt like a new species at a zoo exhibition. Everyone was friendly enough and there was lots of chatter, but the sense of being stared at would not go away.

Lucas had invited her to a barbecue at his partner's house. Kirk Beldon was also a detective at the LAPD and he also lived in Mischief Bay with his wife and son. There were probably twenty or twenty-five people milling around in the backyard. Tables had been scattered around and the barbecue was on the patio. A few young kids ran around and played, chased by a very strange alien-looking dog with fluffy white hair and a pink T-shirt trimmed in rhinestones.

"This is Lulu," Lucas said, scooping up the dog as she ran past. She immediately relaxed into his arms and gave his chin a quick lick. "She's a Chinese crested with very delicate skin. So she wears clothes and sunscreen and probably has her own masseuse." He gestured to a fiftysomething woman sitting with a familiar-looking man with gray hair and a trimmed beard.

"That's Pam, her mom." He frowned. "Pam is also Jen's mom. Jen is Kirk's wife. Their son Jack is the crazy toddler running around and talking up a storm."

Harper tried to keep up. "Jen's the one who's pregnant?"

"They're having a girl in a couple of months." He pointed to a pretty dark-haired woman around thirty with a baby in her arms. "That's Zoe. She's Jen's best friend. See the guy with Pam?"

"Yes."

"That's Miguel. He and Pam are a couple and Zoe is his daughter. She's marrying Pam's son Stephen in September. They have a little girl who's about seven months old."

Harper looked at him. "Jen's best friend is married to Jen's brother and Jen's mother is dating her best friend's father?"

"It's kind of a soap opera."

"There's an understatement." She watched everyone interact. "They seem lovely."

"They are. After I was shot, Jen made me move in with her family while she took care of me."

Because he didn't have anyone else, Harper thought. Lucas didn't have family and it wasn't as if any of his girlfriends would have been capable.

"That was nice of her."

Lucas watched Jen as she checked on her guests. "She's special."

There was something about the way he said the words.

Harper wondered if there was more between Jen and Lucas than either of them wanted to let on. She had her chance to find out a few minutes later when Jen came over and smiled at Harper.

"I'm heading in to assemble salads. Want to help?"

A very innocent question, but Harper had a feeling there would be a test of who could grill the other better.

"I'd love to." She turned to Lucas. "You going to be okay by yourself?"

"I'll manage."

Harper took her glass of white wine with her and followed Jen into the house.

The kitchen was large and well laid out. There was a small table for Jack and plenty of storage. Jen began pulling different ingredients out of the refrigerator. She was barefoot and pretty in cropped pants and a maternity T-shirt with an arrow pointing to her belly. The text on the shirt proclaimed Future Madam President.

"Thanks for inviting me," Harper told her. "This is nice."

"You're welcome. I'm glad to finally meet you. Lucas hasn't said much so we're all curious."

"I'm sure you are."

The two women looked at each other. Harper was still trying to figure out what she could ask without seeming rude when Jen drew in a breath and spoke.

"I'm going to address the elephant in the room," she said. "You're not his usual type."

"You mean I'm not a twenty-year-old airhead? I mean it's not like there aren't plenty of intelligent pretty women in their twenties, but does he date those? Of course not. A lack of brainpower seems to be a prerequisite."

"Right?" Jen laughed. "Although I like to think the smart

ones aren't interested in dating a guy about the same age as their dad."

"Or older."

"So true."

They smiled at each other.

"I can't explain it," Harper admitted. "I'm a virtual assistant. Lucas hired me last year after he'd been shot in the line of duty. While he was in the hospital and living here, a lot of his bills went unpaid. He didn't want that to happen again, so he has me manage that part of his life. We've been friends for a while and now we're seeing each other."

"So you knew about the girls he dates from the start?"

"He would bring them around, which makes him and me totally unexpected."

"I'm glad he found someone normal," Jen told her. "He's a good guy."

"He speaks highly of you, as well." Harper let the words just hang there.

Jen's eyes widened. "Oh, I just got that. No. He and I are friends. Good friends. He was brutally honest with me at a time when I needed to hear the truth, but that's all. Kirk is the love of my life and I'm lucky to have him."

Tension Harper hadn't acknowledged eased. "It's good to have friends."

"It is. I hope you and Lucas make it work."

Harper nodded, but otherwise didn't respond. Her and Lucas? She had her doubts about it lasting. Yes, he was great and she really liked being with him. While the sex was fantastic, she enjoyed his company even more. He was funny, smart, kind and an all-around great guy. She couldn't imagine…

No. No! Absolutely not. She would not, could not, fall for him. She was some pit stop as he made his way through a romantically uncommitted life. All his relationships came with a rapidly dwindling shelf life. She was many things but stupid wasn't one of them. Lucas was not someone who stuck around. He never had. She would enjoy what they had while it lasted, and then happily move on. No matter what.

Becca finished her lunch, then pulled out her geometry book. If she did her final review now, she wouldn't have to take her book home and do it later.

She worked through the first final practice problems fast enough, then stumbled over number nine. There was always one, she thought with a smile.

"What's so funny?"

She looked up and saw Jordan standing by her table.

Becca had taken to sitting outside on the rear patio. None of the cool kids wanted to be there—it was quiet and sort of hidden. When you were popular, it was important to be seen. In the last few weeks, as Becca had found herself more and more ostracized from her friends, she'd taken refuge in the solitude. At least out here she didn't have to worry about anyone noticing that she was alone. After a while, she'd discovered there were advantages to having an extra half hour to do her homework.

"Nothing much." Becca closed her book and slid her homework into her folder.

Jordan surprised her by sitting down. "I never see you anymore. What have you been doing?"

Becca didn't know how to answer that. The reason she and Jordan didn't hang out was because Jordan's boyfriend was a jerk and Jordan was a bad friend. Probably not what she should say, Becca told herself. She searched for a more politically correct truth and decided on, "I'm spending a lot of time with Jazz. We're going to classes so she can be certified as a therapy dog."

Jordan's expression was blank.

"Jazz is the dog Great-Aunt Cheryl left me."

"Uh-huh. So she'll come to school with you and stuff?"

Becca did her best not to roll her eyes. "She'll be a therapy dog, not an emotional support animal. I'm going to take her to the memory unit at a retirement community where she can hang out with the residents there. She had to complete a bunch of training, which is part of what I'll be doing this summer. I've already talked to my counselor about making that my senior project."

Jordan groaned. "That sounds great. I have no idea what I'm going to do. You know they love it when we volunteer. Ugh. I don't want to hang out with a bunch of homeless people or sick kids or anything." She winced. "That sounded meaner than I meant."

"It's okay. I got scared when I first went to the memory unit, but the lady who runs the service animal program says I'll get used to it. Jazz needs to be busy and this is something that can help her and other people."

Becca was surprised at how mature she sounded. It was kind of impressive.

Jordan played with the strap on her backpack. "I've seen you around. You were with some guy last weekend, getting ice cream. Who is he?"

"Ashton. He's my uncle Kit's nephew, the one we talked about before. He's going to MIT in September."

Jordan looked at her. "Are you two together?"

Becca nodded.

Jordan returned her attention to her backpack. "That's nice. Nathan and I..." Her eyes filled with tears and her voice thickened. "He, ah, what he said to you, he said to Ella Powers only she said yes. I caught them together."

Tears spilled onto her cheeks. "It was so horrible. He laughed at me and said I was stupid for trusting him like that. He said every guy is just out for what he can get and I'd better grow up."

Becca didn't know what to say so she got up and circled around the table, then sat next to Jordan and hugged her.

"I'm sorry. He's a total dick. What a jerk. You deserve better than that."

Jordan's body shook with her sobs. "I was so sure he loved me. I thought he cared. Finally, finally someone was there for me. At least that's what I thought, but he was only pretending so I'd have sex with him."

Becca bit her lower lip as Jordan cried.

"Everyone is watching me. They're all talking about me behind my back. A couple of girls have said I deserve it. They're posting horrible stuff about me."

"I haven't seen it," Becca admitted. "I don't check any of that anymore."

Jordan straightened and stared at her. "How can you not look?"

"I'm busy." Plus, it wasn't as if she had a ton of friends right now. Who was going to send her anything?

"I'm sorry," Jordan told her. "I was so awful to you and you were the only one telling me the truth. I should have listened."

"It's okay."

"It's not, but I hope we can be friends again."

"Sure."

The reply was automatic, and was followed by a sense of uncertainty. Becca *wanted* to have friends in her life again, but she wasn't sure if she could trust Jordan not to act like that again. Jordan had always been into drama and being the center of attention.

"So we can hang out?"

"Of course."

Jordan smiled at her. "Thank you, Becca. I knew you'd understand."

Becca smiled back even as she wondered if she'd found her way back to something important or if she'd just set herself up to be screwed a second time.

Chapter Twenty-Seven

STACEY WOKE UP FEELING EXACTLY THE SAME WAY SHE had when she went to bed the night before—swollen, exhausted, achy and crabby. She wanted to pick a fight with pretty much anyone and wished she could get one of those foam bats so she could pound away without hurting anyone. She didn't want to eat or drink or talk, she just wanted to feel better.

She forced herself to shower, then stood in the bathroom and tried to convince herself she would be fine once she got to work. Only for the first time maybe ever, she couldn't imagine dragging herself into the lab today. She called Lexi and told her she was taking the morning off, pulled on maternity yoga pants and a T-shirt, then went into the kitchen, dreading a disgusting breakfast of protein-fortified oatmeal, fresh fruit and herbal tea.

She found Ashton sitting at the table, his tablet in front of him. He looked up when she walked in.

"Morning. You're not going to work?"

"Maybe later. I'm just so tired."

He eyed her swollen belly. "Dragging all that around can't be easy. Can I fix you breakfast?"

His unexpected question almost made her cry. She sank into a chair. "Thank you. That would be wonderful."

"No problem."

He got up and filled the teakettle and put it on the stove. After measuring out the oatmeal, he put it in a bowl, then pulled out a container of cut-up fruit.

"I heard back on the online class," he said, sounding sheepish. "I got an A."

"Congratulations."

"Don't say that. I don't deserve it. I have no idea why I was goofing off like that. It was really stupid."

"There could be a lot of reasons. You're still settling in to living here, so nothing is familiar. You're adjusting to having Becca in your life. You're ambivalent about your mother and guilty about your success when compared to what she's going through so you self-sabotage." Bay wandered into the kitchen, one of her puppies trailing after her.

"You're uncomfortably insightful."

She waved away his comment as she patted Bay. "Just speculating. I'm not sure the why matters so much now that you're aware of what you did. I think as long as you don't let it happen on a regular basis when you go to college, you'll be fine."

He measured loose tea into the teapot before adding the boiling water. He set the pot, a cup and saucer, along with a tea strainer in front of her. He added a container of yogurt, a spoon, some fresh fruit and a napkin.

"I'll get going on the oatmeal."

"Thank you." She felt the strangest need to cry and did her best to push away the tears. Talking about something less emotional than him preparing her breakfast seemed the best way to cope.

"Are you nervous about college?" she asked.

"Some." He measured out water from the kettle and poured it, along with oatmeal, into a pot, then adjusted the temperature on the stove and began to stir the mixture. "Not counting you and Kit, no one I've known has ever gone to college. I'm not sure what to expect."

Finally a topic on which she could excel. If there was one thing she knew and knew well, it was how to get through the maze that was higher education.

"The first thing you have to be prepared for is how huge the campus is. All major colleges are practically their own cities. The dorms have very specific rules about when you can show up and what you can bring, but don't worry about that. We'll go in a few days early so you're completely comfortable with where everything is."

Ashton glanced at her, all the while stirring her oatmeal. "You're coming with me when I go to MIT?"

"Not if you don't want me to, but I'd planned on making sure you were settled. We can ship a lot of your stuff ahead, but some things just aren't practical. I'll have to read the rules for the dorms. Sometimes you can have a mini fridge and sometimes you can't. That sort of thing. Linens matter, believe me. A good desk chair. You're not used to the winters so you'll need several coats in different material to manage the weather. We definitely want to buy those there. Los Angeles is not the place to try to buy a heavy-duty coat."

"Thanks, Stacey. That means a lot to me."

He spoke without turning around and his voice sounded slightly strangled. She wasn't sure what that meant but decided it was better not to ask.

"Once you start school, you have to be prepared for the speed at which everything moves. Academically, you'll start to feel lost within a couple of days. Don't let that throw you—everyone is experiencing the same thing. Find out who the TAs are. Go to tutorials. You're going to have to create your own support group, but don't jump into anything. You want to find out who's smart and who's working hard. They aren't always the same people. Protect your study time. Create a study schedule and stick to it. You can party after you graduate."

He turned around and grinned. "You're saying I'll have temptations?"

"More than you can count. Not just parties, but other activities. Lectures and workshops. They can be just as interesting."

"What were you tempted by?"

She poured herself a cup of tea and took a sip. Bay had settled at her feet. The other puppies had joined the first and now they all climbed over their mother, who seemed content to ignore them. "I went to college when I was fifteen. No one bothered with me, but I saw what was happening around me."

She dipped her spoon into the yogurt, then left it there. "You're as smart as anyone else, but you won't feel it. Just know that they're faking it, too. If you don't understand the assignment, ask. The professors are intimidating on purpose. They want to weed out those who aren't going to stick to the program. There's a reason the class size gets smaller as you move through your studies and not all of it is because the subject matter is harder. People drop out."

She thought about what else she could tell him. "They'll have seminars for freshmen. Go to all of them. Learn about campus life. Once you're in a groove with your studies, you can start to branch out socially. If your roommate parties all night, ask to change rooms. Don't stop asking until you're in a living situation that works for you."

"You know your stuff."

"I went to school for a lot of years." Getting two PhD's had taken a bit of time.

There was more, but she felt an odd pressure in her belly. Something uncomfortable.

She rose. "I'll be right back."

As her pregnancy had her running to pee continually, Ashton didn't ask if she was all right, which she appreciated. She made it to the master bathroom only to realize she didn't have to go at all. Her bladder wasn't full, it was—

She was unprepared for the pain that ripped through her. One of the books she'd read had likened contractions to menstrual cramps, but except for location, these had nothing in common. The sharp, almost-twisting band of tightening muscles had her leaning against the wall and trying to catch her breath. A quick wave of nausea swept over her before fading. The contraction eased, and then her water broke.

What was it with the human body and fluids, she thought as she stared at the mess on the floor. The steady dribble down her legs warned her this wasn't like the movies where there was a clean whoosh and then nothing. Even more significant, she sensed things were going to get worse before they got better.

She dropped towels on the floor, before getting out of her wet pants. She used a sanitary napkin to manage the amniotic fluid as best she could, then put on clean yoga pants and took a few minutes to try to relax and catch her breath before she went to find her phone.

Bay was waiting outside the closed door. The dog whined low in her throat when she saw Stacey.

"I'm okay," Stacey told her. "It's just…"

Another contraction hit. This one was just as intense, just as unwelcome.

"Stacey, are you—" Ashton hovered in the doorway to the bedroom for a second, then rushed to her side. "What's wrong?"

She handed him the phone and did her best to keep breathing. "I'm having contractions. Call Kit." She looked at Bay. "How did you get through this so calmly?"

Bay moved close and licked her hand. Stacey patted her and tried to steady her breathing. "I'm going to be fine," she lied, terrified that nothing would ever be fine again.

Stacey acknowledged that she was most likely not the first woman to be annoyed by the euphemism of the word *labor* to describe what her body was going through. She could actually see her muscles rippling with each contraction and the sensation to push grew with every passing second.

The epidural had helped, but it didn't take away all the pain, nor did it ease her sense of helplessness. The baby was coming and she couldn't stop it. Much of the universe was built on randomness. A single act set forces in motion and once they were moving, they could not be stopped.

She'd met Kit, had fallen in love with him and now she was having his baby. For most women, this day would be the culmination of hopes and dreams—something to be celebrated, not dreaded. But then Stacey had never been like everyone else.

"Look at me," Kit said gently. "You're going to be fine."

Statistically he was telling the truth. Childbirth was safe and, despite her age, she was healthy and had done her best to stay that way through the pregnancy. While there were always unexpected developments that could injure or even kill her, they seemed unlikely. No, her bigger problem would be that everything went well and she delivered her baby. And then what?

Bunny walked into the labor room and crossed to Stacey. "I'm here. How are you doing?"

Their relationship had always been troubled, always difficult. Stacey had grown up knowing she was a chronic disappointment—she didn't want to learn how to bake or sew or decorate for Groundhog Day. She wanted to know why the stars moved and some people were better at math than others. Being the kind of wife and mother Bunny admired had been an anathema. She'd prided herself on being better than her mother, on escaping what she viewed as the trap of Bunny's life.

Only now she was the one who didn't know how to make things work. She was left with nothing but useless knowledge and an unskilled heart.

"I can't do this, Mom," Stacey whispered. "I can't. All those times you said there was something wrong with me? You were right. I'm not like you."

Bunny took her other hand and squeezed tight. "Don't be silly. There's nothing wrong with you. And of course you're not like me. You're your own person and that's how it's supposed to be. If you can cure MS, you can have a baby. Even birds have babies."

"I'm not curing MS, I'm helping reduce the symptoms and birds don't give birth. They hatch out of eggs."

Her mother sniffed. "See how smart you are." She smiled. "Stacey, you're going to have this baby because your body knows what to do. It doesn't matter what your head thinks. In this battle, your body will win." She squeezed harder. "You're not alone, Stacey. I'm here and Kit's here and your sister is on her way. We're going to get you through this."

Her mother's gaze locked with hers. "Not just for the birth, either. We're all going to help you through the whole thing. You're going to do just fine."

"I want to believe you."

"Then maybe it's time you started listening to me. You never have before, so I figure I'm due."

Despite everything, Stacey chuckled. "Thanks, Mom."

Bunny kissed her forehead. "You're my baby girl. I'm not going to let you down and you're not going to let yourself down, either. Now, let's have this baby."

Joule Wray Poenisch lay in her bassinet. She was tightly wrapped in a blanket with a tiny pink cap on her head.

Becca wrinkled her nose. "Is she comfortable like that? I wouldn't like not being able to move around. I think it would freak me out."

"You didn't just spend nine months in a womb," Harper told her, looking at all the babies and letting the wonder of birth fill her with happiness.

"Gross, Mom."

"Is this where I remind you I not only carried you for nine months, but then I gave birth to you through my vagina?"

Becca covered her ears with her hands and began to loudly hum.

Harper laughed. "All right. I'm done messing with you. She's so beautiful."

"She's red and scrunchy."

"That's what newborns look like."

"Not in commercials or on TV."

"They use older babies," Harper told her. "You can tell

by how they cry. It doesn't sound the same. A newborn cry is distinct." She sighed as she sifted through memories. "You cried right away, which was a relief, but you were so small. I was terrified I was going to break you or drop you or something. Plus, I had no idea what to do. The theory of a baby is very different than the reality."

"Was Grandma there with you?"

"She moved in for two weeks and when the time was up, I begged her not to go." She hugged Becca. "That happens a lot, by the way. One day you'll be begging me to never leave."

"Maybe." Becca sounded doubtful.

Harper let it go. There was plenty of time for her to be proven right. "I remember the first time I was alone with you at home. I held you in my arms and you looked up at me and I wondered how on earth I was ever going to know how to be your mother. I was so scared. Sometimes I still am."

Becca looked at her. "Why?"

"Everything is always changing. You're not the same little girl who raced home from school so we could bake cookies together." Harper kept her attention on Joule Wray. "You don't talk to me as much anymore and I've tried to figure out when that changed. Do you know?"

Becca was silent. Harper risked glancing at her and saw her daughter staring at the ground.

"Was it the divorce?" Harper asked quietly. "Were you mad at me for what happened with your dad?"

"Some, but not much." Becca looked at her. "I know you had to get a job and the VA business means you're home a lot, but you stopped being there. You were always so busy and you never had time for me. One day I realized you just weren't listening so I stopped talking."

Each word was like a knife to the heart and some cut all

the way through. She wanted to say it wasn't true—things hadn't happened that way, but what if they had? She wanted to defend herself, to say it hadn't been like that at all. She'd been trying to hold things together, to keep food on the table. She'd been scared and alone and...

And none of that mattered, she reminded herself. Not to Becca. From her daughter's perspective, she hadn't just lost her father, she'd lost her mother, too. At least a little.

Sure she could say that Becca could have tried harder or been more understanding, but Becca was the kid in the relationship. Once the business had started going, Harper had gotten caught up in growing it. They'd fallen into bad habits that had led to more estrangement.

Shame wrestled with defensiveness. "I'm sorry," she murmured. "I never meant to let you down."

"Mom, you didn't. I'm sorry I said anything. It's fine."

"No." Harper faced her. "It's not fine. Given the circumstances, I did okay, but I could have done better. I should have recognized what was happening."

"You were caught up in a lot of stuff. I know you were scared when Dad left."

And hurt and ashamed and whole lot of other emotions her daughter didn't need to know about.

"I was pretty selfish," Becca added. "I think it comes with being a teenager. I don't mean to be, but it's hard to think about other people sometimes."

Harper pulled her close and hugged her. "Maybe we can try to do better." She drew back and smiled at her daughter. "Ignore that. What I meant to say was I'm going to do better. I want us to be close again. I want to know what's going on with school and your friends and Ashton and the classes you're taking Jazz to."

Becca started to cry and hugged her hard. "I want that, too, Mom. A lot."

They hung on to each other for a long time. Harper hoped it wasn't too late, that they weren't just saying words but would actually follow through with their plan.

If it was up to her, the answer would be yes.

The dog agility class was more than a little intimidating. The equipment at the obedience school was a lot more heavy-duty than the used stuff Becca had bought, and the course was laid out differently. Becca had watched a few YouTube videos and done some reading, but still hadn't been able to figure out the best way to use her equipment. She hoped the class would help her with that.

There were eight other dog owners, most of them way older than her. She noticed a teenager about her age and walked over to her. The petite blonde smiled.

"Hi, I'm Shara."

"Becca. This is Jazz."

"Hi, Jazz." Shara patted the black-and-white border collie at her side. "This is Ivan." He was a handsome dog with one blue eye and one brown eye.

Becca kept her grip on Jazz's leash as the two dogs sniffed each other's butts and seemed to get acquainted.

"Is this your first agility class?" Shara asked.

"Uh-huh. I don't know much about it, but I wanted to do something Jazz would like. She's happier when she's busy."

"My aunt is seriously into it," Shara admitted. "She competes and everything. I took one of her older dogs to a couple of competitions and it was fun." She sighed. "My mom raises Yorkies. The house is filled with moms and dads and puppies all the time. We have to socialize them and I know it sounds fun, but it gets to be a drag. I've been asking for a big dog and finally they agreed." She patted Ivan again. "He's stubborn but really smart."

Becca tried to picture Ivan with tiny Yorkie puppies underfoot and couldn't. "He does okay with the babies?"

Shara laughed. "Border collies are herding animals. He's great with them. As soon as they're old enough to start exploring, he goes on duty to keep them safe. The moms totally trust him to handle things while they take a nap. It's pretty funny."

Shara looked at the layout, then back at Becca. "I'm saving to get a few things for the backyard, so I can train Ivan at home."

"I bought some used equipment a couple of weeks ago," Becca said. "I'm still figuring it out. You can bring Ivan over if you want to practice together."

"That would be great. You know, we're really too old to start competing at the junior level. There are seriously little kids out there with their dogs. But I'm still looking forward to trying."

"Me, too."

The class began. The instructor took them through the weave poles and the teeter-totter. Jazz was familiar with both and took her turn quickly and easily. Becca picked up a few tips for training Jazz and met a few more of the dog owners. Everyone was nice and friendly.

When the Corgi mix bolted, Shara sent Ivan after him. Becca couldn't believe how Ivan got in front of the Corgi and herded him back to his owner.

"How did you do that?"

Shara grinned. "Last summer my folks sent me to a cattle ranch where they train dogs and their owners to herd. Ivan loved it and I got to hang out with cute cowboys."

They exchanged numbers and agreed to get together to practice in a couple of days. Becca was just about to start the walk home when Ashton pulled up and called out.

"Hey, gorgeous."

Becca blushed as she waved. Shara sighed.

"Is that your boyfriend? He's totally hot. Seriously hot." She grinned. "Sorry. I don't mean anything by that. It's just how I talk."

Becca laughed. "It's okay. Ashton is kind of hot." And sweet and affectionate and just good to her.

She introduced Shara and Ivan before they left, then opened the back door for Jazz and slid in next to Ashton.

"Did I know you were going to stop by?" she asked after he'd kissed her.

"I'm a surprise."

"Yes, you are."

"How was class?" he asked.

"Really good. I met Shara and Ivan, of course, and we learned a lot. Jazz was an excellent student, weren't you, sweet girl?"

Jazz barked in agreement.

"Shara and I are going to practice together and there's a beginners competition in August the instructor thinks we should sign up for."

"Are you going to?"

"Yeah. It's scary to think about, but why not? It'll be good for us."

He chuckled. "I'm glad the competition is in August so I can be there."

Right, because he was leaving for MIT in early September and would be gone forever.

"Don't," Ashton said quietly as he pulled up at a red light. "It will go fast."

"What?"

"The time I'm at college. One of the reasons I'm working as many hours as I can is to save enough money to fly home for Thanksgiving." He shrugged. "Christmas makes sense— it's a longer break and I'm sure Stacey and Kit planned to send me a ticket, but Thanksgiving is different."

She felt that if she weren't held in by her seat belt, she might float away. Happiness and hope and love all made her weightless.

"To, um, see me?" she asked cautiously.

He reached for her hand. "Yes, Becca. To see you."

She wanted to ask how much he cared about her and if he'd had other girlfriends he'd liked more and where he saw them in two years and if there were other good colleges by MIT because maybe she could apply there, but instead she told herself to breathe and enjoy the moment.

They arrived home far too quickly. As Ashton pulled up in front of the house, Becca saw a familiar car in the driveway. She knew her mom was gone and Dean didn't work on weekends, so her dad had no way to get in the house. She wondered how long he'd been waiting and what he could possibly have to say to her.

"Who's that?" Ashton asked.

"My father."

"You don't look happy."

"I'm not."

Chapter Twenty-Eight

BECCA THOUGHT MAYBE SHE SHOULD EXPLAIN HER reaction to Ashton, then told herself it didn't matter. He, of all people, would understand why she could never be sure what to expect from her father. He said all the right things, but when it came to showing up...he didn't.

All three of them got out of their cars at the same time. Becca walked toward the porch, letting her dad come to her. Ashton was right beside her, as was Jazz. The Doberman kept glancing at Terence as he approached, as if ready to protect her pack from the man who had been so sick on the drive to Mischief Bay.

"Hey, Becca," her dad said as he got closer. "I was hoping to catch you."

Why? Only she didn't ask the question in part because it was stupid and in part because she was afraid he might tell her something she didn't want to hear.

"Hi, Dad." She pulled her house key out of her pocket and opened the door. "This is Ashton. Ashton, my father Terence Szymanski." She held in a smile. "And you remember Jazz, Dad."

Her father kept his distance from the Doberman. "Nice to meet you, Ashton." He nodded at Jazz, who walked through the open door, but stayed close. "Becca, I'd like to talk to you about a few things." He looked from the dog to Ashton and back. "Maybe out here, because of my allergies."

"I'll take Jazz into the backyard," Ashton said. "Just shout if you need anything."

And he would be there to protect her, she thought as he closed the door.

"Who's your young man?" her father asked as he took a seat on the porch steps. Becca settled next to him.

"Ashton is Kit's nephew. He's staying with him and Stacey until he goes to MIT in September."

"Are you two, ah, seeing each other?"

"Yes, Dad. We're dating."

"Oh." Her father stared at his car. "I didn't know."

"Mom does. She's fine with it."

She wanted to say more, like if he ever bothered to see her, he might know things about her life. But he didn't care—not anymore. He had Alicia and their new life.

"Okay, then I guess I'll talk to her."

"Whatever."

"Becca, come on. Give me a break. I've been gone for two weeks on my honeymoon and before that I was getting ready for my wedding. I've had stuff to do."

"Right, and before that you were buying a house and before that you were busy dating and before that, you were moving out and getting settled. It's been two years since you left us. Two years and you never have time for me." She stood and glared at him. "How do you think that makes me feel? You were supposed to help me learn to drive, but you never even showed up. It's not like you have five kids and you can say you forgot. There's just me."

He met her gaze and nodded slowly. "I know. You're right and I'm sorry."

"You always say that. You tell me over and over again you're sorry, but nothing changes. Mom messes up but when she apologizes, it means something. At least she tries."

Her father tensed. "I'd prefer it if you didn't bring your mother into this."

"Why not? She's part of my family, too. She takes care of me."

"I take care of you, as well. Who do you think pays for half the things you have?"

Her eyes filled with tears as she hurried up the stairs and grabbed the door handle. "I'm not something you pay for. I'm your kid."

Before she could go inside, her father reached for her.

"I'm sorry." He touched her arm. "Becca, that came out wrong. Please talk to me. I'm really sorry."

She looked into his blue eyes. They were the same color as hers—a little lighter than her mom's. She wanted to bolt, but told herself that wouldn't fix anything.

"You keep saying it," she whispered. "I wish you'd stop."

"Me, too. Please give me another chance. I swear, I won't let you down. I love you, Becca. You're my daughter and you will always mean the world to me."

More than Alicia? Only she recognized the danger of asking that particular question. She had a bad feeling she wouldn't much enjoy the answer.

"Okay. I will, but you have to promise not to blow me off again."

"Cross my heart. We'll have dinner together next week. That's what I came by to say. That I miss you and want us to spend some time together. So dinner? Does that work?"

She hesitated before nodding slowly. "Sure."

He hugged her and kissed the top of her head. "I'll text you a date and time."

She nodded. He walked to his car, waved and was gone. For a second, she just stood there, willing herself to believe everything was going to be okay between them. That he got it and everything would work out. Only he'd broken promises so many times, she wasn't sure she still had the faith to believe in him.

One week after leaving the hospital, Stacey couldn't believe how much she appreciated and admired her mother. Bunny had always been a ridiculous figure in her life. Even as a child, she'd been dismissive of all the things her mother knew how to do. But after being home with Joule for seven incredibly long days, Stacey knew her mom was more than amazing. She was a hero.

The house was chaos. No reading, no books, no videos had prepared her for the keening sound that was her daughter's cry. Worse, every cry sounded exactly the same. There was no difference between Joule Wray being hungry or needing her diaper changed or wanting to be burped. The adults were expected to figure out what was wrong and fix it. Unbelievably, sometimes she seemed to cry for no reason. None! There was simply nothing wrong and yet there she was with that sharp, ear-piercing scream, tormenting them all.

While Stacey and Kit looked at each other in alarm, Bunny clucked and murmured and sang until JW—as they'd taken to calling her—was quiet again. Bunny had skills and patience and an unnatural ability to exist on practically no sleep. And the most shocking thing of all? She said JW was an easy baby who rarely cried. How was that possible? If JW was one of the good ones, how had the species survived? Wouldn't other mothers have either run away or refused to have more children?

Stacey finished cleaning the kitchen. She'd already eaten and showered and dressed. She liked to keep busy, so as to avoid JW as much as possible. Bay wandered through the kitchen.

"I don't know how you do it," Staccy told her dog. "It's a nightmare."

Bay gave her a calming look, as if saying it would get better. After all, her puppies were already weaned and being adopted. In a couple more days, Bay would be an empty-nester and life was good.

"It's not like that for me," Stacey told her. "Kit and I are going to have JW for the next eighteen years."

Bay wagged her tail.

"Easy for you to say."

For some reason, Bay wasn't bothered by the baby's cries, nor was Ashton. He'd already mastered feeding and had no problem with diapers, regardless of their contents. Like Bunny, he had an ability to calm JW and soothe her back to sleep. Stacey might be able to help people with debilitating diseases, but when it came to her own daughter, she was useless and preferred to stay out of the way.

She was about to retreat to her bedroom to check her work email when Bunny cornered her in the kitchen.

"JW needs to be fed," her mother told her.

Stacey hoped she didn't look as terrified as she felt.

"You can do it." Her mother sighed. "I'll prepare the bottle. You go get her."

Stacey wanted to tuck her hands behind her back and refuse. She wanted to say it was Kit's turn, only it wasn't and he'd gone to school to finish up some paperwork for the end of the semester. He'd mentioned going to lunch with a couple of his friends and Bunny had encouraged him, no doubt because he was a man.

JW began to whimper in her crib. Stacey tried not to wince as she walked down the hall and into her daughter's room.

The nursery decor had turned out well, she thought. The cool gray walls had just a tint of pink to them, which went nicely with the cream-colored furniture. Cheerful prints hung on the wall and Kit was talking about painting some kind of mural. But all that faded in the background as Stacey approached the crib. Fear clawed at her throat, making it difficult for her to breathe. Adrenaline triggered her fight-or-flight response and she had no intention of fighting.

"Just a baby," she chanted softly to herself. "Just a baby, just a baby." Somewhere she'd read those words were supposed to help, the assumption being a baby wouldn't judge. Stacey had yet to find the words the least bit comforting.

JW lay on her back, tightly swaddled in a blanket, her eyes closed, her mouth opened as if she were going to start crying for real. Panic joined fear. Stacey hurried close and wrung her hands as she said, "It's okay. I'm here and your grandmother is just in the kitchen."

JW opened her eyes. Stacey knew that her daughter's vision was still blurry and there was no way she was reacting to Stacey's voice directly, so it was all circumstantial that JW stopped whimpering at that exact moment, but it was gratifying, nonetheless.

"Hi," Stacey whispered. "I'm your mom. Your dad is going to be much better than me, but he's out right now. I'm sorry about that." More sorry than JW would ever know. "I need to pick you up and feed you. Your grandmother has you on a schedule. Everything I've read said schedules are important and I can support that. Your cooperation would be appreciated."

JW began to cry.

All right, it was obviously too soon for reasoning, Stacey thought as she sucked in a breath, then bent over to pick up her daughter.

Despite several lessons in the hospital and Bunny showing her over and over again, Stacey still had trouble getting her hands and arms in the right position. Plus, even while swaddled, JW tended to move. Stacey couldn't imagine the horror of trying to bathe her. As far as she was concerned, Kit could deal with that.

She cradled her daughter the way she'd been taught and slowly walked over to the rocking chair. After sitting down, she got JW in position just as Bunny appeared with a bottle.

Stacey tested the temperature of the formula. Her mother would have done that already, but Bunny would lecture her if she didn't do it herself, then she pressed the bottle to JW's tiny mouth and hoped her daughter would take the meal.

There was a second of nothing, then JW opened her mouth and latched on to the bottle. Stacey relaxed.

"See," her mother said. "You're doing just fine."

Stacey thought maybe *fine* was stretching it, but she allowed herself to relax a little. JW drank steadily while Stacey held her and slowly rocked back and forth.

This wasn't so bad, she told herself and tried to believe it. It wasn't that she didn't care about her daughter, it was that she was ill equipped to deal with her. Babies frightened her—especially her own. She felt inadequate and helpless—not emotions she enjoyed.

Ashton and Bay wandered in just before JW finished her bottle. He sat cross-legged on the floor and Bay flopped next to him. Seconds later, the last remaining puppy raced in and threw himself at his mom.

"You're getting it," Ashton said as JW finished the bottle. He leaned over and grabbed a small towel from the changing table, then held out his hands for the baby.

"I wish." Stacey glanced toward the door and lowered her voice. "This is a nightmare. I can't do this for the next eighteen years. I can't."

Ashton grinned as he shifted JW into position, up against his chest and shoulder, then began to gently pat her back. "You don't have to. From what I hear, she'll be eating solid food by at least five years old. So that's thirteen years of no bottle feeding."

"You think you're funny."

"I am funny."

Stacey glared at him, but didn't speak.

JW burped twice. Ashton kept her in position for a few more minutes.

"I heard from my mom again," he said.

Stacey stared at him, trying to read his mood. "Are you okay?"

"No, but I'm dealing. She wanted money again and I told her no again. I said that I loved her and wanted her to get better, but I wasn't going to help her buy drugs. She started screaming at me so I told her I was going to have to let her go until she wants to talk to me because I'm her son and not just to get money."

"What did she say?"

He looked away. "Nothing I want to repeat."

"I'm sorry."

"Me, too. I love her but I can't let her drag me down."

There was something about his voice. She stared closely and wondered if he was crying. Did men his age cry? Kit almost never did, although he had teared up the night he'd proposed and again when she'd told him she was pregnant.

Stacey sat in the rocking chair, feeling awkward and ridiculous. Ashton had done the right thing—he would be fine. Only...

She slid onto her knees, then leaned forward to hug him. He wrapped his free arm around and held on tight, JW nestled between them. After a couple of seconds, he drew back and smiled at her.

"Thanks."

She had no idea for what but decided to take the easy way out. "You're welcome."

Ashton offered her JW. "Want to hold her?"

"Do I have to?"

He grinned. "Not for me. I'm happy to carry her around forever."

Which was wonderful except, come September, Ashton would be gone. Bunny would leave even sooner, then Kit and Stacey would be on their own. It was going to be a level of hell she couldn't begin to imagine.

Becca couldn't stop smiling. She'd aced her driving test with what she thought was an impressive 91 and now was able to drive her car anytime she wanted, as long as it was okay with her mom and she followed the rules of her provisional license. But still!

Her mother had suggested a dinner out to celebrate and

told her she could invite Ashton. Lucas had joined them, as had Bunny. They were at Pescadores, a local seafood restaurant in town.

"I'm so proud of you, I'm ordering myself a glass of champagne," Bunny declared, her smile impish. "Although part of the celebration is that Kit and Stacey are home alone with the baby for the first time. I suspect I'll be getting a lot of texts."

Harper shook her head. "Mom, don't. You know it's terrifying to have an infant in the house. You must have been scared when you first had me."

"Don't get in the way of my fun. I've earned it."

Becca's mom ordered a glass of red wine while Lucas had a Scotch. Becca and Ashton each got a soda.

"School's out, you have your license and a new job," Lucas said, grinning at Becca. "It's pretty good to be you."

"It is. I'm excited about the summer. I've got a lot going on."

Harper leaned toward her mother. "Did Becca tell you she's getting Jazz certified as a therapy dog? She's going to take her to the memory unit at your retirement community."

"She did tell me and I think it's wonderful." Bunny smiled. "You can come visit me when you're done with your volunteer work so I'll get to see a lot more of you."

Harper caught Becca's gaze and gave her a sympathetic glance. Becca smiled. She wouldn't mind seeing her grandmother a little more, but stopping by every time she went over with Jazz would be difficult. Of course Bunny was super busy with her friends, so maybe she wouldn't always have time.

Lucas said something and her mom leaned close to hear what it was. As Becca watched, Lucas touched her mom's arm.

It was no big deal—just a light brush of his fingers, but there was something about it that made her feel funny. Like her stomach was upset, but different. She told herself she was acting crazy, only when her mom straightened and saw Becca looking at them she got the strangest look on her face—like she'd been caught doing something wrong.

Becca felt her mouth drop open as she stood up. "You're dating!"

Everyone stared at her and she blushed. She didn't know what to think or say or do, but somehow she knew this was all Lucas's fault. He was supposed to be her friend, not her mom's. Everything about this was wrong.

"Becca," Ashton began, but she shook her head, then turned and ran out of the restaurant. When she got to the parking lot, she realized she didn't have anywhere to go. She'd come with her mom and Lucas. Ashton had brought Bunny. She could walk home but the house was far and she would feel stupid the entire way.

She pulled her phone out of her pocket. She and Jordan were supposed to be friends again. Maybe Jordan could pick her up. Or—

"Becca, I'm sorry."

She put her phone back in her pocket and started to walk away from her mother, weaving between parked cars. "I'm not talking to you."

"Becca, please. I'm wearing heels and I'm going to hurt myself."

Becca slowed, then turned. Her mother walked over to her, her mouth turned down at the corners. They were between a Mercedes SUV and a Lexus sedan.

"A lot of people in Mischief Bay have money," she said, folding her arms across her chest.

"Yes, they do."

"But not us."

Her mother gave her a slight smile. "We are more in the average income range." Her mother drew in a breath. "I feel like an idiot. Not just because we're talking out here like this, but because I didn't realize how much you'd grown up. I treated you like a kid and you're not. I should have told you about Lucas."

"So you are dating him?"

Her mom hesitated. "We're seeing each other." Her tone was cautious.

"What does that mean? What aren't you telling me? Are you getting married?"

"What? No. God, no. Becca, it's Lucas. He's a really nice man and I enjoy his company and yes we're seeing each other, but it's not anything more than that. Let's all think about his last girlfriend and the one before and the one before that. Which one of these isn't like the other?"

"Because you're—"

"Please don't say old, I beg you."

Becca held in a smile. "So it's just temporary?"

"Yes. I'm getting my dating feet wet again, so to speak, and he's, well, I'm not completely sure what he's doing with me. For now, it's nice."

"Why didn't you tell me?"

"I honestly don't know. It was a knee-jerk reaction because I know it's temporary and I don't want you to think I'm sleazy or anything. Plus, he's the first guy I've seen since the divorce and that's weird."

Becca wondered if they were having sex, then shuddered at the thought. No way she was asking *that* question. Parental sex was just not supposed to happen under any circumstances.

"I was keeping the secret because of me, not because of you," her mother added. "I hope you can understand."

There was something in those last words. Becca groaned. "Because I didn't tell you about Ashton?"

"Did I say that?"

"You didn't have to."

"Mo-om."

Her mother linked arms with her and they started back toward the restaurant. "Maybe it's a thing with the women in our family. Maybe we all keep romantic secrets." Harper grimaced. "God, I hope that's not true. If it is, your grandmother has a secret man in her life, too."

"Grandma's too old to want a boyfriend."

Her mom grinned. "Let's see how you feel about that when you're her age."

"I can't imagine it at all."

"You should enjoy being young. It goes fast." Her mom stopped walking and faced her. "Becca, I really am sorry."

"I know. You can stop saying that."

"I will, it's just we're finally back talking and I don't want to mess that up."

"You didn't. I promise."

"Good." Her mom hugged her. "I love you, sweet girl."

"I love you, too, Mom. And if Lucas breaks your heart, I'll tell Ashton to beat him up for you."

"I couldn't ask for anything more."

The looked at each other and began to laugh, then together went back in to dinner.

Chapter Twenty-Nine

HARPER WATCHED THE CLOCK, WAITING FIVE FULL minutes past the time when she knew Terence would be in his office, then dialed his private number. After a busy morning dealing with clients, she was feeling productive, empowered and a little bit smug about her latest sexual encounter with Lucas.

The things that man could do to her body with just a few well-placed kisses. It was damned impressive.

"Hello?"

The male voice startled her for a second and she had to push away the erotic memories to remember who was on the other end of the phone.

"Terence, it's Harper. I want to talk to you about Becca."

"What about her? Is she okay?"

"If you're asking if she's been in an accident or fallen out a window, then yes, she's fine. If you want to know how she feels about having you as her father, then she's not so great."

"Dammit, Harper, I don't have time for this—"

"I couldn't be more clear on that," she said, interrupting.

"But that doesn't matter. What does matter is your daughter also knows it. You came by to see her. You told her she was important to you. You said you wanted to spend time with her and made her trust you all over again, and then you disappeared." She didn't care that her voice rose with every word until she was shouting at him. "You are the lowest life-form ever. What is wrong with you? She's your kid. You're supposed to love her and if you can't manage that with your selfish, asshole heart, then at least pretend for her sake. She's nearly seventeen. Give it a year, and then turn your back on her."

"You don't know what you're talking about," he began.

"You couldn't be more wrong. Were you or were you not here ten days ago telling her you wanted to have her over to dinner?"

"Yes, but—"

"Did you or did you not promise to text her and invite her over?"

"Yes, but—"

"Did you or did you not forget to do it? Or not mean it in the first place? My God, Terence, you're breaking her heart. Is it fun for you? Is it for sport?"

"I don't need this shit."

"Becca doesn't need your shit, either, but you're her father. Grow a pair and do the right thing."

There was a long silence. Harper was determined to wait him out and hopefully make him squirm and see that what he was doing was hurting their daughter. Becca had tried to play it cool, but Harper had seen the truth—that she wanted to spend time with him.

"I'll get in touch with her," Terence said at last.

"Whatever you do, don't lead her on. The divorce was only

supposed to mean you and I weren't together anymore. Not you and Becca."

"You think I don't know that?"

"You're not acting like you do. She loves you, Terence. You're her dad. It would be nice if you acted like it."

"I have to go."

With that, he hung up.

Harper tossed the phone on her desk and leaned back in her chair. Had he always been like this? Was she finally seeing who he really was? Except for Becca, she wasn't sure it mattered. He'd moved on and she'd moved on.

Funny how when she tried to remember what she'd seen in him, she couldn't. They'd met through mutual friends at a party and had hit it off right away. He'd been a couple of years older and nearly done with his bachelor's degree, while she'd been in her first year of college—a year she'd never finished because she'd dropped out to get a job so she could help put Terence through podiatry school.

She'd been so sure he was the one, so sure she would love him forever and now she honestly couldn't say why she'd married him. She supposed their lies had doomed them from the start—her getting pregnant without telling him, his getting a vasectomy without telling her. His cheating. Maybe, if they'd tried harder, they could have worked things out. Looking back, she had to admit she was glad they hadn't. The divorce had been hard and she'd made a lot of mistakes, but over the past few months, she'd grown so much as a person. Her business was thriving. She and Dean could barely keep up with the work, and except for Terence, things were good with her daughter. Even Bunny moving out had been for the best.

Harper glanced at the clock and realized that while it was fun to pat herself on the back for her accomplishments, time was ticking and her to-do list was probably eighteen thousand items long.

She and Dean spent the rest of the day scheduling clients' work. They'd each signed up for an escrow closing class at the community college, through the continuing education department, so only a single Saturday. They were concerned that wasn't going to be detailed enough, so Dean was looking into online real estate licensing programs. If they weren't too expensive, they would discuss if he should take the whole program, giving them a clearer understanding of what they could do to help Tanya. There were a lot of real estate agents in the area and if things worked out with her, they could easily expand.

Becca got home at her usual time, her new friend Shara in tow. The two teens took their dogs out back and began to practice agility. Thor loped alongside the other dogs, probably in solidarity, Harper thought. Dean headed out at four and somewhere close to five, Lucas let himself into the house.

"Hey," he said as he walked into the family room.

"Hey, yourself."

He crossed to her and put his hands on her shoulders, as he looked into her eyes. He often did that—studying her face as if wanting to assure himself everything was as it should be. Or maybe that was simply her imagination working overtime. Maybe he was thinking she was just so old, but he would deal with it because it wasn't as if she could grow younger.

The thought made her smile, which had him asking, "What's so funny?"

"I'm proud of how well you're dealing with my ancientness."

He kissed her. "I'm an exceptional human being."

"You are."

He wrapped his arms around her and held her close. She closed her eyes and breathed in the scent of him, the heat from his body, how good she felt when he was around.

"Did you rip Terence a new one?" he asked lightly, still hugging her.

"I did. He yammered and swore he was going to do better." She drew back and looked at Lucas. "You know I don't care for myself."

"You're worried about Becca. Hell, I'm worried about Becca. That jerk doesn't deserve to be her father."

His words were nearly as fierce as his tone. Somewhere deep in her chest, she felt a tightening. Nothing unpleasant—more of a warm feeling that he was someone she could trust with pretty much anything. Her work, her daughter, her heart.

"Want some coffee?" she asked, stepped away and turning toward the kitchen.

"It's a little late in the day."

"Oh, right. How about a glass of wine?"

She didn't care what she offered, she only knew she had to keep moving, because to not stay in motion meant she was going to have to deal with what she'd just realized.

In a way she wasn't sure if she should laugh, cry, throw up or run screaming into the ocean. Somewhere between orgasms, she'd fallen for Lucas. What had started as easy and fun had turned serious—at least for her.

"You okay?" he asked, following her.

She turned and offered what she hoped was a bright, re-assuring smile. "Never better. I'm empowered by telling off Terence. I think I should take up karate or something."

Lucas studied her for a second, then smiled. "I'd pay money to see that."

"Interesting. Let me work up a proposal and we'll take it from there."

He chuckled and she reached for a bottle of wine. The crisis had been averted, at least for now.

Becca paused for a full one-two count at the stop sign before driving through the intersection. She was driving in her car, by herself, for only the third time ever. She was both scared and excited and wanted to do a little dance in her seat, but that would mean taking her attention off what she was doing and she couldn't. She turned onto Sepulveda and headed north, toward Hermosa Beach, where her dad lived with Alicia.

He'd surprised her by texting her and inviting her to dinner. After their last conversation, she'd thought maybe he'd changed, but then he'd totally disappeared and once again she'd been forced to see he didn't care about her at all. His text had really surprised her and even though she told herself he hadn't changed and she was dumb if she trusted him, she couldn't help hoping he would want to spend more time with her.

Sometimes Becca wondered if maybe her dad hadn't wanted children at all. She knew her parents had been married for a while before her mom got pregnant, so it wasn't like they'd *had* to get married, but still. In her heart, she wasn't sure what her dad thought about her. He'd always been kind of not there, but things had gotten worse after the divorce and once he'd met Alicia, it was like she didn't exist anymore. Except for the trip up to Grass Valley, she hadn't spent more than a few hours with him in the past year.

She turned left and drove toward the water. Her dad's house was about four blocks from the beach. Parking was impossible, but he'd promised to leave the tiny driveway empty for her to use. She pulled into it, careful to ease her car all the way up to the garage door, then turned off the engine and took a breath.

She'd done it! Maybe, in a few weeks, she would be ready to go on the freeway by herself.

She was smiling at the thought when she knocked on the front door. Alicia answered almost right away. Her new stepmother looked at her, sighed, then called, "She's here," before walking away without inviting Becca in.

Becca hesitated, not sure what she was supposed to do. Did she go in? Wait outside? Before she could decide, her dad appeared.

"Hi, Becca." He held open the door, then hugged her when she walked inside. "The drive okay?"

"It was. Thanks for letting me park in the driveway."

"No problem. You'll get the hang of parallel parking when you've had more practice."

She started to say she was going to ask Lucas to give her more lessons, then hesitated. Her mom and Lucas were dating now, so was it okay to talk about him? She groaned softly. Parents divorcing, dating and remarrying was complicated. They should be more sure before they got married in the first place.

"Come on upstairs," her dad said. "We're going to eat on the rooftop patio. I'm barbecuing."

Her dad's house was typical for Hermosa Beach. Tall, skinny houses were squeezed onto tiny lots, so houses went up rather than out. Only the garage was on the street level. There was a half staircase, then a bedroom, another half staircase to a second bedroom and laundry room. The third level was the biggest with a kitchen, dining area and living room. The fourth level had another small bedroom and a rooftop deck with a view of the ocean.

She and her dad went into the kitchen. Becca didn't see

Alicia anywhere. The other woman had never liked her much and Becca had no idea why. She sure couldn't be mad because Becca's dad spent too much time with his daughter.

Her dad walked to the refrigerator and pulled out a diet soda. "Ice?" he asked as he got out a glass.

"Sure. Thanks."

He poured her drink, then picked up a glass of white wine before motioning for her to go into the living room. When they were seated on the long sectional, he angled toward her.

"I'm glad you were able to stop by. I want to talk to you about something."

Becca put her drink on the coffee table, careful to use a coaster, then wiped her hands on her jeans. She didn't like how her dad was looking at her or the tone of his voice. He was going to tell her something bad—she could feel it.

Her father cleared his throat. "I don't know if your mom ever mentioned the reason we didn't have more children."

"What? No. Why would we talk about that?" She'd always accepted being an only child. There had been plenty of kids to play with on the street and her mom was always there for her, so it hadn't been a problem.

"Oh, I thought she might have..." He paused. "I had an operation so I couldn't have more children."

"Dad, gross. Stop."

"I'm only telling you that because shortly after Alicia and I started dating, I had the surgery reversed." His gaze grew pointed. "I can have children now."

"I get it," she began, then stopped as an unpleasant possibility seeped into her brain. "She made you do it, didn't she? Alicia. She wouldn't marry you if she couldn't have kids with you."

Her father looked away. "Becca," he began, his tone strained, as if there was more. As if…

"No. No! You can't. It's going to change everything. It's going to make it worse. You're not around now. With a baby…" She felt her eyes burning and started for the stairs.

"Becca, wait. I'm sorry. I didn't think it would happen so fast. I thought we'd have more time to get things right between us."

She stopped on the landing and glared at him. "A baby is going to change everything and you know it."

"Becca, wait. Don't go. Stay for dinner."

"Why? Alicia doesn't even speak to me. She doesn't want me here, and you don't, either. I don't know why you wanted me to come over at all. You could have just texted me."

She ran down the rest of the stairs and out to her car. Once she'd started the engine, she thought for a second about where she was going to go. Not home. She wasn't ready to tell her mom about the baby and there was no way she could get past her without her mom knowing something was wrong.

She checked the traffic before carefully backing out of the driveway, then headed back to Mischief Bay. Twenty-five minutes later, she parked in front of a small house with a well-kept lawn. She'd only been here once before, when her mom had dropped off something. She wasn't even sure why she'd come, although it might have something to do with having nowhere else to go.

She got out and walked to the front door. It opened before she could knock.

Lucas smiled at her. "What's up, kid? Everything okay?"

She burst into tears.

Without saying anything, he pulled her inside and wrapped his arms around her. She had no idea how long she cried or what he had to be thinking. He probably thought she was a pain in the ass, but she didn't care. She couldn't—everything hurt too much. Her heart felt like it had been beat up and the rest of her ached.

Finally, she was able to breathe without crying and stepped back. Lucas brought her into the living room and pointed to the sofa, then disappeared down a short hall. He was back seconds later with a tissue box, which he handed to her before sitting on the coffee table and studying her.

"What?" he asked.

She blew her nose a couple of times and tried to speak. More sobs clogged her throat and blinded her. She covered her face with her hands and tried to tell herself it didn't matter, only it did. It had for a long time and now it was going to be awful forever.

"Alicia's pregnant," she managed to say. "She's going to have a baby and my dad had to have an operation and he did it and now she's pregnant."

She blew her nose again and wiped her face. "He wasn't there before and now he's never going to be there. I've seen Aunt Stacey and Uncle Kit with JW and she's all that matters. Babies get everything. I'm just some kid he used to care about."

Lucas moved to the sofa and put his arm around her. She turned toward him and sobbed into his shoulder.

"I hate him. I'll hate him forever."

"I know, kid."

She looked up. "Aren't you going to tell me it's wrong to say I'll hate my dad? Aren't you going to tell me it's going to be all right? That he still loves me and of course he'll be there for me?"

He tucked her hair behind her ear, then kissed her forehead before sighing. "Would you believe me if I did?"

"No, but adults do it all the time."

"I'm sorry about your dad. I do think he loves you a lot, but he's not handling the situation as well as he could."

She sniffed. "That's it?"

"That's all I've got."

She leaned against him again as she thought about his words. They hurt, but not in a mean way, and in her heart, she knew he was right about all of it.

"It hurts a lot," she whispered.

"I know. It's going to hurt for a long time."

She sat up and glared at him. "You're not very good at comforting people, you know that?"

"So I've been told. Want to go get something to eat?"

She nodded. "I need to wash my face first. And I might cry during dinner."

"I've dealt with worse."

She got up. "Thanks for listening."

"No problem. I'm here for you, Becca. No matter what happens, you can count on me."

"Thank you."

She headed for the bathroom. Funny how she didn't believe anything her dad said, but she totally trusted Lucas. He would be there for her, and at least that was something.

Thursday morning Harper glanced at the caller ID and groaned. "It's Cathy."

Dean looked appropriately outraged. "You tell that bitch we don't serve her kind."

Harper grinned. "You weren't even here for the infamous party bag incident, and the truth is I only have myself to blame, so there." She hit the speaker button on the phone. "Hello, this is Harper."

"Hi, Harper, it's Cathy. I haven't talked to you in forever. How are things?"

"Busy. Incredibly busy. How can I help you, Cathy?"

"I need some gift bags for a party and this is a rush job. It's fifty bags and I need them by next Thursday. It's a really big deal for me so I know you'll make it work, won't you, hon?"

Dean rolled his eyes and mouthed, "Tell her to pound sand."

"I'm afraid I'm booked up for the next few weeks," Harper said instead.

"What? You can't be. Harper, I know you were upset about the order before and maybe I shouldn't have undercut your price so much, but come on. You said you wanted to be paid twenty-five dollars an hour. I think that's a ridiculous amount, but maybe for this one project..."

"That price doesn't include rush work," Harper told her. "To fit you in, I'd have to move some other projects and potentially upset regular clients. There would be a premium for me to do that."

"Let me guess," Cathy said, her voice thick with anger. "It will be amazingly close to what you wanted me to pay you last time."

"I hadn't thought of that, but it's a start." Harper took a breath. "Cathy, I find the work I do for you a lot of fun. The bags are always beautiful and I enjoy the challenge, but like everyone else, I have to make a living. You've always wanted to undercut my prices. You expect me to use the most expensive supplies, take a lot of time making everything perfect, and then not pay for it. I'm unwilling to do that anymore. What I charge is what I charge. If you're not happy with that, then I encourage you to go elsewhere."

"You're going to be sorry you treated me this way."

"Actually, what I'm sorry for is how I let you treat me. I

take responsibility for it—you were trying to get away with something and I let you. Just know it won't happen again. Now, would you like to talk about the bags?"

"Go to hell." Cathy hung up.

Harper pushed the button to end the call, then wondered if she was going to regret losing the client. For a second, there was a whisper of fear, but then her overriding sense was one of satisfaction.

"You go, girl." Dean held up his hand for a high five. "You were polite, firm and told her what for. I love it! Plus, I have no idea where we would find time to make any bags she would want. You showed me the pictures of those ones you did. Lordy, there had to be at least a half hour in each of them."

"It was a lot," she agreed.

"Mom?"

Harper turned and saw Becca in the doorway to her office. Her daughter looked pale and upset. Harper touched her forehead. She felt cool and her eyes were clear.

"What's wrong, sweetie? Is your stomach upset? Do you think you ate something funny at your dad's last night?"

Becca had gotten home close to nine and had taken Jazz for a walk. This morning she'd been up and out early. Harper had barely seen her.

Her daughter's eyes filled with tears. "I'm not sick. It's something else."

Fear twisted Harper's stomach. A million possibilities battled for dominance. Pregnancy, drugs, rape, a car accident, bullying.

"That's my cue to go run some errands," Dean said, walking past them. He patted Becca on the shoulder. "Feel better, little one."

Becca gave him a faint smile.

When he was gone, Harper drew Becca to the chair by the desk. They both sat down and Harper took her daughter's hand in hers.

"Tell me, baby. Whatever it is, we'll figure it out together, I promise. I'm here. Tell me."

Becca squeezed her fingers before pulling back and staring at Harper intently. Tears spilled down her cheeks.

"I'm sorry," she whispered. "Mom, I'm sorry. I didn't know how to tell you."

The fear grew until it filled her chest and made it impossible to breathe. Becca wasn't sick—Harper knew that much. She never went to the doctor by herself and she was under eighteen, so the office would have notified her. If she wasn't sick, then everything else could be fixed.

"Just say it, honey. It's okay."

"Alicia's pregnant."

Harper mentally scrolled through her daughter's friends, trying to come up an Alicia, only to realize her daughter meant Terence's new wife.

"Dad told me last night. He said he had an operation so he could have kids again and she's pregnant." Becca began to cry. "I know it's going to be bad for you and I want to talk about that, but what about me? He's never there now and he's never going to be there again. He's only going to care about the baby."

Harper stood and pulled Becca to her feet, then held her tight. "Oh, Becca, I'm so sorry you're having to deal with this. I wish I could change things. I can't believe he told you all that. It's awful."

"It was gross," her daughter admitted. "I was mad and hurt and I didn't know what to say."

"What did you do?"

"I left."

"Good for you." Harper brushed away her tears. "I know I'm supposed to tell you not to run from your problems but this time, it was the right decision. What were you supposed to say? And then to sit and have dinner with you-know-who? No way."

"You're not upset?"

Harper tried to figure out what she was feeling. Regret? Anger? Disappointment? "Not for myself," she said, figuring it out as she went. "I was mad when your dad got the vasectomy. He didn't tell me until I began to wonder why I didn't get pregnant again. You were easy."

"Please let's not talk about that."

Harper smiled at her. "Okay, I won't, except to say I loved having you so much, I wanted more children. Your dad finally came clean. I guess it hurts a little that he didn't want more children with me, but I'm okay with it now. I have you and that's the most important thing in the world." She hugged her daughter again. "What matters now is you."

"I never want to see him again. He's awful and I hate him."

"You don't hate him."

Becca groaned. "Fine. I don't hate him but I almost hate him."

"You're hurt and you feel betrayed. That's going to take some time to deal with."

Her daughter took a step back and glared at her. "You're going to say I still have to see him."

"I am."

"Even after this?"

"Yes. He's your father and when you're eighteen, you can make your own decisions about seeing him or not. Until then..." Harper thought about all Becca had been through.

"You don't have to get in touch with him if you don't want to. You can wait for him to contact you. If he wants to set something up, you'll go."

"And if he doesn't show?"

A very likely occurrence, Harper thought grimly. "If your dad blows you off again, I'll talk to him. If you want, I'll tell him you aren't willing to see him until he can keep his promises."

Becca's eyes widened. "What if he gets mad? What if he wants to take you to court?"

"We'll deal. I love you, Becca. I want you to be happy and I'm going to keep you safe. I'm more than capable of standing up to your dad for you."

"Oh, Mom."

Becca threw herself at Harper and squeezed so tight, Harper couldn't breathe. But it was a good pain. The best pain. It came from love.

Chapter Thirty

STACEY TRIED NOT TO ACT TOO EXCITED ABOUT HER FIRST day back at work. She knew that Kit was nervous about staying home with JW by himself. Bunny had moved out nearly a week before, leaving the family on their own, and while Kit had taken over the bulk of caring for their daughter, Stacey had always been around to help. She knew he would be perfectly fine—Ashton was due home from work in the late morning and he was always so good with JW, and Bunny had promised to drop by to make sure all was well. Despite that, he looked a little panicked as Stacey fixed her breakfast, and she was doing her best not to break into song at the thought of getting out of the house.

Her body was recovering as expected. She'd been surprised at how sore she'd been and how not nursing had caused its own kind of pain. That was better now and she could move around without discomfort. She could also hold JW and feed her without feeling totally inept, although she preferred for Kit to take care of the baby. Stacey was happy in the more traditional male role, being on the fringes and observing rather than participating. Perhaps when JW was older, she would be more involved.

Kit finished feeding their daughter, then put her on his shoulder to burp her. Stacey finished her breakfast and put the dirty dishes in the dishwasher.

"How are you feeling?" Kit asked. "Any regrets?"

The question confused her. "About?"

"Going back to work." He turned his head and kissed JW's ear. "I'll admit that there's a ton I don't know and the responsibility is overwhelming, but I don't think I could leave her. Not for anything."

Kit had always been so loving and supportive, so she was unprepared for what seemed to be a blatant dig at her lack of maternal feelings. The need to lash out at him, striking him harder and faster, nearly annihilated her. Only years of rational thought kept her in check. Instead of saying something hurtful, she walked out of the kitchen and back to their bedroom, Bay at her side.

She straightened the bedspread and brushed her teeth. To be honest, there was no reason to linger there—she should collect her things and leave for the office. At least there she was safe. Only she couldn't seem to make herself go. Kit had hurt her. Kit never hurt her. What was going on?

"I'm sorry."

She finished rinsing out her mouth and turned to find Kit in the doorway, JW still in his arms.

"I didn't mean that the way it came out." His mouth twisted. "I was trying to reassure you that I'd be fine."

"You think there's something wrong with me. You think I shouldn't want to go back to work. We're near a breakthrough. I do important work."

I never wanted to be a mother.

Only she couldn't say that. She'd agreed to have a baby with Kit because she loved him. The fact that she hadn't thought through the consequences, hadn't realized an infant was more than a theory, was her own fault.

"Stacey, there's nothing wrong with you. I know you love JW. Your way is different, but it's no less valid."

"I don't believe you. You're disappointed."

"You're projecting whatever you think you're supposed to be onto me. I love you exactly as you are and I'm grateful you're comfortable with me staying home with our daughter."

His eyes were so kind, she thought absently. She'd noticed that from the first. That and the way his face and body appealed to her sexually.

"I know what people are thinking," she admitted. "What they're going to say about me. I don't like it."

"They've always talked about you. Why is this different?"

"I don't know, but it is."

He moved close and kissed her. "You'll figure it out. Now go on. You have a disease to ass kick."

She nodded and left. On the short drive to the lab, she did her best to lock away her unsettled feelings. She'd always been able to focus completely on work. Today shouldn't be any different.

She parked in her usual spot and made her way to her office. Lexi was waiting. Her assistant grinned.

"You're here. I half expected you to call and say you were extending your leave, but I'm so glad you didn't. The place is falling apart. Max has been haunting me for the past three days, begging me to give him your home number. His group has hit a snag and they need your help. Karl has been a bear. Your team has made some excellent progress but they have a few questions to run past you and I've been holding it all together with rubber bands and prayer."

Stacey stored her bag. Being back felt right, she thought happily. This was her world and where she belonged. Here she was needed, respected and making a difference.

"We need to prioritize," she told Lexi.

"I've already scheduled everyone. This is the order I'd thought you'd want to see them." She handed Stacey a list.

Stacey scanned it and nodded. It was barely eight o'clock. None of the meetings started until ten-thirty.

"I appreciate the chance to go through my emails and read up on the logs," she said, then grinned. "Is there coffee?"

"A giant pot of it. Want me to bring you a cup?"

"I'd love that, thank you."

Stacey got right to work. She read the summaries on the progress made, making notes as she went. She finished her first cup of coffee and was on her second, when she started to feel…not right. She was too warm. No, she was too hot. She felt a little light-headed and slightly sick to her stomach. Her chest hurt and her throat was tight and she had the strangest need to start crying.

She sucked in a breath and tried to figure out what was happening. The flu? Some other bug? She pressed a hand to her stomach to try to figure out if she was going to throw up. Did she need to—

JW, she thought desperately. She had to see JW. Something was wrong, she could feel it in down to her bones.

She grabbed her backpack and raced out of the building to her car. She drove much faster than the speed limit and made it home in record time, then burst inside, calling out for Kit.

Her husband hurried out of the kitchen. "What's wrong?"

"The baby, is she okay?"

"She's sleeping. Stace, what's going on?"

Stacey ran past him, down the hall and into JW's room. Sure enough, their daughter lay sleeping soundly, Bay on the comfy dog bed next to her crib, keeping watch as she often did.

Stacey hugged herself tight, as if to hold in all the feelings. Kit came up behind her and wrapped his arms around her.

"It's okay," he whispered. "Everyone is fine, even you."

"I don't understand. I just knew something was wrong and I had to get back to see her. I had to."

He chuckled. "You missed her."

"It wasn't that. It was something else." Something she couldn't explain.

He turned her and smiled at her. "Honey, you missed your baby. That's what missing someone feels like."

"I thought I was going to throw up."

"That could be your hormones getting back to normal. Do you feel okay now?"

She nodded.

He kissed her again. "It's nice that you miss her. Do you get that?"

She didn't because nothing about what he was saying made sense. "I guess."

"That was convincing. Missing your child is completely normal. You want to be with her. That's not a bad thing."

It wasn't, she thought. People missed their children all the time. Even the guys at work talked about their kids—the things they'd done together over the weekend and their hopes for the future. It was…normal.

"I missed her," she said, hoping it was true, but not quite daring to believe. "I didn't think I would."

"I did. Now get back to work and heal the world."

He hugged her and she breathed in the scent of him, then patted Bay and touched JW's cheek before going back to her car and driving to work. Lexi was waiting for her in her office.

"You okay?" she asked. "The first meeting starts in ten minutes. You want me to postpone it?"

"No," Stacey told her with a smile. "I missed my baby so I ran home to see her. I'm back now."

"You're the boss."

Stacey collected her notes and walked toward the conference room. The ache was still there, but alongside it was the knowledge that while she would never be exactly like her mother, she was closer to normal than she'd ever thought she would be. She was almost just like everyone else, and she was a mother.

Becca watched as Jordan painted Jazz's nails. Jazz lay patiently, her front paws in front of her. Every now and then she glanced at Becca as if asking if this was really necessary.

"She's so well behaved," Jordan said, finishing the first coat. "I thought we'd have to hold her down or something."

"She's smart and has a lot of training." She rubbed Jazz's head. "Don't you, sweet girl? You're so good."

Jazz's ears went back and her tiny tail wagged.

"I got approval for my senior project," Becca said. "I have to journal our progress this summer, and then produce a video about how Jazz helps at the memory unit."

"Do you remember what we learned from that camp last year? I don't."

"I've made a few videos for my mom's company. I'm going to be working there this summer."

"For your mom?" Jordan wrinkled her nose. "That would be a nightmare for me."

"No, I'll work for Dean. He's really cool and funny."

Jordan's mouth twisted. "You have it all together, Becca. When did that happen?"

While we weren't friends, she thought, then told herself saying that wouldn't help. She and Jordan were finding their way back and she didn't want that to change. She was hanging out with Shara more and more, as well, and that felt good. She knew the summer would be busy, with work and her senior project and her friends and Ashton, but she was so tired of being alone that it was okay. She would make it work. And when Ashton left for college, she would be grateful for the distractions.

Jordan started on Jazz's second coat of polish. Becca petted her dog.

"Are you going to be working this summer?" she asked.

"My mom wants me to intern in her office. I think that's a bad idea." Her mouth turned into a grimace. "They're talking about making me pay for my own gas and stuff, which is totally wrong." She glanced at Becca. "What do you think of Justin Williams? He wants to hang out."

"I don't know him very well. I think he's nice." Nowhere near as popular and cool as Nathan, but that was probably a good thing. "Maybe the four of us could do something sometime."

Jordan nodded and finished the second coat, then put the cap on the bottle and looked at Becca.

"Have you guys, you know, done anything?"

Becca felt herself blush. "No. We talked about it but I'm not ready." And Ashton had been smart enough to figure that out.

Jordan began to cry. "Don't do it, Becca. Wait. I'm sorry I believed Nathan. I'm sorry I trusted him. He just said what he had to say to get me to sleep with him. He never cared at all."

Becca slid across the floor and hugged her friend. "I'm sorry."

"Me, too. I can't take it back. I have to live with what I did for the rest of my life."

Becca had no idea what to say. She felt sick to her stomach and so grateful to Ashton. She'd been willing to give herself to him to be more like Jordan and if he'd been someone else, he would have taken advantage of her.

Jordan sniffed, then straightened and wiped her face. "Okay, this is dumb. It's over and I don't care about him. Come on. Let's go get some ice cream. We can sit outside with Jazz and ignore all the boys who think we're hot."

Becca scrambled to her feet. "Even Jazz."

Jordan laughed. "Even Jazz!"

Harper went outside to help Dean unload his car. He'd taken over dealing with Cathy and had negotiated a deal that covered supplies and their time, along with a bonus for the rush job.

"These are going to be fun," she said, fingering the beautiful paper they would use to line the bags. "Cathy might be hell on wheels to work for, but she has great ideas on how to create the world's most expensive party."

"Oh, the money I could have spent at that store," Dean told her. He'd gone to an upscale craft store in Santa Monica. "I need to remove their address from my GPS or I'll find myself back there again, and Lance will kill me if I bring any more crafts into the house."

"Doing craft projects with kids is fun," she teased. "He should know that."

"Don't enable me, young lady. If anything, I need an intervention."

Harper heard a familiar car driving down the street. She turned, already smiling, as Lucas pulled up in front of her house in his silly, white convertible. Then the smile froze, as did the rest of her when she saw his passenger.

The girl was young, beautiful and blonde. She leaned over and whispered something to him before turning to look at Harper.

The earth tilted and Harper's vision narrowed until all she saw was a pinpoint of light. She couldn't think, couldn't speak, couldn't move. The need to run was powerful, but it was as if her head was disconnected from her body and no messages were getting through.

No, she told herself. This wasn't happening. Couldn't be happening. He'd promised.

"Selfish asshole," Dean snarled, grabbing her arm and pulling her into the house. "I'll deal with him."

Harper knew she should say that she was more than capable of fighting her own battles. That she was a mature, self-actualized woman with a successful business and, thanks to an online class, the ability to fix a leaky faucet. Only she couldn't say anything at all. She could only stand in the foyer and shake.

Dean disappeared outside and returned less than two minutes later. He looked furious and a little intimidating, which she wouldn't have thought was possible for someone so good-natured. Without saying anything he walked up to her and held her.

"He stopped by to say he couldn't pick up Thor until later," Dean told her, his voice thick with anger. "I told him we both knew that wasn't the reason and that he should get the hell out of here while he still could. I told him he was a total dick and that we both expected better of him. I wanted to say more but the little chickie next to him looked scared, so I had to stop with that."

Harper's chest tightened until she thought she might snap in two. Thoughts raced through her brain, one after the other, each more hurtful than the one before. She got the message—he'd stopped by with the girl to show her it was over. Not tell, show. Because they'd had a deal and he'd broken it and rather than man up and say something, he'd been deliberately cruel.

He knew her, knew what she feared. He could have texted her or sent an email. Instead he'd shoved her face in his actions.

"Th-thank you for telling him off," she whispered against Dean's chest.

"Hey, we're a team. More important, we're friends. I'm just so angry at him." He stroked her hair. "I'm sorry, Harper. I didn't expect this."

"Me, either."

She wasn't numb exactly. More in shock. There was plenty of pain, but also disbelief. He'd promised. She couldn't stop thinking that.

Dean released her. "You okay?"

She shook her head and tried to speak, only she couldn't. She sucked in air and knew the tears would come—it was just a matter of time.

She felt humiliated and played but mostly devastated. She knew that theirs was supposed to be a casual, sex-based relationship, only she'd allowed herself to feel more and now she was paying the price.

She looked at Dean and saw him glance at the clock. She registered the time, as well, and forced herself to square her shoulders and look as normal as possible, under the circumstances.

"You need to get the kids," she said. "I'm okay. You go."

"You're not okay. I do have to get the twins. Let me get them and bring them back here."

"No way. I'm about forty seconds from crying and they don't need to see that. It will terrify them." She swallowed and sucked in a breath, fighting the inevitable tears. "Would you take Thor back to his house, please? I don't want Lucas coming by later to get him." She never wanted to see him again, but wasn't sure how to make that happen. Lucas was a client and until about two minutes ago, she would have sworn he was a friend.

Dean nodded and called for Thor. The dog came trotting up. Dean snapped on his leash. "I'll call you in about an hour. Becca should be home, right? Oh, maybe get in touch with Bunny." He winced. "No, not your mother. She'll just tell you everything you did wrong, even if it isn't true." He stared at her. "You know this isn't about you, right? Whatever demons have him chasing those little girls have nothing to do with you. You are perfect and lovely and he's nothing but a lowlife bastard who doesn't deserve to be alive."

Dean hugged her again.

Harper did her best to hang on to the little self-control she had left. She knew the storm was coming but she wanted to be alone when it hit. She hurt all over. She felt empty and sad, but mostly, mostly she felt humiliated. She felt as if every flaw, every fear had been exposed to the world, and the world had pointed and laughed. She'd allowed herself to dream, and that dream had been mocked, broken and ground into dust.

"I'll call you," he promised.

"Text me," she told him. "It will be easier for me to lie and say I'm okay."

He hesitated, then nodded. After the door closed behind Dean and Thor, Harper walked into the kitchen, then went into her office, only to return to the kitchen. The mail sat in a pile on the table.

She picked it up and flipped through it and saw a letter from the IRS.

"Perfect," she muttered. "Just perfect."

She ripped open the letter and scanned it, then stared at the check that fluttered to the floor. She read the letter again.

Apparently she'd made a mistake on her taxes and they were refunding three thousand dollars. Wasn't that an amazing surprise? Shouldn't she be happy?

The trembling returned. She wrapped her arms around herself, sank into a chair and began to rock back and forth. *In and out*, she told herself. *Breathe in and out. Slowly, steadily.* Then her breathing hitched and the tears spilled onto her cheeks. The sobs came next, ripping through her, breaking her until she knew she would never be whole again.

Chapter Thirty-One

SATURDAY MORNING, STACEY KNOCKED ON ASHTON'S half-open door. He looked up from his computer and smiled sheepishly.

"You caught me. I'm doing nerd stuff."

She walked in and sat on the bed next to Bay and stroked the dog. "Which is?"

He pointed to the screen. "I downloaded one of my textbooks and I'm reading it."

"Why is that bad?" She shook her head and grinned. "Never mind. I get it—what's normal for me is nerdy for everyone else. I'm used to it. So I thought we could talk about our trip back east. College starts a couple of days after Labor Day and the dorms don't let you in early. Still, I thought we'd go at least a week in advance. We have things to buy and I want you to be comfortable with the campus. We'll rent a car, so we can buy what we need and get to your room."

She paused to make sure she was covering everything. "Kit's going to stay here with JW. She's just too young to travel and it's not like she can do anything. My mom will move in while we're gone to help with everything, which Kit will love. He gets along with her way more than I do."

"That's because you intimidate her."

Stacey laughed. "Me? Intimidate Bunny? That's not possible. I fail at everything she values."

"You make her aware of what she gave up to take care of her family. That's why she's so hard on you. She's hard on Harper because she feels guilty about encouraging her not to have a career and instead stay home with Becca."

"How could you possibly know that?"

One shoulder rose and lowered. "Kit and I talk about stuff. So do Becca and I. I just put the pieces together, and I could be wrong, but I don't think so."

Intimidate her mother? Was that possible? Sure, it would be nice if it were true, but Stacey couldn't imagine that happening.

"Whenever you want to leave for the trip is fine with me," he added. "My boss knows I'm moving back east. Once we have the dates, I'll let him know when that's going to happen."

"I'll buy the tickets today. What do you want to do about your car?"

He hesitated. "I've done a lot of research and I'm not going to need it at MIT. At least not my first year. If it's not too much trouble, I'd like to keep it here, in the garage. I'll put all my stuff in it, so that's out of the way, too."

She waved her hand. "Sure. The garage is fine. Leave the keys with Kit so he can drive it every few weeks to keep it all working." She frowned. "Why would you put your stuff in your car? Why not just leave it in your room?"

He looked down at the floor. "So the room's empty. You might need it for something."

Why would they want an empty...

Hormones were still messing with her head, so Stacey wasn't even surprised when she felt the burning need to burst into tears. She managed to keep control and only had to clear her throat before she spoke.

"Ashton, this is your room for as long as you want it. Please keep your things where they are. Kit and I assumed you'd be coming back for breaks and in the summer. We want you to come back because this is your home. You're a part of our family and we love you."

He made a low sound she couldn't define, then nodded. "Ah, thanks, Stacey. I appreciate that."

She rolled her eyes. "Get over here and hug me."

He laughed and did as she requested. Bay jumped to her feet and licked them both. Funny how after all this time, Kit continued to give her what she wanted most, even when she didn't know what that was.

Becca had thought the worst thing ever was her parents getting a divorce, but she'd been wrong. Having Lucas and her mom break up was more awful because now she knew what was going to happen. When her dad had moved out, he'd promised nothing would change. She hadn't known he was lying and that he would never be there for her again. And he was her dad. Lucas had even less reason to bother with her and for some reason that hurt way more than she'd expected.

She was trying to be as good as she could, trying to look out for her mom. The house was so quiet and sometimes she could hear her mom crying. Becca was angry at Lucas for being a tool and mad at herself for caring that she would never see him again. Jazz missed Thor and nothing was right. Why did Lucas have to be such a jerk? Was Ashton the only decent guy out there? Okay, Ashton and Kit, but that was it.

She walked into her mom's office, "I'm taking Jazz to agility class. Do you need me to stop at the store or anything?"

Her mother looked at her and tried to smile. Her eyes were red and her face pale. "No, thanks, but I appreciate you asking. Are you home for dinner tonight, or are you and Ashton going out?"

Becca wasn't sure what to say. She and Ashton had plans, but maybe she should stay here. "I thought we'd hang out with you."

"No way. Go out and have fun. I'm totally fine. I promise."

Which Becca wanted to believe, but she wasn't sure. "We'll talk later," she said, then called to Jazz.

After agility class, she got her dog in the car and started for home. Jazz was doing really well with all the equipment. She would never be a champion—while she was well trained, she didn't have the flat-out speed of some of the other dogs—but she gave her all and seemed to really enjoy herself.

Becca came to a stop at a red light and waited for it to turn green. Without warning, a big SUV slammed hard into the back of her car. Jazz was thrown into the dashboard and immediately started yelping. Becca's seat belt locked as her head slammed against the headrest. Before she could figure out what was happening, the SUV backed up and drove past her.

Becca felt dazed and confused and scared. She didn't know what to do, but Jazz's yelps had her panicking. She looked at her dog, all crumpled in the car's foot well, then glanced around and got her bearings. The vet wasn't that far away.

It only took a few minutes to get there. Once she parked, Becca ran inside and called for help. Two of the techs carried Jazz into an examination room and promised they'd look at her right away.

Becca walked out and saw the back of her car was totally

smashed. She tried to figure out if she was hurt, then decided that except for being sore, she was okay.

In her glove box was an envelope Lucas had given her with instructions on what to do if she was in an accident. She hadn't gotten the license plate of the SUV, and she wasn't even sure of the make or model, but she could call the police.

"Mischief Bay Police Department."

"Hi, um, my name is Becca Szymanski. I was at the corner of Bartholomew and Treybal and someone rear-ended me, then drove off."

"Is anyone hurt?"

"My dog, Jazz. I didn't know what to do. She was crying so I took her to the vet. I'm there now."

"Give me your name again and tell me where you are."

Becca did, then was put on hold. A minute or so later, she was told to stay where she was and that an officer would be there shortly to take a report.

By the time she hung up, she'd started shaking. She wanted to call her mom, but didn't want to upset her. Instead she texted Ashton, then went inside only to be told that they'd taken Jazz in for X-rays.

"Something's broken?" Becca asked, her voice a wail. "No, she has to be all right."

The receptionist's smile was sympathetic. "Let's find out what's wrong with her, okay? The doctor wants to be sure before she makes a diagnosis."

Becca tried not to cry as she told herself she had to be there for Jazz. She had to be mature. "Okay, thank you. I'll be outside. If you could please come get me when she's done."

"I will."

Becca paced in the parking lot, trying not to throw up. She desperately wanted her mom and was nearly about to give in and call her when a familiar white Mercedes convertible pulled in next to her.

"What are you doing here?" she demanded, even as she wanted to throw herself at Lucas.

He parked and got out, then held open his arms. Becca knew it was wrong, but she couldn't help rushing to him.

"It's okay, kid," he told her. "I'm going to take care of everything." He stroked her hair. "I have friends at Mischief Bay PD and when you got your license, I put the word out that I was to be notified if you got into trouble. We go way back so they agreed. You called them and they called me." He looked at her. "You all right? Are you hurt? Should we go to the hospital?"

"I'm fine. It's Jazz. She was riding in front and when that guy rear-ended me, she went flying. They're doing X-rays. What if I broke her?"

"You're not responsible for being rear-ended. Tell me about the car that hit you."

"It was a black SUV. Big. Maybe a Tahoe or Escalade. I didn't get the license plate."

"Where did this happen?"

She told him and he began taking notes on a small pad he pulled from his shirt pocket. "There's a traffic camera right there. Maybe we can get the license plate."

She nodded. "I should have had a seat belt on her. I'm going to start doing that and making her ride in the back."

Lucas ruffled her hair. "I'm sure you will. Let's go look at the damage to your car."

He whistled when he saw her crumpled trunk. "He hit you hard. Your car is going to be in the shop for a while."

Becca hadn't thought about the repairs. "Does insurance cover it?"

"Yes. There's a deductible."

And she'd used the last of her savings to buy agility equipment. Still, she was working and if she had to use her paycheck for the deductible, she would.

"Did you call your mom?" he asked.

She ducked her head. "No. She's... No."

"Why didn't you call me?"

Becca glared at him. "You left. You cheated on my mom and made her cry and you left. You abandoned her and you abandoned me. You were just gone, like my dad!"

His face tightened. "Becca—"

"No!" she screamed. "You are not going to tell me it wasn't like that. You're not going to tell me that I'm wrong. I know what happened. I know what you did. You were supposed to love her and you hurt her. You're just like my dad. You're just like him!"

"You done?" he asked, his voice so much quieter than hers.

"No. I hate you. I'll always hate you."

"Then we have a problem because despite what happened with your mom, I'm not going anywhere, kid. Not where you're concerned. I was giving you a couple of days, but then I got the call, so here I am." He moved toward her. "Becca, look at me. When have I lied?"

"You lied to my mom."

"That isn't about you and me."

"It is. It is! She's my mom and you hurt her." She rushed at him and began hitting him. He let her, then drew her against him.

"I'm so sorry," he told her. "I mean that. I'm sorry."

She cried because there was nothing left to say and she was scared and hurt and she didn't know what was going to happen with Jazz. Finally, she pushed away.

"Just go."

"I won't."

She glared at him. "I don't want you here. I don't trust you. You lied and you hurt my mom. We don't need you anymore."

"Becca, please."

Ashton drove into the parking lot and jumped out of his car. "You're not answering your phone. What's going on? Becca, are you okay?"

She ran over to him, trying to tell him what had happened, but she was crying too hard. Lucas followed and filled him in.

"Are you okay?" Ashton asked. "Are you hurt?"

She shook her head. "It's Jazz. And my car."

"Your car can be replaced. You can't."

Becca sensed more than heard Lucas behind her. She had a bad feeling he would stand there forever, if she didn't talk to him.

She turned. "We're done. I'm done with you. I never want to see you again."

Something flashed in his eyes. She thought maybe she'd hurt his feelings, then told herself she didn't care. He was awful and she was better off without him.

"Becca, I get that you're mad at me and that's okay. But know this. I care about you and I'm not going anywhere. You're going to have to accept that."

"No, I don't. You're nothing to me. Nothing. Do you hear me? Do you?" The last words came out as a scream. She pressed her face into Ashton's chest.

"You should go," Ashton told him. "She's upset."

"I'll be in touch," Lucas said, then there was silence, followed by the sound of his car starting.

Becca waited until he was gone to lead Ashton into the vet's office. "I'm scared about Jazz. What if she's going to die?"

"Let's wait to panic until we know something, okay?"

"Ugh, logic."

"I know. I can be such a pain."

They waited for nearly forty minutes, then met with the vet. Becca listened as the older woman talked and showed them the X-rays. Nothing was broken. Jazz was bruised and sore, but otherwise would be okay. She needed rest along with painkillers and anti-inflammatories. It was only when it was time to pay the bill that Becca realized she didn't have any money, or a credit card.

"I'll get it," Ashton told her. "You can pay me back." He handed over a debit card.

Together they carried a drugged Jazz to the car and put her in Becca's back seat.

Becca kissed her dog. "I'm sorry," she whispered. "I should have made you wear a seat belt and ride in back. I will from now on, okay. Because you're my girl and I love you."

Jazz licked her cheek.

Becca straightened. Ashton touched her arm.

"I'm going to follow you home. Your mom is going to freak and it will help if I'm there to be a buffer. Once she's calm, I'll take your car to the body shop for an estimate while you call your insurance company."

All things she'd never thought about having to deal with. "Thank you."

He kissed her. "This is the only place I want to be, Becca. I hope you know that."

She nodded and leaned against him for a second, then sighed. "If this is what it feels like to be a grown-up, then it totally sucks."

He chuckled. "You're going to have to get used to it, kid. You can't stop the process now."

She got into her car and waved, but all she could think about was how Lucas always called her "kid," and how much she was going to miss him. Unlike her dad, he'd totally been there, right until he'd turned into a lying weasel dog and hurt her mom.

"We have to talk," Dean said as he took his seat in the desk that faced hers.

Harper didn't think she had one hit left in her. Lucas's betrayal had about taken her to the edge and Becca's accident had pushed her over. Honestly all that was keeping her from plunging into the abyss was her grip on some spiny plant. The second she let go, she would fall and never be seen again.

"All right," she said, hoping she sounded more confident and upbeat than she felt.

She told herself it would be fine. Becca wasn't hurt, Jazz was healing and she was getting over Lucas. Okay, that last one was a lie, but as she was only talking to herself, who was going to call her out on it?

"I've been making some calls," he told her, opening a folder. "There are at least a dozen real estate agents who have expressed interest in our services. I think we should hire someone to primarily work on doing that with both of us being backup."

"Hire someone? That's a big step."

"It is. Now brace yourself, because I have something shocking to say."

"I'm braced," she lied, mentally seeing her grip on the spiny plant slip a couple of inches.

"I think we should expand. We already have more work than we can manage and we're growing every week. Let's go for it. I'd like to buy in as a partner. And I do mean buy in.

With cash. We can rent a real office, hire a few more people, form a limited partnership and take the world by storm. What do you think?"

Her head started to spin. "Can we do that?"

"We can if we want to. I've done some research and a preliminary valuation on the business. You've worked hard, Harper, and your company has a lot of value. Plus, there's that old building by Olives martini bar. I talked to the owner and he's going to sell in maybe three years. Which is perfect for us. It's cheap rent for now, because nobody wants that short a lease. Yes, we'll have to move later, but later we'll have more clients and more money, so we can afford something nice. Or we can buy the building ourselves. The partnership is easy and Lance knows a really good accountant. What do you think?"

Move Harper Helps to a real office building? Hire more people? Take Dean on as a partner?

"I'm stunned. Intrigued, but kind of in shock."

"Intrigued is good, because there's more." His gaze intensified. "You're working too hard. You pretty much deal with the business 24-7. You need a break and you need separation. Moving the business out of your house would help with that. If we do this, I'd want us to both agree how much we're going to work from home. I'm hoping it's only in a crisis because we both need to spend time with our families. I waited too long to find Lance and have kids to screw that up now and I know you want to be with Becca before she heads off to college."

The tears weren't as prevalent as they had been, but they were darned closed to the surface. Harper felt her eyes burn. He was right about all of it. She'd taken on too much and paid the price for it with her daughter. Dean's plan solved both problems.

"If I say I love you, will you take it in the spirit I mean it?" she asked.

Dean smiled. "I will. We're great together. We can do this. Expand the business, run an empire and still have time for what matters. We have synergy. Let's take advantage of that."

"Okay," she said slowly. Her gaze fell on Jazz sleeping in her bed. "On the condition the office is dog friendly."

Dean laughed. "I agree. Jazz is family, too. We can't just leave her alone by herself." His expression turned anxious. "So do you want to think about it?"

"No," she told him with a laugh. "You're right. This is what we should be doing. Let's go for it."

Dean grinned. "Yay! But I have to say, we need to have one firm rule." He drew his eyebrows together and shook his finger at her. "No more sleeping with clients!"

Harper's mouth dropped open, then she started to laugh. "I promise."

Chapter Thirty-Two

BECCA LAY STRETCHED OUT ON THE FLOOR NEXT TO JAZZ. Ashton was on the sofa nearby.

"I took her back for her recheck and she's fine," she said, petting her dog. "We went over the X-rays again and it was so cool to see them." She bit her lower lip, and then blurted, "I've been thinking about college and what I want to study. I'm thinking I want to either go to veterinary school or be a radiologist. I know, I know, it's a lot of work and I'd have to stay in school for like the rest of my life, but when I was calm and we were talking about the X-rays, it was so interesting."

She sat up and faced him. "I already made an appointment with my counselor. She's there for another week before she goes on summer break and she's fitting me in. It means I'd have to change my classes next semester and take another science class and I'd have to take calculus, which I wanted to put off, but it's worth it." She stopped before asking, "What do you think?"

"Hmm. I don't know. My girlfriend's brain." He closed his eyes as if he were thinking, then looked at her. "I like it."

She laughed and moved toward him. He leaned close and kissed her.

"You know," he said, "there are a lot of great schools near MIT. You could apply to a couple of them."

"I could. I might."

"Good."

He kissed her again, lingering this time. Her phone chirped and she glanced at the keyboard, then pushed it away.

"Lucas?"

"Whatever. He wants to take Thor for a walk and invited me along."

"How often is he getting in touch with you?"

"Every day." She rolled her eyes. "It doesn't mean anything. He's..."

"What? He's faking wanting to spend time with you?"

"No, it's just... He hurt my mom."

"He did and he's a dick for doing that, but what about you, Becca? I thought you guys were tight."

"We were, but I can't be friends with him now."

"Is that what your mom said?"

"No. I didn't ask her." She hadn't wanted to mention Lucas at all. Her mom was finally doing okay with the business expansion. She and Dean were packing boxes and had hired a full-time person. Things were good. Why bring up something from the past?

"Having someone care about you is a good thing," Ashton told her. "You might want to think about that before you throw it away."

"You think I should talk to him."

"I think you should give him a chance. Yes, he hurt your mom, but he didn't hurt you. He cares about you. I'm going to be gone at the end of summer. I'd feel better if I knew Lucas had your back."

"You are so annoying."

"Maybe, but I'm not wrong."

She groaned, then reached for her phone. "Fine. I'll talk to my mom and if she says it's okay, I'll go walk my dog with him, but I won't like it."

Harper taped the box shut and moved it to the growing stack. She and Dean were moving into their new office in less than two weeks. Starting a limited partnership took a lot of time and paperwork, but she knew in her gut, she was doing the right thing.

She couldn't believe that by expanding the business, she was actually going to have more time for herself and her daughter, but that was how things were shaping up. She and Dean had drawn up an agreement, spelling out responsibilities for each of them, along with the hours they intended to work. Harper had promised him and herself she would stop working on Sundays and only bring home projects for Saturday morning. The evenings were to be spent on things other than calligraphy and making gift bags.

She was in a good place, at least for that part of her life. Yes, she still missed Lucas—far more than she'd thought she would. The damned man had stolen into her heart and no matter what, she couldn't seem to dislodge him. But she was moving forward and telling herself everything was going to be fine.

"Mom, can I talk to you for a second?"

She looked up as Becca walked into the office. "Sure, honey, but I thought Ashton was here."

"He went home. We're getting together later." Becca shifted

her weight from foot to foot. "I didn't tell you everything about the accident."

Harper froze. "What didn't you tell me?"

"That when I called the Mischief Bay police they got in touch with Lucas and he came to check on me."

The response was both better and worse than she'd imagined. "Okay," she said slowly. "And?"

"He wants to be friends with me. He says he cares about me and whatever happened between the two of you isn't about him and me. Ashton says Lucas has always been there for me and I shouldn't throw that away, but he hurt you, so I'm not talking to him, only he won't go away and I don't know what to do."

Harper collapsed into her chair. Becca looked worried and hopeful and the most heart-wrenching combination of adult and child.

She knew what she wanted to say. She wanted to tell her daughter that under no circumstances was she to see, text or speak to Lucas. That he was the devil and with luck the next time he got shot, he would die. Only... Only...

Lucas had been a far better father than Terence had bothered to be, especially since the divorce. He'd taken care of Becca, taught her to drive, insisted she understand her car and demanded good grades for the privilege of her license. He'd been consistent, fair and unfailingly patient. All Harper's complaints about him were personal.

"Ashton is right," she said slowly. "Whatever is going on between Lucas and me has nothing to do with you. Go talk to him. Listen to what he says. If you don't like it, then walk away."

"You sure?"

Two words that told her what Becca really wanted, or

maybe she'd always known. With Terence gone, Becca had a dad-sized hole in her life and she'd found someone to fill it.

"I'm sure." Harper smiled. "I promise."

"Thanks, Mom. I'm going to text him back right now."

Her daughter danced out of the room. Harper returned her attention to her packing, then glanced up at the ceiling. "If you're listening, God, I deserve a whole lot of credit for that one. Let's all try to remember you owe me the next time some guy asks me out."

Becca drove to the park. Jazz whined from the back seat, but Becca was firm.

"No. You're going to ride back there. It's safer. Do you know how lucky we are that the air bag didn't go off? Not that it would have from a rear-end collision, but still. It could have, and then you would have been hurt. This is better."

Jazz yipped.

"Don't you take that tone with me, young lady," Becca said with a laugh.

She pulled in the parking lot of the dog park and opened the door for Jazz. Her dog jumped down, sniffed, then began to whine. Becca figured her excitement was a lot more about Thor than Lucas, but knew that both were nearby. She turned and saw them approaching.

He was there, just like he said he would be. Just like he'd always been. She dropped the leash and ran toward him. He caught her and hugged her so hard, she couldn't breathe, but that was okay.

After a couple of seconds, she looked up at him. "I'm still mad about my mom."

"I know."

"You were a dick. You still are."

"I know."

"I talked to her. Do you know how great she is? She said it was okay for me to hang out with you. That's how much of a mom she is."

He nodded without speaking.

"But you've been good to me, and there for me, so I'm here. I guess people are complicated."

"I've never had kids," he said, his voice gruff. "I thought I would for a while, but then I realized it wasn't going to happen. I kind of wish things had been different, but they are what they are." He cleared his throat. "What I'm trying to say is that I think of you as the daughter I never had. I love you, Becca. No matter what, I'll be here for you. You can always call me, day or night. Whatever it is, I'll be there. I'll keep showing up. I give you my word."

She knew what his word was worth, at least when it came to her. He wouldn't be like her dad. He wouldn't forget her or get too busy or even drop her when he broke up with her mom. She trusted him.

"Thank you," she murmured, not ready to say the *L* word, but kind of feeling it on the inside. She turned and called for Jazz, who immediately walked to her side. Thor returned to Lucas and the four of them strolled along the boardwalk.

"I got an A in European History. My teacher was really impressed with my report."

"See what happens when you do the work?"

She sighed. "Can you just say congratulations? Does every second have to be a life lesson?"

"Pretty much."

"Fine. Yes, if I'd done the work, I wouldn't have had to do the report. But I really enjoyed it and I learned a lot. War is awful. We shouldn't do that anymore."

"You're right. We shouldn't. Anything else?"

"I'm not sure how I'm supposed to know when it's okay to have sex with Ashton."

Lucas swore under his breath. "We are *not* having that conversation."

"I have to talk to someone and we both know my mom would totally freak out. Although I guess I should talk to her. I should probably be on birth control. I mean I agree with Ashton that we should wait, but he's pretty hot and what if I can't control myself much longer?"

Lucas swore again. "You're killing me, kid."

"Good. That was my plan."

People complained about being in a routine, but Stacey found comfort and happiness in the sameness of her days. When she got home from work, she spent a half hour with JW while Kit finished making dinner. If Ashton was home, he cleared the table and cleaned up the kitchen. When JW went down for her evening nap, Stacey and Kit hung out or watched TV or worked on a jigsaw puzzle. Stacey handled the eight o'clock feeding and the one at midnight, Kit took care of the rest.

She was happy—a state she'd experienced since meeting Kit but not one she'd expected after they had a baby. She'd been so afraid of what would happen, of being replaced, of not being enough. Although no one would accuse her of being the greatest mother on the planet, she could manage a few basic things. Feeding, changing diapers. Perhaps as JW grew, Stacey would feel inadequate in other areas of her mothering, but for now, she was doing okay.

She had so much—her job, her family, her husband, Ashton and JW—and so much of that was because of Kit. Yes, she would still have her great career without him, but if she was by herself, it would consume her and that wasn't healthy. Without him, her mother would have made her even more unsure and she wouldn't have met Ashton or had JW. Kit was, as always, the best part of her.

As he studied their half-finished thousand-piece puzzle, she felt her love for him grow inside of her until it was all she was. Just love for her husband. JW lay in her chair on the table, staring at the mobile turning above her head. This moment was so perfect, she wanted to thank him and show him how much he meant to her. Only he would say that having her and their baby was enough. He would say he already had everything he wanted in the world. That he was perfectly happy and leaving her with no way to express her feelings of—

"I need to check to see if Max emailed me," she lied, coming to her feet. "Can you watch JW for a second?"

"Sure." Kit smiled. "Tell Max hi from me."

"I will."

Stacey hurried to her desk and opened her iPad. She typed in her search question, then sent the list and the paperwork required to their shared printer. Papers in hand, she returned to the dining room.

Kit was still studying the puzzle. With his right hand, he picked up a small piece and set it in place. With his left hand, he rocked JW. His hair was too long, his T-shirt rumpled. He was kind and sexy and fun and the best man she had ever known.

"Kit?"

He looked at her. "What's up?"

"I love you."

"I love you, too. Very much."

She sat next to him and set the papers on the table. "We

decided it would be best to give JW your last name. Hyphenating it was going to be too much of a burden for her."

"Did you change your mind? Stacey, I don't care if you want to hyphenate her name. Whatever makes you happy."

"I don't want to do that. I want to hyphenate mine, at least at work because I've been in the field for so long. But in the rest of my life, I want to just be your wife. I'd like to take your name."

"Are you sure? You don't have to do this for me."

"I want to. I want everyone to know I'm your wife."

He smiled and kissed her. "I think of myself as your husband, but whatever makes you happy."

"You do. Always."

Harper had just loaded another box in her car when she heard a familiar sound. Her stomach clenched and the urge to bolt was incredibly powerful. Still, she stood her ground as Lucas pulled up in front of her house.

The top was down on his convertible and once again he had a passenger, only this time, instead of some twenty-year-old woman/girl, a tall, black-and-tan Doberman rode proudly in the passenger seat.

Thor looked both regal and ridiculous. Then he caught sight of her and his expression changed to one of happy excitement. *So much for regal*, Harper thought, telling herself that focusing on the dog meant she would be okay. Thor wasn't the problem at all.

She hadn't seen Lucas since the last time he'd been by. Dean had handled returning all his things to him and had closed out his account with their business. She'd deleted all the passwords she'd kept for him, had taken him off her phone, but no matter how much purging she did, the stupid man continued to hang on to her heart.

If only he weren't so handsome. If only she didn't like spending time with him, or how he was with her daughter, or the sex. If only the sex had been bad.

She'd been a fool, she acknowledged, falling for a guy like him. She'd known better and had done it anyway. Lucas had never pretended to be other than he was. She'd been the one to assume he could be normal. Oh, he deserved all the blame for doing everything she'd asked him *not* to do, but believing in him—that was on her.

He nodded at Thor, who gracefully jumped over the door and onto the grass. He trotted up to Harper to greet her, then ran to the front door. Harper followed and let him in. She heard Jazz come running, then the frenzied gallop that told her they'd already started their favorite chase game.

She briefly thought about shutting the door behind her and locking it, but the gesture would only be satisfying for a moment, while the knowledge that she'd been childish would live on much longer. So she stood still until Lucas walked into the house, then crossed her arms over her chest and waited.

"You're still mad," he began. "No, not mad. *Hurt* and mad. I broke my word. You asked me for one thing and I didn't do it. I betrayed you and hurt you. I get that." He shoved his hands in his front pockets, then took them out.

"I'm sorry for what I did and how I hurt you. I apologize for my actions and I didn't have sex with her. The girl."

"Thumper? Was that her name?"

One corner of his mouth turned up. "Not Thumper. I don't even know why I asked her out and I sure as hell don't know why I brought her here."

"Oh, please." She dropped her arms to her side. "You know

exactly why you did it. We all do. You are as transparent as glass. You liked what we had. You thought it was great and that scared the crap out of you. You're so afraid of making another mistake, you won't even try. You play at relationships with women without actually having one, and somewhere along the way you convinced yourself that what you're doing is plenty. That you don't need more."

She poked him in the chest. "But you know what? You're completely and totally wrong. You desperately want more. That's why you were always hanging around here. You like being a part of something, so one day you took a chance and it was better than you thought. So much better you got scared. But did you have the balls to talk about that with me? Of course not. Instead you lashed out like a five-year-old and you deliberately set out to hurt and humiliate me. Don't for one second think that is something I'm going to forgive or forget."

His dark green gaze settled on her face. "There's no fooling you."

"You got that right."

"I was fully in the wrong."

"You were."

Telling him off had been empowering. She felt strong and more than capable of taking care of herself. She didn't need a man, certainly not Lucas. He was nothing to her. She'd moved on. *M-o-v-e-d* on.

"I love you."

Her stomach hit the floor as her brain shut down. "W-what?"

"I love you," he repeated, his gaze steady. "I love you, Harper."

Silly, foolish hope flared to life. She did her best to squash it, but it refused to die. "You're just saying that because you want to get laid."

He didn't smile. Instead he said, "Before I got shot last year, I told myself I had it all. A job I loved, friends, hot and cold running women. Everything was easy and exactly how I liked it. Then I nearly died. While I was recovering, I had a chance to think. I stayed with Kirk and Jen and I saw what they had. I saw what it meant to have someone to love and know you had their back while they had yours. I remembered what it was like to be part of a family. Slowly, I began to want that for myself. Then I met you."

She told herself to remember she'd moved on, that there was no way she could trust him. Only she really, really wanted to.

"You were so earnest and so determined to do a good job. With your matching napkins and homemade everything, you were charming. Your mom made you crazy and you had the best daughter in the world and slowly, so slowly I didn't see it happening, I fell for you."

"That's a nice story," she began, even as her resolve began to crumble.

"It's not a story." He moved closer. "I had to screw it all up to see it, but that doesn't change the truth. I love you, Harper. I'm kind of crazy about your daughter, too, but that's totally different."

He put his hand on her upper arm. "I know I have a lot of ground to make up. You have no reason to forgive me or believe me. I need to earn your trust again and I'm willing to do whatever it takes. I want to be here for the long haul. Forever. For always."

Harper wasn't sure how she was supposed to resist him. Yes, he'd been beyond stupid, but she understood why, and she believed that he'd learned his lesson. She thought about how things had been before and how they were now. She thought about the plates at the table and knew she really wanted there to always be at least two. His and hers.

Theirs.

"Well, damn," she murmured, right before she kissed him. "I guess I love you, too."

"Good." He grabbed her around the waist and grinned. "Want to have a baby?"

"What? Dear God, no! We're too old."

"What about a cat? Want to get a cat?"

"We have Dobermans. I'm not sure a cat's a good idea. Unless it was maybe a bobcat."

"Want to marry me?"

Her heart stopped, then started up again. Certainty replaced any lingering doubts, then happiness overwhelmed everything else.

"Maybe," she teased.

"Maybe?" He nibbled on her bottom lip. "Just maybe?"

"Okay, yes. But not right away. We have stuff to work through."

"Want to go make a spreadsheet? You know how that makes you happy."

"You make me happy," she told him. "When you're not being stupid."

"You make me happy all the time."

She took him by the hand and led him toward her bedroom. "Good to know. And just to be clear, I'm going to be fifty in eight years. You need to be able to handle that."

"I can handle it just fine."

"Maybe I'll start getting BOTOX."

"Maybe I'll research bobcats."

She was still laughing when he pulled her into his arms and

silenced her in the best way possible. There was time to deal with the BOTOX/bobcat issue and everything else. They had the rest of their lives.

Epilogue

"WE SHOULD TALK ABOUT THE WEDDING," BUNNY SAID as she put down her napkin and picked up JW. "I've been thinking about it."

Harper glanced at Lucas, who squeezed her hand. With luck, her horror and fear didn't show.

"It's that or the fact that you used store-bought hot dog buns at dinner," he murmured, leaning close.

"I was never expected to *make* hot dog buns," she told him. "It's the store-bought relish I'm in trouble for."

"It's hard to keep track."

"Tell me about it."

"Excuse me," Bunny said, her eyes narrowing. "This is a serious conversation. You've been engaged nearly a month. You have to make a decision about the wedding. People are starting to ask questions."

"What people?" Stacey looked confused. "Who else matters but family?"

Kit grinned. "That's my girl."

They were all in Harper's backyard on a warm summer

evening, the first weekend of August. In a few weeks Becca would be back to school and Ashton would be heading off to college. There would be the usual fall rush with the business, then the holidays. Time moved quickly.

"Lucas and I haven't talked much about the wedding," Harper admitted. Mostly because what they had now was so good. They'd settled into a comfortable routine with lots of evenings together, great dinners with Becca and Ashton or Stacey and Kit, and enough sex to keep her body finely tuned and happy.

At first she and Lucas had been discreet about their intimacy. They'd never done anything with Becca in the house and Lucas had gone home every night. Two weeks after he'd given Harper a stunning engagement ring, Becca had sat them down and explained that while she might not be ready for sex, she was perfectly comfortable with them doing it, as long as it was behind closed doors and she didn't have to hear anything. In other words, she was comfortable with Lucas sleeping over.

Harper had been more caught up in what a funny, sweet, sensible adult her baby girl had turned into while Lucas had nearly fainted from shock. Two nights later, he'd stayed and had pretty much been living with them ever since.

Bunny sniffed and returned her other granddaughter to her bassinette.

"When are you getting married?" she asked. "What kind of wedding will it be? This is a second marriage for both of you."

Stacey frowned. "Why does that matter?"

"It's all about what's the proper thing to do." Bunny smiled. "Harper, you'll want something small. Your first wedding was a backyard affair, so that's out, and you'll want to wait a few months. You won't want to rush into anything."

"So people won't think we're getting married because she's pregnant?" Lucas asked, putting his arm around Harper.

"Hardly. Harper is far too old for that." Bunny pulled out her phone and began flipping through pictures. "I'm thinking sometime in spring. The retirement community has a lovely rec room we could rent." She handed over her phone.

Harper looked at the picture of the large space. There were high ceilings and a lot of windows, but still, it was a rec room in a retirement community. Not exactly the venue of her dreams.

Lucas passed the phone back. "Bunny, it's our wedding and our decision."

"It's a family decision, and let me remind you, I'm the mother of the bride."

"I'm the groom," he said calmly. "I have some ideas of my own."

Bunny's lips pressed together. Harper knew her mother was torn between wanting to respect a man's opinion and telling Lucas that his job was simply to show up when told and marry her daughter.

"What ideas?" Bunny asked, her teeth slightly clenched.

"No rec room, no homemade food, no 'this is Harper's second wedding.'" He used one hand to make air quotes.

"It should be a party," Becca said. "A fun one with everyone you guys love."

"Dean and his family for sure." Harper wondered if she should get a pad of paper and start making a list.

"No children." Bunny's voice was firm. "It's not appropriate."

Stacey looked at her sister. "This isn't going to go well at all, is it?"

"Nope."

★ ★ ★

Two weeks later Harper found herself at a bridal boutique, looking at dresses. She wasn't exactly sure how it had happened. One minute she'd been trying to decide if she should take her mother's call and the next she'd found herself driving to meet Bunny at a store in Culver City.

Her mother had arrived before her and already had several dresses waiting in a dressing room.

"Oh, good," Bunny said when she spotted her daughter. "I was talking to the saleslady about how you're having a second wedding and you're thinking about something casual in the rec room."

Before Harper could respond, or scream, or run, Stacey hurried in.

"Am I late? Did I miss it?"

"We're just getting started." Harper hugged her sister. "Shouldn't you be at work?"

"I took the afternoon off. I want to be a part of this. Mom said you'd decided on the rec room for your venue." Stacey's tone was doubtful.

"I haven't," Harper said, her voice low. "Lucas and I don't know where we're getting married, but it's not there. We haven't even picked a date. I don't know why I'm here."

"Because you have trouble telling your mother no." Stacey linked arms with her. "I'm here and together we'll be strong."

"I hope so."

They went into one of the large dressing rooms. Harper studied the gowns on the rack. Most of them had long sleeves and relatively high necks. They were beige or taupe, with too much lace and big skirts.

"I honestly haven't thought about a dress," Harper murmured, "but if I had…"

The saleswoman joined them. "Your mother said you wanted something modest. A lot of ladies of a certain age don't want bare arms or a low décolletage."

"I can show my arms." Harper looked at her mother. "Why wouldn't I show my arms?"

"You're over forty, dear."

"Yes, but I still look good." She glanced at Stacey. "Don't I?"

"You look great."

The saleswoman smiled. "I've also put aside some lovely pantsuits for you to try."

Harper held in a groan. "No pantsuits. This is a wedding, not a business meeting."

"Harper, you have to get organized. You've picked your venue, now you can—"

Harper felt her self-control starting to slip. "Mom, there's no venue, there's no wedding date and I'm not wearing pants to my wedding."

She looked at the assortment of dresses. Maybe they would look better on.

"A dress is a better choice," Bunny told her. "I only offered pants as a suggestion because you like to do things differently than I would." She reached for a long-sleeved, overly lacy dress. "Try this one on first. My friend Carrie wore it when she got married last year. I've seen the pictures and she was stunning."

Harper tried not to whimper as she gazed at the monstrosity. "How old is Carrie?"

"Eighty-two. Why?"

Harper told herself she would get through the afternoon and when she got home, there would be a handsome man and plenty of wine. "No reason, Mom. No reason at all."

★ ★ ★.

"I've never staged an intervention before," Stacey said as soon as Becca let her into the house the following Saturday afternoon. "I did role-playing with Kit and he said it will go fine."

Her niece laughed. "It's not really an intervention. We just have to help Mom figure out what she really wants. I love my grandmother, but no one wants to wear the same dress as an eighty-two-year-old. It's crazy. I did a lot of research and so did Lucas."

Stacey held up her tablet. "I come armed with information, as well."

Weddings had never been important to her. As a little girl, she'd never dreamed about her dress or the flowers. She'd been more interested in intellectual pursuits. But she understood that she hadn't been normal then and she wasn't normal now, which was fine. She was happy with herself and her life, and if her sister wanted a wedding, then Stacey was going to do everything she could to make that happen.

Stacey and Becca went into the family room. Lucas was already there, as were Thor and Jazz. Harper was in the kitchen, studying the three-ring binder where she kept her favorite recipes.

"So we're agreed," she said. "I'll batch cook a couple of times a month and—" She stared at Stacey in surprise. "Hi. Did I know you were stopping by?"

"This is an intervention," Stacey told her. "I'm here to help."

Harper looked from Lucas to her daughter. "What?" she asked, coming to her feet. "No. Come on, I've been good. I've kept to my schedule. I don't bring work home at night, I'm never on the phone with Dean after seven unless it's an emergency. I know I haven't decorated for Labor Day yet, but I didn't think anyone cared."

Lucas patted the cushion next to him. "This isn't about work. It's about the wedding."

Harper groaned. "Anything but that. I swear, I'm not buying that hideous dress. Or a pantsuit."

Stacey and Becca took seats. Becca and Lucas exchanged a look before Becca said, "Mom, here's the thing. Grandma's ideas aren't right for you. All those rules. Why wait until spring? You two should get married now so you can start living your lives."

"Now? You mean this fall?"

Becca and Lucas exchanged another glance before looking at Stacey, who grinned.

"We're thinking Labor Day weekend."

Harper's mouth dropped open. "Wh-what? That's in two weeks. Are you insane? No! It's not possible." She turned to Lucas. "Are you in on this? Do you want to get married that quickly? What about the planning? What about my mother?"

Lucas grabbed her hand. "I want what you want. Having said that, I'm worried Bunny is going to guilt you into something you *don't* want. This is about us, Harper, not her." He winked. "Besides, I think Bunny is going to be distracted for the next few weeks. I introduced her to a retired detective friend. They had their first date last night and I heard it went well. Bunny is going to be busy with her new man at least long enough to get this thing done." He stared into her eyes. "But only if you want this to happen."

"I want to marry you," Harper said, then bit her lower lip. "But two weeks... I don't think it's possible."

"It's more than possible," Stacey told her firmly. "As long as we apply some simple rules of project management to the process. The wedding has three large components. Venue, food, dress. The rest can be filled in."

Harper looked as if she was going to faint, but instead she nodded. "All right. How do we deal with those three?"

Becca spun her tablet toward her mother. "Party boat. There's one out of Long Beach that holds a hundred and sixty people. It's available the Saturday of Labor Day, which is weird, but I think it's a sign. Anyway, that's big enough, there's plenty of parking by the dock and the company works with a caterer."

"A party boat?" Harper asked, looking at Lucas. "It sounds kind of fun."

"That's what I thought." He kissed her. "It's very us. I know it's not one of the three, but I know a guy who's married to a woman who owns a bakery. She can make us a cupcake wedding cake with no problem."

The front door opened and closed. "Am I late?" Dean called as he raced into the family room. "I had to take Mandy and Miranda to a birthday party and one of the mothers there wanted to talk about a project." He sat down and groaned. "I tried to explain it was *not* the time, but she wasn't having any of it. Where are we?"

"Party boat with caterers, and the cake," Becca said. "Stacey explained we have plenty of time if we stay on track."

Dean grinned at Stacey. "We have had several very productive phone calls about this. Honey, if the whole medical-research thing doesn't work out, you have a future in our firm."

"Thank you," Stacey murmured, doing her best to accept the compliment in the spirit in which it was meant.

"We're calling in favors for the flowers," Dean said. "That florist we always use? Deloris said she will make our botanical dreams come true. Lance and I have a DJ we always use and he just had a cancellation."

"Another sign," Becca said happily.

Stacey knew there weren't signs or omens, but people enjoyed them so she simply smiled and nodded.

"Lance, for reasons we are not going to discuss in public, is an ordained minister," Dean offered. "He says he's happy to marry you two." Dean glanced at his list. "Venue, food, music, flowers." He looked at Lucas. "You're in charge of the honeymoon."

"I have that covered. What else?"

"The invitations will have to be electronic," Dean mused. "I can design those today. Are you two registering for gifts?"

"We'll do a charity instead," Harper said. "People can give in our name."

"Then that's everything," Becca said happily. "So, Mom, do you want to get married in two weeks?"

Harper's happy expression faded. "I don't have a dress. What if I can't find a dress?"

Stacey cleared her throat. "I bought you one."

Everyone turned to stare at her. Dean's eyebrows rose.

"Hon, don't take this wrong, but you?"

Stacey looked at her sister. "After that horrible afternoon with Mom I went online and I found what I think is the perfect dress. At least I hope so." She'd been so sure when she'd seen it and when it had arrived, she'd known Harper would love it. Only now, with all eyes on her, she suddenly felt awkward and unsure. Who was she to think she could buy her sister a wedding gown? She'd obviously made a mistake.

"Show her," Becca urged.

Stacey tapped on her tablet and turned it so Harper could see the screen.

The dress was ivory lace over a nude lining. There were spaghetti straps with a deep plunging neckline in front and a higher V in the back. The lace fell to midcalf but the lining stopped about midthigh. It was sassy, sexy, and the second Stacey had seen it, she'd known it was the one.

"Well, I like it," Lucas said.

Harper's eyes filled with tears. "Stacey, it's perfect. I love it. Did you really buy it?"

"It's in the trunk of my car. Want me to get it?"

Harper nodded, stood and rushed over to hug her. She wiped away tears, then waved her arm.

"Get over here, all of you. You're amazing and I love you all."

"Is that a yes to the wedding?" Lucas asked.

"Absolutely."

Two weeks and four hours later, Harper stared into Lucas's dark green eyes and said words she'd never imagined she would utter again.

"I do."

He slid a simple platinum band on her ring finger—because, hey, a two-carat solitaire deserved to get all the attention—then leaned close enough to whisper, "That dress is killing me. It's a lot lower than I thought it would be. How long do we have to stay at this party?"

Instead of answering, she laughed then kissed him. "You are a ridiculous man and I love you very much."

"Good. You can prove it later."

"I plan to."

"You're not supposed to be talking," Bunny called from the front row. "This is a wedding."

The burly man sitting next to her took her hand in his.

"Now, Bunnykins, you know how kids are these days. We have to let them be."

Bunny beamed at him. "Yes, Burt. You're completely right. I'm sorry, Harper. You talk away."

"It's a Labor Day weekend miracle," Lucas whispered before turning back to a grinning Lance. "So are we done here?"

"You are. I now pronounce you husband and wife."

Lucas kissed her. "I was going to ask him to say man and wife, but I figured you'd kick me in the shin for that one."

"Probably," she said with a laugh.

The captain of the boat honked twice to let them know they were about to get underway, then the boat eased out into the harbor and servers began passing glasses of champagne.

Everything had turned out perfectly. The dress, the boat, the menu, the flowers, the cupcake cake. Tomorrow Stacey and Ashton would leave for MIT—a couple of days later than originally planned, but Stacey had already arranged for everything to be purchased and waiting at their hotel. Bunny would leave Burt's side long enough to help Kit with JW, who had slept through her first wedding. Once Stacey was home and Becca had started school, Lucas and Harper were off to Hawaii for a two-week honeymoon. Becca would stay with her aunt, as would all three dogs. It was going to be a madhouse and Harper knew they would love it.

She and Lucas mingled with their guests until her feet were killing her, then she went into the private cabin and exchanged her gorgeous but very uncomfortable shoes for a pair of ivory-colored flip-flops that she'd embellished with seed pearls and little lace flowers. She and Becca had completed the project together, then had made a pair for Becca to wear.

Lucas followed her into the bedroom and locked the door.

Even as she started to tell him there was absolutely no way they could, you know, he was unbuttoning his shirt.

"We can't," she said, despite the tingling that spiraled out from her belly.

"Five minutes," he told her. "It won't be my best work, but it will be thorough."

"It's so bad. No. We shouldn't…"

But he'd already reached for the back of her dress and was tugging down the zipper.

"I really think we should."

As she gave herself over to him, she knew their lives would always be like this. Funny and unexpected and delicious and filled with family and friends, not to mention illicit sex. And later, there would be cake!

Once her breathing had returned to seminormal and she was getting dressed, she smiled at him. "You're the best husband ever, Lucas. I want you to know how much I love you."

Instead of smiling, he touched her cheek. "I love you, too, Harper. This is only the beginning. For both of us. Forever."

And it was…

★ ★ ★ ★ ★

SISTERS LIKE US

SUSAN MALLERY

Reader's Guide

Suggested Menu:

Glazed Ham

Potatoes Grand-Mère
(recipe follows discussion questions)

Strawberry Avocado Salad
(recipe follows discussion questions)

Lemon Meringue Pie

1. With which sister did you identify most strongly? Why?

2. When asked what inspired this novel, Susan Mallery said:

> I watched a documentary called *The Last Man on the Moon* about astronaut Gene Cernan, and it got me thinking about all of the astronauts in the early years of NASA, and how much their families must have sacrificed. The rewards were heady, I'm sure, but a kid still wants her daddy at her birthday party. In *Sisters Like Us*, the sisters' maternal grandfather was an astronaut, and their mom resented the time he spent away from home, and that he was willing to die and abandon his family forever. Those feelings about her childhood colored how she raised the girls, of course, leading to their struggle with questions of what is the right amount to love your job. How much can you give to your work before you start taking away from your family?
>
> I was interested in the idea of legacy, of how events of the distant past impact events of today in a thousand

subtle ways. *Sisters Like Us* isn't about astronauts at all. In fact, their grandfather is only mentioned a couple of times. But his impact on their lives is huge because of the way their mother *perceived* her childhood.

How did this play out in the story? Are there any other ways that their grandfather's time as an astronaut affected Harper's and Stacey's lives? What events from your parents' childhood do you think affected yours?

3. Why was Becca so unhappy at the start of the book? Do you think she had a right to be? Why or why not?

4. *Sisters Like Us* has three main characters: Harper, Stacey and Becca. What were the major turning points of each character's story? Did the events of each story line affect the others and, if so, how?

5. What did you think of Lucas? If you've read the first book in which he appeared, *A Million Little Things*, did your opinion of him change? Why do you think Lucas was attracted to Harper, and vice versa? How did you feel when he brought another woman to Harper's house, despite his promise not to? Harper forgave him—did you? What did you think of his relationship with Becca?

6. Why did Harper choose to work as a virtual assistant? Do you think she made the right decision? What would you have done differently?

7. Discuss Becca's reaction to finding out that her friend was no longer a virgin. At what age do you think a girl is too young to lose her virginity? Do you have a different opinion about how young is too young for a boy?

8. Bunny has some very firm ideas about men and women.

How have gender roles changed over the years? Do you think Stacey and Kit's marriage is unusual, in the roles each plays in the family? Why or why not?

9. Were you happy with the ending? Why or why not?

10. On her Facebook page (Facebook.com/susanmallery), Susan Mallery sometimes invites readers to suggest names for characters or pets, then promises to include in a book the last name of the reader who made a suggestion she chose. The name Bay was suggested for one of the dogs by a reader with the last name Szymanski, who was sure Susan would never use her name in a book. Not only did Susan use it, but she used it for a main character, which means it appears prominently in the cover copy. What did you think when you first read this last name? How did you pronounce it? Why do you think Harper kept her ex-husband's last name instead of going back to Bloom? Have you ever seen your last name in a book?

Potatoes Grand-Mère

4 baking potatoes, peeled and cut into 1/8-inch slices
Salt and pepper
2 Tbsp butter
1/2 cup diced onion
1 clove garlic, minced
2 Tbsp flour
1 tsp dry mustard
1 cup half-and-half
1/2 cup shredded Parmesan cheese, divided

Layer potatoes in a greased 8-inch-square baking dish, seasoning each layer with salt and pepper to taste. Melt the butter over low heat in a medium saucepan. Sauté the onions until translucent. Add garlic. Mix together the flour and dry mustard, then sprinkle over the onion mixture, stirring thoroughly. Add half-and-half a little at a time, stirring constantly, until thickened. Remove from heat and stir in half the cheese. Pour over the potatoes.

Cover and bake at 350°F for 45 minutes. Remove the cover, add the rest of the cheese and bake until cheese is golden brown, about 15 minutes longer.

Strawberry Avocado Salad

6 cups baby spinach
1 cup fresh strawberries, sliced
1 avocado, diced
2 oz Parmesan cheese, sliced
1/4 cup chopped pecans
Balsamic vinegar and olive oil to taste
Salt and pepper to taste

Toss together the spinach, strawberries, avocado, cheese and pecans. Serve with vinegar, oil, salt and pepper.